TURBULENT JOURNEY

Hilda Petrie-Coutts

Copyright © Hilda Petrie-Coutts 2023
All Rights Reserved

All the characters in this book are fictional and any similarity to any actual person alive or dead or place is purely coincidental.

Chapter One

Geraldine Denton straightened up easing her stiff knees to glance down reflectively over flower beds on which she lavished so much effort. The lupins, roses and peonies were especially fine this year, ceanothus smothered in blue flowers attracting the bees, and honeysuckle's rich fragrance wafting on the breeze. If only David were still alive to enjoy it with her. She sighed, tucked a strand of silvering hair back from her damp forehead and turned her head as she heard the sound of a vehicle drawing up outside the neighbouring cottage that had remained empty for some months now. She moved closer to her low front hedge in surprise.

It was a small black van she noted, the driver and assistant opening the back and waiting as a grey car drew up behind them. Geraldine stared with unconcealed curiosity as a shapely, blonde-haired, young woman in blue jeans and a casual jacket stepped from the car, helping a small girl to stand nervously at her side, a pretty child with fair curls and a solemn face. Neighbours—she was going to have new neighbours she realised and drew in her breath in delight. As though sensing the woman's gaze, the girl glanced across at Geraldine and gave a slight smile, before opening the gate and walking briskly along the pathway, unlocking the front door, and disappearing inside with the child ahead of the delivery men.

Over the next five minutes, the workmen carried in the woman's few belongings, and eventually, the van drove away. Geraldine hesitated. Should she offer a welcome to this new arrival in the village? She went indoors, stared at her recently baked chocolate cake cooling on a rack, and on inspiration eased it onto a plate and set off. She knocked and waited. No one answered, so she knocked again, louder. At last, the door was cautiously opened and Geraldine found herself being examined by a pair of slightly apprehensive blue eyes.

'Good afternoon, my dear,' smiled Geraldine. 'I saw you arrive earlier. Moving in such a tiring process, so thought I'd welcome you and that you might enjoy a slice of chocolate sponge with a cup of tea,' and she held the cake towards the girl, whose lovely face bore a guarded expression as she examined the caller, then reached out a slim hand to accept the unexpected offering.

'Why that's very kind of you, Mrs..?'

'Denton—Geraldine Denton, your next-door neighbour. I'm so glad this dear cottage has a new owner.'

'Actually, I'm only renting for now but with an option to buy. But won't you come in Mrs Denton? I have a box of groceries with me—so there should be milk, sugar and a packet of tea somewhere. Oh, and my name is Anna Lindstrom.' She stood back allowing Geraldine to enter, clicking the lock after her. They made their way along the passage past the few boxes of belongings and into the small homely kitchen.

'I'm glad the previous owner left her electric kettle behind,' said Anna frankly. 'Not sure I brought mine with me.' She looked around tiredly. Geraldine came to a decision.

'Strikes me you need a hand with all this, my dear. I know my way around this place as though it were my own. Daphne Pearson was one of my dearest friends for over ten years, and I was devastated when she decided to join her son in New Zealand—leaving all her furniture and everything behind. Still miss her you know, the more so since I lost my beloved husband David last year.' And she sighed.

'So, you live alone next door?' Anna inquired and seemed to relax as her visitor nodded assent. Geraldine sensed a nervousness in her bearing and wondered why.

'I noticed you have a little girl?' said Geraldine. 'It will be so good having a child about the place. My young grandchildren are far away now—a little village in the north of Scotland. My son Colin works in the oil industry and his wife Mary is a school teacher there.' She noticed that Anna did not appear to be following her quiet chatter. The poor girl must be tired, she thought. Then the newcomer responded at last.

'Yes, I have a young daughter. Her name is Susan,' she said softly. 'She's four years old and rather shy and exhausted after our journey—fallen asleep on the sofa,' she added.

'And your husband, he will be joining you soon,' Geraldine inquired and saw the shuttered look cross the young woman's attractive features.

'I am a single mother,' she said shortly.'

'Oh, forgive me—I didn't mean to pry,' Geraldine said gently. 'Now where will I find that packet of tea?' She followed Anna's gaze towards a box on the pine table. Minutes later she opened the small cupboard where her previous neighbour had kept her crockery, quietly placing cups, saucers and plates on the table. 'Shall I pour?' she asked. 'Do you take milk and sugar, Anna?'

'Only milk.' The girl watched as Geraldine sliced the chocolate cake, handing her a plate. She took a small bite.

'This is delicious—thank you, Mrs Denton.'

'Just call me Geraldine, dear.' She glanced at her new young neighbour over her teacup. The girl was quite lovely she decided, with a smooth oval face, finely arched brows over those deep blue eyes, almost a hyacinth blue—well-shaped nose and a determined mouth with a slightly full lower lip above a dimpled chin. Her long hair was of a shade of corn gold and worn tied back behind her head. Geraldine had also noticed she was well-spoken and wondered curiously what had brought Anna to this remote village, with a few shops in its single street and little in the way of excitement.

'Now would you like a hand in making up the beds?' she inquired as they rose from the table. 'The linen is kept in the airing cupboard at the top of the stairs, so shouldn't be damp.' Anna shook her head, dismissing the offer of assistance.

'You have been more than kind, Geraldine, but I will manage from here on,' she stated, 'I'll always be grateful for your welcome today!' and her visitor was too wise to press her services. She turned to leave, sensing Anna's relief at being left alone. She heard the click of the lock as the door of Bramble Cottage closed behind her. She made her way to the garden gate and bit her lip, as she returned to her own home, pondering over the anxiety Anna Lindstrom had evinced during their short time together.

In her earlier years, whilst employed in a particular secret department of the civil service, she had learned to detect those undergoing suppressed emotions—for whatever reason. Amongst these, she had at times encountered women displaying a similar slightly strained manner to that she had noted in Anna Lindstrom. Sometimes it is presented in women suffering from emotional or physical domestic abuse Seemingly her new neighbour was a single parent—but this of course did not mean that she hadn't faced problems with the father of her child.

She closed the pale blue front door and made for her comfortable sitting room, with its deep-seated, three-piece suite fitted with floral loose covers in soft pastel shades, and the upright piano she loved to play, while the table bore a silver rose bowl now full of white and gold blooms from the garden, and a glass-fronted cabinet displayed treasured delicate miniature blue and white ornaments David had bought her from Holland over the years, together with other mementoes of their overseas travels.

David, how she missed him she thought wistfully, as she sank back in her favourite chair and rested her head against a cushion, gift embroidered by her son Colin's wife Mary. She stared at the opposite chair, remembering how her doctor husband had relaxed there after a busy day's work, and where on his retirement they had continued to enjoy an evening game of chess. She stared at the antique ebony chessmen on the little oak table now placed against the wall. Life was rather like a game of chess she decided, however carefully you considered the next move you might miscalculate, as fate chuckled its checkmate!

How was her new neighbour managing, she wondered now? Perhaps she might get a sight of Anna's little four-year-old daughter tomorrow! She had briefly glimpsed the child getting out of the car on their arrival and had appeared nervous. Well, that was natural enough for a little one, to find herself in a strange place. She must contain herself in patience until tomorrow—and in the meanwhile, what about some music? She rose and slipped a disc into the music centre, then sank back to enjoy Mendlesohn's Fingal's Cave. They had been there once, whilst on a trip to the Hebridean islands, and she remembered clambering carefully into the cave's interior at David's side, sharing the feeling of deepest awe at nature's wondrous setting.

But despite her initial absorption in the music, Geraldine found her thoughts returning to the young woman who was now living in Daphne Pearson's 'Bramble Cottage' and wondered what mystery surrounded the girl. Obviously, Anna had not possessed the contents of her own home, else why move into a fully furnished cottage?

This would not do she chided herself. She was being too imaginative about the new arrival. But when two cottages nestled so close to each other, and about at least ten minutes walk from the rest of the village, it was inevitable that their residents should take a close interest in each other and be mutually supportive, as had been the case between her widowed friend Daphne Pearson and herself. To lose her beloved husband David and have Daphne leave for New Zealand at much the same time, had been difficult to cope with—this place suddenly so quiet—so alone, yet so full of memories.

The girl who was occupying Geraldine's curious thoughts, breathed a sigh of relief when the pleasant elderly lady who had made herself known to her with such unexpected kindness, had taken the hint and disappeared back to her own home. It was the very remoteness of Bramble Cottage from all neighbours but one, that had persuaded her to accept advice and move here with Trudy, who must now be known as Susan. Would the little girl always remember her new name, and understand how vital it was never to disclose her former identity?

She glanced at the sofa where she had hastily draped her jean jacket over the sleeping child earlier. She must prepare a bedroom for Susan—and always call her little daughter by this new name, and equally important to remember she was now Anna Lindstrom. She had decided on her late great-grandmother's name as being easy to slip off the tongue.

The people in the refuge had been supportive, and kind beyond all expectations. Perhaps in time to come, she might involve herself in similar work, and repay the wonderful caring she had received by reaching out in turn to others who had endured what she had. But right now, it was of the greatest importance to rebuild her life and provide a secure future for Susan. She bent over the child, kissing her lightly before running up the unfamiliar red-carpeted stairs to explore the bedrooms.

The following morning the cottage was already beginning to feel like home, however strange it was to take over the everyday essentials someone else had put in place over a possible lifetime. If the previous owner Mrs Pearson was similar to her friend Geraldine Denton, the amazing old lady next door who had called on her yesterday with her chocolate cake, then she must have been a special person. Bramble Cottage certainly felt like a happy place she decided.

She had woken to the sound of birdsong in the garden and stared about her in confusion until she recalled she was in her new home. She slipped out of bed and opened the door of the smaller of the two bedrooms on the other side of the landing and smiled to see her little daughter beginning to stir.

'Good morning, my darling,' she said softly, as Susan opened her eyes staring around in bewilderment at her strange surroundings. The child's tousled blond curls framed a winsome young face, her eyes the same vivid blue as her mother's.

'Mummy—it's a new bed,' she exclaimed.

'Yes, darling—and a new home where we will be safe and you can grow up without anything to worry you,' she said gently.

'I think I remember getting here in the car—and feeling very tired,' said the child quietly. 'Is this my new bedroom then, Mummy?' She smiled as she saw her favourite doll on the pillow beside her, and looked around curiously. 'He won't find us here?' she said anxiously.

'No Susan darling, we are going to start a whole new life here, make some new friends. You're going to have lots of fun exploring Bramble Cottage once you are up and dressed. First, I'll show you where the bathroom is, and after a wash we'll have some breakfast in the kitchen. Up you get then!'

The child slipped into her mother's warm embrace with a trusting smile, then ran across to the bedroom window and looked down.

'Why there's a lovely garden out there and flowers,' she stated in delight.

'Yes, we're still in the countryside, Susan dear—just like that big house, we stayed in with that nice lady Amber whom you liked. Come on now—bathroom!' she said firmly.

After a bowl of cereal followed by scrambled eggs on toast, Susan ran from room to room exploring. Anna followed at her side. It was such a relief that the child had taken to her new home so easily. She hoped it was indeed true that he would not find them here. She wanted to believe it, but the stress of the last few years still clung to her mind, as did the threats he had made of retribution should she ever attempt to leave him. But it was done now, the worst was over she reassured herself. She would never have to see his hard, dark eyes staring at her again, as he uttered one of his scathing remarks criticising her appearance, or the meals she carefully prepared, cruel little jibes meant to hurt and to control. It was difficult to accept that she was finally free of the man who had terrorised and manipulated her life for so long.

'May I go into the garden, Mummy?' Susan demanded. Anna considered her and nodded.

'Well—all right then. The kitchen door opens onto the back garden. You go out there and have fun, whilst I wash up and finish unpacking our bits and pieces!' smiled Anna. She watched from the window for a brief moment, as Susan wandered across the lawn, clutching her doll by one arm, exploring this wonderful place where birds sang and there were so many flowers, and a wooden bench overlooking a small pond backed by a rockery. It seemed like a dream the child thought, as she placed her doll on the bench and sat beside her.

'Yes, I have made the right choice,' Anna murmured, turning away and smiling as she saw Susan so happy. 'However tough this new life may prove to be, wild horses never drag me back to that gilded trap!'

Susan sat staring in fascination as a small goldfish broke the surface of the pool, near a clump of water lilies. Then the child slipped off the bench as a cat appeared and rubbed its back against her legs.

'Hallo cat, what's your name?' said the child as she bent and stroked its silver grey, tabby fur, to be rewarded by a loud purring.

'His name is Marcasite because of his colour,' said a quiet voice. Susan glanced around and saw a woman with greying hair, smiling at her from the other side of the low garden fence.

'Is he your cat,' asked Susan shyly aware that she had to be careful of whom she spoke to.

'Yes, my dear, I've had him since he was a kitten, over nine years ago now. You must be Susan. I spoke with your Mummy yesterday—I believe you'd fallen asleep soon after you arrived. My name is Geraldine!'

'Geraldine, that's a nice name,' replied Susan trying it on her tongue;

'Why thank you. You know Susan, the lady who used to live in your new home was my best friend and I hope you and your mother will be very happy here.'

'I love it already,' replied Susan shyly. 'It's so quiet and beautiful and all these flowers!'

'You like flowers, Susan? You must ask Mummy if you can both come over and see my garden one day, once you are settled in.' And with a cheery wave of her hand, Geraldine moved away, as the grey cat streaked across the grass and leapt the fence to join her.

'What a lovely little girl,' murmured Geraldine, glad to have met the child. As she approached the door she heard the phone ringing, lifted it and sat down in delight as she recognised the mobile number, but was surprised to get a call from Scotland so early in the day.

'Mary! It's so good to hear from you. So how are you dear—and how is that son of mine?' To her surprise, there was no answer just the sound of a desperate sobbing. Geraldine paled.

'Mary? Mary—what's wrong, dear?' she asked in concern. At last her, daughter-in-law made a faltering reply.

'You had better sit down, Geraldine,' came the trembling voice

'I am—but you're worrying me. Whatever is the matter, Mary?' And suddenly she guessed. 'Colin—is it Colin?' she demanded urgently. There was a whispered affirmative.

'Yes. I'm so sorry—but Colin's dead. His helicopter went down returning from the rig. There were no survivors—and no sign of his body yet. They rang me from base half an hour ago—and I don't know what to do. It doesn't seem real—it can't be!' came Mary's heartbroken wail.

Geraldine stared at the receiver in stunned silence. It couldn't be true—that her only son Colin was dead? She felt her heart start to pound erratically and tried to suppress the scream at the back of her throat. She had to remain calm and try to support the young woman weeping so inconsolably at the end of the phone.

'Oh Mary, Mary love—what a dreadful thing to happen. I'll come up there. You will need help with the children,' and her thoughts went out to the twins, little seven-year-old Charles and sister Melanie.

'They don't know yet,' sobbed Mary. 'How can I tell them that their Daddy is dead! I'm ringing from home, the Headmistress told me to leave my class when the phone call came—but the twins are still back there in school. Mrs MacArthur is going to drive them here at the end of the afternoon.'

'Oh, Mary! What you must be going through. But I know you will find the right words to speak to Charles and Melanie—that their Daddy was such a brave man—he's in heaven now and loving them both still and always will.' Geraldine tried to keep her voice steady, knowing she had to be strong for Colin's grieving wife and little ones. But it was hard, so hard, when dealing with her own shock on learning of her only son's death.

'Can you really come up, Geraldine?'

'Of course—I'll need to make arrangements for the cat first. Have to get to Southampton airport and fly up to Aberdeen—get a taxi from there.' Geraldine was beginning to make logical plans for the journey. It all seemed so unreal. One moment she had been happily making friends with that delightful little girl next door—and now this terrible catastrophe. There had been problems with certain helicopters before, but all were supposed to have been fixed. Oh, Colin—Colin! She tried to concentrate on Mary's voice.

'I must go, Geraldine—someone at the door. Oh, I'm just so grateful you're coming, dear.' She called off, and Geraldine sat looking down at the phone in stunned silence. To have lost David last year—and now this new heartache. She made herself stand up. She must find out the flight details—pack a small bag. But what about Marcasite? Dare she ask her new neighbour Anna Lindstrom to care for him for a few days—little Susan had liked him—so?

Anna heard the knock at the door, opened it almost apprehensively and smiled in relief to see her neighbour's face. But Geraldine was not smiling today, her eyes showing signs of recently shed tears.

'Why Geraldine? Come in—is something wrong?' she asked and listened sympathetically as the woman blurted out the terrible news that her son had just died in a helicopter accident and automatically her arms went about Geraldine's slim shoulders, as she led her inside and into the kitchen. 'Here—sit down—I've just made a pot of tea.' She poured a cup for the badly shaken woman who had treated her with such kindness yesterday.

'Is there anything I can do to help?' she asked quietly. Geraldine fixed damp grey eyes on her.

'Well, I hardly like to ask—but it's my cat. I've told my daughter-in-law Mary that I'll fly up there. She has to tell the children—is distraught. She needs me, so I must go. There will have to be a funeral, only I don't know if they will be able to find Colin. Seems the sea was so deep where the copter came down.' Geraldine was trying her best to control her shock. 'But I can't leave Marcasite—haven't time to find a cattery.'

'Marcasite? Of course, Susan told me she had met him in the garden. I don't know too much about cats, but yes, I'll look after Marcasite, no problem. Just tell me what to feed him.' She saw the look of relief spread across Geraldine's face.

'This is a spare key to my cottage. If you come back with me I'll show you where I keep his tins of cat food and he'll need fresh water each day and...' her voice tailed off as she fought back tears, and raised the cup to her lips. The tea helped, and she took the tissue Anna held out to her. She gave the girl a grateful smile and rose to her feet. 'Anna if you are sure, then perhaps you can come over with me now.'

'Just let me call Susan—she's still out in the garden.' Minutes later, Anna with her small daughter at her side followed Geraldine hurriedly across the short distance separating the two cottages, and in through the blue front door. Anna glanced around curiously.

'What a lovely room,' she cried, as Geraldine showed them into the sitting room, before leading them through to the kitchen and opening the cupboard where tins of cat food were stacked and packets of treats.

'This is Marcasite's dish,' said Geraldine. 'And his water bowl is here. Oh, you'll need the tin opener.' She was fighting to regain control, perhaps the discipline of giving these simple instructions was helping her maintain calm.

'Look, just go and pack and make your flight arrangements,' said Anna firmly. Geraldine nodded gratefully. At this moment they heard a sharp meow as the tabby stalked into the kitchen and looked curiously at the strangers, recognised the little girl and purred as she knelt and stroked him. Anna bent, gently stroking him in turn, and after stiffening for a moment the cat accepted her and continued purring.

'He likes you,' said Geraldine forcing a smile. 'Right, I'll pack now.'

'I'll find out about flight times for you in the meanwhile,' suggested Anna, pulling her phone from her pocket.

An hour later, Anna watched Geraldine drive off for the airport in her beige Ford. She experienced an unexpected feeling of loneliness that the elderly lady she had known for so short a time had suddenly disappeared. Poor woman, she must have experienced such a terrible shock on hearing her son had died, lost somewhere in the remote icy waters off the northeast coast of Scotland. Anna shuddered then called to Susan, and locked the blue door behind them as they returned next door to Bramble Cottage.

'How will Marcasite get into the garden, if the door is locked?' asked Susan. Anna smiled at the child's concern.

'Seems there's a cat flap in Geraldine's back door—the cat will be fine! Now it's time I started preparing lunch—and you should sit down and read your Mandy Loo book—it's through there on the sitting room table. Call me if you get stuck on any of the words!' The little girl smiled and disappeared. Anna glanced after her fondly. Teaching Trudy to read at an early age was a wise decision—no that was a slip, not Trudy—but Susan! She must always remember to think of her child as Susan,

'Susan and Anna,' she made herself repeat the words like a mantra, as she peeled the vegetables. 'Susan and Anna Lindstrom—not Trudy and Erika Nicolson!' She set the soup to simmer on the cooker and sat down to consider how best she was going to make a new start here in this village she hadn't yet explored. She was going to need a job, that was obvious. True she had that small sum of money in her private account, originally earned through her nursing duties, and dating back from the time before she had met Malcolm Greer, and which thankfully he had not guessed she possessed. When she had left him, she had thought it was lost together with her father's legacy, but on advice from those in the refuge, it had been accessed with help from the bank officials. But this would keep her going for a few months at the most. So, nursing again? But records of her nursing career were in her real name—Erika Nicolson. Dared she take any future hospital authority into her confidence—no, nursing was too risky for Malcolm would guess she would return to the profession she loved and had only given up at his insistence.

As she sat there, she began to mentally review all that had happened over the last four fraught years—made herself face those disturbing memories analytically.

Strange to think it was during her nursing career that she had met him in the first place. As a staff nurse on male orthopaedics at St Phil's, she had paused by the bedside of a new patient who had just arrived on the ward, recovering consciousness after surgery, screw fixation for a right Pott's fracture, tibia and fibula both fractured at the ankle. She had glanced at the name above his bed—Malcolm Greer, and greeted him, asking how he was feeling as she checked the bed cradle.

'What have they done to me,' he inquired, as he stared at her, taking in the sympathetic blue eyes in her attractive face, the golden hair drawn back beneath her nurse's cap. 'Thought I would just be put in plaster and allowed home!'

'That was not possible. You received a serious injury, Mr Greer, but the operation has been successful and you should make a full recovery.' She had been aware of his dark eyes examining her quizzically beneath arched brows, as he bent a warm smile up at her.

'So, I've had surgery?'

'Yes, as I explained, you sustained a Pott's fracture, that is broken tibia and fibula at the ankle—have received surgery and now need to lie as still as possible.'

'It's damned painful!'

'I'll bring you some medication to help—then you should try to sleep.'

'What's your name, nurse?' he demanded.

'Staff Nurse Nicolson.'

'And your first name?' She had not replied but moved on to her next patient, but was aware of his gaze following her. She checked his details in Sister's ward book. Malcolm Greer was a property developer, thirty-six years old, unmarried and owned a mansion on the outskirts of

Lynchester. A few days later, he was visited by a respectful, swarthy-faced man, who had brought him his computer—then took notes from Malcolm who gesticulated as he gave orders. They both stopped talking as she approached the bed and the swarthy man left soon afterwards. She had felt slightly curious but Malcolm Greer was just one patient in a busy ward.

Malcolm Greer remained in the ward for another three weeks and was then discharged in a walking plaster, to be seen by outpatients in two weeks' time. She was slightly relieved to see the handsome patient finally leave, as a porter pushed him through the swing doors to be driven home in hospital transport, had not expected to see him again. For Malcolm had been persistent in trying to discover more about her and had suggested they should meet once he was mobile, all of which overtures she had tactfully ignored. It was an unwritten hospital law that nurses did not cross the professional barrier between staff and patients.

She had almost forgotten Malcolm when two weeks later he appeared unexpectantly in the hospital forecourt and leaning on a cane, just as she was leaving by the staff exit. She was talking with her colleague Lilian Brown as he approached them flashing a warm smile at her.

'Staff Nurse Nicolson—Erika—a small token of my gratitude for your recent care of me!' and he had tendered a magnificent bouquet of red roses, definitely not acquired in the hospital shop. Lilian glanced from one to the other of them and left with a smile.

'Why thank you, they are lovely but quite unnecessary,' she had replied awkwardly as she took the flowers. 'It was a pleasure to care for you as it is for all patients who pass through the ward.'

'But we are no longer in the ward,' he had stated. 'So, I take it you are now free to accept an invitation to dine with me—it would give me great pleasure if you were to agree.' She knew she should refuse, had a feeling that there was something unpredictable about the tall, good-looking man with his arrogant bearing. But as he looked down pleadingly at her, she softened. After all, what harm could it do, he was no longer a patient, so not against protocol.

If only she had refused that first meeting lunching at a good restaurant, years of misery might have been avoided. Apart from one brief light love affair in her teens, Erika had thrown herself wholeheartedly into the nursing profession she loved. Although not necessarily ambitious, she knew she would enjoy future promotion to ward sister—worked towards this. Perhaps the fact that her late father had been an outstanding surgeon had been a deciding factor in her decision to become a nurse.

When Professor Alexander Nicolson had been diagnosed with an inoperable brain tumour, Erika's world had come tumbling down—for six months later her beloved father was dead. He had been her sole parent, for her mother had died giving her birth, and her only connection with the sadly unknown Lois Nicolson was the beautiful photographic portrait of the lovely young woman that hung in her father's study. A month after her father's funeral, at eighteen years of age, Erika had enrolled as a student nurse at the hospital where his memory was revered. That had been just over five years ago and she had never regretted her choice. When the other young nurses enjoyed dances and trips to the cinema in their off-duty time, Erika had studied hard. She also loved literature, the classics in particular and poetry and would make occasional visits to the theatre. And then suddenly Malcolm Greer had come into her life—and everything changed.

Erika had no slightest intention of intimacy between them when he invited her to spend a precious day off visiting his mansion. He assured her his elderly housekeeper and other members of staff would be present at Enderslie Court, and he would drive her back to the nurses' home well before 11 pm.

The old mansion house set in its attractive grounds lay several miles from the small town. As Malcolm showed her around its many rooms, she saw all was luxuriously appointed, and in perfect taste, had looked around in amazement, never expected his home to be such as this. She could never recall much of what had occurred later that evening, except that the dinner was delicious and served by the swarthy-faced man who had visited Malcolm during his stay in the hospital. She rarely took alcohol, but the wine that accompanied their meal, was light and cool, and she took a couple of glasses—and then found herself becoming abnormally sleepy.

Erika awoke the following morning in a strange bed, head feeling slightly muzzy. She realised she was naked, and pulling a sheet around her, slipped out of bed, and looked anxiously around—became aware of a certain soreness and gave a cry of distress.

'Good morning, Erika darling,' came a voice at the door, and looking round she saw Malcolm smiling across at her in amusement. 'Thank you for the most wonderful night,' he said gently.

'What do you mean—and where are my clothes?' she had demanded in outrage.

'The maid is pressing your blue suit, will bring it up immediately. The bathroom is through that door if you remember—so if you'd like to freshen up, shower—we'll then have breakfast when you are ready.'

'What happened last night,' she demanded angrily.

'It is not exactly flattering, that you should have forgotten the delights we shared in bed so soon, Erika.' He was resting his back indolently against the door frame.

'Are you saying we slept together—how can that be when I have no recollection of it happening?' And as she looked at him, the answer shot into her mind—the wine, and feeling so strange afterwards—then nothing. 'Did you drug me?' she asked in horror. 'Was that it—what kind of man needs to treat a woman in such a way? You disgust me!' She saw his face change as the amused smile froze to sudden cold malevolence. It passed almost immediately as his bland smile returned. He drove her back to the hospital and she walked away from his car without a backward look. He had looked after her thoughtfully. Malcolm Greer had, at last, found a woman he desired to share his life with—and who amazingly in this modern world, had come a virgin to his bed.

She had never intended to see Malcolm Greer again, throwing herself back into her work with determined energy and devotion, attempting to blot out the memory of the man's sexual assault—for such she knew it to be and found it so hard to understand. On the few occasions on which she had accompanied him on visits to the local art gallery, cinema or theatre, prior to the devastating occurrence at Enderslie Court, Malcolm had always proved kind and considerate

Shortly after what had in effect been his rape of an unconscious girl, his offerings of flowers and chocolates had begun to arrive for her at the nurses' home, to be scornfully tossed into the bin. How dare he try to contact her again after his outrageous behaviour!

Then one evening two months later, as she crossed the hospital forecourt, making towards the nursing home, Malcolm Greer suddenly appeared.

'Erika—I need to speak with you—please say you forgive me!' He stared at her pleadingly. She glared back at him in shock and attempted to walk past, but he caught at her arm. 'Wait—please wait. I deeply regret my behaviour towards you, and most humbly beg your pardon. Please give me another chance?' She jerked her arm away and stared at him angrily.

'Nothing you can say could ever excuse your treatment of me. I feel nothing but contempt for you, Mr Greer! Another two nurses were passing and looked at them inquiringly.

'Listen—what I did was wrong—but you see, I am in love with you. Cannot get you out of my mind!' His dark eyes swept over her face searchingly, looking for any slight softening in her attitude.

'Love—you think behaving dishonourably to an unconscious woman is love? Then I can only say I feel very sorry for you,' she said in a low voice.

'I have never felt the way I do about you for any other woman. I suppose I thought that once we had made love—that you might return my feelings. I want to marry you, Erika!' She heard the passion in his voice, sensed that however twisted his reasoning, he was telling the truth as he saw it.

'Goodbye Malcolm Greer,' and she walked away. To her relief, he did not follow her and Erika sat down in her small bedroom, heart pounding as she attempted to regain her composure, realised she was shaking. She had been feeling slightly nauseous these last few days, tummy upsets could happen when working on the wards but she hadn't reported it. Now this sudden confrontation with the man she hoped never to see again caused disturbing memories to resurface—and an impossible thought came into her head. The nausea she had experienced over these last few mornings—surely it wasn't possible that she was pregnant? A simple urine test taken the following morning confirmed her suspicion to be fact. But it couldn't be happening, she couldn't be carrying Malcolm Greer's child. Panic set in!

How could she have a baby and continue with her nursing career? There was always the option of abortion, but Erika knew this was not a choice she could make. But what then, leave before her condition became apparent, give birth and place the child for adoption? It seemed to be the logical answer. Her father had left her well provided for, so money would not be a problem. Many nurses took a break in their careers and with her excellent record, she should find it relatively easy to return to St Phil's or perhaps another hospital and make a completely new start. The more she thought about it, the more it seemed the correct way forward.

Two weeks later Erika tendered a month's notice, much to the regret of the senior nursing officer, who said that should the staff nurse wish to return she would receive a welcome. She experienced a pang as she left the nursing home for the last time, stowing her bags into the boot of her white Vauxhall. She was unaware of being watched from across the hospital forecourt. Malcolm Greer was sitting there in his silver BMW, had been waiting in hope of a glimpse of Erika when he saw her pushing her bags into her car boot, and driving off. He had followed, noted the Vauxhall draw up before a substantial house with a fine garden, watched as she parked the car in the driveway, then removed her belongings from the boot, unlocked the front door and disappeared inside.

So, she owned a house of her own in an expensive area. Suddenly he realised how little he knew about the young woman who had obsessed him for the last few months. He sat there, considering it was unlikely she would come out again soon. He must try to find out about the house she had entered, took note of its name on the gate 'The Laurels' and drove off. He did not realise Erika had noticed his silver BMW on the road below her, as she opened the door. The sight of it had made her feel very uneasy.

As she relaxed in the comfortable bedroom, so familiar since her childhood, Erika's thoughts returned to Malcolm Greer, the father of the babe growing beneath her heart. Well, he would never have the joy of knowing his child, she thought firmly. As she turned her head on the pillow, wondered for the first time if she was carrying a boy or a girl. But what did it matter as the child was to be adopted? But suppose the adoptive parents were not kind to the little one and she felt a sudden fierce sense of protectiveness towards it.

Another month had passed, during which Malcolm Greer had discovered that Erika's late father had been a renowned surgeon, no doubt had left all he possessed to his only child. So why had Erika needed to work as a nurse? Such work was understood to be sadly underpaid in the Health Service. He was puzzled, and could only think she had needed a challenge. He liked that. But why suddenly leave the work she so obviously enjoyed to retire to 'The Laurels'? Was it to escape his attention?

A business most believed as a property developer took up most of his time, but occasionally Malcolm would drive over to The Laurels on the off-chance of seeing the lovely, golden-haired young woman with her challenging blue gaze. He cursed himself for his treatment of her, not through any remorse, but because he had not realised she was different to those women he had casually toyed with in the past.

Then one morning in early August, he parked across the road from the house to be rewarded by the sight of Erika leaving the house. She was wearing a loose finely pleated silk shirt above a navy skirt. As she walked down the front steps, the light summer wind, blew her shirt revealingly about her figure, and his eyes narrowed as he noticed the slight thickening at her normally slim waist. Was it possible that Erika was pregnant? His mind thought back to the date on which she had spent the night with him at Enderslie—over four months now—and she had been a virgin! Could she be carrying his child? It would explain why she had left the work she loved at the hospital.

He took a decision, got out of his BMW and crossed the road to intercept her before she could get into her car parked at the curb. Her eyes widened in shock as she saw him.

'What are you doing here?' she demanded in annoyance.

'Erika—we need to talk!' he pointed a finger at her waistline. 'I think you know why.' She drew in her breath and faced him defiantly.

'I have no idea what you mean Mr Greer. Please leave, or I will call the police and report you for harassment!'

'A father at fault for showing concern for the mother of his child?' She blanched at his words, opened the car door and switched on the ignition. He stared after her as she drove away, her expression had confirmed all he suspected—and he smiled satisfaction. He must plan now.

Erika did not see him again for three weeks when he waylaid her once more as she was about to get into her car. He inclined his head to her and smiled courteously.

'Please may we talk, Erika,' he said softly. 'Afterwards, I promise to leave immediately if you so wish, but I think for the sake of our future child there are matters we need to discuss.' She knew there was no hiding the evidence of her pregnancy now, but had no intention of confirming his paternity.

'Whether or not I am expecting a child is no business of yours, Malcolm. Please leave!' she said in a low voice. He saw the implacable expression on her face and his eyes hardened.

'Listen to me, Erika. When the baby is born, a simple blood test will reveal whether or not I am the father. The law will allow this test. You can either decide for us to bring up our child jointly in a caring relationship—marriage if you wish or face a more difficult future where I will demand regular access to our child. Think it over Erika. You know that I love you and am in a position to offer you every comfort. We could be very happy' he said persuasively.

'Thank you, but no! My child is to be adopted, all arrangements made.' Her heart was pounding as she drove away, for she realised he would not accept her decision lightly. So now what—move to another town, leaving all that was familiar behind?

The scan had shown the child was a girl. Could Malcolm legally prevent her plans for adoption from going through she wondered, as the doctor at the clinic emphasised that her blood pressure was higher than normal? The woman asked if anything was worrying Erika, who shook her head dismissively, not ready yet to trust anyone with the truth of the situation.

What about her baby's future—was she being hard-hearted in denying the child a father's love? What would life be like if she gave in to Malcolm and agreed to marry him? But it did not need to be marriage, she could always become his partner. Then she dismissed such thoughts as ridiculous but knew she was feeling very tired these days.

As the weeks sped by, Malcolm Greer made frequent visits to the door of the house, bringing small gifts and gradually Erika began to weaken as he demonstrated an apparent genuine concern for her. Eventually, she invited him in one afternoon, when he stared curiously around the comfortably furnished house that still showed masculine imprints of her late father from the many medical books, some fine seascapes on the walls, a pipe placed on a side table next to a deep leather armchair. Professor Alexander Nicolson had obviously had a great influence on Erika's life, thought Malcolm. Once Erika was under his control this house should be sold, the money so realised placed in a joint account to eventually disappear. She must become totally reliant on him.

Gradually, almost imperceptibly Erika developed an affection for Malcolm, even trying to justify his drugging her that night at Enderslie in her mind, as the action of a man who had allowed passion to overcome all normal behaviour. She was unaware that she was being skilfully groomed.

Then one day Malcolm invited her to visit his town flat. As she got awkwardly out of the car, eight months pregnancy disturbing her usual grace of movement, he tucked her hand under his arm, as they stepped in a lift and ascended to the second floor of the building, immediately above a fashionable jewellery shop. Erika glanced around as he watched her reaction to the subdued elegance of the sitting room, then led her to explore the kitchen and bedrooms and then opened a door into a pretty nursery with a delightful white cot, panels painted with nursery rhymes, a mobile with silvery chimes, a cushioned rocking chair and shelves displaying a wonderful collection of soft toys.

'For our little Trudy,' he said quietly. She looked at him.

'You are taking matters for granted, aren't you? I have not even agreed to live with you yet, but you have already chosen our future daughter's name?'

'You do not care for the name Trudy? It was my mothers,' he said softly. 'What do you think of the flat? I can change the colour scheme if it does not please you?' He gathered her into his arms gently and kissed her. She stiffened at first and then began to relax. He smiled satisfaction, knew that he had prevailed—Erika was his.

'Come—let's go into the sitting room where you may make yourself comfortable Erika darling.' He had never used the endearment before, but she did not seem to notice, as he arranged cushions behind her head as she sank on the cream velvet settee, and put her feet up to ease swollen ankles.

'Did you like the nursery?' he probed.

'Well—yes. It was delightful,' she murmured, as she tried to visualise a tiny baby lying there. A warning signal flashed momentarily through her mind. Was she making the correct decision for her little one's future? Then his dark eyes were looking at her caressingly as he smiled at her lovingly, and the moment passed.

A month later just after Christmas, after a long labour, the child was born at St Phil's, and as Erika relaxed on her pillows and looked down with tired wonder at the tiny daughter in her arms, Malcolm Greer leaned over her hospital bed and kissed her in satisfaction.

'She is beautiful, Erika darling—our little Trudy has your golden hair and blue eyes.' he said as he stared possessively at the baby. 'In a few days, you will both be home. I am engaging a nursemaid to help look after our daughter, so that you may soon regain your strength.'

'But I do not need a nursemaid,' Erika protested in surprise. He smiled at her soothingly.

'Trust me, it will be for the best, my darling. Now I must go, business calls!' and his voice was firm.

Erika arrived back at the flat that was to be her new home, holding baby Trudy tenderly in her arms, and stepped out of the lift at Malcolm's side. She made her way to the nursery, as he opened the door for her and stared uncertainly at an attractive girl wearing a white apron over a blue dress, who rose from the cushioned rocking chair and smiled at her politely.

'This is Sarah Lofts, our little Trudy's nursemaid,' he said lightly. 'She has the highest references and should be a great help to you, my darling!' Erika experienced a sense of annoyance as she stared at this person who had been engaged with no reference to her but forced herself to return Sarah's greeting smile.

'May I see your little Trudy?' asked the girl, walking confidently towards Erika. 'Oh, why she's adorable,' she exclaimed softly. 'Ah— would you like me to change her nappy—I think that perhaps..!' Her pert nose suggested the need and Erika found herself handing Trudy over to this unwanted nursemaid, who laid the babe on a small table covered with a soft padded changing mat and despite the small cry of protest as Trudy sensed a stranger, began to deal with the situation with gentle deft movements, and Erika had to admit that she was indeed very efficient.

'Let's leave Sarah to deal with Trudy, while I make you comfortable next door,' said Malcolm, slipping an arm lightly about her shoulders as he led her away from the nursery and into the sitting room, and over to the cream settee, piled with cushions. 'There now, sit and just relax Erika, darling.' As she sat down she glanced around, saw the vases of expensive red roses placed about the room, wondering why his efforts to please did not bring her any real sense of delight, then told herself she was being ungrateful, that the future would bring happiness as they brought up their little daughter.

Their first real disagreement happened when he tried to persuade her to stop breastfeeding the baby.

'After this first month, Trudy will manage very nicely on a bottle like most babies in this modern age,' he had ordered. Erika had disagreed with barely concealed annoyance.

'No Malcolm! It is a personal decision for me to take,' she had replied. 'Breastfeeding offers protection against infection during a baby's early months, and strengthens the bond between mother and child.'

'But I want to invite some business associates here to meet my lovely wife—don't want to risk seeing your gown stained in the front with milk!' he protested angrily.

'That never happens—I'm always, most particular, as you are well aware! Apart from which I am not your wife, but your partner,' she retorted indignantly.

'You spend too much of your time with the child—it's time for you to take up your duties as my well—companion, and allow Sarah to deal with Trudy. After all, that is what I pay her for!' He had left the room slamming the door after him and waking an indignant Trudy who cried out in protest. He had shown a side of his nature Erika had not come across before and she was troubled.

He brought her flowers that evening and an expensive diamond bracelet.

'Well—do you like it,' he demanded as he slipped it on her wrist.

'Thank you—it is very beautiful,' she acknowledged.

'Joseph Lindt assured me it was one of his finest,' he said in satisfaction.

'You mean it comes from that jewellery shop below the flat?'

'Why not, it is a very fine jeweller, after all, I own it!' She stared at him in surprise.

'You never mentioned it before! But I realise you are quite wealthy, Malcolm. You have always said you are a businessman—a property developer?' she looked at him questioningly.

'My business dealings are no affair of yours, my dear Erika!' he said harshly. 'They would merely bore you. You will never lack for anything, let that suffice.' He drew her roughly into his arms and caressed her, but her response was automatic, her mind troubled. Had she made a most terrible mistake in allowing Malcolm Greer into her life? Would she perhaps be better to leave at this stage, and move back into The

Laurels? But what about baby Trudy? How would he react in such circumstances—had once indicated he would always demand regular access to the child if she attempted to pursue an independent life for herself, which meant she would never be free of him! She secretly acknowledged that there was something in Malcolm that she feared, and surely this was not natural in a normal loving relationship.

He was all kindness over the next few weeks and Erika began to relax. He insisted on buying her elegant stylish clothes from the branch of a top fashion house, and several beautiful evening gowns, with jewellery and accessories. She had never had any interest in such matters before, but it seemed to please him she realised and began to accept this different lifestyle. They would often visit exclusive restaurants, and Malcolm smiled at the admiring glances thrown at Erika. He had recognised the girl's exceptional beauty when first he had noticed her from his hospital bed. With her shapely figure, deep golden hair and hyacinth blue eyes she was arrestingly lovely. But Erika still possessed a strong will of her own, and he had the feeling that she might take herself off one day. How to prevent this from happening he wondered. She had been adamant in refusing his offer of marriage, despite his suggestion that it would be better if matters were legalised for the sake of the child.

She still owned that house that had been her family home and he knew that while she retained this, she would be in a position to move back there at any time. Something had to be done to cut off this escape route, in case Erika was ever so unwise as to leave him.

'We are going to move into Enderslie House for a few weeks,' he said casually one morning as she sat with six months old Trudy on her lap, ruffling the baby's soft blond curls framing her small piquant face, as the child made a grab for pearl necklace about her mother's throat.

'No, Trudy sweetheart,' laughed Erika, gently releasing the small hand, and kissing her. She turned and looked across at Malcolm now, as his words about moving registered in her mind. Enderslie—she had not been there since that night when Malcolm had drugged and then raped her—for there was no other expression to describe what had happened.

'I don't think I am ready to return to that house again yet,' she said now in a low voice. 'You go if you need to Malcolm—and I will remain here with Trudy until you return.' His face darkened with anger at her response.

'You are my wife, will do as I bid!' he said coldly.

'On the contrary, I am not your wife. Our arrangement is entirely voluntary, and I must say I find your present dictatorial attitude towards me offensive. You do not own me, Malcolm Greer!' She had said it now, resentment she had stored up now pouring out audibly. No sooner were the words out than he strode across the room and seized her by the throat.

'We may not be married, but you owe everything to me, Erika! And you will obey me if you know what is good for you!' and he shook her violently. Somehow, she managed to retain her hold on little Trudy who screamed in fright! Then suddenly Greer released her, the pearl necklace breaking, the pearls scattering across the carpet. He stood looking down at her, then turning on his heel, swore savagely and left.

She was left trembling as she tried to soothe the frightened baby.

Chapter Two

She was not aware of what happened subsequently, as one night after she had fallen asleep, Malcolm Greer went through her handbag and smiled satisfaction on finding an envelope containing her monthly bank details. He photocopied details of this and other data he had earlier discovered in a small box of letters, documents and photographs she had brought with her from her family home, and concealed them under a few sweaters on the top shelf of the wardrobe. He studied the copy of her father's will and noted the amount of money she had received on the renowned surgeon's death, together with the deed of inheritance for The Laurels.

The next day he met with Frank Dalton, a lawyer whom he always paid handsomely to carry out his legal requirements.

'Tell me, Frank, how can I acquire a house and sell it without the owner's knowledge or consent?' He looked intently at Dalton as the lawyer raised the generous glass of whisky he had accepted and lifted an amused eyebrow, at Greer's question.

'Not possible,' he replied. 'Why do you ask?' And Malcolm Greer told him in cool decisive tones. Dawson stared back at him.

'There is only one legal way I can think of—but it would only apply if the woman was judged unable to deal with her own affairs for shall we say, a disturbance of the mind! A power of attorney might then be used.' Malcolm considered the suggestion and shook his head.

'No—I do not wish to cause irreparable damage to our relationship but need a way to prevent her from leaving. Without the security of her substantial home and the money her father left her to fall back on, she would face an uncertain future.' He leaned across the table and stared into Dalton's narrow, expressionless face. 'So, think—think!'

'The house is worth at least 800k you say. You need the money?' he inquired.

'What kind of question is that? I'd be a fool to forgo such a sum, but on the other hand, I do not actually need it—why do you ask?'

'Suppose the house should burn down! I notice from these papers that insurance on the property is due for renewal. Should an accident happen to The Laurels before the insurance is renewed, then Erika will be unable to get compensation!' He gave Greer a penetrating stare. 'What do you say?'

'Arson? Suppose it could be traced back to me? Too risky!'

'For a sufficient fee, I can provide a man who will deal with the situation and leave no slightest evidence behind. But you will need to make your mind up quickly, as no doubt both the insurance company and her bank will be in touch with their client to remind her to renew her commitment. Perhaps you should watch her post?' He smiled at Greer and held out his glass for a refill. 'Excellent whisky by the way!' He watched Greer's face and saw his client had come to a decision.

'Very well, I agree—arson! It would seem to offer the best solution.' The conversation continued, a sum agreed on, and both men smiled satisfaction as they parted.

Erika was still deeply shocked at his recent treatment of her. True he had been all apparent contrition the next day, offered her flowers and a fine turquoise necklace, her pearls to be repaired, but a barrier had been breached. She had to face the fact that the father of her child could be violent—was dangerous. She must take little Trudy and leave, sever all contact with him—but how could this be achieved when he would undoubtedly track her down and demand paternal rights over their small daughter? Perhaps she needed to see a solicitor, and get some legal advice? Even that would be difficult, for she also had the feeling that the attractive nursemaid, Sarah Lofts, was watching her movements.

A week later Erika had a phone call from the police. After checking she was the legal owner of The Laurels, the officer's grave voice announced that there had been a severe fire at the house, its origin unknown, but the fire service was of the opinion that it had been caused by an electrical fault.'

'How badly is the house damaged?' she had asked through trembling lips.

'I'm very sorry, madam—but the place is a complete right off! You will need to claim on your insurance,' the officer said sympathetically. She put the phone down, trying to come to terms with the fact that the lovely old house that had contained so many memories of childhood and her father's love had been destroyed. She had been planning to move back there taking Trudy with her—so what now? The insurance—she must put in a claim.

'Is something wrong, my dear?' inquired Malcolm's suave voice as he came quietly into the sitting room. She told him, trying to keep the shock from her voice. He was immediately all deep concern. 'You must let me help you place a claim on your insurance,' he said. 'It was a fine house, a sad loss.'

'It was my home,' she whispered.

'Was—yes. But now you have two new homes, Erika—this flat and Enderslie House. And I shall make it my delight to see that you always have all you can possibly need,' he said soothingly. She made no reply.

When it was discovered that her insurance on The Laurels had expired a week before the fire, Erika was stunned. Why had the insurance company not reminded her—or her bank? Both assured her letters had been sent to her new address, which was obviously untrue. Or was it? A faint suspicion entered her mind that perhaps Malcolm might have intercepted her mail. Then she told herself she was being paranoid. The loss of her family home had to be accepted, and new plans were considered for a future new home for herself and her baby daughter. At least she still had a comfortable sum in her bank account, thanks to her father's legacy.

For the next week, Malcolm treated her with kindness and courtesy, there were little gifts and a visit to the theatre. Gradually Erika began to relax, telling herself that she had been judging him too harshly, that he was now attempting to behave as a loving partner, not a dictator. But it had been too good to last, for as Erika was preparing breakfast, he seated himself at the kitchen table watching her.

'You will not need to cook our meals tomorrow, my dear. At Enderslie House the staff will attend to all such chores. So, after breakfast start packing any clothes you want to bring with you and Sarah will attend to all little Trudy's things. We leave at midday.' He spoke firmly and met her indignant gaze with an implacable stare.

'We spoke of this before, Malcolm when I made it clear that I do not want to live at Enderslie House—it holds unfortunate memories!'

'Since it was where our daughter was conceived, I do not share this opinion. You will learn to love the place, Erika. Many women would be proud to live in such a delightful residence!' he stared at her haughtily.

'Then perhaps you should select one of them to accompany you there—for I am adamant that I will not!' she declared hotly. He sprang up from his chair and put his hand on her shoulder, fingers pinching painfully into her flesh. She dropped the spatula in pain, stepped back from the frying pan where eggs and bacon were sizzling, and wrenched herself free from him.

'Lay a hand on me again and I will leave you!' she announced, eyes flashing.

'You may do so—but you will leave without our daughter! Sarah Lofts will come with me to care for the child, and you my dear will be seen to have decided to desert little Trudy!'

'You would not dare!' she said aghast. He smiled at her mockingly.

'If you are not ready to leave by mid-day, you may judge for yourself whether I make baseless threats. Now be sensible, Erika! You will have a comfortable life ahead of you if you behave reasonably—and little Trudy has the best that money can buy.' He walked out of the kitchen as she stood there in shock. What should she do? Perhaps she must have the courage to take Trudy and just leave now—move into a B&B as a temporary measure. Once she was at Enderslie House it would be far more difficult to get away, the place so remote.

Erika went to their bedroom, started to throw her clothes into a couple of cases, snapped the locks, and then went to Trudy's nursery. She looked at the empty cot in disbelief. Where was her baby? She called Sarah's name, but no one came. Perhaps the nursemaid had taken Trudy into the sitting room—rushed through there and realised was no sign of Sarah or her beloved baby. Her heart was pounding uncomfortably, frantic tears coming into her eyes when she heard a sudden laugh behind her. She turned to see Malcolm staring at her in cool amusement.

'You were looking for little Trudy, my dear? I have sent her on before us in your Vauxhall with Sarah driving, all her necessities are carefully packed. She will be waiting for us at Enderslie—unless of course, you have decided not to join us there?' He smiled indolently, obviously convinced of her compliance. She looked back at him with contempt, tears sparkling on her lashes. She had no alternative now but to give in, at least for the time being.

As Enderslie House came into view from the car window, Erika stared towards it stonily. Yes, it was an imposing building, set in lovely grounds, but to her, it appeared as a prison. But at least she would soon be reunited with her baby. It was apparent that she must pretend to accept the invidious situation for now, but one day she would escape from the man she now disliked and feared. She prayed that day might arrive soon.

It was to be almost four years before Erika finally managed to evade Malcolm Greer and those he employed in Enderslie who kept her under constant if unobtrusive scrutiny. They were long years during which Malcolm alternated between acting as a charming companion, but whose mood changed to freezing disdain should she ever request to go into town. On those occasions when in sheer desperation she demanded to leave and lead her own life again, he would lash out with physical violence. Afterwards, he would try to appease her. She had everything she could possibly want here in her beautiful home, she should be content with a lifestyle many women would envy her.

In the meanwhile, little Trudy progressed from baby to delightful, lively toddler, then into a somewhat subdued small girl. Nursemaid Trudy had been replaced by Mrs Carrie Beecham, a middle-aged nanny whom Malcolm had engaged to care for Trudy for the greater part of each day. At first, Erika had protested the presence of this steely-eyed woman, with her silver hair tucked back beneath a lace cap, who seemed intent on dampening any show of spontaneity the child evinced. She seemed like a character out of Dickens, Erika thought.

As for Moira Banks, the elderly housekeeper, she was polite enough but distant. had seemingly enjoyed her position for over forty years, originally working for Malcolm's parents, from whom he had supposedly inherited his wealth. Erika learned that twenty years ago when their son had just achieved his MA, the couple died of pneumonia within days of each other. Malcolm Greer returned to Enderslie and installed a new member of staff as his personal assistant, a dark-skinned individual with an inscrutable expression, who carried out his employer's orders with quiet efficiency. Erika had disliked Hassan from the first moment she had seen him on her original visit to Enderslie House when Malcolm had drugged and raped her.

Apart from the housekeeper, Nanny Beecham and Hassan, there was also the cook Martha, a couple of maids and a gardener. All of the people employed there seemed completely devoted to Malcolm and she soon realised there was not a single one she could take into her confidence or seek help from. On the surface it might have seemed that she led an idyllic existence, Malcolm always showing a kindly concern for the beautiful mother of his little girl when others were looking on, whilst displaying a darker side of his nature when they were alone. And always the man Hassan watched her when his master was away, and she knew that Malcolm had ordered him to do so.

About two years ago soon after Nanny Beecham had arrived to take up her duties with little Trudy, Erika began to feel very fatigued, usually in the early afternoons.

'You should lie down for a little, Madam,' Nanny said with apparent compassion, and Erika had felt too tired to refuse. But why was she suffering from this unusual tiredness? She was usually full of energy, but now it was becoming difficult even to think clearly at times. It had been on one of these afternoons that Malcolm had appeared where she was lying back on a couch, bent and kissed her.

'I'm sorry to disturb you, my darling,' he said lightly, 'but I need your signature on this form.' She had looked at it foggily, the words seeming to shimmer oddly beneath her eyes. She looked at him.

'What is this, Malcolm?'

'Oh, a mere formality. It is a request to your bank to allow your money to be transferred into a new joint account I am setting up. It seems the most logical thing to do now that we share all things together, don't you agree?' She frowned, her eyes troubled. The few thousands her late father had bequeathed, would provide a lifeline should she ever manage to get away from Enderslie and its despotic owner.

'I have no wish to set up a joint account with you, Malcolm!'

'I find that difficult to accept when I provide everything for you and our child! It is with Trudy in mind that I am doing this—as in the case of my demise—or yours, then all will be placed in a trust fund for her upbringing. Now, what is wrong with that?'

'It just feels wrong,' she said. He merely smiled at her.

'You need to trust me, my dearest Erika. Ah, you haven't finished your milk,' and he leaned over the small octagonal table, handing her the glass. She lifted it to her lips automatically and drank, as she continued to stare at him, she knew she was growing ever sleepier. He placed a pen in her hand and guided her fingers down onto the form. 'Just sign it, darling, and then you can relax and go back to sleep,' he said and smiled satisfaction as she complied. It was done. Now if ever Erika tried to leave him, it would be without a penny to her name.

The following day she tried to remember what had happened and was appalled to realise what she had done. Why had she been so foolish—and why this constant feeling of tiredness? When Nanny Beecham handed her that usual glass of milk that day, she thanked the woman, and was about to lift it to her lips when a thought struck her. She remembered how Malcolm had drugged her that first night at Enderslie when Trudy had been conceived—was it possible?

It was at this moment, that Mitzi, the little Russian Blue cat Malcolm had bought her, arched its back and purred as she bent to caress it. She stared down at the little animal, then on sudden inspiration poured some contents of the glass into a saucer, and put it down for Mitzi to lap. Not long afterwards, the little cat fell deeply asleep and did not stir when Erika tried to wake it.

A feeling of fear gripped Erika by the throat as she faced the reality that Malcolm was having her drugged on a regular basis. What was he using—could it be something addictive, she worried. She lifted the saucer and replaced it under the glass, and settled back in the chair. Nanny Beecham came in, glanced at her approvingly, not even noticing the sleeping cat at her feet, and left the room again. Later Mitzi was removed.

She had stiffened when he had attempted to make love to her that night.

'What is wrong, Erika?' he inquired.

'I do not feel like it.'

'That is unfortunate, for I do,' he replied and forced her shoulders back against the pillows mounted and entered her without care or consideration. He expended himself, rolled back and fell into snoring sleep. She choked back a sob. It couldn't continue. Somehow, she had to get away with little Trudy and make a new life for them both. But how could it be done? Some months ago, he had said her car was dangerous to use, and had it removed. The house was about five miles from the town, it was a distance she could manage on foot if necessary, but what about Trudy? No, the little girl was just over two years old, too young to walk any distance and just how fast could Erika go carrying her?

She must make a sensible plan—but what? Without money or anywhere to go what were her possible options? She must wait until Trudy was a little older. In the meanwhile, she must try to set Malcolm's mind at rest, pretend to have an affection she did not feel, and stop taking that drugged milk. Nanny Beecham looked at her uncertainly when Erika refused to take any more milk.

'It does not agree with me, Nanny—and perhaps you may guess why!' Whether the woman informed Malcolm she never knew, but the heavy feeling of tiredness that had beset her had disappeared.

Another eighteen months passed. Malcolm now regularly invited his business associates to be entertained at Enderslie, and it was her duty to act as the perfect hostess. The gowns he bought for her were extremely lovely, with exquisite jewellery to further enhance her appearance. It gave him enormous satisfaction to see envy in other men's eyes when they saw their host's beautiful partner. Erika found that performing her duties to his satisfaction meant a lessening of friction between them, and gradually as the months passed he began to believe that at last Erika had given up all thought of trying to leave him. Despite this, he could still lash out at times, or make derogatory remarks about her appearance.

After she had pleased him by playing the gracious hostess to some important foreign guests one evening, she was surprised the following morning to be told he was taking her to the theatre that night, they would be driving into Lynchester, would spend the day there and she could take time doing some shopping if she wished. It was an unusual occurrence and Erika felt a throb of excitement, almost sensing a change was on the horizon.

'May we take Trudy with us.' she asked hopefully. He shook his head.

'No, she would only get tired. She will be happy enough here with Nanny Beecham,' he said firmly. She sighed and tried not to make her disappointment apparent. This was going to offer a rare opportunity to seek help. She had often planned what she would do if the chance presented itself.

During her work at the hospital a few years ago, she had heard talk of a women's refuge somewhere in Lynchester. But how was she to discover its whereabouts, and contact those who ran it? When he had first installed her at Enderslie House, she had curiously lost her cell phone. Her request for another one had been dismissed. She could use the house phone if necessary. It had been just another means of cutting her off from anyone she might know.

She had often thought about the possibility of seeking out a women's refuge, wondered whether she dared borrow his computer, and use the search facility to look for one in the area, but knew he might be able to check any new data appearing on his mac, could not risk his discovering her plans. Then there was Hassan, his rather cruel dark eyes always following her. Once she had slipped out not the grounds, staring at the delivery van that was about to leave after delivering the weekly groceries. Suppose she were to grab Trudy one day and ask the driver for a lift. The man was closing the van's doors as she stared at it speculatively.

'You wish to speak to the driver about a missing item perhaps, madam?' said Hassan's sibilant voice. She turned and shook her head.

'No—just need some air, will take a walk in the garden,' she had said innocently, felt his eyes following her as she walked across the lawn and sat on a bench under a flowering cherry tree. Wherever she went she knew Hassan was observing her. It was an impossible situation.

The thought of a possible escape never left her mind. So now as she sat beside Malcolm in the BMW she was determined to seek help if the opportunity presented n
itself, but knew she would have to be very careful.

'You are very quiet, Erika,' he said suddenly.

'I do not like to disturb you when you're driving,' she replied.

'You shouldn't worry—I am an excellent driver,' he said loftily. 'I will drop you off at the flat, as I have a business meeting in the Stag Hotel. Feel free to visit Dora's gown shop and purchase something special—put it on my account. I will return to the flat in a couple of hours, and take you out for a late lunch.' He was ordering her as he did Hassan, she realised. But this was the first time that she was going to have a precious two hours to herself, would not waste this opportunity.

He parked long enough for Erika to get out, watched as she approached the door to the flat and sped off. She wondered what this business meeting was about, and sensed it was something important. As she was about to put her key into the lock, she heard her voice called, turned around and saw an old nursing colleague, Lilian Brown waving to her.

'Erika! It is you, isn't it?' cried this friend from her past, her eyes taking in Erika's elegant, maroon suit, pearls at the throat of her cream silk shirt, the dainty high-heeled shoes.

'Lilian! Oh, it's so good to see you!' exclaimed Erika.

'We haven't met since you up and left the hospital! Where have you been?'

'Oh, I share my partner's home a few miles out of town,' replied Erika. Lilian stared.

'Well, how is it that I haven't seen you around? I was sure you must have left the area, dear.' She smiled at Erika. 'Look, I was about to get coffee and a pastry at Claudette. Care to join me?' Erika was about to refuse, so indoctrinated had she become by Malcolm, but taking a deep breath she smiled in agreement.

As they sat in the café in a corner seat, exchanging a little light talk, Erika took a decision.

'Lilian—I need help—need it badly,' she said in a low voice.

'Thought you seemed tense—so what's wrong, Erika?' Nurse Lilian Brown had seen the distress in Erika's blue eyes and sensed this friend she had not seen for the last four years, was scared. She reached out a hand and took Erka's reassuringly. 'Look—whatever it is, I will do all I can to help.'

'It means trusting you with something I find very difficult to disclose. But the fact is, that my partner Malcolm Greer, has been forcibly keeping me in a mansion he owns called Enderslie House, refuses to let me leave him, and says he will keep our little daughter Trudy if I ever attempt to get away. There are people in the house watching me all the while—and I am desperate, Lilian!' The words poured out through trembling lips. As Lilian listened appalled.

'Where is your little girl now?' she asked, her brown eyes brimming with sympathy

'At Enderslie House with her nanny, a gorgon of a woman who suppresses all dear little Trudy's natural sense of fun. Then there's a manservant called Hassan, who watches my movements at all times when Malcolm is away.'

'Right, so you have to get away from this dreadful situation,' declared Lilian hotly. 'What you have just described is domestic abuse, you know that!'

'I suppose I have never put a name to it before—but you're right! I have fantasised about snatching Trudy and escaping to a women's refuge. But I don't know how to contact one, am not allowed to have a cell phone or use a computer.' Lilian looked at her in consternation.

'Well, I'll get you a mobile. I also will contact a social worker I know, as well as another woman who runs a refuge. I believe we were meant to meet this morning, Erika! You finish your coffee while I pop to the store next door and buy a cheap mobile. Won't be long!' Erika stared after her, hardly daring to believe that she had taken the first step to freedom!'

When Malcolm Greer returned to the flat, it was to find Erika examining the contents of two carrier bags bearing the name of Dora's gowns. He smiled. She had done exactly what he had told her and felt content that at long last Erika had accepted their life together. It was also proving to be a very successful day. His business meeting had gone off better than he had hoped, and he was set to gain a cool million through his initial modest investment in the country house they had jointly forced the impoverished owner to sell. But it was other businesses conducted in Eastern Europe that brought in greater profits.

Erika had barely taken in the theme of the drama they watched together later at the theatre, and after he had made love to her that night, had lain quietly next to him as her thoughts explored the reality of actually getting away from him at long last. But she would have to be careful, so very careful.

In the end, happened very quickly. She had taken Trudy out into the garden and as Nanny Beecham sat staring disapprovingly nearby, she played ball with her little girl as they got ever further away from the wooden bench from which the woman surveyed them. The phone in her pocket vibrated, and she bent down casually as though to examine her shoe.

'The car will draw up in the courtyard in five minutes if you are ready,' came a strange voice. She swallowed in excitement.

'I'll be there,' she whispered. Then calling Trudy to her picked her up and started to swing her about, as the child laughed in delight. She put her down as she heard a disapproving cry from Nanny Beecham, and whispered into Trudy's ear.

'Trudy darling, we are going to play a special game, have an adventure. But you mustn't be scared if you hear people shouting. Just hold my hand tightly—and when I say run—then run very fast—understand?'

The little girl looked up at her trustingly and reached out a small hand.

'Yes, Mummy,' she said.

'Good—now then, Trudy! Run—run!' and Erika suddenly tossed the ball in front of them as far as she was able, and set off after it, Trudy at her side. Nanny Beecham let out a loud cry of protest as they disappeared from the back garden, rushing round the side of the house to the front courtyard. Almost simultaneously a car drove up, a man leapt out, assisted Erika and Trudy onto the back seat of the nondescript vehicle, and was back in his driving seat within a couple of minutes, as there was a furious shout from the front steps of the house, where Hassan stood gesticulating violently, and watching in incredulity as his master's lovely mistress and small daughter were driven away!

Erika clutched Trudy to her and kissed her wondering little face.

'Where are we going, Mummy?' she asked, enjoying feeling the security of her mother's arms about her.

'To start a new life, Trudy sweetheart! Where there will be no cross-faced Nanny Beecham—we will have lots of fun,' she reassured her gently.

'What about, Papa—is he coming with us? He gets very cross too,' said Trudy tellingly. She stared up at her mother. 'He shouts at you sometimes and it scares me.' The child had never spoken of this before and Erika blinked back tears as she realised the effect Malcolm's behaviour had been having on little Trudy.

'We will not be seeing your father again, my darling,' said Erika softly.

'Not ever—are you sure Mummy?'

'Not if I can help it—no!' declared Erika, and they heard an approving laugh from the driver. Erika glanced towards him for the first time.

'How can I thank you for your help,' she said in a low voice. 'You have been brilliant coming to get us in this way. I can hardly believe it's happening!'

'Well, it is—and names Roddy Forester, by the way! Now tighten your seat belt Erika—we are being followed—green Land Rover. The driver looks like that nasty bit of work I noticed standing on the front steps of the house as we left,' he said evenly. She gasped in dismay.

'Hassan! He's Malcolm's personal assistant—part of his duties is to watch over me! I have always feared him,' she whispered and bit her lip as she turned her head to confirm the identity of the car speeding behind them.

'Here we go then,' said Roddy and giving her a quick reassuring glance before suddenly accelerating, as their car shot forward at amazing speed along the country road. Trudy clutched anxiously at her mother, as Erika held her close. Suddenly a field gate was opened at the side of the road, and as they swept past, a herd of black and white cows were driven onto the road by a farmhand. There was a loud screech of brakes as the Land Rover was forced to a stop. Roddy chuckled as glanced in his wing mirror and drove on.

'What an amazing coincidence,' cried Erika, looking back as the herd of cows continued to constitute a solid blockage across the road. 'Bless that farmer!'

'Danny is a good fellow,' agreed the driver. 'Seems to be having quite a problem sorting out the livestock!'

'You know him?' she asked incredulously.

'We have met. Ask no questions!'

'Are you involved with the refuge, Roddy?'

'My wife Norah runs it. But you won't be staying with us for long. The place is as close a secret as we can make it—but perhaps too near to this area. You will be moved on, possibly towards the coast.'

They had turned off the main road now and were bumping along a rough lane, banks on either side overhung by bushes. They drove on about a mile until an old farmhouse came into view when the car slowed down and braked.

'This is where you get out, Erika,' said the driver, opening the car door. She stepped from the car curiously, as Roddy lifted little Trudy out to stand solemnly at her mother's side, as the farmhouse door opened and a red-haired woman wearing blue jeans and a jacket and with a wide smile on her attractive face, beckoned a welcome.

'Erika—Trudy! Come in my dears! Any trouble Roddy?'

'Some objectionable fellow tried to follow us. Danny's herd were crossing the road at the time—delay didn't do the bloke's blood pressure much good I think,' and he kissed her and turned to Erika.

'My wife, Norah,' he introduced. 'Let's get you settled inside.' Erika stared from one to the other of them, eyes brimming with tears of relief.

'Thank you both—oh, thank you,' she breathed and followed Norah in through the farmhouse door. She wasn't quite sure what she had expected, as she gazed at the comfortable sitting room with several well-worn couches and easy chairs where an assorted group of women sat talking quietly together, several small children playing with toys on the carpet, all seemed very normal she thought. The women looked up as she came in.

'Our two latest new guests everyone,' smiled Norah. 'I'm just going to show them into their room—they will join you later. You can introduce yourselves then.' They waved at Erika as Norah led her away.

'How many women do you help here?' asked Erika.

'Oh, it varies according to need. But up to twelve. Some arrive badly injured, others traumatised after years of abuse, and some psychologically damaged. All have one thing in common, they have reached breaking point, and found the courage to walk away from their abuser!' She saw the worried look on Erika's face. 'What's wrong?'

'I feel a fraud in as much that I've received no violent injuries—at least nothing that shows,' said Erika in a low voice. 'Just four years of being held in my partner's mansion against my will, threats to keep our little girl if I attempted to get away, constant criticisms of my appearance, sometimes punched, slapped, but always expensive gifts offered afterwards with apologies, the whole cycle repeated time and again. He engaged a dragon of a nanny to care for Trudy, and there was a man called Hassan who kept me under constant surveillance when

Malcolm was away on business!' And suddenly her tears started to fall, and Norah slipped a compassionate arm about her.

'What you have just revealed is truly dreadful, Erika. Your friend Lilian contacted me and filled me in on some of this and I'm just so glad that we were able to move to help so quickly. I've heard of Enderslie House, that the man who owns it is very wealthy but has a questionable business record. You are well rid of this bully and I hope the courage you have shown, will lead to a new and happier future!' She gave Erika a quick hug, and the spontaneous gesture touched her as Norah then knelt down beside Trudy. 'So, this is your little daughter. What a lovely little girl—she has your eyes and hair. Trudy—my name is Norah,' she said and diving a hand into her pocket produced a sweet and offered it.

'Nanny said I shouldn't eat sweets! She said it would make my teeth fall out!' said Trudy seriously.

'Well dear, you don't have to worry about that grumpy old nanny anymore! Ask your Mummy, she will tell you.' She smiled as Trudy popped the sweetie in her mouth. 'Now come this way, please. We need to do a little paperwork in the office, then you can relax in your room. But first what about refreshments—there's a pot of tea and cakes—milk or fruit juice for this young lady! You will be staying in the farmhouse—some of our guests have rooms in one of the restored barns you know.'

It all seemed like some strange dream thought Erika, gratefully sipping her tea, as she sat in a small office with Norah who took a few notes—then looked at her inquiringly.

'Have you considered changing your name, Erika? If you are to make a new life for yourself then I suggest a change of identity will be essential. Trudy too will have to get used to a new name and the sooner you both start the better. From what you have told me of Malcolm Greer, I would say that he will not let you disappear easily. A change of name will just be the beginning.' Her brown eyes met Erika's troubled blue gaze.

'You are quite right, Norah. And I think I know the name I'll use. Anna Lindstrom! It was the name of my Swedish great-grandmother. Malcolm has no knowledge of my predecessors, so quite safe to use it.'

'Good—as it is a family name you will be less likely to forget it under stress. What about Trudy?'

'I am not sure.' How could Trudy be anyone else but Trudy, she thought? Norah glanced down at the little girl thoughtfully.

'What about Susan or Susie—it has a slightly similar sound to Trudy. She would soon get used to it.' Erika nodded. Yes, Susan would serve as well as another, she decided.

'Good—then that is agreed, the first positive step towards your new future taken. Now, I'll show you the room you will use while here. Come along, my dear!'

Erika looked around the clean, basically furnished bedroom and felt it to be a palace, for now, at last, she was free of Malcolm. As Norah left closing the door behind her, she sank down on the bed and pulled Trudy onto her lap.

'Is this our new home, Mummy?' asked the child, looking up at her earnestly. Erika stroked her soft curls and smiled.

'Yes—well, maybe not for very long. We'll have a new home of our own one day, but for now, we must get ready to meet new friends—and there will be no Nanny Beecham to stop you from having fun!' she promised

'Good!' declared Trudy. 'I just want you to look after me, Mummy!' Erika hugged her, then looked down at her seriously.

'There is something else I have to tell you, dear. Your father may attempt to find us and try make us return to Enderslie. But we are not going to let him find us! That's why we are going to change our names. I am going to be known as Anna Lindstrom—can you say that, darling?' and she repeated it twice. Trudy tried it on her tongue and smiled.

'I like it, Mummy. Anna Lindstrom! Have I got a new name too?' she asked.

'Yes. You are now Susan Lindstrom—or Susie if you prefer that.'

'I like Susan,' she said slowly. 'Susan Lindstrom,' and she began to say the name aloud in ever more confident tones. Erika—or Anna as she must now think of herself, kissed her daughter in relief. This was proving easier than she had feared.

'Just remember—if anyone asks your name from now on, you must always say Susan Lindstrom—forget you ever had another name!'

'Susan—Susan—Susan!' chanted the child and slipping off her mother's lap, started to march around the room, shouting her new name at the top of her voice. And looking at her, the mother realised she had never heard her small daughter raise her voice before. She was beginning to act like a normal child for the first time. An hour later Norah came to collect them.

'Time to meet the others,' she said, as they returned to the sitting room, where they were introduced to the assorted residents of the refuge by their new names and received a warm welcome from these women of different age groups, and varying backgrounds, as a small boy with a scar on his face, came up to Susan now and tugged gently at her dress.

'Come and play,' he said. 'I'm Ben.' She looked at him uncertainly, then glanced across at the toy garage he was pointing at.

'I'm—Susan' she said shyly. 'Yes, I'd like to play.' And Anna watched the little exchange in delight, realising that the child had used her new name automatically.

Dinner was cooked and served by Connie Forester a pleasant-faced, rosy-cheeked, older woman whom she learned was Norah's mother-in-law. It was almost as though she had been introduced to a whole new family she thought as she saw how the other residents helped with the washing up, chattering away companionably together. There was one girl who didn't engage with the others. She was pale, withdrawn and appeared quite listless when addressed.

'Doris is still traumatised,' said a quiet voice beside Anna. It was Norah. 'She has only been with us for two days—suffered rape and has two broken ribs. She was referred by the police.' She drew Anna aside and spoke quietly.

'Poor girl,' exclaimed Anna in concern. 'Was it a random attack?'

'No. Her employer a solicitor, instructed her to remain in the office to finish some vital documents. She tried to fight him off—but he was drunk, almost killed her!'

'What a beast!' cried Anna hotly. 'What will happen to him?'

'He's been charged and allowed out on bail. He faces trial and eventually, I hope, a long term of imprisonment and will inevitably be struck off.'

'Has Doris received hospital treatment?'

'Yes. He was only allowed bail after we accepted Doris here.'

'Her ribs must be so painful.' Her former instincts as a nurse were coming to the fore as she imagined how difficult every movement must be for the girl. Norah nodded.

'Her mental scars from the rape will take longer to heal than her ribs,' she said quietly and wondered why Anna had become very quiet. 'Anna?'

'On my first visit to Enderslie House I was drugged—then raped,' said Anna slowly. 'It was how my little daughter was conceived. I woke up shocked and bewildered, to find myself in a strange bed—and challenged Malcolm with what he had done. He laughed—said he adored me, and this was why he felt entitled to take this action. I swore never to see him again. I refused to see him for a few months. It was when my pregnancy became noticeable that he put pressure on me to move in with him. Said if I refused he would constantly demand access to his child—would it not be better for the baby to be brought up in a secure home? I was tired and confused. The rest you know.'

'Anna—you have been most cruelly used, my dear,' Norah had listened appalled.

'I once had a house. It was our family home left to me by my late father, a well-known neurosurgeon—who tragically died of a brain tumour. As well as the house, Dad also left me well provided for financially.' She looked at Norah in distress as she continued. 'My house was suddenly burned down at a time when the insurance had just expired—I had not received notice it needed to be renewed.'

'That was dreadful—sounds no coincidence! But at least you still have money in the bank?' suggested Norah.

'Not now. Nany Beecham was in the habit of giving me a glass of milk every afternoon—it was drugged. At first, I couldn't understand why I was getting so inexplicably tired every day. Malcolm came to me one afternoon while I was resting, and demanded that I sign a form informing my bank that my money was to be transferred into a joint account he was setting up. I hardly knew what I was doing when I signed my money away Norah!'

'His behaviour towards you has been criminal. He should be brought to court to account for his actions—bastard!' She looked at Anna, brows knitting together as she considered the situation. 'Look, Anna—we are situated only a few miles from Enderslie. Dangerously close! I have discussed the situation with Roddy and he agrees that we need to move you further away. I have also just phoned Beth Ellis, the social worker we liaise with, and the upshot is that tomorrow morning you will leave for Dream Echo, about sixty miles from here and where you will receive every care and help you need to seek a secure new future.' She saw Anna's face drop as she realised the refuge she had begun to feel of as home, was to be snatched away so soon.

'I will do whatever you advise, Norah,' she said quietly. 'Whatever happens in the future, I will never forget your kindness to me—and Roddy's wonderful help in getting me away from Enderslie House.'

'Personally, I wish we could have kept you here longer. But your safety and that of your precious little daughter has to come first.' She pointed to Susan playing happily with Ben. 'At least you now know how adaptable young Susan is. Roddy will be ready to drive you away at 5-30 tomorrow morning. So, I suggest an early night!'

The following morning Anna dressed Susan in the clothes Norah had supplied for her the night before. Instead of yesterday's expensive little pale blue velvet dress with lace collar and cuffs, the little girl now wore green dungarees and a white sweater, a green peaked cap over her fair curls. As for Anna, she sported blue denim jeans and a casual jacket, with serviceable loafers, on her slim feet, blonde hair tied back under a white and navy scarf. At a quick glance, their appearance was entirely different to yesterday and Norah smiled satisfaction as after a quick breakfast she embraced them as they walked out of the farmhouse door towards Roddy's car. Anna turned, holding something out.

'Norah—I want you to have this,' said Anna quietly and slipped a turquoise necklace into her hand. 'I wasn't able to lay my hands on any money when I left but snatched up some of the jewellery he gave me—left the most valuable pieces behind. Little enough, considering he took all of my father's legacy, leaving me penniless.'

'But I couldn't take this. It looks very valuable,' Norah objected. But Anna smiled firmly and insisted, as she got into the car and buckled Susan's seat belt.

'Good luck—and God bless you,' cried Norah softly, watching as the car disappeared from view, bearing yet another abused woman towards a new future.

All of this was being reprocessed through Anna's mind, as she sat in her new, unfamiliar kitchen. She jerked herself back to the present, as her thoughts flew to her new friend Geraldine, who was proving such a kindly neighbour. It was terrible the elderly lady should have lost her only son in such tragic circumstances. She hoped Geraldine would arrive at the airport in good time to catch her flight to Scotland. How would the woman's daughter-in-law Mary manage now—and oh, how very difficult it would be to tell those little twins they had lost their father. The name father had two such different meanings to her, on the one hand, the memories of her kindly parent, the gifted neurosurgeon with his great love of humanity—and then the parent of her little daughter, the cruel manipulative bully who did not deserve the name of father.

Susan was already beginning to forget the man she had called Papa of whom she had always felt nervous. Although Malcolm had treated the child with casual kindness at most times, Anna knew he had no real love for his little girl—but treated Susan as a bargaining pawn to prevent Anna from ever escaping his power. She remembered how she had been prevented from showing the normal loving influence on the child, by his engaging the stern disciplinarian Nanny Beecham.

Why had she allowed it all to happen? Why had she not just grabbed her child and fled? But being so many miles from the town, where could she have run to, with Hassan watching her every move? It was no good going over it all again in her mind. She had to deal with the present and just be grateful to all those wonderful people at that amazing refuge Dream Echo, and the girl even younger than herself who owned and ran it.

She had learned a lot during her six weeks at the refuge and now knew that however difficult her own life had been, there were millions of women around the world suffering far worse domestic abuse from their partners or fathers—still finding it incredible that statistically, one in four women suffered abuse from men at some stage in their lifetime.

'Mummy—Mummy! I've found a frog,' called Susan excitedly from the garden. 'Come and see!' Anna smiled and let herself out through the back door. 'He's very small,' said Susan, opening her cupped hands. Anna stared down at the little creature and pointed.

'Look, Susan, see that little bit of a tail your frog has—that shows he has recently changed from being a tadpole, probably started his life in that garden pool—would have been a tiny little egg, to begin with.' And as the child listened in fascination Anna realised that they were, at last, embarking on the natural relationship between mother and child, and enjoying that special closeness that Malcolm had done his utmost to prevent. Why had he acted so cruelly? Was the possible reason, that he had wanted her attention to be focussed solely on him, hence the imposition of the soulless nanny? Well, she was free of his presence at last—but sensed it might take longer to shake off the psychological shackles with which he had bound her. She watched now as Susan bent and released the frog, joining in the child's laughter as it leapt frantically away.

'Will Geraldine be high up in the sky now?' queried Susan. 'I hope she comes back soon, I really like her, Mummy!'

'Yes, she is a lovely person,' agreed Anna. 'She may be away a few days, her daughter-in-law Mary needs her help,' she explained.

'Why does she need help?' demanded Susan curiously. Anna hesitated. 'Well, something very sad happened darling, which is why Geraldine needed to fly to Scotland. Her son died in a helicopter accident.' Susan looked at her questioningly.

'What is a helicopter?' Anna glanced down at her in surprise, realising how limited the child's general knowledge was following her sheltered existence at Enderslie House.

'It's a sort of plane, dear, with a large propeller on top and a small one on its tail. They are usually very safe—but this one fell into the sea!' Susan's face was puzzled and to avoid further questions on the subject, Anna made a quick suggestion.

'How would you like to help me bake some fairy cakes?' she asked and minutes later they were back in the kitchen, exploring the cupboards, as for the first time her small daughter got flour on her hands and learned to spoon cake mix onto the trays that looked as though they had given many years of service.

Later, they went next door and fed Geraldine's cat, and changed his water. The little animal purred satisfaction, seeming to take a special liking for Susan. She stroked him fondly.

'I wish we could take him back with us,' said the little girl. 'I thought we had a cat once—a cat called Mitzi.' Anna looked at her in amazement.

'That was when you were a very small girl, darling—when Nanny Beecham first came to live with us. I'm surprised you can remember Mitzi.' Susan was barely three years old then thought Anna. The little girl frowned slightly and persisted as she stared at Anna.

'You said he went to sleep—and didn't wake up?'

'Yes, but let's forget all the sad things that happened at Enderslie House. We won't talk about any of it again!' and thankfully Susan said no more about the ill-fated cat. But Anna found memory flooding back once more of the terrible tiredness she had undergone for many weeks back at that time, and of the afternoon when she had realised that the glass of milk Nanny was encouraging her to drink every day, was possibly drugged, had poured some of it into a saucer for Mitzi to confirm her suspicions. To her dismay the little cat had not survived, its body was quietly removed and never mentioned again by either Malcolm or Mrs Beecham. But the drugging ceased.

'I like our new home, Mummy,' said Susan, as Anna tucked her into bed that night. 'Will you tell me a story?' Anna sank to the side of the bed and started on Cinderella, and within minutes the little girl closed her eyes. Anna bent over stroked her hair and kissed her.

'Mummy, we really are safe here, Papa will not find us—or Nanny Beecham?' came a whisper as she was about to leave. Anna blinked back tears as she tried to reassure her.

'Hush now, no one is going to find us, I promise! Now go to sleep, Susan dear.' And this time the child did so. As she walked downstairs, Anna faced the fact that it was going to take her small daughter some time yet to let go of the past, and a sense of anger against Malcolm Greer shot through her. He had done so much damage.

She sat in the cosy little sitting room that evening, wondering about the woman whose home this had been for most of her life and yet left all behind when she decided to move to New Zealand to be with her son. It had felt very strange at first, moving into a fully furnished home, almost as though she were an intruder. But already that feeling was disappearing, and Bramble Cottage offered the security she needed to plan a new life for Susan and herself. One day soon she would have to consider taking a job—and would need someone to care for Susan. Maybe there was a nursery in the village? She certainly was in no position to engage any paid help at this stage.

She sat there thinking for some hours before seeking her bed, murmuring a quiet prayer of thanks to God who had brought them safely to this remote cottage. She then added a prayer for her kindly neighbour now somewhere in the north of Scotland, grieving the loss of her only son, and trying to bring comfort to her widowed daughter-in-law, then at last, she relaxed and fell into a deep sleep.

Chapter Three

Geraldine arrived outside the solid granite stone house, paid the kindly taxi driver who helped her with her travel bag, and then drove off, leaving her staring across the front lawn towards the downstairs windows where curtains were drawn. A fine smirr of rain was beginning to fall as she walked up the path and rang the bell. None of it seemed quite real—just couldn't be, that her dearest son was lying dead somewhere deep on the cold seabed. The door opened and she saw Mary's anguished face and knew she had to accept reality and put aside her grief to comfort her daughter-in-law, whose normally calm and good-looking face was swollen from copious tears shed from reddened eyes.

'Mother G—come in, oh, come in,' said Mary in a broken voice. 'I'm so glad you are here!' and they fell into each other's arms.

'Mary love, I'm so sorry. I can hardly believe it,' said Geraldine in trembling tones. 'Have you heard any more? Have they found him?' Mary shook her head, as she choked back her tears. She fought for control, and taking Geraldine's arm led her into the living room, where they sank down together on the worn leather settee.

'No, Mother G, they think it unlikely they'll be able to recover Colin's body—the copter came down over that deep underwater trench, miles to the south of the platform,' and Mary looked at the older woman with compassion. If she had lost a beloved husband, Geraldine had also lost her only son, and less than a year since her husband David's death.

'Where are the children,' asked Geraldine, looking around. 'Do they know yet?' Mary nodded and dabbed at her eyes with a tissue.

'The minister's wife Molly is with them in the playroom. She has been wonderfully kind. The twins were completely bewildered when I told them about their Daddy. They're only seven and..' The tears started to fall again. Then she looked at Geraldine's stricken face and rose to her feet.

'But what am I thinking of—I'll make us some tea, Mother G—take you up to your usual bedroom first. She looked around, 'Where's your bag.'

'Hallway. You make the tea, dear, I'll make my own way up upstairs.'

'Somehow, they got through that first night with Geraldine putting comforting arms about her little grandchildren, twins Charles and Melanie when Mary led them in to see her. '

'Our Daddy's been drowned, Granny,' said Melanie. 'But I want him to be back here with us!' Geraldine looked down compassionately into the sorrowful little face.

'I know, darling. But Daddy's in heaven now, and his love will always be with you, even though you can't see him,' she murmured gently.

'But where is heaven,' asked her twin brother Charles. 'I asked Auntie Molly, but she just said we would all know one day!' He fixed questioning grey eyes on his grandmother. She was very wise, so? Geraldine didn't reply directly, instead put her arms about both children and held them close.

'Hush, my darlings. Daddy would want you to be very brave now, and to help your Mummy all that you can.' She looked at them seriously. 'Always remember that your father was a very brave man—and that he was very proud of you both!'

'Why did the helicopter crash,' demanded Charles now. 'What went wrong with it?' He needed answers which Geraldine wanted too. 'It shouldn't have happened!'

'Charles dear—there will be a lot of people trying to discover what caused it to crash, and until then we can only be patient.' And she kissed them, with a promise to tell them a bedtime story later, as Mary led them off upstairs.

Geraldine looked at Mary as they sat together again on the settee.

'How many people were in the copter,' she asked now.

'Only Colin and his colleague Jonathon King,' replied Mary absently, 'And the pilot of course. Kevin was very experienced and had never had the slightest accident in the past. And the copter not one of the routine ones, but a new smaller model from what I'm told.' She shook her head. 'The weather was fine too, none of the sudden squalls you can sometimes get. I've been up with Colin a couple of times, and was never scared, although aware there had been occasional fatal incidents over the years. But all procedures had been tightened up, careful checks made on all craft.'

'Have they found the wreckage yet,' asked Geraldine.

'No—a distress signal was received, then nothing. They have been scouring the apparent area ever since—but no trace!' said Mary hopelessly.

'What was Colin doing—I mean, what did his work involve?' Mary drew her brows together and shook her head pondering slowly.

'He mentioned a new find—the place they'd been exploring three hundred miles to the west, and from what he said, this new field if ever drilled, would make all that has previously been extracted from the North Sea, so much chicken feed! He wasn't supposed to have mentioned it to me—official secrets etc.' She raised her eyes and met

Geraldine's gaze. 'Do you think—but no! I cannot believe I even thought—would be too terrible to contemplate—but Colin and Jonathon were the only two who were party to the secret, apart from those heading the company, or so he told me.'

'But surely Colin's loyalty to the company could never be doubted,' cried Geraldine, then looked at Mary searchingly. 'So, what is it? What are you not telling me?'

'Colin has been deeply concerned about global warming and the devastating effect it is going to have on the world. It is said that over the next twenty years—or sooner—as the ice caps melt ever faster, the sea level will rise by fifty feet. Do you realise what that could mean Mother G?'

'I have often heard this spoken of on the TV of course, read the papers, seen pictures of children in massive protests in different countries,' said Geraldine slowly. 'If it is true, then it would mean that great swathes of low-lying land would go underwater—some islands disappear. But even if Colin believed such reports to be true, how would that impact on his work?'

'Don't you see, Mother G—climate change is caused by the use of fossil fuels! The new oil field if it goes ahead, due to producing billions of barrels of oil would be worth untold millions of pounds to the economy—nothing could be allowed to stop it going ahead—and no one, certainly not an over-zealous employee!' she said bitterly.

Geraldine regarded Mary's agitated face in consternation.

'Had Colin spoken to other people about his concerns? Is it possible his employers got to hear about his thoughts on the matter?' Mary nodded in affirmation.

'He told me that he had arranged a meeting on the rig with the millionaires funding the project, his assistant Jonathon to accompany him—would ask them to reconsider going ahead because of the danger their huge new oil field would cause in accelerating global warming.'

'So, he actually confronted them?' confirmed Geraldine.

'Yes—it was scheduled for yesterday morning—he flew out early. He phoned me briefly after the meeting, just before taking that last fatal return flight back from the rig. He said they had been polite, but dismissive. Kevin was to fly them back in another smaller helicopter.'

'But Colin could not have done anything to make them halt matters—nothing to cause them to—well, let's say it then—to get rid of him?' Geraldine was turning over the possibility in her mind, that her beloved son had been murdered.

'But I believe they did,' whispered Mary. 'That they killed him!' Geraldine listened appalled. She slipped an arm about the trembling woman's shoulders.

'Listen, Mary—right now we must wait in hope that the wreckage of the helicopter will be recovered—and the bodies of those three who lost their lives. There is nothing we can do tonight—you are distraught my dear and no wonder. You should go to bed—need sleep.'

'I couldn't sleep,' returned Mary.

'You go on up. I'll bring you a milky drink and a couple of sleeping pills. Tomorrow we will discuss everything again—possibly have news by then.'

Eventually, Geraldine sought her unfamiliar bed but did not sleep until the early hours. Thoughts of Colin kept swirling through her head—and Mary's wild suspicions. She tossed and turned restlessly, then for one brief moment her thoughts strayed to the lovely fair-haired woman and little daughter who had moved next door to her cottage—was it only a day ago? She remembered how happy she had been to meet Anna Lindstrom and young Susan—the shock this morning of receiving the terrible news that had caused her to fly up here to the north of Scotland. Then Colin's face flashed across her inner vision—a smile on his handsome, rugged face. She murmured his name lovingly—and at last, she slept.

The following morning, Molly MacKinnon arrived, her hazel eyes brimming with sympathy, as she offered to take the twins over to her home in the manse for the day, as they would not be ready to return to school for a while yet.

'Won't Robin find them a distraction,' ventured Mary.

'By no means—Robin suggested it,' replied Molly. 'He also wondered if you would like him to visit you today Mary?'

'Perhaps not today,' said Mary awkwardly. 'My mind is so full of questions I need to be answered. Later in the week then, Molly?'

'I'll tell him—he will quite understand. If there is anything either of us can do, you have but to say.'

'Looking after the twins is the most wonderful help you can give Molly dear!' She watched as her children went off unquestionably with Molly MacKinnon, then turned to look at her mother-in-law.

'I'm sorry I was so emotional last night, Mother G!' she said quietly.

'We had both undergone the most terrible shock, my dear. But what you told me about Colin and his dealings with the oil company has raised many questions in my mind. Where did he keep all his private papers, Mary?' she asked.

'In his office—why?'

'Perhaps we should go in there and have a good look—see if we can find anything to help justify your suspicions! What do you say?'

'Let's do it. This way Mother G.' Mary seemed much calmer this morning as she opened the door to the small office. They glanced around. His computer lay on his functional desk with several drawers.

'Do you know his security code, Mary?'

'Yes—it's papapenguin!' and she opened the Mac, and typed it in. The two women looked at the data revealed with baffled eyes—facts, figures—statistics. Masses of data, some seemed to be in code. Whatever it meant, was undoubtedly of some importance. Geraldine looked at Mary with sudden inspiration.

'Mary—do you have a spare memory stick,' she inquired.

'Yes—in that drawer with all the paper clips and bits and pieces.' She produced one and handed it to Geraldine, who inserted it into the side of the Mac.

'We need to leave it for a while. I remember seeing David using a memory stick as a backup. Now let's see if there is anything else with a bearing on Colin's work!'

There were a great many books on climate change, reports from around the world describing unusual and severe weather conditions—floods and forest fires—fearsome twisters leaving a trail of devastation in the USA—heavy snow storms, ice—and winds sweeping across the planet. They looked at each other. This was certainly proof of Colin's profound interest in global warming. Had this concern led to his death?

'Here is the memory stick—keep it safe,' said Geraldine, removing it from the Mac and proffering it to Mary. 'You know, I think we should have one each. I'll put another in, just in case!' She didn't say in case of what, but they both sensed that whatever secrets the computer held, should be protected.

'I hadn't realised you were so conversant with computers, Mother G,' said Mary in surprise, as both left the office.

'Why, because of my age?' asked Geraldine. 'I used to help David in some of his work, a busy doctor has to place great reliance on his computer. For years before my marriage, I was a civil servant, you know.' As Mary glanced at her as she realised how little she knew of Colin's mother, whom she had met a few times before their marriage and this was only the second time Geraldine had visited their home in this quiet coastal village in Northern Scotland. 'I suggest you keep your memory stick somewhere very safe—not in this office,' she added.

'Why not. The children never come in here?' Mary looked at her tiredly.

'But someone else may! Think—Mary! If you are correct in what you suspect and Colin was deliberately killed, then whoever was responsible may very well want to lay hands on his private papers.' She fixed her direct grey gaze on the younger woman

'But that is ridiculous,' said Mary uncertainly. Or was it, she thought and suddenly she felt afraid. 'Geraldine—what shall I do?'

'Put that stick in a secure place—as I shall with mine. If we are wrong about all this, no harm is done. But believe me, my dear, it is better to be prepared!' Mary nodded, surprised at that new note of authority in her mother-in-law's voice. 'Now, let's check through that filing cabinet in the corner.'

Half an hour later, they returned to the sitting room and prepared to examine a folder they had discovered underneath a pile of brochures in the bottom drawer of the filing cabinet. Suddenly Mary broke down into a paroxysm of choking sobs.

'I cannot cope with any of this, 'she sobbed wildly. 'My darling Colin lying dead in the sea—and we are going through his correspondence instead of mourning him.' Geraldine put her arms about her, fighting off her tears.

'Hush now, Mary. We are trying to do what Colin would have wished. Try to be calm, dear and—oh!' she paused as the doorbell rang. She rose to her feet, walked over to the window, looked out and saw the group of official-looking men standing there. 'Mary! You have visitors—some sort of officials! They may have news. Shall I let them in?' As she spoke she hastily grabbed the folder and ran next door into the kitchen, thrust the folder into the swing bin, then went to the hallway and opened the door as the bell rang a second time.

'Mrs Denton?' began one of the men.

'Yes,' she replied. 'I am Mrs Geraldine Denton—but perhaps you need my daughter-in-law, Mary Denton? I'm afraid she is deeply distressed at the moment.'

'You are Colin Denton's mother?' checked one of the men, portly, slightly balding, with hard dark eyes. 'May I offer our sincere condolences on the death of your son, dear lady? All in the company are deeply shocked by the news of the terrible accident.'

'Have you found the wreckage yet,' she asked quietly. He shook his head, as another man tall, well-built, with somewhat arrogant features, inclined his head gravely to her.

'I'm Richard Lancaster—managing director of Sea Giant. I have come to see what I can do to help at this desperately sad time. You live here with Mary Denton, madam?'

'No. I flew up from the south of England yesterday when Mary phoned me with the awful news! As I told your colleague, she is deep in grief.' He looked at her, saw her own eyes were damp and switched on a commiserating smile as he looked at the elderly woman.

'I can only guess how terrible this must be for you as a mother and for Colin's widow. But I would be extremely grateful if we could exchange a few words with her—to come in for a short time?' he asked suavely. Geraldine stepped back and ushered them through to the sitting room, where to her relief she saw Mary had regained her composure.

'Mary dear, these gentlemen are from Colin's Head Office, and wish to speak with you.' She watched as the four men bowed gravely to Mary, again murmuring their condolences.

'Has the helicopter been found yet—the wreckage I mean?' she burst out. They shook their heads sombrely and saw the despair on her face. Lancaster sized her up swiftly—bowed.

'Richard Lancaster—MD of Sea Giant,' He smiled at her. 'I've come personally to say how appalled we are that this should have happened—the loss of a man so greatly esteemed for his dedicated work for the company. We wish to offer a generous compensation package to help you in the immediate future. You have twin children I believe?' She looked at him helplessly.

'Yes. Charles and Melanie. They are being cared for in the manse by the minister and his wife. They are only seven years old—can you imagine trying to explain what has happened to them?'

'I think we need answers, Mr Lancaster,' put in Geraldine now. 'What caused an apparently new helicopter to crash? Also, is it usual for a craft to be carrying as little as two people?' Lancaster switched his attention to the elderly, silver-haired woman who had posed such questions. It was the portly, narrow-eyed man who answered.

'Mrs Denton—I am Ross Chambers, in charge of company security. Sadly, these disasters do happen, despite the rigid manner in which our helicopters are maintained. At this time, we have no evidence as to the cause of the crash—possibly pilot error—or freak weather conditions.' He shook his head with apparent despondence.

'But the weather was absolutely fine yesterday,' burst out Mary in frustration. 'And I know the pilot Kevin MacDuff had an unblemished safety record!'

'Ladies—understandingly you're both suffering from shock,' said Lancaster smoothly. 'Now we have no intention of outstaying our welcome at this sad time. But there are a few details we have to attend to and would ask your cooperation.'

'What details are these?' demanded Mary, very alert now as she stared at him.

'Well, we need to remove all company documents Colin may have had in his possession. Some of these are covered by the Official Secrets Act and are vital to our work. Where did your husband keep his papers, Mrs Denton? If you show us, we will quietly collect all such and cause no disruption at this difficult time.' He smiled at her sympathetically.

'He had an office perhaps?' Mary exchanged a glance with Geraldine, who stepped forward and stared authoritatively at Lancaster.

'I find it absolutely heartless that you should make such a demand when Colin has not even been declared dead yet! Suppose that by some miracle he has survived?' She eyed him in disdain. 'You should be ashamed of yourselves—I'm almost inclined to call the police!' she flashed. But Mary placed a restraining hand on her arm.

'It's all right, Mother G. Let them take whatever it is they have come for and just go!' She stared at the four men. 'This way gentlemen—but I find your lack of good taste at this time to be extremely hurtful.' They smiled at her in relief, completely ignoring Geraldine's baleful glare as they followed the sad-faced widow through to the small office. Mary left them there and closed the door behind her.

She hurried back to the sitting room and looked gratefully at Geraldine.

'You were right, Mother G! If we hadn't taken record of the Mac on that memory stick and removed Colin's personal documents when we did, it would have been too late!'

'Hush, Mary dear. They may come back at any minute, behave normally.'

'Where did you put that folder?'

'Tell you later—it's safe.' Geraldine glanced around and noticed a photograph album lying on the coffee table beneath some magazines. She lifted it and opened it on her lap as she gestured for Mary to look at it with her. 'Why these are the twins as babies,' she breathed. 'How alike they were at that age.' Mary sank down next to her appearing to concentrate. They looked up as there was a light knock on the door. It was Richard Lancaster.

'We seem to have all we need,' he said lightly. 'Bye, the way, we are borrowing Colin's computer and will return it when we have removed any company data from its hard drive. Oh, and may we have your husband's security code for the Mac?'

'I do not know it,' lied Mary.

'Well, that cannot be helped. Now, I wonder if Colin might have left any of his more recent work anywhere else in the house. In here, perhaps?' he asked, scanning the room carefully. 'Maybe—over there,' he suggested, pointing to a pile of folders on a stool.

'No Mr Lancaster. I am a schoolmistress—and that is my pupil's work waiting to be marked. It's good that you reminded me of my normal activities,' and she walked over to the folders, and gestured to them. 'You are welcome to glance through them,' she said in a shaky voice.

'Sorry, Mrs Denton! It is just that we had expected to find more in your husband's office than we discovered there. What about your bedroom? Might Colin have left anything there, do you suppose?' Mary looked at him in outrage.

'This way then,' she said icily, and he followed her upstairs, leaving Geraldine waiting below. Minutes later they returned, Lancaster looking somewhat abashed. Geraldine snorted angrily as she confronted him.

'Well, Mr Lancaster—if you have finished investigating my daughter-in-law's bedroom, perhaps would you care to examine the kitchen next—or the playroom?' she asked scornfully, hands on her hips as she glared at him.

'My apologies to you both, ladies,' said Lancaster looking out of countenance. 'I will collect my companions and leave you in peace. We will be in touch the moment we receive news of any sightings of…!' He turned awkwardly away and they heard him call to the others still in the office. All four men trooped out of the house and a little later drove off in their white Bentley parked at the curb, next to Mary's blue Audi.

Mary, watched from the window as the car disappeared, and burst into exhausted tears. Geraldine handed her a tissue.

'Thank you, Mother G. If it hadn't been for your advice they would found whatever they were looking for—and I don't think it was the computer. I sensed something very wrong about those men—and I'm scared.' She wrung her hands restlessly together. Geraldine nodded understandingly.

'Come and sit down, my dear. We must talk.'

'I think I need a cup of tea—or something stronger to settle me,' said Mary unsteadily.

'Then let's go through to the kitchen. Apart from anything else, I need to retrieve that precious folder,' said Geraldine. Mary stared in wry amusement as Geraldine produced the folder from the kitchen swing bin.

'I would never have guessed it might be there,' she exclaimed softly. 'Mother G—what is really going on? And why did Colin have to die—surely it wasn't merely because he didn't approve of fossil fuels? If they thought his beliefs were incompatible with his employment they could just have fired him!' She went to a cupboard and produced a bottle of whisky. 'It's Colin's, I don't usually touch the stuff, but…!' She poured two glasses of the amber liquid and handed one of them to Geraldine.'

'Thank you, Mary. I think Colin would have approved,' she said quietly. 'Let us drink to a beloved son, husband and father.' They sipped the whisky slowly, and then both pairs of eyes fastened on the folder that possibly contained many secrets—secrets for which those hard-eyed men had been searching so assiduously.

Two hours had passed and Geraldine stared reflectively at the folder the exposed contents of which had flung down a gauntlet before them. Was it one they could pick up? They sat in silence for a few minutes.

'I can hardly believe such duplicity is possible,' breathed Mary at last. 'No wonder those men were so intent on discovering all of Colin's papers. But now what? I am an ordinary school teacher, have never been involved in what I can only suppose would be referred to as espionage. Colin wanted these matters exposed—and he died for his beliefs. I loved my husband, Mother G—but I have two young children to care for and provide for. So, what now?'

'Mary—all I can suggest is that you allow me to carry on Colin's investigations where at all possible. As you say, you have those beloved twins to care for—they must be put first! Forget this folder. I will take it back home with me, see that other relevant people are made aware of it—and deal with the situation.' Mary looked at her with troubled eyes but knew a deep sense of relief that Geraldine was prepared to take care of such difficult matters.

'If you are absolutely sure, Mother G—but please be extremely careful. I know that those men are dangerous, fear they may come back to check through the house again!' Geraldine's grey eyes studied her kindly.

'Relax Mary. I am taking the folder with me. They will find nothing here of any interest to them should they return. Now little Charles and Melanie will probably be home soon and you must be ready for them. They are going to need all of your reassurance dear.'

'Yes, you're right. I'm just so grateful to you for all your help. Look, I will drive round to the manse now and collect them and thank Molly for all her kindness.' She gave Geraldine a hug and slipping on her jacket, checked the car keys were in her pocket then minutes later Geraldine heard the sound of Mary's blue Audi driving off. Geraldine carried the folder up to her bedroom, unzipped the lining of her travel bag and slipped it inside, then returned to the sitting room.

What was that? Geraldine rushed to the window and looked out. There had been the sound of a crash—or explosion! She had a sudden premonition that something awful had happened to Mary and tried to reject the thought. She sat there taut with nerves, waiting for—what?

When the doorbell rang, she steeled herself to open it and saw the bluff, the concerned face of a middle-aged police officer.

'Would you be the mother-in-law of Mrs Mary Denton, madam?' he asked gently.

'Yes, I'm Geraldine Denton! What has happened, officer? Mary set off for the manse a little while ago to collect the twins. I heard an awful sound—explosion?'

'May I come in, please,' he said. 'I think you need to sit down, Mrs Denton.'

'Just tell me,' she whispered, as she sank onto the settee she had shared with Mary such a short time ago. He sat beside her, took her hand, and forced the words out gruffly.

'Mary's dead. The car was seen out of control—it crashed into the side of the low bridge over the burn. Her petrol tank must have exploded, the car was in flames. I'm so very sorry to tell you this. There will be a proper investigation, her remains are being moved to the mortuary.'

'May I see her,' she whispered. He shook his head.

'No—that will not be possible. She was badly burned you see.'

'Oh no—no!' cried Geraldine wildly. 'It was only yesterday she had news of Colin's death, and now this horror!' She tried to restrain her trembling. 'The twins—little Charles and Melanie! How do we tell them they have lost both parents?'

'Where are they now?' he asked. 'I'd thought perhaps they might have been kept off school, be here?' he asked.

'No officer. Molly MacKinnon came early this morning and offered to take them back to the manse for the day. Mary was on her way to collect them and bring them home.' It was difficult to speak logically to the police officer, yet it helped.

'Had Mary complained of any difficulties with the car recently? I mind she bought it only a few months ago.' Geraldine shook her head.

'She made no mention of anything wrong with the car to me. It was parked outside the house on the road, but I barely noticed it. But as you will appreciate, news of Colin's almost certain death when his helicopter crashed yesterday, filled our thoughts to the exclusion of all else. I arrived from the south of England yesterday evening. We spent today trying to come to terms with the shock. Then those men from the oil company came here this morning.' He looked at her curiously.

'Is there any news, have they found the wreckage yet?' he asked quickly.

'No officer. They seemed inordinately concerned about Colin's private papers, and demanded his computer.' He looked back at her keenly, detecting a strange tone in her voice.

'Did they say why they wanted the computer?' he asked curiously.

'Something about the Official Secrets Act? Mary and I were completely baffled. Colin's work was certainly involved with oil exploration—and Mary mentioned there has been another recent find that may offer an extraordinary yield. But how secret that might be when all such matters end up in the newspapers and TV—well!' He frowned as he looked at her.

'Who were these men? Did they identify themselves?' he asked.

'Two of them did so. One was the MD Richard Lancaster, the other said he was in charge of company security—Ross Chambers!' She saw him taking notes. He rose to his feet.

'You are being extremely brave at what must be a terrible time for you, Mrs Denton. I will be in touch with you again soon. How long will you be staying here?'

'I'm not sure. I had thought it would be until the wreckage of the helicopter was found—to confirm Colin's death and that of the other two poor men. But I must return to my home eventually—had to ask a new young neighbour to care for my cat. Colin was my only child, you know, his death was such an awful shock. His father, my dear husband David, died only a few months ago—and now Colin—and Mary?' her voice shook.

'Would you be able to take on care for the children if necessary—if there are no other relatives to step in?' he questioned. He saw her grey eyes widen in shock as she faced the situation. Her answer came clearly, without hesitation.

'Yes, of course, I will undertake the care of my little grandchildren. Charles and Melanie will come back home with me,' she said softly. He bowed his head to her and left. As he got into the police car he felt troubled about what Geraldine had stated regarding the arrival of those representatives of Sea Giant, demanding Colin's computer, and this before he had even been officially declared dead. It sounded strange, suspicious—but what could be behind it? Was there a possible connection between Colin's supposed death followed so closely by that of his wife, the esteemed schoolmistress Mary Denton? It sounded like something from a TV movie—only it had all happened—was deeply disturbing.

He must discuss the problem with his sergeant, who might wish to take the matter higher. In the meanwhile, he could only hope that their police mechanic might be able to establish what had caused Mary's little blue Audi to seemingly career wildly out of control according to a witness—then the fatal crash. And why had it immediately burst into flames?

The phone rang. Geraldine picked it up and heard Molly's tearful voice.

'You have heard, Geraldine?'

'Molly, the police officer has just left. Do the children know?' she asked

'Yes, we've told them and they are heartbroken. They are asking for you, want their granny—are scared that something might happen to you too. Robin is with them—but poor little things, what is to happen to them now?' Molly's voice trembled with emotion.

'They will be returning to Hampshire with me. They already know the cottage and have spent occasional holidays there. There is a good village school and they will soon make new friends. Better they have a completely new start far away from the dreadful trauma they are experiencing now.'

'I suppose you're right. But are you sure you will manage—at your age I mean?'

'Perhaps the number of our years is of less importance than the use to which we put them. I won't say it will be easy—but they are my grandchildren and very precious.'

'Well, anything that Robin and I can do to help in the meanwhile! There will have to be a funeral for Mary—and I suppose a memorial service for Colin.'

'The police officer said someone saw Molly crash the car and that it had been careering out of control?'

'Yes. That was Archie Pratt. He was walking his dog when it happened. He said he ran towards the Audi when it hit the parapet of the bridge, but it burst into flames almost instantaneously. Mary would not have had a chance. Just so dreadful! What I do not understand is that it was a good car, a new one—I can't think why it should have happened.'

'I agree. Something is very wrong! Molly, are you bringing the children over now?'

'Well, it might be better to let them sleep here tonight. Give you a chance to come to terms with all that has happened. I'll drive them over after breakfast tomorrow. And Geraldine, my heart goes out to you, my dear.'

Geraldine checked that both front and back doors were locked that night before she went uneasily upstairs to bed in the granite house. She lay there listening to the tick of the clock on her bedside table, going over in her mind all that had happened since first she arrived in the house yesterday evening. Every single exchange with Mary—their decision to copy the data on Colin's computer on those two memory sticks—the arrival soon afterwards of the Sea Giant officials, every question they had asked—their concern that they had not found all they were searching for in Colin's office. Then Mary drove off to collect the little twins—the sound of that explosion! Why? She did not doubt in her mind that Mary had been cruelly murdered. But why had it been thought necessary? Over and over again she explored the last few hours.

Had those officials suspected that Mary had secreted some of her husband's secret documents away somewhere—and she was filled with dismay as she thought of the folder she had personally hidden in the inner lining of her travel bag. Had she been responsible for Mary's death?

If she had not alerted Mary to the possibility that Colin had been disposed of because of his concerns over global warming and the damage that this newly discovered enormous oil find could inflict on future generations—then Mary might not have agreed to explore his office—and take a copy of his computer data on those memory sticks. But then, Mary already had her suspicions about Colin's death.

But at least Lancaster and that other fellow Chambers could not have known they had inserted those memory sticks into the computer—or was it possible that the men checked the Mac so closely that they had become aware of the activity on it earlier that day? That must be it! And she went cold as the suspicion unfolded in her mind and with it the realisation that they had acted with such speed and utter ruthlessness. Someone must have tampered with Mary's car where it was parked outside on the roadside. And there were no immediate neighbours to have noticed—Mary's house slightly on the outskirts of the village

Did this mean that her own life was now in danger? Hopefully, there was a chance that they merely regarded her as an elderly woman out of touch with the modern world. As she had only arrived in Scotland the day before, it would have seemed unlikely to them that she would have been involved in checking through Colin's computer data, never mind copying it onto a memory stick.

'I must take the children safely away with me tomorrow,' she murmured.

She rose early after a sleepless night, made a bowl of cereal and a pot of tea—and proceeded to look for suitcases. She found them in a store cupboard adjoining the kitchen and carried them upstairs to the children's rooms. She packed their clothes and a few books and toys. Good, now to book their flights. She was offered one leaving Aberdeen airport at 2 pm. It would be tight getting there but there was nothing else available until tomorrow.

Now she forced herself to go into Colin and Mary's bedroom. She opened the wardrobe and passed her hand lovingly over one of her son's suits, choking back a sob. Next, she checked around the room for any private papers. Found what she sought in the chest of drawers, tucked beneath some sweaters. There was a sealed envelope marked Will—bank statements, letters and a diary. She also picked up a framed photograph of Colin and Mary with the twins. She packed all these in her travel bag, together with the photograph album.

She had barely completed the job when the doorbell rang and Robin and Molly stood in the porch, each holding the hand of a tearful child.

'Granny—Granny!' cried the twins. 'Our Mummy's is dead—she's dead like Daddy!' and they ran into her arms, sobbing. She knelt between them, holding them close, then led them inside followed by the sympathetic couple who had been caring for them.

'Children, I want you to wait in the playroom for a little, while I talk with Molly and Robin.'

Yes, Granny,' they nodded and walked slowly off, young faces white and tear-stained.

'Molly tells me you plan to take the twins back to England with you,' queried the minister gently as they seated themselves. 'It is a deeply caring decision—and I think the right one for the children. A new start away from a place which will hold such tragic memories for them, to live with a grandmother they love.' She stared back at them both, at rosy-cheeked Molly kindly face framed by dark curls, and her husband Robin with his steady blue eyes, wavy hair greying at temples and quiet smile.

'I believe it is a decision Colin and Mary would have approved of,' replied Geraldine. 'A lot of what has happened is very disturbing—the police are aware of my concerns. Mary's death coming so closely on that of my son—and no sign of any wreckage from the helicopter yet! I have booked flights from Aberdeen. Must leave soon. I'll book a taxi to get to the airport.'

'My dear Mrs Denton—Geraldine, forget a taxi! Molly and I will gladly drive you to the airport. If you give us your home address and phone number, we will keep in touch with you—send on any correspondence that arrives and let you know of any developments with Sea Giant.' She sighed in relief.

'Robin—that would be amazingly kind,' she said gratefully.

'Listen, Geraldine. Your son spoke with me on a matter that was troubling him, and which I may not discuss with you as it was within my capacity as minister. But let it suffice, that I think your decision to remove yourself and the twins is a very wise one.' Geraldine looked at him curiously, wishing she could persuade him to disregard the bonds of secrecy, but sensing a request would be unavailing. This was a man of integrity. She opened her bag.

'This is my card, Robin. For my part, I ask that you do not divulge my details to anyone else, except to the police if needs to be.'

'You have my word,' and he slipped it into his pocket She glanced from both him to his wife, trying to think coherently.

'Now look, I know arrangements will have to be made for Mary's funeral—and Colin's if they recover his body.' It was so difficult to shape the necessary words, to discuss her present heartbreak and bewilderment at events so devastating. But her little grandchildren's needs must come before all else—and they must be safely removed from this place.

'Geraldine, I imagine you may not feel able to return for these two sad farewells,' put in Molly, her face full of sympathy. 'And it would probably be too much for the children. But you have my word that Robin and I will ensure that all is done the very best way we can. The whole village will be joining in our grief—and Colin and Mary always remembered with love.'

'Thank you,' said Geraldine quietly. 'I will pay whatever expenses are incurred in all this. You must just let me know.' She got up. 'I must go to Charles and Melanie, prepare them for their journey—and it is going to be such a help having you drive us to the airport.'

'Perhaps we may just bow our heads in prayer for a moment—to ask our Heavenly Father's help and protection for you and the little ones.' The words he spoke touched Geraldine's heart, breaking through the almost icy control she was displaying. She blinked back her tears and murmured a quiet amen. None of it seemed quite real—like a nightmare she was trying to wake from. Then a calm seemed to encompass her as resolutely she went to prepare the waiting children.

The journey was uneventful, the change of planes straightforward, and by the time they arrived at Southampton airport and collected their bags Geraldine's mind was beginning to clear, as she spoke reassuringly to the two tired, overwrought children. She pushed the trolley with their bags to the carpark, found her beige Ford and settled the twins in the back seat before pushing the bags in the boot. They were off, and now at last Geraldine realised she was back in control of events.

An hour later they drew up outside her cottage and she drew a deep sigh of relief. The two small, fair-haired children clambered out as she opened the car door, and looked around, remembering this place where they had spent such happy holidays with their grandmother in the past.

'Come along then, my dears!' Geraldine led them up the garden path and unlocked the blue front door. They followed her in slowly.

'Look, it's Granny's pussy—Marcasite!' cried Charles, bending and stroking the cat that arched its back and purred, as Melanie bent down beside him too. Then the cat stared at Geraldine in cooler greeting, was displeased at her absence she realised.

'Sorry, Marcasite,' she whispered, nor did it seem illogical to apologise to her pet. Oh, it was so good to be back in Rose Cottage and what passed for normality again.

She busied herself making up twin beds for the children in one of her two spare bedrooms. She unpacked their suitcases and found their cuddly toys that she had brought with her, placing them on their pillows. Then she put away clothes and essentials hastily gathered from their past familiar home, laid out pyjamas, and placed their toothbrushes in the bathroom. The two solemn youngsters watched her, still trying to understand the sudden frightening disruption in their normal lives.

At last, they were tucked up in bed. She sat beside them in a wicker chair, talking gently and humming a lullaby, until they fell asleep, and she crept out. By now Geraldine felt completely exhausted and wished her husband had still been alive to have helped her through the nightmare of recent traumatic events she had endured.

'Oh, David—David,' she whispered. 'How I need you dear.' She sighed, sank down in her favourite armchair, her head resting against an embroidered cushion, and as she did so, recognised it was a gift from Mary. So hard to acknowledge she would never see Mary's kindly face again, hear her soft Highland voice—and even harder that she would not feel her son Colin's strong arms about her shoulders in one of his affectionate bear hugs. It had been difficult enough coming to terms with the couples moving so far north because of Colin's involvement with the oil industry. But the shock of this sudden double bereavement impossibly hard to bear.

She was dozing off in her sitting room chair, too tired to go to bed when the doorbell rang. She sat up glanced around almost fearfully, and then realised she was safe home in the cottage. She rose and opened the door cautiously, and saw the attractive face of her new neighbour, Anna Lindstrom.

'Anna—come in, dear,' she managed. The girl followed her through to the sitting room.

'I saw the car earlier, knew you were back, Geraldine. Just wanted to see if you are all right. Look. I should have waited until the morning—and mustn't leave Susan alone for more than a few minutes, she's sleeping. Wanted to check if you need anything?'

'No, but it's good to see you, Anna. But actually, I am extremely tired—will tell you about everything tomorrow. My daughter-in-law Mary—well she died in a fatal road accident yesterday—just one day after Colin's helicopter crashed.'

'What! But that's absolutely awful,' gasped Anna, blue eyes widening in shock.

'I've brought my two little grandchildren back with me,' continued Geraldine. 'I'll be their official guardian from now on. It would have been too painful to have left them up there, with two funerals so soon to take place. So, I managed to book flights and they are fast asleep upstairs now.' Her grey eyes focussed on Anna's face. 'Your little Susan will have two young neighbours— twins Charles and Melanie.' For answer Anna put her arms around Geraldine and felt her suppressed trembling.

'Geraldine—I will do everything I can to help you and your little grandchildren. But go to bed now, you must be exhausted.'

'Yes—I think I will go up. And thank you for coming—and caring, Anna.' She watched as Anna left quietly, and locked the door after her.

She had just drifted into a troubled sleep when she was awakened by the sound of crying. She switched on her bedside lamp as the door opened, and two small figures stood on the threshold.

'Oh, my dears—come here, then!' She pulled the duvet aside and beckoned, and they climbed in the double bed beside her—and at last, all three slept.

Morning dawned, and birdsong woke the children who found Geraldine was already up. They rushed through their morning wash in the bathroom and made their way down to the kitchen, where they could smell, eggs and bacon frying.

'Good morning, Granny,' they chorused, trying hard to smile, although it was obvious tears were still not far away. They ran over and pressed their heads against her, as she bent and kissed them.

'Sit down, darlings,' she said, 'Cereal and fruit juice first, and then a fry-up!' And gradually the children fell back into a remembered routine from previous holidays at Rose Cottage. They each took a tea towel and wiped up the dishes as Geraldine washed. She knew how important it was for their security to involve them in everything in their new home. Inevitably there were questions, to which she found it difficult to provide answers.

'What made Mummy's car crash, Granny?' asked Charles urgently, his serious grey eyes fixing on her face. 'It was a new car—and Mummy was a good driver!'

'And why did Daddy's helicopter fall into the sea?' demanded Melanie. 'I thought the Sea Bird was very safe.' She spoke with maturity for such a young child, who had always been the slightly more serious of the twins.

'Children, the police will be examining Mummy's car to see if anything was wrong with it—and these things can take time. As for the helicopter, divers will have to find the wreckage, and this may be difficult as they believe it came down in very deep water.' She looked at them sadly. 'All of this is so hard for you both—I know how much you loved your parents. I loved them too. So, we will all just have to do our best to be brave, as they would want us to be. One thing I promise, you will be safe and deeply loved here with me, and one day you will be happy again.'

They looked at her trustingly, their hearts too full for words. Then Charles glanced towards the window.

'May we go out in the garden Granny?'

'Of course, Charles, my darling—off you both go!' She sat down at the kitchen table glad of a moment's peace to think. At some stage, she must find time to examine the contents of that folder she had rescued and was still in the lining of her travel bag—and then there was the memory stick. What secrets did that contain that caused the top officials of Sea Giant to come to her son's house and demand Mary hand over his computer? And what else were they searching for? And why was Mary murdered, for she was convinced the car crash had been no accident?

'And how safe am I?' she murmured, as she sat there going over everything in her mind. But was she being paranoid—for those hard-faced operatives from Sea Giant had no way of knowing that Geraldine Denton had once been a senior member of MI5. No all they would have seen would have been an elderly, silver-haired woman grieving her son's death. Hopefully, they would view her abrupt departure as resultant of her extreme distress at having to remain in a house where both occupants had tragically died. What more natural than to have removed her grandchildren away from such a scene?

Well, we have to carry on—even when overshadowed by life's thunderclouds, she thought. And surely those two children for whom she was now responsible, represented a rainbow of hope for the future. With a fresh glint of determination in her eyes, she got up from the table and went into the garden.

'Where are you both?' she cried.

'Over here, Granny. There's a little girl next door. She says her name's Susan,' cried Melanie. 'May she come over and play with us?'

'I don't see why not—if her mummy agrees,' said Geraldine and waved as she saw Anna Lindstrom near the fence. 'Anna, why don't you both come over?' she called, would have preferred to have had a few peaceful days to come to terms with the sorrow of her double loss, but had taken to her new neighbour, felt she was someone she could trust.

Ten minutes later Anna and Susan joined them in the back garden, and sat down next to Geraldine, on a rustic bench banked by flowering shrubs. She introduced them to the twins.'

'Anna, are you always going to live next door to Granny?' asked Charles curiously.

'I hope so,' she replied gently. 'It will be so nice for Susan to have two new friends.'

'Where is Susan's daddy?' asked Melanie shyly.

'Susan does not have a daddy,' replied Anna lightly. 'It's just the two of us, my dear.'

'Did her daddy die, like ours?' asked Charles. At this point, Geraldine interrupted firmly.

'Charles—it is not polite to ask so many questions,' she gently reproved.

'No—that's all right,' said Anna forthrightly. 'You see children, all families are different. Sometimes there are two parents—but sometimes just a daddy or just a mummy to look after the children—sometimes a granny or granddad. What is important is that there is lots of love.' They looked at her and nodded, their minds still struggling to come to terms with the loss of their parents and all that had been normal and familiar. None of what was happening now seemed real, more like a strange dream from which they would wake to find themselves back home with their father and mother. Only it was real—and they would never see their beloved parents again.

'There's a swing under that big tree at the end of the garden—come along Susan, we'll show you,' and Charles held out a hand to the little girl, who took it shyly.

'That went very well,' said Geraldine. 'Poor young things, it has been incredibly difficult for them to accept the situation. I hope I took the right decision to bring them down here, but I thought a complete change of scene might help.' Anna looked at her sympathetically.

'Geraldine—I can only guess what you are going through right now. The sudden death of a dear one can be so devastating. I remember how I felt when my father died—the loss, emptiness.' She stopped abruptly, realising that she was speaking of a past that she no longer was able to acknowledge. She sensed Geraldine was watching her appraisingly, and knew she had to be extremely careful not to divulge any facts of her past. Her future safety and that of her little daughter rested in her ability to maintain her new assumed identity. But she was aware that Geraldine was also hugging a frightening secret to her, guessed it related to the tragic death of her son in that helicopter accident—and then the extraordinary coincidence of her daughter-in-law's fatal accident immediately afterwards.

'If you should want to discuss any personal problems, either now or in the future, then I will always be ready to help or advise in any way,' said Geraldine quietly, reaching out a hand to Anna. 'It is obvious you also, have been through a very stressful time, dear.'

'Sometimes it is better to leave the past in the past,' replied Anna. 'Look, if the time comes when I need some advice, then I can think of no one I would rather trust than you, Geraldine. But right now, I simply want to settle down in my new home—and find a job eventually.' She hoped her reply was not too defensive, but Geraldine merely smiled understandingly.

'If and when you are ready—I'm always here, just remember that,' she said quietly, then the children called and they rose to their feet.

Chapter Four

Molly MacKinnon answered a knock at the manse door and stared at the tall, commanding figure who stood there, a polite smile on his hard, good-looking face.

'Mrs MacKinnon?' he asked politely.

'I am—and who are you?' she demanded uneasily.

'Roger Armstrong, from the board of Sea Giant. I believe you are caring for the children of Colin and Mary Denton—thought their grandmother Geraldine Denton might also be here with you. I called at the Dentons' home, but no one seemed to be in?'

'Well, you are too late, Mr Armstrong! As I am sure you are aware, Mary Denton died two days ago in a fatal car accident. Geraldine and the children left the village later the next day.'

'That was a surprisingly sudden decision,' he said taken aback. 'Perhaps you could let me have Mrs Denton's address? I need to contact her.'

'That will won't be possible, as she did not leave her address,' she stated calmly. He looked at her almost disbelievingly.

'Well, I assume she will return for her daughter-in-law's funeral,' he said. 'Can you at least tell me when that is to be held?'

'As yet the police have not informed us when Mary's body will be released for burial, so no date arranged. I believe Mrs Denton thought it best to remove the twins from such a deeply upsetting situation. I am sure you understand. I consider it unlikely she will return soon.' He looked as though he would say more, but at that moment Molly's husband appeared. He looked towards the stranger inquiringly.

'We have a visitor, my dear?'

'This gentleman is from Sea Giant and is just leaving. He came asking for Geraldine Denton. I have just explained that she left yesterday—and we do not have her address,' stated Molly. The minister glanced pleasantly at Armstrong.

'I fear you seem to have had a wasted journey, sir,' he said. 'May I ask if you have discovered the wreckage of the missing helicopter yet—and the three men aboard?'

'Not yet—but doing all in our power to do so,' replied Armstrong, glancing from one to the other of the couple, and wondering if they really did not have Geraldine Denton's address. He noted Robin's dog collar and shrugged. 'Look, this is my card. Be kind enough to let me know if Mrs Denton contacts you.' He inclined his head to them and walked away.

'I didn't like the look of him,' said Robin reflectively. 'Seemed upset that we were unable to furnish him with Geraldine's address?' and raising his eyebrows he glanced at Molly questioningly. She gave her husband a straight look.

'Robin as you know, Geraldine believed there might be a connection between her son Colin's death and Mary's subsequent fatal accident. All too much of a terrible coincidence! She didn't want anyone to learn her whereabouts—but left details with me in a sealed envelope so that I could pretend no actual knowledge of her address.'

'Yes, and I have her card Something quite frightening has been going on, Molly.' He stared at his wife's troubled face and put a comforting arm about her. 'You were quite right to send that fellow away. When you think about it, why should an important operative of Sea Giant wish to speak so urgently with an elderly woman who has just lost both her son and daughter-in-law?'

'Why indeed?' agreed Molly. 'Especially since as I told you, four other men came to Mary's house early on the day of her accident and went off with his computer and other papers. We're possibly looking for further documents. Was Mary killed because she had knowledge of some aspect of Colin's work they wanted to be kept secret?' They stared at each other uneasily.

'Sometimes I wish mankind hadn't this obsession with fossil fuels—polluting the atmosphere and increasing global warming—then the innumerable plastics, by-products of the oil industry, fouling up the world's oceans! And all for the profit of a few greedy individuals.' He shook his head. She lifted a hand and stroked his wavy greying hair.

'The trouble is Robin, that a great many men now rely on the oil industry for their employment, possibly earning much larger salaries than previously available to them in their earlier occupations. We all know of the worry countless families endured when the oil prices suddenly fell over the last years and men lost their jobs in thousands.' Her cheeks were burning as she spoke. 'And it wasn't only working on the oil rigs themselves, but the collapse of the other smaller industries supporting their work.' They walked slowly into the homely manse kitchen, sank down at the scrubbed pine table and looked at each other in concern.

'My dearest, let us lay these troubles too great for us to deal with, before the Lord. And Robin bowed his head in prayer firstly for the souls of their friends Colin and Mary and their orphaned twin children, now living somewhere in the south of England with an elderly grandmother, who had displayed so much courage in dealing with her own grief as she reached out to little Charles and Melanie. He went on to ask forgiveness for mankind currently exploiting the riches of the earth to increase their power and wealth and leaving a trail of destruction across the world.'

'Amen,' added Molly gently. 'Now let me see—you have a christening this afternoon?'

'Aye, the Roberson's wee babe. I'll to the kirk now and see all is in readiness.' She watched him go lovingly. She was very blessed in her husband. At that moment the phone rang.

'Molly—this is Jean MacArthur,' came a soft voice. 'I just want to ask after the little Denton twins, heard you had been caring for them? And we are all devastated at the news of Mary's death. What now for those poor bairns?'

'Their grandmother flew up to be with Mary when news of the helicopter crash reached her. Was in their house when she heard the sound of Mary's car exploding—such a terrible shock coming one day after losing her son! Mary was on her way over to the manse to collect Charles and Melanie when it happened.

'It is so hard to take it all in. How are the twins coping?

'Their grandmother has already taken them back down south with her—will become their official guardian. I believe she thought it best to remove them from what will be the ongoing stress of funerals. Robert and I will miss the whole family so much.'

'Where does the grandmother live?'

'I don't know is the answer to that—but she is a wise and responsible lady. The children will be safe with her.'

'So, their names must be removed from the school rolls. I will tell the headmistress. She is desperately looking for someone to take over Mary Denton's duties. She was a wonderful teacher. You wouldn't be able to give a few hours of your own time to help out in the meanwhile?'

'Wish I could—but life as a minister's wife is busy, to say the least.'

'Yes—of course. When you learn the children's new address, let me know. Their details will need to be forwarded to their new school.' And the school secretary rang off. All around the village of Grantly people exchanged their feelings of shock at the loss of a much-liked and respected couple, as well as the two other men missing in the helicopter disaster.

Richard Armstrong joined his colleagues in the opulent head office, where they were seated on black leather swivel chairs around the glass-topped table set in rose granite, a whisky decanter and glasses before them, as they studied a chart of the sea bed.

'Armstrong! How did you get on with Geraldine Denton?' Richard Lancaster asked curiously. Armstrong reached for a glass and shrugged!

'You won't believe this, but the woman has already up and left, taking the kids with her! Seems she decided to leave soon after news of Mary

Denton's sad demise reached her. I spoke with the minister's wife, who was not exactly helpful. Said Geraldine Denton had not left her address. Could be true, but seems odd.' Lancaster frowned. 'Why would she have withheld her address?'

'Possibly forgot to do so in all the upheaval,' suggested Ross Chambers. 'No doubt she will be in contact with the minister—MacKinnon, isn't it, to arrange the funeral service for Mary Denton—and some sort of memorial for that fool Colin!'

'In the meanwhile, we need to get back into the Denton's house to check for whatever device was used to back up that computer early yesterday morning. One thing for certain—it wasn't used by Colin Denton!' smiled Lancaster.

'Could it have been the grandmother—Geraldine Denton?' asked Armstrong.

'Very doubtful—met her, an elderly woman, probably far from computer literate, even if she possesses one,' snorted Lancaster. 'No, my opinion of her was of a grieving female shocked at her son's death and protective of her daughter-in-law and didn't exactly welcome our visit. I imagine she was so deeply shocked she just wanted to get the youngsters safely away.'

'So whatever gadget was used and my guess is a memory stick, it must still be somewhere in that house then. Unless of course, Mary Denton was carrying it on her person when she was involved in her er—unfortunate accident. In which case, we have nothing to worry about!' put in Chambers. 'However, we had better make a careful check there, which should be easier now Geraldine Denton has conveniently removed herself.'

'What about Colin Denton's colleague, Jonathon King, who shared his unfortunate views?' asked Armstrong. 'He went down with Denton of course—but what if he had left anything around at his flat?'

'We've already checked the place,' replied Chambers. 'His girlfriend allowed access. Nothing of note was found. His computer was missing. The girl said he had it with him—so at the bottom of the sea now!' he added with satisfaction.

'But we're still unsure as to whether Denton or King divulged our secret project to any other person?' said Lancaster slowly. 'Well, we need someone to take the Denton house apart. Luckily it's on the outskirts of the village and stands suitably far away from curious neighbours.' He smiled, 'Well, your good health gentlemen!' He raised his glass.

'How likely do you think it is that Scotland will become independent,' asked Armstrong suddenly. They looked at him in surprise.

'Can't see it myself,' replied Lancaster. 'Westminster would never allow it, too much to lose, their oil revenue not the least of it, eh!'

'Got a feeling it could happen though,' said Chambers thoughtfully. 'There is a new restlessness. The Scots have always regarded themselves as Europeans. This Brexit business has really stirred them up. We should keep the full extent of the new field under wraps for the foreseeable future. We need to know who we will be dealing with long term.'

'Which is why we need to make sure we have left no loose ends from recent regrettable events,' said Lancaster firmly. 'Well, you all know what we need to get on with now,' he said dismissively. He glanced towards the heavy glass door as they rose from the table. 'We'll speak again later—in the meanwhile, I have a special call booked with our chap in Shanghai.'

Anna was brushing Susan's fair curls. The little girl looked longingly towards the window and could hear the sound of the twins in the garden.

'May I go out now Mummy—please!' she asked, and Anna smiled.

'Yes, darling, of course, you can. Off you go and I'll be out there soon when I've tidied the kitchen.' She watched her daughter scamper off, looking cute in a pale blue top and jeans, and for a moment she recollected how only a few months ago, Trudy as she was known then, had been a solemn-faced child, formally dressed in expensive little outfits, appearing like a small adult and supervised by the stern, unyielding Nanny Beecham.

She frowned. Why had it taken her so long to take the plunge and make an escape from Malcolm Greer's dominance? She gave a quick shudder as she remembered his arrogance, the complete control he had taken of her life. Well, she was free of him now, and would always feel the deepest gratitude to those who had helped her escape with her daughter, and invented a new identity for them both. It had been difficult at first to accept her new name, but now she felt more Anna than Erika—and luckily Trudy had readily taken to the name of Susan. But she would have to be careful that her little girl never mentioned any details of their past life.

The fact that Susan had instinctively disliked Malcolm Greer, and although so young had noticed his harsh treatment of her mother and certainly was immensely relieved to be away from the rigid rules of Nanny Beecham, all of this made it easier for the little girl to realise she must never say anything that would put their new happiness at risk. And Anna realised how fortunate she had been to find Bramble Cottage, with such a kind and caring neighbour as Geraldine Denton.

She thought of Geraldine now. How difficult it must have been for the woman to have faced the death of her only son, with the added shock of her daughter-in-law's fatal car crash. To have then taken on the responsibility for her seven years old twin grandchildren was all the more remarkable. But there was something about Geraldine that intrigued her. Although appearing such an innocuous older lady, she detected the woman had a very keen mind, and wondered about her earlier background. Maybe her agreeable neighbour would open up to her one day. Perhaps she also might display enough courage to share with Geraldine the details of her recent escape from an abusive relationship, had the feeling that she would understand, and be supportive.

Geraldine meanwhile was busily studying the data transferred from the memory stick onto her computer. It all seemed as incomprehensible as when she had glanced over it with Mary, as they examined it before the visit of the four representatives of Sea Giant. She wondered briefly what had happened to the memory stick Mary had retained. She remembered seeing her drop it into her handbag, so possibly Mary had taken it in the car with her when she left on her last brief journey to collect her children—a journey ending so tragically.

She did not know the key to unlock the code in which these files were presented. But they must be of supreme importance to Sea Giant who had killed twice to protect them! However, there was someone from her past who might be able to help her, but she hesitated to contact him.

She glanced out of the window and saw Charles and Melanie sitting on the cushioned bench, heads bowed over a beautifully illustrated storybook she had found that once belonged to their father. Next week they would start school in the village and hopefully settle down well. So far, the little orphans were finding it hard to deal with the traumatic loss of both parents, one moment playing normally, the next bursting into tears as the reality of the huge change in their young lives swept over them. But they also seemed to draw strength from each other with that special bond that could exist between twins.

Geraldine sighed. Should she wait until they were in school next week before contacting Tom Lanscombe? Like her, he was officially retired from the Secret Service but still kept his hand in when called upon. Then there was his lovely wife Lottie Lanscombe, a talented author who had also helped her husband in certain cases. Better to wait perhaps—but it could not harm to make a quick call now, to start the ball rolling. A warm well-remembered voice answered her call—Lottie!

'Lottie, do you remember me—Geraldine Denton who was Geraldine Court before marriage?'

'Geraldine—of course, I remember you, dear. How are you? It's been quite a time since we met. How is David?'

'You hadn't heard—he died just after Christmas—heart,' replied Geraldine quietly.

'Oh, my dear—that is so very sad,' came Lottie's sympathetic reply. 'I know Tom will want to add his condolences to mine. You had a son though if I remember rightly—Colin?'

'Colin lost his life a few days ago when his helicopter disappeared over the North Sea. He had been living in the village of Grantly near Aberdeen and working in the oil industry, at a company called Sea Giant. He had—certain issues with them. Lottie, my son's dear wife Mary also died, when her new car went out of control and crashed, this on the day following Colin's death. It happened shortly after representatives of the company had arrived demanding Colin's computer—said something about the Official Secrets Act?'

'This is all quite shocking, can hardly take it in Geraldine!' said Lottie slowly. 'Are you suggesting that Colin and Mary were murdered?'

'I believe it to be so. I was wondering if Tom could help me. You see, I took a copy of the data on Colin's computer before those men came—memory stick. Have been trying to make sense of it, but it is all in code.'

'Can you come here and spend a few days with us, Geraldine?'

'Would love to—but it's not possible. Colin and Mary had seven year's seven-year-old twins—Charles and Melanie. There were no other relatives, so I brought them back to live with me in Rose Cottage, and have become their official guardian.'

'Oh, Geraldine! What you have been going through? Look—if Tom agrees, perhaps we could come to you—book a B&B in the village.'

'I have a spare bedroom—would be wonderful to see you both.'

'I'll have to check with Tom, but sure he will agree. What is your address again?' She listened. 'Rose Cottage, Ravensnest, Hants—got it!' Why did the place sound slightly familiar,' mused Lottie as she scribbled the address on a jotter, 'I'll ring you back once I've spoken with Tom! Will do all we can to help, that I promise.'

Geraldine was aware of a great wave of relief as she put the phone down, knowing she couldn't wait to see them. As she sat there, she recollected Lottie's kindly blue eyes, and rosy cheeks, her face framed by hair prematurely white—and Tom's rugged features and penetrating gaze beneath shaggy brows. Remembered nostalgically cases they had been jointly involved with in the early days. Yes, she had taken the right step, she assured herself.

Feeling a sense of relief that she would soon have the support of the esteemed ex-colleagues she had not seen for many years, she went out in the garden to speak with twins and found them standing next to the garden fence calling across to the little Susan

'Granny—may Susan come over and play?' asked Melanie.

'Of course, if her Mummy says so.' As she spoke, Geraldine peered over the rustic fence where yellow roses and honeysuckle swarmed above the flower bed and bees buzzed over lavender, pinks and stocks and butterflies fluttered and saw Anna coming towards them. She watched as the little girl ran to her mother and looked up at her pleadingly.

'Is it all right if I bring her round,' called Anna. 'I don't want to impose when—?' she glanced at the twins.

'You'll both be very welcome, dear. I was hoping to speak with you, wondered if you would like to come to the village later? We can all take my car, make things easier. I'm sure you could do with some more groceries by now and I'd love to show you around the place—not that it will take long!'

Anna held Susan's hand, as she walked behind Geraldine and the twins along the cobbled high street, staring curiously at the small shops they passed. She had been putting off venturing out to the village, and the provisions she had brought with her when she had first arrived almost a week ago certainly needed replenishing, was almost out of milk and bread.

As she entered the village store with Geraldine, she drew a sigh of relief. It was not proving as frightening as she had feared facing the outside world for the first time away from the safety of that wonderful refuge where she had spent so many weeks regaining her confidence and realising that a new future could be hers if she had the courage to face it in her new identity.

Her first step had been their arrival at Bramble Cottage—then meeting Geraldine and all that had happened since. Perhaps watching her new friend cope with the shock of losing her only beloved son in strangely suspicious circumstances, followed by the death of his wife, and taking the brave decision to take guardianship of her little grandchildren, when she should be sitting back and enjoying retirement, all this had helped Anna to face an independent future.

'I am Anna Lindstrom,' she heard herself saying to the polite storekeeper. 'I have moved into Bramble Cottage with my daughter Susan. Mrs Denton says that if I phone an order in future, you will deliver?'

'Ted Masters—I own the store. Glad to meet you, Mrs Lindstrom. Yes, it will be a pleasure. Good to know that lovely cottage is occupied once more.' She smiled at the pleasant, balding man, who offered an apple to Susan. Yes, she really could manage to start again in this little village. Geraldine who had been watching her sensed the new confidence in the girl.

'I am dropping into the school to speak to the headmistress,' she said. 'I think the twins should start next week—and you could always have a word about Susan's future while we are there. They have a nursery class for four-year-olds if you are interested?' Anna hesitated. Was it too soon? Suppose Susan let slip details of her past. Perhaps she should wait until the child was more familiar with her new name.

'Yes, a good idea. I'll think about it—but not just yet. Susan had had a lot of changes recently you know.' Geraldine nodded and did not attempt to press the point.

'Well, you can put her name down for a year's time,' she suggested casually. 'But at least you can take a look at the school now and see what you think of it.'

The headmistress, Mrs Joan Walters, received her visitors cordially, already knew Geraldine well as the widow of their much respected and badly missed doctor, and looked with sympathy at the serious-faced twins sitting at Geraldine's side. To have lost both their parents so suddenly and to be removed from their parental home and school, was challenging in the extreme, but Mrs Denton was a kind and responsible person, and little Charles and Melanie were fortunate in their grandmother. She resolved to see her two new students receive every help.

'Charles and Melanie, I look forward to welcoming you to school next week. I understand that you have been going through a very difficult time, but I'm sure you will be very happy here,' she said kindly. She then turned her attention to her younger adult visitor whose small daughter was watching her curiously.

'So, Ms Lindstrom, you would like to enrol your little girl in primary one next year. What is your name dear,' she asked the child gently.

'I am Susan Lindstrom,' she replied clearly.

'How old are you, Susan?'

'I'm almost four. How old are you?' she asked politely. Mrs Walters kept a straight face.

'That is a question children do not ask grownups,' she explained.

'Why not?' inquired the little girl.

'Hush, Susan,' said Anna firmly. 'Perhaps, we might discuss Susan attending nursery once she has settled into our new home. She can already read and write you know.'

'Splendid,' said the headmistress. She smiled at Susan. 'Your Mummy has been teaching you, dear,' she said approvingly.

'Yes, and my Nanny—' Susan began and stopped awkwardly. She glanced at her mother, who had taken her hand, and pressed it warningly. Listening to the little exchange, Geraldine quickly intervened to prevent more questions. It was time they were leaving, she explained, needed to do some shopping! A few minutes later, they left the Head Mistress's office, while Mrs Walters gazed after them thoughtfully. She had sensed something unusual about Anna Lindstrom and Susan. But those poor little Denton twins—they would need a lot of support. She sighed, children's lives were so heavily influenced by the behaviour of their parents and others who had the care of them.

Anna stowed away the groceries in the cupboard and fridge and turned to Susan who was sitting at the kitchen table, busily colouring her painting book with the new crayons her mother had bought her.

'What did you think of the school, Susan darling,' she asked. The child lifted her head

'I'm not sure,' she said. 'There were lots of children in the big playground—they made rather a lot of noise. It was a bit scary you know, Mummy.'

'They were enjoying themselves. I liked the headmistress—she's a very nice lady,' she added. Susan put her head on one side.

'She asked questions, Mummy—it was difficult.'

'You did very well, sweetheart. Just remember, we must never talk about anyone we knew at Enderslie House.'

'Like Nanny Beecham—I'm sorry Mummy. I almost forgot.'

'I know you will be more careful in future. We both have to be, dear. It's very important!' She stooped over Susan and kissed her. 'I love the colours you are using. You are going to be quite an artist!'

'Are we really safe here, Mummy—Daddy really won't be able to find us?' checked Susan. The mention of Nanny Beecham had brought the frightening past back into consciousness. Anna kissed her remorsefully, worried that she had uncovered disturbing memories.

'We are quite safe, darling. And just think, we have our lovely new friend Geraldine next door, and young Charles and Melanie. Listen, when you are old enough I promise you will enjoy that school we saw today. Just try to remember not to speak to anyone about Enderslie House—never mention your father, nor Nanny Beecham!'

'I won't, Mummy.'

'Good! Soon it will just be like a bad dream, just fade away altogether.' Her blue eyes gazed down tenderly into Susan's matching gaze. Anna could see no trace of Malcolm's hard features on her daughter's face and was thankful for it. But people would eventually ask questions about the child's father and she must have a reliable answer ready.

A week had passed and Geraldine was eagerly expecting her visitors. Tom and Lottie Lanscombe were to arrive that afternoon and now she checked all looked welcoming in the cottage, fresh flowers in the vases, cushions plumped up, their bedroom prepared. It was going to be marvellous having the support of those who had been such close friends, but also esteemed colleagues in that special department of the civil service dealing with UK security.

There was a ring at the door. Surely it was a bit early for her guests—found it was Anna Lindstrom standing there, with Susan at her side.

'Geraldine—I wonder if it would be possible to speak privately with you later—when the children are playing together perhaps?' She looked hopefully at Geraldine who sensed the anxiety behind the request.

'Of course—come in my dear. The twins have started school today, hence the place is quiet! But I am expecting house guests this afternoon. Friends of mine I haven't seen for many years. Look, why don't we let Susan play in the conservatory? We'll put some modelling clay on the table there for her—she loves that doesn't she, then you and I can talk in peace in the sitting room.'

They seated themselves together on the sofa, and Geraldine looked encouragingly at the young woman whom she had guessed was carrying a secret from her past. For a moment there was silence, and then she took Anna's hand.

'Perhaps you want to speak of the reason that brought you to this remote little village? I guessed that life had been difficult in your recent past, that you had escaped from a fraught situation. If I am wrong then please forgive my mistake!' She watched Anna's face and saw her swallow, as the girl lifted her eyes, looking at Geraldine directly.

'I had not realised it was so obvious, but you are quite correct. I escaped from an abusive relationship with a man I hated and feared. He was Susan's father—she was born of rape.'

'Just tell me—take your time. Anything you share with me will always remain secret, that I swear,' replied Geraldine protectively.

'I don't know where to start!' faltered Anna.

'Well, how about your real name—it's not Anna Lindstrom is it?' asked Geraldine.

'No—it's Erika Nicolson—and my little girl, Trudy. The people at the first refuge who aided my escape, suggested I change our identity. I chose Anna Lindstrom as it was the name of my Swedish great-grandmother, but unknown to my abuser.' Now she had started it was like a dam bursting as Anna started to pour out details of those years of abuse she had endured at the hands of Malcolm Greer.

Geraldine listened with growing anger towards the man who had treated this fine young woman with such cruelty. She looked at her encouragingly.

'You say you were a staff nurse on a busy surgical ward. This means you will have no trouble finding another suitable post when you are ready to work. I take it you will need a regular income sooner or later?' Geraldine probed gently.

'Yes! The problem will be that all my nursing records are in my real name Erikson. I daren't use this, because Malcolm will check for it at all hospitals in his search for me. He'll guess nursing will be my obvious choice of work—may also realise that I will take another name. He has the money and the power to get others to investigate on his behalf. So, you see why I may not resume the career I love. Did I tell you that my late father was a famous neurosurgeon? My mother died giving birth to me—my father and the medical profession were the backgrounds of my childhood years,' explained Anna sadly.

'Have you changed your appearance, since leaving this man?' inquired Geraldine. 'That lovely golden hair of yours is natural I think?'

'Why yes. I could dye it, cut it short I suppose, but I cannot change the shape of my face, the colour of my eyes. And why should I have to do so!' said Anna hotly. 'No, I will have to find another type of work and it has to be soon. As I told you, Malcolm took all my money—but was unaware of that small savings account that remained from my nursing days. This is what is keeping me going at the moment.'

'Anna, I'll do all I can to help you—need time to think. Now as I told you, my friends are arriving soon. Have I your permission to discuss your problem with them—they are well qualified to advise and completely trustworthy?' Anna looked slightly apprehensive at the idea but nodded.

'Yes, providing you trust them, then I am happy to do so. Geraldine dear, I will leave for now—just so grateful for your support. It means a lot. You are a very special person.' She rose to her feet and called to Susan. The child was bending over the clay she was working on.

'Look at the cat I have made Mummy!' she said, pointing to the little clay model. 'Do you think it looks like Marcasite?' Anna looked at her tenderly.

'It certainly does—well done, Susan! We must go—it's time for lunch.' She waved to Geraldine as they let themselves out of the blue door. She drew a sigh of relief that she had taken the plunge and shared her history with her kindly neighbour, and felt lighter already. There was something about Geraldine Denton that inspired confidence and wondered curiously about the earlier life of this elderly woman with wise grey eyes.

Malcolm Greer! Geraldine bent over her computer attempting to discover details of the business background of the scoundrel who had so foully abused an innocent woman who had devoted her life to the nursing profession she loved. Her eyes narrowed at what she read. Next, she brought up an image of Enderslie House and stared at it long and hard, realising how isolated the house was from any other habitation. It must take a great deal of money to maintain a place that size. While her priority at this time was to establish the motives of those who had murdered her beloved son Colin, and his dear wife Mary—and hopefully expose the unscrupulous operatives of Sea Giant for their crimes, she would also do all in her power to help Anna, had developed an almost motherly affection for the young woman and her small daughter. It was as though Anna and little Susan, together with her orphaned grandchildren, had now formed a cohesive family unit—her lonely existence following her husband's death replaced by such unexpected new responsibilities.

At just after 2 pm Geraldine heard the sound of a car drawing up outside the gate. She glanced out of the window—yes, it was Tom and Lottie, her much-anticipated visitors, and she hurried to the door. She glanced at them as they came up the pathway towards her, and despite the passing of time, recognised Lottie's rounded figure, snow-white hair and rosy cheeks and Tom's rugged face.

'You found me! Oh, it's so wonderful to see you both,' she cried in delight. Within minutes they were embracing as she ushered them inside Rose Cottage.

'Why this is delightful, Geraldine,' exclaimed Lottie glancing curiously around the comfortable living room, her eyes lighting on the silver-framed photograph of a kindly, good-looking man, lips parted in a quizzical smile. She looked at Geraldine sympathetically.

'That's a great photo,' she said gently, 'We were both so sorry to learn David had passed away. He was such a vital person, a kind and marvellous doctor—and as I remember, had a fine sense of humour.' Geraldine nodded and blinked away a quick tear.

'Yes, I do miss him you know, but strangely it sometimes seems as though he is still in the room,' she said quietly. She smiled at them, 'But I am so glad our friendship has endured and so grateful you have come, for I badly need advice!' Tom reached out a hand and put it on her shoulder.

'Anything we can do to help, we will! And not mere words either,' he reassured. 'I can hardly believe ten years have gone by since last we met, Geraldine!' He shook his head reflectively. 'Time seems to pass ever more quickly as our years advance.'

'I wasn't even sure you would still be in that beautiful home of yours near the church—Ivy Cottage!' she replied. 'Just took a chance and phoned! Look, sit down both of you and I'll make tea—or would you prefer coffee?'

An hour had slipped by, during which Geraldine filled them in with every relevant detail of what had occurred since receiving that fatal phone call from Mary, informing her that Colin's helicopter had crashed—with no survivors. They listened intently as she related all that Mary had told her of Colin's deep concern over global warming, his worry that the opening of yet another major oilfield could only accelerate an onrushing situation where the world would be subject to violent forms of climate change, with tremendous storms, flooding, and raging forest fires—and great areas suffering drought, starving indigenous nations seeking refuge in the West. She glanced at them and saw how intently they were listening.

'And it has already started, hasn't it,' she said quietly. 'Every day we hear of tornadoes, earthquakes, mudslides burying villages, low lying areas subject to widespread flooding. And the icecaps are melting at an ever-increasing pace, sea levels ultimately rising twenty to fifty feet! Why is mankind so blind!' Her cheeks were burning as she poured it all out. 'Colin was acutely aware of this, and apparently took the directors of Sea Giant to task, asked that they reconsider going ahead with their latest discovery, a field that would produce billions of pounds worth of oil.' She paused and glanced from one to another of them.

'It was very brave—perhaps even foolhardy of Colin to attempt to sway men whose only philosophy is to make an even greater profit from black gold,' said Tom gravely. 'You say that this new field is still secret as far as the general public is concerned?' His shaggy brows drew together over his sharp eyes as he checked the point with her. Geraldine sighed.

'I only know what I've gleaned from the data I found on Colin's computer and what little Mary was able to tell me in the few short hours we spent together before she too was killed. I wish Colin had been in touch with me and trusted me with his concerns. I can only think it must have been in consideration that I was still in grief for his father's death. But to be honest, he never shared any information with me about his doings in the oil industry. Once he had settled in that little village near Aberdeen with Mary and the twins, I heard little from either of them. Young folk have their own lives to lead, so!' and she shrugged and sighed.

'You say that you did not give your address to anyone in Grantly?' asked Lottie.

'Only to the minister's wife, Molly. I wrote it down for her in case she needed to get in touch with any fresh news and gave Robin my card. Both she and her husband, the Rev Robin MacKinnon, are completely trustworthy. They were caring for the twins when Mary's car crashed and caught fire.' She swallowed as she recollected the terrible event, then suddenly glanced at the clock. 'The twins!' she exclaimed. 'I must drive over to the school and collect them. Will you be all right?'

'Off you go, we'll be fine,' said Lottie.

To their surprise, she was back within a couple of minutes. She smiled at them and explained.

'My new young neighbour offered to collect them for me—a lovely young woman who has recently escaped from an abusive relationship.' She saw Lottie's face light up with interest.

'Of course—this village is called Ravensnest! Tell me, is your new neighbour named Anna Lindstrom by any chance?' She saw Geraldine's face drop in bewilderment.

'But how could you know that?'

'Well, it is an incredible story! Do you remember a certain Antonia Marsden, an autocratic elderly woman living in an imposing old mansion house, Sweet Meadow? Actually, it belonged to her stepson Robert Marsden, although Antonia liked to give the impression it was hers!' Geraldine looked at her and frowned reflectively.

'Yes, I do vaguely. Rather pompous, white hair, pearls and a cane.'

'Summed up beautifully! Well, to cut a long story short, Antonia encouraged the marriage of her stepson to a younger version of herself, equally cold and calculating, named Veronica. It was a disastrous marriage resulting in divorce.'

'Go on!' Geraldine was listening intently.

'Robert Marsden was an investigative journalist, dedicated to his work. Two years after his divorce, he met and fell in love with a lovely Welsh girl, Amber Williams. They were expecting a child, when a mere month before the expected birth, Robert set off for the Arctic to cover the work of a weather station investigating global warming—he suspected a rogue American company, Oleumgeldt, of planning to damage the ice caps to give easier access to rich oil deposits. This could well have accelerated that very global warming that your son expressed concerns about.' Geraldine looked stunned.

'Did he find the evidence he sought?' she asked.

'Before he could send the report back, an attempt was made on his life—he was standing on a huge ice cliff. It was mined—Robert disappeared into a fifty-foot chasm. Amber had been rushed into hospital, and had just given premature birth to their baby when news of Robert's death was mentioned in a TV news report.'

'What a tragedy! Poor young woman' exclaimed Geraldine. 'Were they married?'

'No. Robert had proposed, but Amber was not sure. Her own parent's marriage had been difficult. Now suddenly, the man she loved so dearly was dead and without even seeing their baby son. She was shortly contacted by Robert's solicitor, invited to be present at Sweet Meadow for the reading of Robert's will. Robert had previously introduced Amber to his stepmother, who was far from welcoming. Now she made a second visit to that cold formal mansion house, to find that a memorial service had just been held for Robert, in our dear little village church. She had not even been informed of the occasion.

'What a heartless woman that Antonia is,' exclaimed Geraldine. 'What happened at the reading of the will?' It was Tom who answered.

'Robert made the will just before his trip to the Arctic. In it, he left Sweet Meadow and a considerable sum to Amber. His mother who was already wealthy in her own right was to move out once she had acquired another residence. I wish I could have seen her face!' and he chuckled. Lottie took up the story.

'We befriended Amber and invited her to stay with us at Ivy Cottage until she could move into Sweet Meadow. So now, this lovely and very courageous young woman, mourning the death of the man she loved, possessed a large mansion house and extensive grounds, its only occupants herself and baby son, and a young girl previously employed as a maid by Antonia, whom Amber engaged as her personal assistant!'

'What did she do with that huge house?' Geraldine leaned forward, completely enthralled by the story.

'She took a most extraordinary and generous decision. Sweet Meadow was wonderfully restored and modernised—and is now a refuge for abused women! The place remains a close secret, where women are helped to recover from abuse, guided into a new and happier future, and make a solemn promise never to reveal the existence of Dream Echo.'

'It's a truly inspiring story, but why are you telling me about it now?' demanded Geraldine curiously. Then she stared at the couple as the answer came to her mind. 'You asked if my new neighbour was called Anna Lindstrom! Was my Anna helped by this amazing young woman Amber at Dream Echo?' Lottie smiled as she answered.

'Yes, my dear. You see, Tom and I also help Amber to run the refuge, together with several other dedicated and well-qualified people. Up to twenty women are cared for there at any one time.'

Geraldine gasped in surprise. How amazing these two dear old friends are. ex-colleagues from her time in MI5 had become involved in helping to run a women's refuge at a time when they might have been expected to enjoy a peaceful retirement!

'I think you are both amazing!' she said gently. 'The work must be extremely taxing, but how rewarding to see damaged women find the confidence to take up their lives again. I truly admire you.' She would have said more, but at that moment the doorbell rang—and she hurried to let the twins in, together with Anna and little Susan.

'Anna dear, thank you so much, for bringing the children home,' she cried.

'It was a pleasure, Geraldine. I won't stay as you have visitors to attend to. See you tomorrow, perhaps?' She made to leave.

'No—stay. I believe you may already know my friends!' She saw the baffled look on the girl's face, as Anna reluctantly followed her into the sitting room, and glanced hesitantly at the couple seated side by side on the sofa. Her eyes widened as she recognised them.

'Mr Lanscombe—Lottie! What are you doing here?' she demanded shakily.

'Anna! I remembered your new address was to be Bramble Cottage at Ravensnest
—what I had not realised was that it was immediately next door to Rose Cottage and our friend Geraldine Denton. But I promise you there couldn't have found a kinder, more supportive neighbour!' said Lottie warmly. 'How are you settling in my dear?'

'Very happily,' replied Anna. 'And so is Susan,' she added softly. 'I will never forget all the kindness we received at the refuge.' They saw the new confidence in her face and bearing

'It's good to see you again, Anna,' put in Tom heartily. 'We wondered how you were getting on.' He looked down at Susan, 'And how are you, my dear? Do you like your new home?' She smiled and ran over remembering them both and clambered on Tom's knee.

'We have a lovely cottage,' she confided, 'And I have some new friends to play with. And Geraldine has a cat called Marcasite.'

'So, these are your grandchildren,' said Lottie glancing at the twins, who were wondering who these visitors were. 'They're beautiful.' She smiled at the twins.

'Hallo Charles and Melanie! We are Tom and Lottie, friends of your grandmother and have come to stay for a few days.' She glanced at Tom, as both sensed the deep sadness beneath the youngsters' polite smiles. Poor little souls, to have lost both father and mother so suddenly at only seven years of age. They were such fine-looking children, both fair-haired with solemn grey eyes.

'We hope you're going to be very happy with your granny—she is a very special lady,' said Tom. 'We know some very sad things have happened recently—but life will get better my dears, you'll see.' He turned to Geraldine. 'They're wonderful kids,' he said quietly, 'As is little Susan.' Geraldine glanced from Tom and Lottie to Anna.

'I had not realised that you knew each other, Anna?' she questioned. The girl inclined her head and smiled self-consciously.

'Geraldine, I did not mention the name of the refuge where I received such amazing support and kindness. I had promised never to reveal it. But seemingly you are acquainted with two of the kind friends I made there—Tom and Lottie!'

'You did well to keep that promise,' said Geraldine. 'Now I have been brought up to date with my friend's more recent activities which I heartily applaud, I quite understand the need for secrecy. What a happy coincidence that of all the places on the map you should have moved next door to me! It is as though it was meant to be!' And she took Anna's hand and pressed it warmly. Lottie turned to her husband as they watched the little scene.

'Of course, that was why the name of the village—Ravensnest, seemed familiar when Amber mentioned this was where accommodation had been found for Anna. I'd almost forgotten it was where Geraldine and David had moved to ten years back.' She looked at Geraldine. 'I do so regret we lost contact with you for so long, and how very poignant that the present circumstances have brought us together again!'

'Look Geraldine—I'll take Susan home now,' said Anna quietly. 'You need privacy to discuss family affairs with your friends.' She rose to her feet and scooped Susan from Tom's knee. 'Geraldine, would you like me to take the twins next door with me for a few hours—give them their evening meal?' Charles and Melanie looked up eagerly.

'That would be wonderful,' exclaimed Geraldine. 'Thank you, my dear.'

'We are here for a few days, so look forward to seeing you soon again, Anna,' said Lottie, as they watched her make for the door with the three children. 'She's a lovely girl isn't she,' she said to Geraldine. 'I hope the skunk who caused her such misery will receive his just deserts one day soon. Tom's been investigating his business affairs, suspects involvement in people trafficking!' Geraldine's grey eyes focussed on Lottie's face aghast.

'Anna gave me a brief account of her previous life under the rigid control of that vile, unscrupulous individual. I must say I wondered how Malcolm Greer had accumulated his wealth. According to what he told Anna it was from his business as a property developer.' She turned to Tom. 'So then, you suspect people trafficking, Tom?' He nodded.

'Yes—young girls from Eastern European countries, brought here with offers of well-paid domestic jobs, and end up forced into prostitution. He works with several other lowlifes and is thought to mastermind the organisation! His supposed work as a property developer is just a sham to mask his real activities.' He shook his head in disgust.

'Thank goodness Anna managed to make her escape from him. She mentioned that he often entertained business associates at Enderslie House, where she was supposed to act as hostess,' Lottie added. 'So, a fine mansion, a beautiful partner and a delightful little daughter providing the perfect background for this supposed pillar of the community, who sometimes donated sums to good causes.' Her blue eyes smouldered as she spoke.

'What are the chances that Greer will face justice fairly soon?' Geraldine demanded. 'Anna is anxious to find work but frightened that he will track her down. I've grown quite fond of her although we have only known each other a short while—and little Susan is a real little sweetheart,' she added. Tom smiled at her words.

'They were favourites at Dream Echo you know. It's great you've been befriending them both. I feel they have a good future before them—and deserve it after all they've endured.'

'Anna couldn't have been more helpful when I had the phone call from Mary with the dreadful news that Colin's helicopter had gone down with no survivors, and since I got back with the children she has been marvellously supportive.' She was trying hard to restrain her tears, and Lottie rose to her feet and bent over her, slipping an arm about her shoulders.

'Geraldine dear, I have the feeling that you have not had time to grieve properly yet—and you must. Need to acknowledge your pain and deal with it. You've busied yourself in the care and comforting of your little grandchildren, helping the poor little souls accept their parents' death, all this in the most selfless way imaginable—plus your support for Anna and her little one.' She spoke soothingly but her words seemed to go unheeded, for Geraldine merely sighed and shook her head.

'I will not spend time grieving until I have the answers I seek and uncover the motives of 'Sea Giant' in his murder, and that of dear Mary. Tom, I am hoping that you will be able to make sense of the data on the memory stick! Please say you will do your best?' she begged passionately and pointed towards her computer.

'You have my word! And if I require assistance, will call on one of our colleagues still active in the service—Charles Latimer, you remember him?' His eyes met hers and Geraldine relaxed and managed a smile.

'Charles—yes, of course, I do, and thank you, Tom. Now it's about time I remembered my duties as a hostess—you must be starving! Please forgive my being so lax. I'm off to the kitchen.' Lottie glanced at Tom who was already lifting Geraldine's computer.

'I'll come with you, lend a hand!' she said firmly. 'We can chat at the same time.' She looked approvingly around the homely country kitchen with its pine table and cushioned chairs, shelves of gleaming copper pans, and quaint china ornaments on the windowsill framed by cheerful red curtains. All looked very inviting. She watched as her hostess began busying herself beating up egg, milk and flour in a pudding basin.

'How is Charles Latimer now?' asked Geraldine, as she switched on the vegetables and checked the joint of roast beef already partly cooked, as she popped in the Yorkshire pudding. 'I still recall him—handsome features, hair prematurely grey, reputed to be extremely courageous, possessed a keen mind and was highly thought of in the service.' Lottie chuckled at a description both concise and accurate.

'You have summed Charles up well—and of course, time has placed its touch on him as it has on Tom and myself in the years since we worked together. Although Tom retired a while back they still keep in touch and Charles was of help to Amber, the young woman who runs Dream Echo, the refuge we told you about.'

'I missed it all when I left MI5, the challenge and yes, the excitement—but I'd spent far too long away from my husband David, who was always tolerant of my work, but I knew it was unfair to him. It was different for you Lottie, for although you had become a famous writer, you were still part of the team, and could work with Tom.' As the words poured out Geraldine realised it was the first time she had acknowledged the sense of loss experienced on leaving the service. Lottie watched her friend's face and saw the conflicting emotions.

'Geraldine, I went through exactly the same thing when I resigned—and as for Tom who carried on working for much longer, he started to busy himself in his garden, but was obviously missing it too. That's why helping out at Dream Echo has been so fulfilling and we both couldn't be happier.' It was clear from Lottie's expression how much she was enjoying her new occupation.

'Speaking with you like this has brought it all flooding back,' said Geraldine musingly, as she reached into a cabinet for dinner plates. She turned and glanced at Lottie. 'Richard had a colleague who worked with him—Paul—er?' She sought for his surname. 'Younger than Richard, six feet, dark hair, blue eyes, could be reckless?' Lottie nodded and breathed a sigh.

'I believe you mean the late Paul Trent.'

'Trent, yes, that's the name—but you said late, Lottie?' asked Geraldine in consternation, noting the expression of sadness in Lottie's blue eyes.

'Yes, he died three years ago, was engaged to be married and about to resign was asked to take one last case. He was shot dead,' replied Lottie soberly. 'If I give you some details it has to be in complete confidence.'

'But of course, Lottie dear. That goes without saying.' They seated themselves at the kitchen table, and Geraldine listened to an account that moved her almost to tears.

'Poor Paul—and I was going to say poor Amber too, except that her story has had such an amazingly happy ending after such traumatic happenings,' she said softly.

'Yes. And a new beginning with Robert Marsden, her first love, and father of her baby son. He returned alive from the Arctic, rescued by the Inuit when the ice cliff he was standing on was mined, explosion causing him to fall into a deep crevasse and nearly taking his life,' explained Lottie and continued, 'It's an incredible story of the courage of two extraordinary men, and the unwavering resolve of a wonderful young woman, who continues to welcome abused women into the home she has adapted into an amazing refuge—now with the help of her husband Robert at her side.' She smiled at Geraldine. 'So, you understand what a special place Dream Echo is and why Tom and I take joy in doing a small part to help.' For a moment there was silence as they sorted out cutlery, table cloth and napkins to take through to the dining room.

'I wonder how Tom is getting on with that Sea Giant data on your computer,' pondered Lottie as they laid the table. 'Strange to think that both Robert Marsden and your dear son Colin were both involved in attempting to uncover the uncaring, selfish behaviour of those who for personal gain are involved in accelerating global warming.' Geraldine looked at her and sighed.

'If only Colin's efforts could have had the same happy ending as Robert's,' she said in a low voice. 'Alas, there was no escape for my dear son when his helicopter took that fatal plunge to the bottom of the sea.' It was said with no slightest self-pity, only a sad acceptance of fate. Lottie looked at her sympathetically.

'I know, my dear. Sometimes we try to understand why such things happen to good people, those we care about so deeply. But I do believe that God knows our struggles and pain and gives us the power to carry on, sometimes opening up life in a way we could never have visualised before.' She looked at Geraldine, hoping her words didn't sound trite but saw a sweet smile on the older woman's lips.

'You're quite right, Lottie dear. And I am prepared for whatever life throws at me next and will do all I possibly can to expose those who murdered my darling son and his wife—and will always care for and protect their young children.' They smiled at each other, checked the table and called to Tom in the adjoining room that dinner was about to be served.

'Would you like me to carve,' he said seating himself and eyeing the joint of roast beef and on a nod from Geraldine proceeded to do so, as she dished up the Yorkshire pudding and Lottie the vegetables—then horse radish sauce and gravy.

'Have you managed to make any progress with the Sea Giant stuff?' asked Lottie.

'Yes, indeed I have. Geraldine my dear, I hope you don't mind, but I've also invited Charles Latimer to join us tomorrow.'

Chapter Five

They heard a knock just after they had cleared the table. Anna had brought the twins back.

'These two have eaten well, Geraldine and are ready for bed!' she said, as the two sleepy children followed her into the living room. 'Would you like me to take them upstairs?'

'No, Anna—you've done quite enough already. You go back and put your little daughter to bed, and thank you for being so wonderfully helpful!' She gave the girl a hug. 'We'll meet up again tomorrow,' she said quietly, watching affectionately as Anna led Susan away and they heard the door close.

'She has come on amazingly from the traumatised young woman who first arrived at Dream Echo,' said Lottie approvingly. 'When our residents leave to take up their new lives we often wonder how they are doing!'

'Yes, I would say Anna is more than ready to resume her work as an orthopaedics staff nurse,' mused Geraldine. 'But it would make life much easier if that brute Malcolm Greer was safely behind bars. Anything you can do to expedite matters there, Tom?'

'If not personally, then I will encourage those who can,' he replied with a grin. He turned to Charles and Melanie. 'Time you two were in bed,' he said. 'Your granny is waiting.'

Geraldine tucked them in bed, told them a bedtime story, and as their eyes closed was about to slip quietly away, when Melanie's little form was shaken with tears. Charles also was grieving, head buried in his pillow.

'I want my Mummy and Daddy,' she sobbed. 'I like it here with you Granny, but I miss them so!'

'And I do too,' came Charles's muffled voice.

'Darlings, I know you do and If I could bring them back I would. But they are safe in God's heaven, and I believe their love is with you always—know they would want you both to be brave.' She sat down beside them again, cuddling and soothing them until they relaxed at last and managed smiles once more. As she walked downstairs to her guests, Geraldine was consumed with deep anger towards those who had caused such havoc in her family and vowed she would do all she could to bring them to justice.

'They're asleep now?' queried Lottie. Geraldine nodded, her face betraying her disturbed emotions.

'They are fine youngsters,' said Tom. 'How are they coping?'

'I thought they were starting to settle down well, but they broke down just now, and although I tried to say all the right things, I just felt so helpless,' Geraldine admitted. 'If I could get my hands on the fiends responsible for Colin and Mary's death, I won't say what I would like to do! I still recall the faces of the four men who came to the door and demanded to see Colin's papers and took his computer!'

'Give me their names again,' said Tom quietly, leaning forward in his chair.

'Richard Lancaster, MD of Sea Giant. Tall with arrogant features, I sensed he was ruthless. Then there was a man called Ross Chambers, overweight, with hard eyes, who introduced himself as being in charge of company security. The two others didn't give their names, some sort of underlings. But I am convinced that one or other of the four, ordered Mary's car tampered with.'

'Proving it will be the next job. Have you had any contact with your friends at the manse, since you have been back home here?' he pursued. Geraldine shook her head.

'They are to let me know when Mary's body is released for burial but understand I will not attend the funeral. As I mentioned, Robin and Molly agreed not to reveal my address to anyone there,' said Geraldine quietly.

'And I suppose no trace of the wreckage has been found yet—or anything else,' he asked gently. They both knew he referred to Colin's remains.

'As I told you, the word was spread that the helicopter had come down over a deep trough—might prove dangerous for divers to work at such depths. No, I've already let go of my beloved Colin and made myself face the actuality of what happened. But I'll never cease trying to uncover the reason for his death!' Tom and Lottie stared at her with quick sympathy.

'Geraldine lass, we'll all work together to discover the secret Sea Giant have killed to protect and once we have established the identity of the perpetrators, see that they face justice!' Geraldine blinked back tears of relief, taking heart from their support.

'Well, let's speak of happier things now—maybe you'd like a coffee or something stronger? I've got some of David's good brandy in the cabinet—and there's vodka, and some decent wine,' she offered. And the rest of the evening passed happily as they reminisced about their time together in the Secret Service. And that night when Geraldine went to bed, she slept peacefully for the first time since tragedy had struck.

The following morning, they had just finished breakfast when there was a knock at the door. It was Anna, with an offer to drive the children to school, which Geraldine gladly accepted, noting that young Charles and Melanie seemed brighter today. After feeding the cat and sorting the breakfast dishes, Geraldine suggested they might like to explore her garden since the weather remained fine and sunny.

'This is another thing we share in common, our love of gardening,' exclaimed Lottie, bending to examine a particularly fine, yellow rose bush, 'You have a real talent for it, Geraldine! Tom does most of the work in ours, whilst I enjoy the fruits of his labour!'

'Well my love, since you provide me with such splendid meals, I believe we have a fine balance in the domestic field,' and he slipped an affectionate arm around his wife's shoulders. Geraldine looked on wistfully, remembering how often she had walked through this little garden with her husband David. But life goes on, and offers new challenges, she told herself firmly. Her most important status now was as grandmother to little Charles and Melanie.

As she stood there staring at the roses, her mobile rang. She pulled it out of her pocket.

'Geraldine—is that you? This is Molly. You gave me this number in case anything should happen here.'

'Molly dear—it's good to hear your voice. How are you and Robin?' she asked, wondering what news the minister's wife might have.

'We are well thankyou—but more importantly, how are bearing up under all that's so tragically happened? And how are you coping with your dear little grandchildren?' Molly's soft highland voice was warm and full of sympathy.

'The twins are gradually coming to terms with their loss,' said Geraldine. 'They break down occasionally, but on the whole show the amazing resilience children can display. They have started at their new school and settling in well.' There was a pause then Molly spoke again.

'Geraldine—there has been a development at Sea Giant. Seems they employed a special diving cylinder mounted with a camera. It's reported they have found the wreckage of the missing helicopter—and two bodies, the pilot Kevin, and that of Jonathon King—but sadly no trace so far of your dear son Colin.' She paused as she heard Geraldine gasp. 'I'm so sorry Geraldine, but due to the crash and the strong currents, it's said he might be anywhere.'

'Thank you for letting me know, Molly. Perhaps you'd be kind enough to pass on any future news. I realised there was no hope of course, but it's still a shock to have the worst confirmed. I'm very grateful to both you and Robin for all your help and support.'

'Mary's body has now been released—the service is to be held in two days' time. I know you will not be here with us, but I promise you all will go as you would wish and be held with love and respect for a very special lady.' Molly's voice trembled slightly. 'One thing more I should mention—the day after you left with the children, a representative of Sea Giant came to the manse, asking to speak with you. He had been round to Colin and Mary's house seeking you, and getting no answer guessed you might be here with us.'

'What did you say,' asked Geraldine alertly.

'The truth—you had taken the twins away with you the day before, as the stress was too much for them. He wanted your address. I said we did not have it—he was persisting when Robin came to the door and sent the fellow on his way. We didn't like him, sensed something very wrong was happening.'

'Molly, you have done exactly the right thing. Under no circumstances mention this address or my phone number to anyone whatsoever. Perhaps one day we will have the answer to all that's happened. For now, I must concentrate on making a secure and happy home for little Charles and Melanie.'

'Trust me, Geraldine—my lips are sealed. But always remember Robin and I are here if you need us. Goodbye for a wee while dear.' And she called off. Geraldine slipped the mobile back into her pocket and saw Tom and Lottie looking at her questioningly.

'That was Molly MacKinnon—the minister's wife,' she said quietly. 'The wreckage has been found—some sort of underwater camera—and two bodies. The pilot and Colin's colleague, Jonathon King. But no sign of Colin.' The couple exchanged glances.

'Let's get you sitting down inside, Geraldine. You've just had a shock,' Tom put a strong arm about her and led her back across the lawn.

'I'll make coffee,' said Lottie, helping her into her easy chair. And making towards the kitchen. But Geraldine shook her head and looked at her urgently.

'Just let me tell you something else first,' she insisted. 'The following morning after I'd left with the twins, an official from Sea Giant arrived at the manse. He'd already been round to the family house looking for me. He asked for my address. Molly and Robin said they did not know it. But why did he want to see me? I can only guess he may suspect I have a copy of Colin's data. I'm beginning to feel extremely uneasy—suppose he does find out where I am? I'm not scared so much on my own behalf—but the twins need me, they have no one else to care for them!' She swallowed a sob.

'Now none of that!' said Tom firmly. 'Nobody will find you here—but should you have further worry on that score, then the answer is simple, you will come to Ivy Cottage and stay with us for however long needs be.' And Lottie added her encouragement.

They sat sipping their coffee and discussing the latest news when the doorbell rang. Geraldine looked up—possibly Anna she thought.

'I'll go,' said Tom and they waited expectantly—then heard a voice Geraldine remembered from a few years back, as Tom led a handsome, silver-haired, keen-eyed man into the sitting room.

'Geraldine, our friend Charles Latimer has arrived,' said Tom heartily, as Geraldine rose to her feet, to be caught in a warm embrace.

'Charles—it's been a long while,' she said unsteadily. 'It's so good of you to come to help. Tom told me he had contacted you.' He looked down at her, his eyes expressing his sympathy. She looked a little older he thought, but still had that determined glint in her eyes.

'I'm glad to see you again Geraldine—but sorry it has taken such a cruel chance to bring it about. Tom told me about your son Colin's tragic death—and that of his wife, in what were suspicious circumstances.' He greeted Lottie, then seated himself in a chair facing Geraldine. 'Just tell everything,' he said quietly.

'You must have some refreshments first,' she exclaimed.

'I'll see to it,' suggested Lottie.

'Just coffee perhaps, I had a snack at a café on my way here.' He smiled at Lottie, then turned his attention on Geraldine.

'Shall we begin?' he asked gently. Then, falteringly at first, Geraldine related all that had happened since that distressing phone call from Mary telling her that Colin's helicopter had come down, with no survivors. She relived every relevant detail in her mind as she spoke, the training she had received long ago as an officer in Special Branch helping her present a concise account of events, as she kept emotion at bay. His questions were equally direct and pertinent. At last satisfied that he had extracted all information regarding the deaths of Colin Denton and his wife Mary, he brought the conversation around to the memory stick on which Geraldine had harvested the data on Colin's computer.

'I installed it on my Mac,' she said and produced the silver computer from beneath her chair. 'Tom's already had a look, personally, I couldn't make head nor tail of it. Lots of graphs, and figures. But whatever it all means was of sufficient importance for Sea Giant to kill twice to suppress it.' At that moment Lottie came back carrying a coffee decanter and a plate of shortbread

'Coffee everyone?' she asked glancing around and placing the tray on the low table between them. Charles lifted his cup to his lips, then set it aside as he opened the computer and sat quietly head bowed over it intently.

Tom watched him. From what he had personally gleaned on quick examination, Sea Giant were right to have been perturbed at the information becoming public! Not only would it destroy their reputation, exposing their duplicity in dealing with those who if not actually classed as enemies to the UK, were certainly not regarded as friends by the West, whilst also revealing the true extent of the new field and the largesse it might provide to those who accessed it.

But it was the information they had accessed from elderly German scientist Ernst Morgenstern, stealing his files with details of his new technology enabling oil to be extracted more speedily at a fraction of the cost and therefore worth. billions on the world market that they had sought to protect. They had made their secret deal with the Chinese in exchange for the considerable funding necessary for Sea Giant to develop the new field.

Lottie was aware of the questioning glance Tom directed at Charles as the MI5 agent raised his head and nodded to him.

'I was right?' asked Tom.

'Yes—and thank heavens Geraldine had the foresight to copy the data she found on Colin's computer onto a memory stick.' He looked gently at Geraldine. 'I want to discuss some technical stuff with Tom—is there somewhere we can go to chuck some dry facts and figures about between us?' he asked. She nodded but looked hurt that they should wish to exclude Lottie and herself from their deliberations.

'David's study is next door,' she said. Lottie gave her a reassuring smile as the men rose and retired to further study the Mac. Suddenly Geraldine gasped.

'Lottie—I have been so totally absorbed with the data rescued on the memory stick, that I forgot the folder!' Lottie looked at her inquiringly.

'What folder is that?' Lottie asked quickly.

'One which I brought back from Colin's house. When Mary and I made that hasty search through my son's study, I found a folder hidden beneath some brochures. I discovered it just as the Sea Giant officials arrived at the door—hid it in the kitchen swing bin. The men were searching for something other than the computer, demanding to look through the sitting room and bedroom in case Colin might have left something of importance there. They went away disappointed. I suggested to Mary that I should bring the folder back down south with me and pass it on to those who might understand its contents.' Geraldine bit her lip. 'How could I have been so forgetful!' Lottie stared at her in compassion.

'Geraldine dear, you have been under unimaginable stress, suffering deep grief over your dear son's death—and his wife's almost certain murder—all this while taking over the care of your grieving twin grandchildren! You have been brilliant in bringing back the data on that memory stick. If you have additional information on these matters in the folder you rescued, let's get it now, perhaps Tom and Charles can make sense of it.'

They went upstairs and Lottie watched as Geraldine retrieved the suitcase from the top of the wardrobe, unzipped the lining and produced the folder—looking at it, remembered how her dear son's hands must have handled this just before he took that last fatal flight. She blinked back the tears that threatened to fall.

'Here it is—take it,' she said steadily to Lottie, who nodded and smiled satisfaction.

'Let's see what the men make of it,' she said. 'Mind you, I we could as easily manage to assess it ourselves—however!' and she raised her eyebrows.

They returned to the study. Charles Latimer took it from Lottie's hands and glancing at Geraldine's face, saw signs of her recent distress. She stared at him.

'I'm sorry I forgot to mention this folder earlier. It's the one I hid just as the men from Sea Giant arrived at my son's house demanding to see Colin's papers and computer. Afterwards, Mary agreed I should bring it back with me in order to see if anyone could make sense of it. But after all that happened subsequently—I was so completely absorbed by whatever the memory stick should reveal that I neglected to show this.'

'It's marvellous that you brought it back with you, Geraldine,' he said quietly, as he opened the folder, Tom leaning closer to examine the contents with him. They began to glance rapidly through each batch of papers, spreading them out on the table before them. Their faces became sterner as they faced the incontrovertible conclusion such proof suggested.

'No wonder Colin was determined to expose Sea Giant!' muttered Tom, stabbing at one of the documents in disgust—a photocopy. 'They are obviously without any scruples or sense of loyalty to this country, but prepared to sell the stolen work of a German scientist enabling oil to be extracted more speedily and at a fraction of the cost from the seabed, and as we have seen the secret worth a fortune on the world market. Incidentally, a few months ago this Ernst Morgenstern was found dead in suspicious circumstances. How could they deal so with those from a part of the world opposed to us in matters of politics, trade and principles.' He shook his head, as Charles swore vehemently. He raised his head and looked sympathetically at Geraldine.

'It was for his knowledge of all this—and their fears he was about to reveal it to the authorities, that sealed Colin's death warrant! He was a brave man Geraldine, a son to be proud of. As for his wife Mary, they decided to kill her, rather than risk any knowledge she might have of these secret matters.' He looked at Tom. 'Do you consider Geraldine has anything to fear from them?' he demanded.

'Perhaps, if they have reason to suspect she too was involved. But I would hardly think so, Charles. They will merely perceive a distraught mother, grieving her son's sudden death, and whose daughter-in-law suffers a fatal car crash leaving two helpless children. Her swift action in removing her grandchildren from such a distressing situation was understandable in the circumstances. Geraldine had not had recent contact with Colin, so in total ignorance of the new oil find and of their plans to exploit it.' He glanced at Lottie. 'Do you agree, my love?'

'I do,' she replied, 'but although unlikely, Geraldine should beware a possible visit from Sea Giant, if merely to reassure themselves she gleaned no evidence of their plans whilst staying with Mary.' She glanced at Geraldine's troubled face. 'Luckily they will have no notion of the calibre of Colin's mother—and background!' And as she regarded her ex-colleagues appearance, she decided that Geraldine presented the perfect picture of a kindly, slightly reserved, elderly lady. Only those quick grey eyes gave a hint of the acute brain she had previously used in her country's service.

'You know, I have a premonition Sea Giant will send one of their people here to Rose Cottage,' said Geraldine quietly. 'With so much to lose if their ambitious deal faces the danger of being thwarted—project exposed to the government, they'll be totally ruthless in swatting aside any who might have even the slightest knowledge of their plans!' She rose to her feet and walked over to the window. 'I am not concerned so much on my own behalf—but for my two bereaved grandchildren. I owe it to their parents to keep Charles and Melanie safe!'

The three others in the study glanced at each other. They knew that she was possibly correct in fearing a visit from the rogue company. Would she be able to outface anyone who arrived here to interrogate her—or would it be wiser to move her to a safe house? But this of course would involve a further disruption in the lives of the twins who had just settled into their new school and felt secure with their grandmother. It was a difficult situation and one on which ultimately only Geraldine herself could make such a decision.

She turned, feeling their eyes on her. She smiled at their concerned faces.

'Well, it needs quite some thought,' she said slowly. 'In the meanwhile, I am going to prepare lunch for us.'

'I'll help,' said Lottie, and followed her through to the kitchen.

It was the third day of Tom and Lottie Lanscombe's stay—Charles Latimer had already returned to London to place his information on Sea Giant's activities before other members of the Secret Service. As for the Lanscombes, they needed to get back to Dream Echo by the end of the week, the refuge taking up much of their time, but were loath to leave Geraldine with so much unresolved. Apart from the neighbouring Bramble cottage, her home was worryingly remote from the rest of the village.

'Do you know the local police sergeant?' inquired Tom who was in the sitting room. Geraldine. She shook her head.

'Not personally—just smiled whenever I have passed him along the high street, but never found the need to contact him with problems His name is Sergeant Will Evans,' she added. Tom drew his heavy eyebrows together reflectively. He did not want to alarm her, but if Sea Giant did manage to discover her address, she would be quite vulnerable here.

'You mentioned that a Grantly police officer called on you with news of Mary's death while you were at the house—did he ask any questions about the Sea Giant fellows who called on Mary?'

'As it happens, he did—took notes. He seemed disturbed that those men should have demanded Colin's computer and papers.' She sighed. 'I don't remember too much about that afternoon, the shock of Mary's death following so quickly on Colin's helicopter crash so difficult to contend with. But why do you ask?' she inquired.

'Just wondered if the local police up there in Grantly were aware of the suspicious circumstances surrounding the two deaths? If so, they may have passed on their concerns, to others more highly placed.' He smiled. 'Look, Geraldine, I think it may be advisable to contact the police sergeant here in the village and ask him to keep an eye on Rose Cottage. Just in case, you understand! Bye, the way, how much of all this does Anna Lindstrom know?' Geraldine glanced at him.

'Why, only that my son and his wife died in tragically close succession, which was why I brought my young grandchildren back here. I didn't wish to involve her in any of the matters I have shared with both you, Lottie, and Charles! She has had enough to contend with in her own life.'

'Do you trust Anna?' he asked directly. She did not hesitate in her reply.

'Absolutely. She is a fine young woman, making a good recovery from the abusive relationship she endured for the last few years. But you must know her reasonably well yourself Tom since you dealt with her at that women's refuge you're involved with and where she received such excellent care.' She smiled. 'I know Lottie genuinely likes her and is next door at Bramble Cottage with her now. I must also admit Anna has been wonderfully supportive since I returned here with the twins.'

'I am wondering whether it might be advisable to take her into your confidence on these matters?' he suggested. 'I spoke it over with Lottie last night, and we both feel you need someone to rely on in case of emergency.' She looked at him questioningly.

'But is it fair to put a young woman who has only just escaped from such a fraught situation in more possible danger?' Her face was troubled as she placed the question.

'Put it this way, Geraldine,' he replied. 'We all require help at times—and having received it, should be prepared to extend assistance to others when called on. From what I know of Anna, she will be only too glad to support you should the need arise.' She looked at him doubtfully and leaned forward in her armchair.

'I hesitate to place such a new burden on her, but at the same time must admit that it would be good to have someone to rely on—help with the children in an emergency,' she said slowly. 'Well, all right Tom—I'll take your advice.' As she said this they looked around as they heard the front door open and Lottie came in and stood smiling, with Anna and little Susan at her side.

'Susan wanted to see Marcasite,' she explained. 'Seems she is very taken with your cat, Geraldine, so I suggested Anna bring her over.' As she spoke she glanced questioningly at Tom, wondering whether he had broached the subject they had discussed last night in bed—that Geraldine should take Anna into her confidence. He nodded slightly and she relaxed.

'Marcasite is in the kitchen, Susan,' said Geraldine, giving the little girl a warm smile. 'Go through and play with him if you like, darling.' She looked at Anna, watching as the girl seated herself on the sofa with Lottie. 'I'm glad you are here Anna because there is something I want to discuss with you. But before I do, I must ask your solemn word not to reveal what you are about to hear to anyone else!'

Anna's blue eyes widened in surprise, as she nodded assent.

'Of course, I give my word Geraldine. Is something wrong?' she demanded curiously.

'A lot has been happening that is very wrong, Anna,' replied Geraldine quietly. 'It was for this reason that I invited my two old friends Tom and Lottie to visit me to ask for their help and advice.' Anna glanced from one to the other of the kindly couple she had previously met during her stay at Dream Echo and saw their faces were grave as they returned her look.

Over the next ten minutes, Anna absorbed the salient points of what Geraldine Denton's family had suffered at the hands of Sea Giant—that Colin and Mary's deaths were not tragic accidents but deliberate murders. She also quickly grasped the fact that her kindly neighbour was herself in possible danger. She looked at her protectively.

'Geraldine—I feel so sorry you had to deal with all this on your own before Tom and Lottie arrived. I only wish you had taken me not your confidence earlier. One thing I promise, if those Sea Giant thugs come here looking for trouble, they will have me to deal with as well!' she declared. Geraldine reached out a hand to her in gratitude, while the Lanscombe's glanced at each other in relief.

'Anna—thank you, my dear,' said Geraldine. 'I hesitated to involve you—you have been through such a lot yourself and you have that dear little daughter to think of.' Anna smiled, back at her, blue eyes firm.

'You have helped and supported me so much as I've settled into my new life here in the village—a mother could not have been kinder. Although we've only known each other for a short while, I treasure you as a special friend.' She paused. 'So, just tell me Geraldine—what exactly can I do to help?'

It was Tom who replied. He leaned forward an urgent look on his face.

'I am going to speak with the local village police sergeant—tell him enough to make him aware that Geraldine could be in danger from Sea Giant. It is always possible that the Scottish police may have passed on concerns to the forces south of the border. Right now, we are not sure if Sea Giant will try to contact Geraldine again. I feel they'll wish to be sure that she has no inkling of the secrets Colin was privy to—and for which he paid with his life. If you see any strangers watching Rose Cottage, or approaching Geraldine, I want you to phone me immediately. If necessary, call the local police.'

'Do you think we can rely on you for this, Anna?' asked Lottie earnestly, sitting next to the girl on the sofa and taking her hand. Anna regarded her honestly and lifted a determined chin, as she replied to the woman who had helped and advised her during her recovery at Dream Echo refuge.

'Of course, I'll do it and more, to help protect Geraldine from those skunks!' she said. 'You have my word.' She glanced from Lottie to Tom. She felt instinctive that the couple visiting Geraldine was involved in more than helping Amber Marsden to run her women's refuge, wonderful though their contributions were to this vital work. Tom in especial held an air of authority, his wife Lottie a well-known novelist, let her gentle mask slip at times.

'I have to ask—Lottie, are you and your husband involved with the police in some way?' she ventured and flushed, wondering if she had overstepped the mark. They glanced from one to the other before Tom answered. He leaned forward in his armchair and gave Anna a straight look.

'Shall we put it this way, Anna? Although officially retired, we were previously in a certain secret branch of the civil service—as was Geraldine. You must never mention this fact to another human being, under any circumstances. To do so could cost lives.' Anna swallowed and inclined her head in agreement.

'I have the feeling that whatever is going on now is rather scary stuff, certainly, all that has happened to Geraldine's family is shockingly cruel. I am aware that I have my own little daughter's safety to watch over, but the larger picture is surely that ruthless companies like Sea Giant need to be prevented from destroying the lives of those who attempt to halt them when they put the desire for wealth and power above the safety of hundreds of thousands around the world!' Her blue eyes flashed with emotion as she poured this out. It was Tom who spoke for the others.

'Anna, I knew instinctively that we could rely on your help and support for our friend Geraldine. I wish Lottie and I could remain longer to watch over her, but we're both needed back at Dream Echo in the work you know of there—in addition to which, I must contact other individuals to deal with Sea Giant.' He paused and looked approvingly at the lovely young woman who had not hesitated to promise her help when called upon. One day in the not-too-distant future, when Malcolm Greer had been dealt with by the law and deservedly languishing in prison, it was to be hoped that Anna Lindstrom might meet another man who would bring true happiness into her life. He exchanged a satisfied glance with Lottie, as Anna looked up quickly and made towards the door.

'Susan's calling,' she said. 'I must go to her,' and she hurried through to the kitchen. Minutes later having collected the little girl she took her leave, knowing Geraldine would wish to spend precious time with her friends. Her mind was in turmoil as she led her small daughter back to Bramble Cottage. Would those representatives of Sea Giant present themselves here in this quiet little village—threatening violence to Geraldine and the twins? As she walked up the pathway, she heard the familiar sound of doves cooing in the trees, all seeming so perfectly normal—but how long would this precious peace last?

Tom Lanscombe strolled up to the reception desk at the village police station. A young woman PC looked across at him curiously.

'Good morning, sir. How can I help you?'

'I would like to speak with your sergeant if I may. Name's Tom Lanscombe,' he added.

'Oh yes, he is expecting you, sir. This way if you please,' and she led him through the connecting door to a small office, where a middle-aged man with greying hair and a ruddy face, was seated behind a desk.

He smiled a greeting to Tom and asked him to be seated. Some ten minutes later he raised a troubled face from the notes he had just taken, his intelligent dark eyes, regarding Tom questioningly.

'I must say this is all quite a shock, sir! We don't normally have to deal with matters of such magnitude in our quiet village. From what you have told me of this oil exploration company, they are a disreputable lot, to put it mildly—and if they are proven guilty of murdering three innocent people, I hope they are put away for a considerable time!'

'I agree,' replied Tom. 'My immediate concern is that they may arrive here in Ravensnest and threaten Geraldine Denton. She is already grieving both her son Colin's apparent death by drowning and her daughter-in-law's unexplained fatal car accident—while bravely taking on the care of her twin grandchildren. I just want assurance that you will keep an eye on Rose Cottage.' Tom's steady eyes met those of the officer before him.

'You have my word that a discreet eye will be kept on Mrs Denton's cottage,' he replied.

'Good man,' said Tom gratefully. 'This is my card—ring me if you have any concerns.'

Geraldine breathed a sigh as she watched the Lanscombe's driving away from the cottage. It had been reassuring to see her old friends again, memories stirring of her time in the Secret Service—and a great relief to freely discuss conviction that the deaths of her dear son and his wife had been ordered by certain officials of Sea Giant. Then there had been the brief appearance of Charles Latimer who was still actively employed at a high level in MI5. Now at least the whole affair was in the hands of those who would leave no stone unturned to arrive at the truth. Well, time to return to the normality of everyday life—only none of it could be described as really normal again, could it?

Anna Lindstrom was a little quiet for the next few days. It had been good to see Lottie and Tom again, but the meeting brought back into focus her recollection of the trauma she had experienced on escaping Enderslie House from Malcolm Greer the man who had forced her into an abusive relationship. She had just begun to put it all behind her as she settled into Bramble Cottage with little Susan. Now memories of the kindness and encouragement she had received at Dream Echo from the amazing young woman who owned it, and her dedicated team of helpers including the Lanscombes returned to raise questions in her mind.

Why was it that some people found it acceptable to impose their will upon others—not only for personal gratification as with Greer—but worse as with Sea Giant, casually taking the lives of those who might expose their evil—even placing a kindly retired lady such as Geraldine in fear of the future? Such villainy must be dealt with by the law. But whereas such thoughts were laudable enough, surely it was down to every individual to reach out and help neighbours subjugated to threats against their lives and of those they loved.

She thought of Geraldine as she collected the children from school. She had become very attached to the twins now who were gradually beginning to relax and smile a little and were always happiest when playing in the garden with Susan. It would take time for such young children to come to terms with the abrupt loss of both parents, but they were blessed in their grandmother's love and protection—and perhaps caring for them was helping Geraldine deal with her own grief.

As she sat in her car waiting for the pupils to come pouring out of the village school, she considered how much stronger she felt these days, the fear of Malcolm Greer which had gripped her mind for so long banished like a weird nightmare. Geraldine had been a factor in this, for in the short time they had been acquainted they had become very close—almost like mother and daughter. It was as though they were meant to have met, with little Susan and the twins forming a small family unit. It was sad that the children would grow up without a father's presence, although unlike Susan, little Charles and Melanie would always retain fond memories of their Daddy. What had he been like, Colin Denton? She sighed, as she thought of the silver-framed photograph of Geraldine's handsome son, wife and children, placed next to that of his late doctor father on the mantelpiece in the comfortable living room at Rose Cottage. She looked up as she heard the pupils noisily exiting the school door, swinging satchels and making for the playground gate. Thoughts of Colin vanished as she opened the car door and beckoned the twins inside where Susan sat impatiently to see them.

The man with badly bruised features did not stir as the woman stooped and stroked his fair hair, worried that after such a worryingly long time he was still suffering a lack of consciousness. Greta Schiffer shook her head, staring at him pityingly. Just two weeks ago, their fisherman son Sven had suddenly arrived in the early hours, as with the help of his steersman and friend Karl, they carried the stranger inside this old timbered house situated on the lower forested mountain slope above the Norwegian fiord where his small vessel was anchored.

'He needs a doctor,' stated Sven to his bewildered parents.

'But who is this poor man, Sven?' asked Greta's husband, Hans, peering down at the couch where Sven and Karl had placed this unexpected guest. 'A new member of your crew—and what happened to him?'

'No, he's not crew, father—it's quite a story.' He drew Hans aside and stared steadily at his father's strong, angular face. 'Look—I need your word not to reveal what I'm going to share with you with anyone else.' Hans's brown eyes regarded his son in surprise.

'Tell me,' said the older man quietly, while his wife Greta produced some faded pyjamas as with Karl's assistance they removed the soaking wet clothing the casualty wore. Good clothes, she noticed, fine quality and he wore an expensive wristwatch. He might have been good-looking before his face suffered that extensive bruising—and his arm seemed in an awkward position—was the shoulder dislocated? He made no groan as they attempted to make him comfortable, a pillow beneath his head.

'Well father, as you know we are fishing in waters where permission to do so is debatable—fairly close to the new activity by that big oil company. We had a good catch and were about to turn the boat for home when we heard the sound of a helicopter. It all happened so quickly—the craft was obviously out of control. Suddenly it started to descend, struck the water and sank!'

'But how terrible!' exclaimed Hans, face shocked.

'Nothing we could do—no sign of wreckage, so I guess it must have gone straight to the bottom. It was Karl who noticed something bobbing in the waves. We swung the boat about—reached out a boat hook, attempted to drag the survivor closer—got him aboard. We thought he was dead at first. How he had managed to get clear of the copter when it hit the water was a miracle.' He paused and stared at his father's troubled face. 'I cannot report the crash, or where we found this man for obvious reasons. We should not have been there!'

'So, you just brought him back with you! Well, he needs medical help—but what do we tell the doctor when he comes—or other officials?' demanded Hans.

'We say we found him drifting in the sea,' Sven shrugged. 'After all, the currents could have carried him miles from where the copter went down. No one can dispute the matter. Might have been better if he had died, less of a problem. But it's second nature to save a fellow human being.' He glanced across at his friend Karl's weather-beaten face, as the man stepped back from the couch, having assisted Greta to do all that was necessary.

'What now?' asked Karl, glancing from one to the other.

'We ask my father to kindly fetch the doctor! Now listen—we keep to the tale we discussed. We saw no sign of a helicopter if asked—merely found this fellow floating half-dead in choppy waters.'

And this was the story they reported to the friendly, elderly doctor shortly later Hans was brought back from the surgery two miles away.

'What do you think, Doctor? Will he live?' asked Sven, as the physician straightened up. He smiled at the captain of the small fishing boat, knew Sven well, and had delivered him as a baby almost thirty-seven years ago in this very house. A good family, making their living from the sea as was common along the coast. Fish was the staple diet, keeping a man healthy.

'He is deeply unconscious. Amazing he survived being in the sea in that state. He has obviously suffered some trauma and I suppose we will have to wait for him to regain consciousness before we get answers. I'll report this to the police unless you prefer to do so?'

'No—want to take the boat straight out again. Wasted enough time on this fellow. My mother will care for him in the meanwhile. Any idea how long he will remain in this state?'

'Difficult to say. Would you rather I had him transferred to the hospital?' inquired the doctor. It was Greta who replied after a quick glance at her husband Hans.

'No, we will care for the poor man. Just tell me anything I need to do—and perhaps you could call back in a few days doctor?' She pulled the deerskin rug around her patient. It was unusual to have anything exciting happen here in this quiet place. Accordingly, it was left that way. The doctor took himself off. After a good meal, Sven and Karl disappeared back to the boat. Hans and Greta were alone with their unresponsive guest.

Now, well over two weeks later, Greta was beginning to wonder if they should indeed have had the patient transferred to the hospital. True they had help, a nurse came daily to administer a liquid food and he had a drip. But suppose the man never regained consciousness—remained in a coma for the rest of his life? She discussed it quietly with her woodsman husband Hans and realised he merely seemed agreeable to let matters carry on as usual for now.

'If only we knew his name! You would have thought he would have carried a wallet in his jacket pocket—some identification,' said Greta, a small frown knitting her brows, blue eyes puzzled. Hans shrugged.

'The force of the current—slapping of the waves, would have sucked anything of that sort out of his pockets.' Hans put his beer mug down and came to stare at the patient with her. His brown eyes widened in surprise. 'Greta—did you see that? His eyelids fluttered!'

'I cannot see anything,' she replied bending down beside him. Then she gasped. 'You're right, Hans! He is waking up!' Two minutes later, the patient's grey eyes opened briefly—then closed again. As they watched his eyes opened once more, as he struggled to regain consciousness. Now he stared straight ahead of him, face expressionless.

'Hallo, my friend. How do you feel?' inquired Hans gently. There was no answer. The man merely looked unseeingly ahead. Hans tried again, this time he decided to try another language, remembered Greta had mentioned the man's clothing had British markings.

'Hallo—are you feeling better? May we know your name?' asked Hans. This time he thought he saw a flash of intelligence in the man's grey eyes. He stirred slightly on the couch as his gaze gradually sped around the room, settling on the faces of the two people bending over him. He looked at them blankly.

'Where am I?' he asked in English, voice a hoarse whisper.

'A small village on the Norwegian coast, a few miles from Bergen,' said Hans quietly. 'You were discovered floating in the sea—my son has a fishing boat, rescued you—brought you here.' The man shook his head, unable to make sense of what he heard.

'I do not understand,' was the whispered response.

'Do not worry, friend. You have been unconscious for more than two weeks. It will probably take a few days more for your mind to clear. In the meanwhile, you are our guest. My name is Hans Schiffer and this is my wife Greta. May we ask your name, sir?'

'It's—its? I don't know!' The patients face registered agitation. 'The sea—you say I was found in the sea? How did I get there?' Hans looked at him and patted his arm comfortingly.

'All will come back, be patient! Now—the doctor dealt with your shoulder—it was dislocated. It may feel stiff, experienced it once myself. I'm a woodsman.' He realised the man was no longer responding and had fallen asleep. At least it was now a natural sleep, he guessed hopefully.

'We should phone the doctor, and tell him the man has regained consciousness.' suggested Greta. She was greatly relieved to see the man was recovering at long last. They should let Sven know when next he anchored nearby. It would be good to have answers to the mystery. Hans had not revealed their son's disclosure to her. Better so he had thought, she might have worried.

Chapter Six

The physician returned the next day, delighted to find the stranger had come out of his coma. As he entered the living room he observed him sitting upright on the sofa, his head in his hands. He straightened as the doctor appeared and submitted listlessly to careful examination. But to all his questions, the patient made little reply, obviously still confused, unable to recall his name or how he came to be found in the sea so far from land. It was a mystery.

The doctor spoke quietly with Greta in the kitchen out of the man's earshot. She looked at him expectantly. Had he made any progress in discovering the man's identity?

'Do not worry, Greta. It may take a few days yet for his memory to return, possibly longer. All such cases vary. But at least he is in your very capable hands. You say he is eating and this is good news. The body often recovers more quickly than the mind.' He shook his head. 'A strange affair. You would think someone would have noticed his absence and reported it. We do not even know his country of origin for certain.' He readjusted his spectacles over his bony nose

'I am sure it must be the UK—he responds to English doesn't he,' she said reflectively, then smiled. 'He is not bad looking now that the horrible bruising is fading from his face!' She looked up as her husband came in.

'Hans—the doctor is pleased with the man's progress, but if only we knew his name!'

'Well, at least he is awake now,' said Hans. 'Doctor—I wonder if you might have a look at my hip? A heavy branch caught me as I felled a larch—pinned me down. It's uncomfortable.' The doctor looked at him quickly, recognising from the tone of his voice that Hans was in pain.

'Let's be having a look at you, Hans my friend.' He helped Hans lower his trousers and made careful examination with sensitive experienced hands. 'Nasty—nasty! Luckily no fracture, but I think you've badly bruised the bone. You must rest up for a few days. I will leave this salve for Greta to apply—after I've dressed that graze.' He left Hans some painkillers before departing to visit the next patient in this thinly populated village clinging to the forested hillside. Later, as Hans gingerly attempted to tuck his red tartan shirt into the top of his jeans, Greta put a restricting hand on his shoulder, her green eyes firm.

'No, leave it. Do as the doctor suggested, Hans my darling, change into a dressing gown—be comfortable and rest!' she instructed. He forced a smile, moved and awkwardly kissed her.

'But you do not need two invalids, woman!' he objected. As she helped him upstairs to their bedroom they were unaware of the change in the man who had been sitting on the living room couch.

It was as the patient's eyes sped uncomprehendingly about the unfamiliar room once again, that it seemed as though a shutter suddenly lifted in his mind. Distorted remembrance surging back—and with it, an enormous fear! He was going to die! They were going down—no time to think, to act. As the copter struck the water, he murmured a prayer, instinctively thrusting his shoulder against the thick Perspex dome that fractured as they had hit, water rushing in. He was aware of agonising pain, his head feeling as though it would explode and his shoulder excruciating. Somehow, he struggled to kick free of the restraints of the seating—was out of the copter and found himself sinking down—down. Lungs were filling with water. Then with last desperate ounce of strength, forced himself to thrust upwards, and had a brief glimpse of the blue sky—before all went black.

The man began to shake as he rose to his feet. He walked over to the window with its cheerful yellow curtains and stared outside. Where had that man said he was? A small Norwegian village close to Bergen! His eyes focussed on all the view from the window—the wooden chalet was surrounded by trees, land sloping steeply downwards—and he glimpsed the sea far below. How did he get here—and who were the kind people who were caring for him? He tried to concentrate on that last remembered moment in the sea, lungs paining him, gasping for air. But—he'd cheated death, was alive!

Little by little his mind cleared—and he recalled his name. Colin! He was Colin Denton. He had a wife Mary—and twin children and a widowed mother. He walked curiously to the front door, out in the fresh air, the sharp fragrance of the pine forest wafting about him on the breeze. He did not recognise the place. He tried to remember why he had been in the helicopter. Part of his mind was still a blur—pieces of the jigsaw missing. He seated himself on the rough wooden bench set outside the chalet in the small half-wild garden and tried to force memory back. It felt as though a veil was protectively screening his mind, but from what?

He absorbed his surroundings. A butterfly hovered over the clump of straggling roses nearby. He looked at its red and gold markings, his eyes followed as it fluttered upwards and away. What must it feel like to spread gauze-like wings—and seek the sky? Thoughts of the helicopter returned—and the face of pilot Kevin, that sudden anguished cry he had given—the scream of the other man sitting beside Colin, his colleague and close friend Jonathon King. Were they dead now? He felt a constricting sense of guilt that he had survived. Slowly but surely memory returned. His meeting with Sea Giant's executives prior to his flight, their smiling dismissive attitude when he had reiterated his concerns over the damage their huge new oil deposit could pose to the already fragile state of global warming. He remembered being told to take the small helicopter to return to the mainland, the larger regular craft he had arrived in needed for a party of ten due to return later. His comrade Jonathon King was to return with him. Their pilot Kevin was also a friend and highly experienced. Colin had not experienced the slightest anxiety when settling himself next to Jonathon.

It was as Kevin had shouted they were going down, something wrong with the controls and making a desperate mayday, that the thought darted through Colin's shocked mind. This was no accident—but an attempt on his life! No time to think after that—only determination born of violent anger to survive. Now as all came flooding back he uttered a groan of despair. If he was right, then it was his efforts to persuade Sea Giant to think again, that was responsible for the deaths of two fine people! Tears came into his eyes. But how had he got here—in this unfamiliar place? What of his wife Mary? He realised she must be grieving his death and what of the children? He had to get back to Grantly. Then another thought assailed him. If he was right and what had happened was attempted murder, then what? If he reappeared in the village, he'd be vulnerable again—but worse, his wife and children might also suffer harm.

Greta left her husband to rest and returned downstairs, walked into the living room—noticed the empty couch that had served as a bed for their previously unresponsive guest. Where was he? She checked the kitchen, and bathroom—opened the front door and glanced around the windswept garden. He was sitting on the bench and she sighed in relief.

'Ah—there you are, sir! You are feeling better—that is good.' She looked down at him. 'May I join you?' and she seated herself next to him and waited. He turned his head and gave the first real smile she had seen. He had not properly registered the woman before, now noting that she was in later middle age, stoutly built, with greying fair hair, broad forehead and intelligent green eyes that were regarding him curiously.

'Thankyou—I fear I do not know your name, only that you have been caring for me,' he queried.

'I am Greta—Greta Schiffer,' she put in delighted that he was speaking logically. 'Do you recall your name yet, sir?' He nodded, wondering how much to reveal to her.

'Yes. My name is Colin Denton—but I do not want my identity mentioned officially yet, for reasons I cannot explain,' he said, his grey eyes watching her face as he spoke. She stared.

'Perhaps you would like to speak with my husband, Hans? He is a woodsman—hurt his hip earlier and is resting upstairs. We have been caring for you for almost three weeks now—since the night our son Sven brought you here. He has a fishing boat—found you floating in the sea miles from anywhere as I understand it. A miracle you survived. Sven and his crew saved you. He will be so glad you are recovered.' Her words were spoken in heavily accented English and he warmed to her open friendliness.

'I am sorry your husband is injured—is it bad?' he asked sympathetically. 'Can I help?'

'In his work, such things occur. He'll be fine in a few days—I am sure he would like to talk with you.' Men often found it easier to discuss things together she thought. 'Come,' she said, and obediently he followed her back into the comfortable pine chalet. He knew he must give some explanation to the couple—but how much to reveal? He mounted the stairs as she led him up to the bedroom, where he saw the man he had previously observed whilst in his confused state, lying on top of a large feather bed. Hans had been dozing and opened his eyes, astonished to see the erstwhile patient standing there with Greta. He sat upright and swung his legs stiffly over the side of the bed.

'You are recovered, sir? he asked and saw the answering glint in Colin's eyes. The man looked different now, Hans decided, alert. He stood up and held out his hand. reintroducing himself. 'I am Hans Schiffer—and this is my wife Greta. Are you able to recall your own identity yet?'

'Yes, Mr Schiffer—everything is starting to come back to me' He began but the other interrupted him.

'Hans, please just call me Hans!'

'Hans then—my name is Colin Denton—from Scotland. But as I've just told your wife, I do not wish my identity revealed to others at this time.'

'We will respect your confidence,' replied Hans instantly.

'Then I will try to explain what happened. The helicopter I was travelling in came down in the sea, and I've reason to believe it was no accident but an attempt on my life! I hope I may trust you to keep this information private for now!' Hans opened his mouth in shocked surprise at this statement, as Greta sank down on the bed beside him, looking equally aghast.

'But this is extraordinary—the helicopter deliberately downed you say? But by whom—and for what reason?' Hans was regarding him in astonishment and with growing concern that he was being involved in matters that were disturbing in the extreme, wondered if any of this might bring danger to him or his family.

'Tell me—how many more people know I am here?' asked Colin urgently. The couple looked at each other. It was Hans who answered, aware of the apprehension the man was displaying.

'My son Sven of course and his crew who saved you—brought you to us here. Then there is our doctor and the local nurse who attended you while you were still unconscious.'

'That is all?' Colin probed. Hans drew his heavy brows together as he thought.

'Well, I believe the doctor made mention to the police of a man who'd been rescued from the sea, but carrying no identification on his person. Such can happen at times—seamen from many lands are employed as crew in the fishing boats. Sometimes a man is lost overboard, and!' he shrugged. 'Certainly, no one official has come here to inquire about you.' He sank back down on the bed, his damaged hip causing discomfort and stared up at this stranger who had made the startling statement that an attempt had been made to take his life. Was the man's mind wandering—but if true, who would be powerful or wicked enough to down a helicopter in order to commit murder?

Greta, now listening carefully to the exchange, seated herself beside her husband, and took his hand, her green eyes worried. The agitation the man standing before them portrayed on return of his memory was palpable. He had endured a terrible time, bad things happening to him. But what was to happen now? Suppose those responsible discovered he was here—and brought their violence into their quiet home? She looked at him nervously.

'Colin—what are your plans now?' she asked gently. 'Perhaps you have relatives grieving your supposed death on learning that helicopter went down? They should be reassured. Do you intend to return to Scotland?' She felt slightly guilty at suggesting he should leave. She had much sympathy for him—liked him, thought him an honest man.

It was Hans who managed to put aside instinctive concern on the wisdom of harbouring a stranger caught up in who knew what strange affair. The man was a guest, under their roof, and needed whatever help and protection they could offer.

'Do you wish to share the reason you assume an actual attempt was made to kill you?' he asked quietly, nodding towards an upright chair by the bed. Colin drew it closer and seated himself. He glanced at Greta, having sensed her worry at any involvement.

'Are you sure you wish me to tell you?' he asked, his grey eyes studying their faces.

'Just be plain, my friend,' said Hans, and Greta took her lead from her husband.

'We are listening,' she said quietly.

Colin leaned forward in the wicker chair, his hands placed on knees covered by jeans meant for a shorter man, the checked wool shirt probably one of Hans he realised. He owed so much to this couple and their son, probably life itself. Where to start?

'So, Hans and Greta—what do you know of climate change—global warming?' They raised their eyebrows at the question. It was Hands who answered.

'We understand it is the greatest danger facing mankind at this time—and being largely ignored by those with vested interest protecting their wealth obtained through fossil fuels—and also in destroying the forests of the world,' he replied, the directness and accuracy of his response taking Colin by surprise.

'That is completely correct,' he approved, as Hans looked back at him expectantly.

'Why do you ask this question, sir? What connection does it have to the attempt on your life?' and the woodsman waited.

'Your son Sven—he owns a fishing boat you say—well from where I imagine he must have picked me up, he will have noticed a large oil exploration installation nearby called Sea Giant?' he asked. Hans did not reply at first. He remembered that Sven had mentioned that they had been fishing in waters not officially permitted, did not want to get his son into trouble—but he sensed that Colin would not expose this secret.

'What of this Sea Giant?' he asked, looking squarely at Colin's face. And then Colin began briefly to explain his involvement in the oil company, with whom he had been employed for some years. Recently however became involved with those who understood the urgent need to slow down global warming as far as possible. He knew that it was difficult to marry his earlier dedicated work on the discovery of a new field—together with all he now knew of the dangers every new large oil discovery presented to the escalating danger of global warming.

Sea Giant's new oil find was lar than anything previously discovered in the North Sea—worth billions! For political reasons, they've been keeping the news under wraps. But there was another related matter, he explained. There was reason to believe that Sea Giant was negotiating with the Chinese offering the stolen secret of a new inexpensive method of extracting oil from the sea bed worth a fortune, in exchange for the huge sum required to fund their planned new installation.

Colin looked at Hans and saw the woodsman's instant understanding.

'So—dealing with a foreign power? Go on—go on!' breathed Hans, as Greta merely looked stunned.

Colin continued 'I knew that eventually, I must decide to leave Sea Giant—a man cannot ride two horses at the same time. But in my naivety, I hoped that by going to the company directors, putting my concerns about the increasing impact that this new find would place in the increasingly dangerous acceleration of global warming, there was a chance they might decide to draw back from their plans—or at least to constrain them. My friend and colleague Jonathon King came with me to that meeting—he shared my views.'

'So, what did the bosses of Sea Giant say?' Hans asked.

'That other means would present themselves to slow global warming—oil was a necessity of modern life etc—provided employment to a huge amount of people. They were suave and treated me with amused contempt. I was advised to return to the mainland and consider my position and my employment—the future of my family!' He paused, 'I had arrived with Jonathon in one of the normal regular helicopters—now I was informed it was needed later to take a large party back—a smaller one available.'

'The one that crashed? You think what happened was deliberate?'

'Yes—and now my friend Jonathon is dead at the bottom of the sea—where I would be lying also, had not your son Sven rescued me!' He finished and watched for their reaction.

'They should be exposed for the dangerous rogues they are!' exclaimed Hans angrily. 'But what to do now? I imagine they consider you are dead—so if you reappear, will you not be at risk once more?'

'Very possibly,' replied Colin grimly. Hans screwed his brows together in thought. What is best to be done? He looked at his wife—remembered her words.

'Greta mentioned earlier, you may have family back home in Scotland grieving your death. They should have their minds put to rest. But the news would need to be kept very quiet if those men are as dangerous as you have indicated.' Hans was viewing the situation analytically. 'What kind of a place is your home?' he inquired.

'A small village in the north of Scotland, not far from Aberdeen. My wife Mary teaches at the local school—and we have seven years old twin children—Charles and Melanie. I cannot bear to think what they must be going through,' he said heavily. 'You are right—I must let them know, but I dare not return to the village yet—it might put my family in danger.'

'You have other relatives, Colin?' asked Greta.

'Why yes—an elderly mother who lives in the south of England, many hundred miles from Grantly. She must be grieving too. We lost my father not long ago, can only guess how distressed she too will be at the news of my death. Those bloody, murdering Sea Giant executives!'

He jumped to his feet. 'Hans I can only think of one man in Grantly whom I can trust with news of my survival—the local minister. He already knows of my concerns regarding the doings of Sea Giant. If only I could ring him—ask him to let my wife know I've survived and warn her not to reveal the news.'

'Then you should make that call, Colin my friend. Later inform the Scottish police—tell them what has happened!' He rose to his feet. 'Give me the minister's number and I will ring him—perhaps better than attracting attention in the first place.' He looked at Greta. 'We go downstairs, my dear. Before anything else, we need a strong drink!'

Robert MacKinnon and his wife Molly were relaxing in their comfortable, worn, tan leather armchairs before the glowing peat fire in their comfortable sitting room in the manse. The old stone house adjacent to the church had been home to them for ten years now since Robert had been officially invited to become minister of Grantly village church to serve the small, community of worshippers who had taken quickly taken the kindly couple to their hearts.

They were discussing the yearly exhibition of patchwork. The cushions, wall hangings, and quilts were to be displayed in the church, created by the local women's group, and sold to raise funds to repair the church roof.

'Look at this bedspread,' exclaimed Molly admiringly. 'It must have taken old Mrs Stewart months to have completed and with her bad eyesight, a true work of love!' Robert leaned forward and nodded.

'Ay, it's very fine. But I rather like that cushion with a leopard's head—thought I might buy it for you, Molly dearest!' He sighed. 'Remember the delicate baby quilt Mary Denton submitted last year. Hard to realise we will never see either Colin or Mary again—they were such special friends. I wonder how Geraldine is coping with the grandchildren. A fine and very courageous lady.' They sat looking reflectively into the fire.

'I'll make us a drink of hot chocolate,' said Molly rising and putting the quilted bedspread aside. He nodded and remained sitting there, thinking of the terrible events that had shocked the entire village over three weeks ago. Would the truth ever come out, he pondered? Suddenly the phone rang. He lifted his mobile—heard a strange voice, heavily accented, and wondered who this might be.

'Is that the Reverent MacKinnon?'

'Yes, who is this?'

'Just call me Hans. I have a friend of yours with me. Are you alone at this time, sir—what follows must be kept private!' the voice continued. Robert frowned in surprise.

'I am a minister of religion. Anything you say will be held in confidence,' he replied.

'Good—good. I hand you over to your friend now!' said the guttural voice. Robin waited in perplexity. At the sound of the next voice he heard, he almost dropped his phone in shock.

'Robin—this is Colin. It's Colin Denton.' It was quite impossible. The words he heard were an illusion—he was imagining things!

'Would you repeat that please?' breathed the minister. 'I cannot understand. The man whose name you use is dead!'

'Only I'm not. I escaped the helicopter—was picked up by a fishing vessel, and taken unconscious to Norway. I have only recently regained my memory!'

'Why. thank the dear Lord—it's a miracle,' whispered the minister through shaking lips, trying to concentrate as the caller continued.

'I need you to listen carefully, Robin. Do you recall those matters I discussed with you recently? Acting on my own initiative, I flew out to the rig for a meeting and spoke with the SG top brass. Was asked to consider my position, and ordered to return to the mainland. Jonathon King and I were allocated a smaller helicopter for the flight back, Kevin was the pilot.' The speaker's voice faltered and Robin bit his lip in sympathy.

'We heard of the terrible accident, Colin.' he said quietly.

'It was no accident, minister. I believe the control panel had been tampered with—something Kevin cried out as he made a mayday! They wanted rid of me!'

'But that is—horrendous,' Robin replied, knowing in his heart that he believed Colin's words.

'Robin, l must ask your help' Colin continued. 'I need you to let Mary know I am alive. I have been frantic thinking of the shock and sorrow she and the children experienced on learning of my death! Will you go to her—explain that I dare not show myself at this stage, for to do so might provoke another attempt on my life and worse, put her in danger herself.' He waited for a reply. Wondered at the delay, had they been cut off? At last, he heard Robin's soft highland voice again.

'Alas, Colin my friend—I cannot do as you ask,' came the words spoken in sorrowful tones.

'But why ever not?' asked Colin bewildered.

'There is something I must tell you. Let me start from the day the copter went down. Mary phoned your mother with the dreadful news—and Geraldine flew up and arrived late that same evening. The following day, while Molly and I were caring for your little ones at the manse, Mary and your mother has an early visit from top officials of Sea Giant, who insisted on removing some of your private papers—and your computer. Later, in the afternoon, Mary got into her Aldi to drive over here to collect the twins. She never arrived.'

'What do you mean?' asked Colin suddenly paling.

'The car came down the brae and crashed against the parapet of the bridge. No easy way to tell you this, Colin. Mary did not survive the accident.' He had forced the words out with difficulty, and could only guess at the anguish they would cause the man who had already suffered so much. He heard a wail of despair at the other end of the phone.

'Mary—dead? No—no! It just cannot be true,' choked out Colin wildly. 'An accident you say—but how? And what of my children—where are Charles and Melanie?'

'Your mother took them back to England with her. She is acting as their legal guardian, and I know will be taking the most wonderful care of them. She left precipitately for reasons you may guess at. We drove her to the airport.'

'Do Sea Giant know her address?'

'Not as far as I know. We refused the information when they came here asking for her. Since then, Molly and I have been in touch with your mother on the phone. The twins are well and have started at the local village school there. I wish I could tell you more.' He waited.

'Mary's Aldi was new—a fine car, and she had never had an accident in her life!' burst out Colin's thoughts swirling through his head. 'Was it an accident?' he asked suddenly, as his mind began to reason. 'Oh, dear heavens—is it possible—did Sea Giant do this to her? Did she die because of me?' And as he blurted out the words, knew instinctively that they were true. Why had he interfered in their affairs however corrupt? Why had he exposed his dear Mary to those fiends? Then his thoughts flew to his mother. Had he put her in danger also—and the twins? Robin heard sobbing at the end of the phone.

'We held a fine funeral for Mary, all of the village attended. She was much loved here.'

'I thank both you and Molly for all you have done,' managed Colin in broken tones. 'I must contact my mother. Will not risk visiting her yet—it might put her in danger. But I need money to repay the kind couple who have cared for me here in this remote area—have been incredibly good to me! I have to get back somehow, but with no money or passport?'

'I'll arrange to get money over to you—forward it to the family caring for you there. You must give me the address. Yes, and perhaps their fishing boat could arrange to put you down somewhere remote. I have good friends on Skye. If you can manage to get there, I'm sure they will keep you safe, until arrangements are made for you to report this terrible business to the authorities.'

'Robin—how can I thank you? Now, will you tell my mother? When I think what she must have been going through,' his voice hardened in anger.

'Leave it to me, Robin. Do nothing until you hear back from me. But how amazing that out of all this sorrow comes the sheer miracle of your own survival—what incredible joy this will bring to your mother and the bairns.' Colin murmured words of thanks—and rang off.

The reverent MacKinnon bowed his head and whispered a heartfelt prayer of gratitude for the miraculous way in which Colin had escaped death. Molly found him sitting so, as she returned with two steaming mugs of chocolate.

'I thought I heard you speaking,' she said as she put them down on the low table between them. She nodded at his mobile lying on the arm of his chair. 'The phone? I hope you are not needed out again just yet, my dearest?' He smiled at her, face still showing signs of the shock he had received. Should he tell her? He almost decided against it, in case those sharp-eyed officials from Sea Giant should return with more questions about Geraldine's whereabouts. But Molly knew her husband.

'What is it? Something is troubling you!' she persisted. He shook his head, gave in and announced the astounding news that he had spoken with a man presumed dead on the phone! She listened in absolute amazement, as conflicting emotions of joy and sadness crossed her open face.

'Oh, thank the good Lord,' she burst out. 'What incredible chance that Colin survived. But Oh, Robin—did you tell him about Mary?'

'Had to—hardest thing I've ever had to do. He was devasted. But Molly darling, you must not mention this to anyone yet. Seems it's as his mother suspected, that the copter crash was no accident—but a deliberate attempt to silence Colin permanently. I must ring Geraldine—and then make arrangements to get money to Colin.' She nodded, still finding it difficult to accept the miracle that had occurred. She handed him his steaming chocolate drink, tears of emotion in her eyes. The wee twins Charles and Melanie had their daddy back! Such wonderful news, she thought—but what sad chance that Mary was not still with them to rejoice in it. Only Molly was certain that her friend Mary's death had been no accident—but murdered by those who had tried to kill Colin. She sat quietly as Robin lifted his phone.

The children had just gone to bed, and Geraldine was sitting before the piano thinking of David, and wistfully playing a few bars of Fingal's Cave when she heard the phone ring.

'Hallo—who is this?' she asked cautiously.

'It's Robin MacKinnon. How are you keeping, Geraldine—and the children?'

'They are fine, making good progress at school and gradually recovering from their grief. But how are you and dear Molly?' she replied, wondering what prompted his call.

'You have not been contacted by Sea Giant?' he asked quietly.

'No, thank goodness. But still fear they may discover this address. I know it would not be hard if they really tried,' she replied soberly.

'Listen Geraldine—I have the most marvellous news. But sit yourself down to hear it.'

'What do you mean?' she asked puzzled, wondering what unusual event in his small village had so excited him. She sank back on the piano stool, grey eyes curious. 'So, tell me, what is this news?'

'No other way to tell you but the truth—and it's amazing! Geraldine dear—your son Colin is alive! He escaped the copter crash—was rescued from the sea by a Norwegian fishing boat and taken unconscious to the boat owner's home in a wee village near Bergen. He has only just regained memory!'

It took a few seconds for his words to register, and then Geraldine gasped in trembling delight, almost dropping the phone in shock.

'It is true— you are sure?'

'I've actually spoken with Colin on the phone. He told me that after attending that meeting scheduled for him to speak with the Sea Giant executives aboard the rig that morning, he was told to return home. The bosses were dismissive of all he said. He believes that the controls of the small helicopter were tampered with before the flight. That the apparent accident was indeed attempted murder.'

'I knew it—so did Mary, bless her!' she drew in her breath shakily. 'I can hardly believe this most wonderful news, Robin! Thank you for letting me know—Oh, but did you tell him about Mary?' she asked in quick dismay.

'Yes, he knows—is devastated as you can imagine. He wants to see you as soon as possible. But not for a wee while—news he is alive must not get out yet, you understand.'

'So, I shouldn't tell the children?'

'Wiser not to. Those Sea Giant men are dangerous in the extreme. If they have any idea Colin is alive they may attempt his life again—and your own safety might not be assured. But at least you know your dear son is alive.' His words swirled through her brain, tears running down her cheeks. She tried to think logically.

'He is still in that Norwegian village?'

'Yes—but without money or means of returning and not sure where to go if he does manage back,' explained Robin. 'I've offered to send money over to the folks who have been caring for him. I have their names and address. I made a tentative suggestion that if he could make it to the Isle of Skye, I've friends there who would take him in. Iain and Fiona MacLeod are completely trustworthy—we go back a long way to my student days.'

'Robin—there are no words to thank you! As for money, let me have your bank details and I'll forward what is necessary. Listen—there are friends I must contact now from a certain special branch of the civil service.' He grasped her meaning.

'Excellent. Remember Geraldine, do not let anyone suspect the good news yet!' he said quietly. 'I'll ring you back tomorrow.'

'May I have the number he called you from? I must speak with him,' she demanded urgently. He gave her Hans Schiffer's mobile details and smiled as he put the phone down.

Hans Schiffer looked curiously at his guest. He and his wife had left Colin alone to speak in private with his minister friend on the phone— Hans returned now expecting to see Colin looking much happier. But it seemed to be otherwise, the man's face a picture of despair.

'What is wrong?' asked Hans in concern. And Colin told him— explained brokenly that his much loved, wife Mary was dead—a suspicious car accident the day after the copter went down. Hans looked at him in horror.

'I am so sorry, my friend! What a terrible shock. You suspect your Mary's death is connected to that bloody oil company?' He placed a comforting hand on Colin's shoulder, trying to assess the implications for Colin's immediate future. 'You said you have children—a boy and a girl?'

'Charles and Melanie—seven years old twins. My mother has taken them back to live with her in the south of England—and I fear for any dangerous repercussions this may have for them,' said Colin anxiously. 'Look Hans—I will take myself off as soon as I can. The minister is going to send funds—will send a bank draft to you...' But Hans interrupted him.

'Enough of this talk of money. Right now, you need a drink, man. Such a series of disasters—and all down to that villainous Sea Giant! They must be exposed—prosecuted!' His bluff face expressed his outrage that such atrocities could occur, as he produced a couple of cans of lager.

'The minister said he has friends on Skye—an island in the Hebrides. They will help me if I can manage to get there,' explained Colin. Hans's face brightened at this. If all that was needed to get Colin to safety was a boat trip, well Sven could surely arrange that. He got up and stared keenly at the map on the wall behind the table. Yes—there it was—that irregularly shaped island, Skye! He had never been there himself but heard of it. So many indentations of the sea around its coastline, all offering a quiet place to drop Colin off, and none to question it!

'I suppose your minister friend needs to speak with his friends on Skye first—see if they are happy with the suggestion. Once he confirms it, Sven will take you there in the boat,' he said, smiling with satisfaction that all should be relatively easy. Colin looked at him, almost too full for words.

'What can I say, Hans! It's hard to believe you would do all this for me—a comparative stranger?' he said.

'Stranger no more, but friend—good friend! Greta and I will always regard you as such—and once those who have wrought such harm in your life are brought to justice and you are free to take up normal life again, you must bring your young children to visit us!' He looked at Colin commiseratingly. Poor man, he had just learned of his wife's death, not even been able to attend her funeral to say his goodbyes. This is in addition to surviving an attempt on his own life. He shook his head and went through to the kitchen to collect a few more cans of lager. It might dull the raw hurt for a while. But he sensed that this Colin Denton was a fighter. He would come out of this tragedy a stronger man—perhaps find new happiness in the future.

Greta looked up from her baking as Hans came in and grabbed a handful of lager cans.
She saw by his face something was wrong.

'Did Colin manage to speak with his minister?'

'He did—and received terrible news. His wife Mary is dead.'

'What is that? His wife—but how?' she asked in dismay, resting floury hands on the table.

'Seems she died in a suspicious motoring accident the day after the helicopter came down. He is devasted. Drink the only medicine to help at the moment,' and he set off with his armful of cans. Greta glanced after him, eyes troubled. Was it possible that those who had tried to murder the poor man, had also killed his wife? And what of his children? She had no heart for her cooking, but continued—they must eat.

Geraldine meanwhile sat taking in the implications of the wonderful news she had received. Then she called the number Robin had given her. There was no answer at first—then a man answered in Norwegian, his voice sounding somewhat inebriated;

'Is that Hans Schiffer?' she asked. 'I believe you have someone very dear to me staying with you. My name is Geraldine Denton.'

'Ah—so! You are his mother? But this is so good.' She heard him calling to someone, then came a voice she had never thought to hear again in this world—that of her son Colin!

'Mum—is that you?' His tone sounded slurred.

'Oh, Colin—yes! Yes, darling—and oh how relieved and happy I am to know you are alive—safe!' she gasped.

'You must not tell anyone yet—could put yourself in danger. How much do you know?' he asked urgently.

'Enough to be aware of most of the truth! Robin rang me—just stay there until we have proper plans in place.'

'I can't come to you—you understand that?'

'I do—and Colin, I'm so dreadfully sorry you've received the sad news of Mary's death. It seems so cruel, just as we know you are safe. But how overjoyed the children will be when we can safely tell them.'

'You mustn't do so yet! Tell no one, Mum,' he ordered. 'Robin is going to let me know when arrangements can be made. So just wait and be patient—we'll see each other one day soon. In the meanwhile, thank you from the bottom of my heart for looking after my little Charles and Melanie.'

'It is a joy to do so. They're doing well at school, and have been so very brave through all of this, 'she assured him and heard him sob. 'I'm going to call off now,' she added quietly. 'This call should be quite safe—however!'

'Look after yourself then Mum and the twins. Take no risks. The people responsible for all this are quite ruthless!' he warned thickly.

'I'm aware of it—you've been drinking?' she said gently, his slurred voice obvious.

'Hans and I are having a few beers. He and his wife Greta have been marvellous—their son Sven saved my life! It's such sweet relief to hear your voice, Mum. Remember—tell no one and do not wear a happy smile!' he advised.

'Don't worry about me. Just take the greatest care yourself, my darling son,' she whispered and put the phone down. Next. to ring Tom and Lottie, she thought.

'Tom—is that you?' she confirmed and heard his well-remembered slightly gruff voice.

'Geraldine? Anything wrong, lass?' he asked quickly.

'Far from it. I've just had the most wonderful, unbelievable news—but it's true!'

'You're not making sense,' he chided.

'I've just spoken to Colin—he's alive, Tom! Was rescued by a Norwegian fishing vessel, is staying with the owner's family!' and she poured the story out. She heard his exclamation of amazed delight.

'Geraldine! This is incredible—Lottie is sitting next to me and we're both overjoyed! You must keep it secret for now—be extremely careful—no slightest change in your normal demeanour. Retain the appearance of grieving mother, however much your heart is dancing with delight!' he advised.

'Colin warned me of the same thing—it will be so hard not to let the children know. What do you think of Robin MacKinnon's suggestion to get him over to those friends of his on the Isle of Skye?' she asked.

'Sounds perfect. Listen—I'll ring Charles Latimer. There are others he will wish to inform, but above all things, we have to keep Colin safe. Certain information he can give vital to the investigation being instigated against Sea Giant!'

'I want nothing more than to see those devils brought to justice!' she returned grimly.

'I'll call you tomorrow, Geraldine! Again, couldn't be happier at such wonderful news!'

Geraldine slept well, her mind relaxing after the many weary, despairing nights she had endured tossing and turning in suppressed grief for her son and his wife. He was alive—Colin was not lying deep down on the sea bed, but safe alive!

She prepared breakfast for the twins the next morning, sitting beside them at the kitchen table and watching fondly as they ate their porridge. She poured glasses of fresh orange juice. How she longed to share the wonderful news with them but resolutely refrained. They were dipping toast fingers into their boiled eggs now. What would happen to them in the future? Would Colin decide to take them back to Scotland—but, with Mary dead, even if the danger from Sea Giant came to an end, and the fiends who had caused such sorrow in the little family were finally arrested, would he want he wish to return to a house full of painful memories?

'You have your satchels?' she checked as she opened the doors of her old beige Ford, helping Charles and Melanie settle themselves in. They looked so cute in their school uniforms, the little red blazers contrasting with their blond curls, their grey eyes at last beginning to lose that look of sadness. She kissed them and smiled as they ran off to join the other kiddies pouring in through the school gates.

Anna Lindstrom was out early weeding the flower bed, in her front garden, when she saw Geraldine get out of the Ford and start up her pathway next door. She called across the fence to her.

'Good morning—wondered if you would like to come over and have coffee this morning?' she asked. Normally her friendly neighbour would have immediately accepted, the two of them now very close. But Geraldine seemed to hesitate.

'Some chores I've been putting off—conscience pricking me,' she called back lightly. 'Perhaps later?' and she hurried indoors. Anna looked after her, perplexed, shrugged philosophically and bent back over her weeding. Little Susan came outside at that moment, brandishing a crayon drawing she had just made. Anna smiled at her young daughter. It was a source of delight to see her so happy and carefree now. All unhappy memories of the strictures of Enderslie House seemed to have disappeared from her mind and she never mentioned Malcolm Greer now.

For a moment, Anna's thoughts sped back to those traumatic years under the man's cruel, controlling dominance. As she considered how she had submitted to his demands, she wondered why she had never made that all-important attempt to escape earlier. But of course, he had always threatened to deny her access to her little daughter if she dared leave him. Bah, that was the past. Hopefully, she would never have to encounter Greer again, and she smiled as she remembered that his illegal business dealings were under police investigation. She had been so lucky to escape his power—to feel free again.

'Susan—I love the drawing—it's very good,' she said admiringly as she hugged the little girl. Susan smiled and jabbed a finger at her work.

'That one is Melanie—and that's Charles,' she explained. 'I wish I could go to school with them!' Anna looked at her thoughtfully.

'Well, you could start at nursery,' she suggested. 'Would you like that?'

'No—real school,' said Susan emphatically. 'I want to be with my friends.' Then she caught sight of Geraldine's cat Marcasite bounding towards them and ran to stroke him, school forgotten for now.

Anna looked after her reflectively. Already Susan was beginning to display a will of her own. What did the future hold for this child who could never be reunited with her father? Somehow, she must manage to make a good future for them both—and eventually, this would mean seeking work again. Well, she reflected, at least Susan had one strong determined parent to love and care for her—and her thoughts sped to Geraldine's acting as an adoptive parent for her little grandchildren and would be quite elderly before they were fully grown, and resolved to assist whenever possible.

She sighed as she resumed her weeding, concerned that Geraldine was facing the responsibilities of adoptive parenthood when she should be taking life easy. Would little Charles and Melanie ever be able to put the emotional shock of losing both parents behind them? She wondered for the first time exactly what Colin and Mary Denton had been like as people. She had seen a fine photograph of the couple in the twin's bedroom, sitting together, lovingly embracing their children.

Mary looked like a warm and lovely person, Colin—strong, handsome—thoughtful eyes. What a cruel loss.

Tom and Lottie Lanscombe were discussing the request received from Charles Latimer at an early morning phone call. Last night Charles had informed his colleagues at M15 of the extraordinary chance by which Colin Denton had escaped his intended watery grave—was safe in Norway, anxious to return as soon as possible. They suggested that when reaching Skye Colin should stay briefly with those friends Minister Robin MacKinnon had recommended—then be collected by helicopter and flown south where they could more conveniently interview him. His possible destination was to be at the women's refuge Dream Echo, where the Lanscombes spent so much of their time assisting Amber, the lovely young woman who had set up the refuge in the secluded mansion house she owned together with her husband, Robert Marsden.

'So—we ask Amber's permission to take on Colin as a member of staff—a temporary gardener perhaps?' asked Tom. His wife shook her head uneasily, frowned. It didn't feel right. She reached out, taking Tom's hand, blue eyes urgent.

'Their attempt to use the refuge is not acceptable. Security is all important for the special work there, as we're both well aware. Amber knows they are fortunate no slightest suspicion of Dream Echo's real purpose has ever surfaced—the cover story of an artist's commune widely believed. I would feel dreadful if we encouraged late colleagues at M15 to bring any slightest unwanted attention upon the refuge.' He looked at Lottie's determined face. He knew better than to go against her instinct on the matter, and actually agreed with her. But where could Colin Denton be safely hidden, for a few weeks at least?

'What about our own place then?' he proposed. 'Charles has visited us here at Ivy Cottage often enough, folks are used to seeing people dropping in and situated right next to the church, it couldn't be quieter.' Lottie looked back at him considering the suggestion. They certainly had the space. He saw a smile soften her lips.

'Yes, I'm agreeable to that, Tom darling. You'd better ring Charles back, see what he thinks? But definitely no to Dream Echo!' She tossed a strand of soft white hair back from still youthful face. He bent forward, kissed her.

'I'll call him now—then we'd better drive over to the refuge and start work, see what new situation is waiting there,' he said lightly, glad the problem was settled.

Charles Latimer was disappointed when what had seemed a logical proposal for Denton's safety was rejected—but immediately amenable to the Lanscombe's kind offer.

'We will say our future guest is my great nephew—recovering from a heart attack,' explained Tom. 'This will explain why he does not get out and about in the village—doctor's orders for complete rest!' Charles listened approvingly. He would have to run it before the team, but sure they would agree.

Far away in the Schiffer's pine chalet, on the high slope above the fiord, Colin Denton was unaware of the different people involved in his imminent return to his home country. There had been another call from Robin MacKinnon, the minister had contacted his friends on Skye. Iain and Fiona MacLeod would gladly care for his friend in complete secrecy, just give them a date.

Sven Schiffer was back from a successful fishing trip, well satisfied with his catch. It was the first time since Colin's memory returned that he had opportunity to meet and thank the dour boat owner who had saved his life. Colin was walking between the densely packed trees above the chalet, when he heard Hans calling him—hurried back down, wondering if there had been another phone call.

'I'm here, Hans!' he said as he reached his host. 'Anything wrong?' Hans shook his head.

'No—all good, my friend. Sven has arrived back, wants to meet you and discuss your return to Scotland. Come—come!' and he propelled Colin before him, ushered him back into the house where a stocky, wind tanned man was waiting.

Sven Schiffer looked curiously at the fellow he had dragged almost dead from the sea just about three weeks ago, brought here for his parent's care, seeming a near corpse at that time! What a difference in his appearance now! This tall good-looking man standing before him, whose steady grey eyes that returning his questioning gaze were intelligent, the man's demeaner confident, easy.

'Sven! Your father told me that I owe you my life,' he said quietly, reaching out hand in firm grasp. 'How can I ever thank you!' Sven clapped him on the back and grinned.

'Why man—buy me a drink one of these days! I'm glad your memory has returned. Father says your name is Denton—Colin Denton?' He stared at him. 'Shortly after we found you, there was radio news of a helicopter crashing into the sea—three names mentioned, and apparently no survivors.'

'So, you knew then?' Colin exclaimed.

'Put it this way, I did not need that broadcast to inform me of the disaster—saw the craft come down from the deck of my boat. When we picked you up, could not be sure if you had escaped it—but what were the other chances of picking up a man from the sea such a huge distance from shore? Couldn't mention it officially. We had been fishing illegally on protected waters.' He shrugged. 'I was not sure you would recover. If you did, all would eventually become clear.'

'You have not told anyone else about saving me—apart from your parents and the doctor here?' confirmed Colin. He had to be sure.

'No. My crew know of course—but they will say nothing. I'm told you say the copter was brought down deliberately. You must have done something to badly annoy those Sea Giant devils!' he said studying him curiously. Hans broke in now making explanation.

'Colin, I've not spoken to Sven of all you privately mentioned to me. I think you should do so now!' Colin nodded instant agreement, as Greta who had quietly come into the living room placed cans of lager on the table and left the men to their talk.

Sven had posed several pointed questions, face darkening in concern. But now hearing of Mary Denton's fatal accident as Colin stated he suspected his wife had been deliberately murdered, he crashed his fist down violently on the table, cans tumbling onto the floor.

'Man—this beyond comprehension—that a supposedly reputable company should resort to such atrocity! Money—power! Their minds distorted by greed, these men must be exposed for their villainy— imprisoned for life, swine!' he ground out. 'If I can do anything to help you, my friend, you have but to say so!' Colin looked at him in gratitude at the offer, as Hans stooped and retrieved the scattered cans of lager.

'He needs to reach the Isle of Skye,' he informed his son quietly. 'Can you take him there Sven?' He handed him a lager, which Sven tossed off, and walked over to the wall map.

'Skye? I know it well. Large island, Inner Hebrides. I can do it, no trouble.' He turned back to Colin. 'I'm guessing you need somewhere safe to lie low. But could you not remain here longer as our guest?' Colin shook his head.

'Your family have been amazingly kind and I thank you from the bottom of my heart. But two small children are grieving my death as well as that of their mother. Then again, I have to reach the authorities back home and lay the facts before them. As you I've told you, little Charles and Melanie are being cared for by my elderly mother—who could also now be at risk. The sooner I can get back to Britain and sort this out the better.' Sven nodded understanding.

'Then let me know exactly where you want to be put down on Skye—and when, and it will be done. Now—tell me more about this global warming. I know it's happening, but just how urgent the matter is, I mean, are we looking at another couple of centuries perhaps—also, what effect will it have on fishing?' Then he listened in shock as Colin spelt it out for him.

'But why has it been left until now for people to start seeking change?' he demanded. 'From what you say, once the icecaps melt in the Arctic and Antarctic, there will be extensive flooding—many low-lying areas, and islands, disappearing under water? And with the increasing heat, crops failing from drought, and people dying of starvation on a massive scale? It sounds horrific, man!'

'Yes, there you have it,' replied Colin soberly. 'The use of fossil fuels accelerates global warming, a fact that is recognised and disregarded by the huge oil companies, blinded by their desire for ever greater profit. Should have had more sense than to think Sea Giant would take the slightest notice of my plea to them. But I fear it was my acquired knowledge of their plans to sell details of a stolen secret method of extracting oil at a fraction of the normal cost, to hostile powers, that signed my death warrant. If they realise I am still alive, they will be fanatical in coming after me. I'm going to have to be extremely careful, but nothing will stop me from exposing them to the police. I need to get back there Sven,' he said urgently. It was at this moment that Hans's phone rang. He lifted it.

'Is that Hans Schiffer? Robin MacKinnon here. My friends on Skye are prepared to help Colin. Is he there?'

'Yes, Minister,' he handed the mobile to Colin.

'Colin?'

'Yes, Robin. What news?'

'Is it possible to be at Portree harbour in two days' time? If so, the MacLeod's will be waiting at the hotel nearby—just five minutes walk from the quay, will pick you up in their car, a navy Nissan.'

'That is the day after tomorrow?' checked Colin eagerly. He glanced at Sven. 'Can you get me to Skye two days' time—at Portree Harbour?' he asked hopefully.

'No problem,' Sven replied, exchanging a quick glance with his father. 'Tell your friend I'll get you there—a promise!'

Colin Denton made wet and windy arrival at Portree harbour, glad to be ashore after the buffeting the stout fishing boat sustained in the voyage. He stood on the quay, regaining his balance after those long hours of continuous motion at sea. Sven looked at him critically. In typical seaman's working clothes, the cap pulled down well over his face, unshaven, he should attract no slightest attention in this remote spot, busy enough though it was with boats arriving to land their catch. He handed Colin a backpack.

'Father put a few items together for you—shirts, underclothes, toiletries,' he handed it to Colin. 'Best you disappear now—just walk off casually. The hotel you want over there—five minutes away.' Colin tossed the bag over his shoulder and turned a grateful face on Sven.

'I will never be able to thank you and your family sufficiently. We will meet again one day, Sven, and make all this up to you, but until then!' he swallowed as he stared at Sven's bluff features.

'Go now—go man! May the good Lord be with you!' and Sven moved away, calling across to his crew. Colin did not hesitate, but walked off along the quay, spitting as he went. No one gave him a second glance. His heart was pounding as he approached the courtyard of the small hotel. Suppose the MacLeods had not arrived? He stood there, glancing anxiously around. A maid wearing a frilled cap and apron came out on the front steps of the old white-washed building and looked across at him. Should he speak to her? Decided against it, lowered his bag to the ground, appearing to enjoy the spectacular view back to the sea. He couldn't just stand here though. It was as he began to experience a slight feeling of panic, that a voice hailed him, as a well-built, slightly balding, grey-bearded man stepped out of a navy car and started to approach.

'Would you be Robin's friend?' the man asked quietly, as he closed the distance between them. Colin nodded relieved affirmation.

'Yes, name's Colin.'

'Iain MacLeod,' said the stranger introducing himself. 'The wife Fiona's in the car. Come away then, best not to linger here.' Colin followed him, and MacLeod opened the car door. He slipped in. A woman seated in the front, next to the driving seat, turned her head and smiled at him.

'Fiona MacLeod,' she said in soft west highland brogue. 'Welcome to Skye, Mr Denton. We are so glad you've made it.' Her husband eased the car neatly about and away. It all seemed like a dream, thought Colin, as they slid smoothly down the slope onto the road, soon leaving the small township behind them as they sped along the forested road.

'It is amazingly kind of you both to help me this way,' he exclaimed, relaxing a little. The woman looked back over her shoulder, fixing green eyes curiously on his face. He looked a wee bit unkempt and needed a shave, but a good-looking enough man, she decided, honest grey eyes with a direct stare.

'Robin and Molly have been our good friends for many a long year. When Robin called Iain and explained you were in difficult circumstances, we had no hesitation in offering our help.' She paused, 'As I understand it, you have been through a dreadful time—and we'll do anything we can to assist you,' she held a hand out over the back of the seat. He took it.

'Thank you, Mrs MacLeod,' he began when her husband interrupted.

'Let it be Iain and Fiona,' he called from the driving seat. 'And I take it we may call you Colin?' And within minutes a new comfortable friendship was formed. They were driving through the hills now, the scenery dramatic in the extreme, lower heathery slopes glowing pink and purple under a brooding August sky, as a shower of rain suddenly swept down, to be replaced by a vivid rainbow.

'Why but it's beautiful here!' Colin exclaimed.

'Aye, Skye's a bonny place,' replied Iain. 'I've travelled the world in my time, seen many fair lands but consider this dear island outshines all such.' He braked, swinging the navy Nissan up a narrow track road leading off to the right. 'Almost there,' he called, 'See—there's the croft!' Colin craned his neck as the whitewashed walls of a secluded stone house came into view, set among birches and rowans, bordered to the left by a fast-flowing burn. It looked idyllic and suitably remote. 'Welcome to our home, Colin!' called Fiona.

Chapter Seven

Robin MacKinnon lifted the phone and smiled in relief as he recognised the speaker's voice. It was Colin Denton, announcing he had safely arrived on Skye and was now with Iain and Fiona at their croft.

'They are a delightful couple,' exclaimed Colin fervently. 'Couldn't be kinder—and so amazing to open their home to a stranger! Thank you from my heart for arranging it for me. You're a very special friend, Minister MacKinnon.' Robin smiled.

'Perhaps we should let Geraldine know?' he queried. 'It will put her mind at rest.'

'That would be great—but please remind her not to display any show of excitement. Just tell her I can't wait to embrace her—and my children.' His voice broke and Robin heard understandingly.

'How was the trip over from Norway?'

'Blustery describes it best! That Schiffer family so incredible in their help. One day I shall return and thank them properly. Must go now, Fiona is just serving up a rabbit stew and it smells good!' The minister turned to his wife.

'Colin's made it to Skye! He's with the MacLeods now.' Molly gasped in delight.

'Robin—that's marvellous. Surely, he'll be safe with our friends in that quiet spot? When I think how dangerous it would be should news of his survival reach Sea Giant, it makes me shudder. I'll never forget that horrible man who came to our door, asking for Geraldine. He had such hard eyes—sensed something evil about him—ughh!' and her face expressed disgust at the memory.

'Luckily at this time they've no slightest clue he was safely plucked from a watery tomb,' replied Robin soberly. 'Once Colin manages to get safely to the authorities, and discloses all he knows, there's no doubt the bosses of Sea Giant will be arrested and dealt with by the law.'

Colin awoke early the following morning, had retired very early the previous evening, exhausted after his journey, and now stared bemused about the unfamiliar bedroom—where was he? Then as memory came flooding back, he swung his legs off the comfortable bed, glancing at unfamiliar pyjamas Iain had thoughtfully provided and walked curiously to the window—pulled back the curtains and looked out.

A smirr of rain was falling, a thin watery beam of sunlight shimmering through a misty dawn. What was that noise? He smiled as he recognised the sound of bleating. How strange life was! One day he was high on a forested hillside, in a pine chalet overlooking a Norwegian Fiord—now here on this remote Hebridean island amid the peaceful sound of sheep.

There was a light knock at the bedroom door and Fiona stood there with a mug of tea.

'Good morning, Colin—did you sleep well?' she greeted solicitously, as he took the tea, and gave her a warm smile.

'I did indeed, Fiona—best night's sleep I've had in quite a while!' he exclaimed appreciatively. 'You have sheep then—can hear them out there.'

'Aye—about a hundred head of sheep, plus six cows, so we've plenty milk and butter, then chickens of course for the eggs. We have fish in the burn, rabbits and pheasants on the hill, and honey for Iain keeps bees. We are practically self-sufficient,' she explained proudly.

'Have you always lived here, Fiona,' he asked, genuinely interested.

'For the last thirty years or so. The croft had belonged to Iain's father. We were in Edinburgh before that—university. You must tell me a little about yourself, once you're dressed and breakfasted. Oh, and porridge is cooked when you are ready—no doubt you'll remember where the bathroom is?' and she walked quietly away. He looked after her. Iain was fortunate in his wife, he thought. Fiona blended a quiet charm of manner with a lively independence, and noting her shapely figure, soft gold red curls and direct green gaze, she must have been quite beautiful in her youth.

He bent down, opening the backpack Sven had pushed at him as they parted, taking out the clean clothing it contained, and looked gratefully at a small bag of toiletries Greta had added. He thought of the unconditional kindness he kept encountering, first from the Schiffer family—now that offered by the MacLeods. After the recent terrible events and facing the stark realisation that his erstwhile employers had tried to kill him as casually as one might swat a wasp—the later shock of learning they were also certainly responsible for his Mary's death, had filled him with despair and bitterness. He wanted if not revenge, at least the satisfaction of exposing their corruption. Now his mood lightened a little.

He knocked at the kitchen door. He found Fiona singing softly to herself as she bent over the stove—he couldn't make out the words. Gaelic perhaps, he wondered. She looked up as he came in.

'Ah, you're ready for your breakfast Colin—I'll give Iain a shout!' She flung the outer door open, calling her husband's name. Minutes later the crofter joined them, and placing a small basket of newly gathered eggs on the dresser he proceeded to wash his hands at the sink.

'Good morning to you, Colin,' he said, glancing approvingly at their guest. He certainly looked much improved from the tired, stressed individual they had collected from Portree yesterday. 'You slept well, I hope?'

'Best sleep in ages!' declared Colin honestly. 'Look, I don't know how to thank you both for your kindness in taking in a total stranger. I'll endeavour to move on as soon as arrangements can be made.' He paused, looking at them seriously. 'But there's something you need to understand. It must never come to light that you have helped me. It might leave you vulnerable to danger from some very corrupt and unscrupulous individuals.' He knew he had to warn them.

There was a minute's silence, as Iain seated himself at the table beside his wife, hanging his jacket on the back of his chair. He stared at Colin from troubled dark eyes.

'We will eat—then you shall reveal whatever you think it right we should know,' he said quietly. To Colin's surprise, the man murmured a swift grace, before taking up his spoon and attacking his porridge. A Christian then—but of course, he was a friend of Minister MacKinnon. Porridge finished, Fiona produced boiled eggs and home-baked bread and butter of her own churning, all washed down by strong tea.

'Well now,' said Iain, as he helped Fiona clear the table, glancing curiously across at his guest from inquiring blue eyes, 'If you are ready, Colin, we are listening!'

'We'll be more comfortable next door,' said Fiona firmly, and led them through to the homely living room, with its worn, brown tapestried armchairs and couch, brightened with colourful cushions, a bowl of cream roses and fern fronds on the low table, some exceptional water colours of the island on the walls, a tall bookcase lining one complete wall, other books stacked beside it, more scattered on an occasional table, and a chess set lay on the window seat.

Colin seated himself on the couch, as the couple took their accustomed armchairs, and looked at him expectantly. He began by sounding them out on their knowledge of climate change wrought by global warming. He found them both to be well-informed and deeply concerned for the world's future. He then spoke briefly on his former occupation in the oil industry—that only when he realised the serious impact fossil fuels were having on swiftly escalating global warming, that he started to question his work.

They were listening attentively as he went on to mention the huge new oil find Sea Giant had discovered, and was keeping secret at this time—the billions of dollars they estimated it would be worth on the world market. He explained how he had conferred together with a close colleague Jonathon King who shared his concerns, made an appointment for them to speak with the directors of Sea Giant on the rig, and was flown out there. He told how he had presented well-researched data on climate change, warning them of the rise in sea level already causing problems in low-lying areas—that every new oil find was contributing to the dangers facing mankind, pleaded with them to reconsider going ahead with their plans at least until they had seriously thought about the consequences.

'I was contemptuously dismissed, instructed to return to the mainland and to consider my position in the company. Jonathon and I were directed to a small, fairly new helicopter for the return flight, were to be the only two passengers, the experienced pilot Kevin, was a close friend. Kevin suddenly shouted something was badly wrong with the controls—made a Mayday! As you know the helicopter crashed Jonathon and Kevin both died—but almost unbelievably I escaped, was floating unconscious almost dead and was picked up by Sven Schiffer's fishing boat. He brought me to his parent's home in a remote spot in Norway. I did not regain memory properly until well over a week later. Look, I firmly believe those controls had been deliberately tampered with. That it was premeditated murder!'

'You were so lucky to be rescued,' breathed Fiona. 'If you are right, then those men are criminals, should be arrested and spend the rest of their lives in jail.'

'It was worse, they went on to kill my wife, Mary,' Colin continued in a low voice—explaining the circumstances as far as he had been able to establish them. He spoke of the assistance received from their joint friends, Robin and Molly MacKinnon. He went on to speak of twin children, seven years old Charles and Melanie, taken back to the south of England by his elderly mother Geraldine Denton. She had flown up to comfort his wife on the same day she received news of his death—and the following morning, together with Mary, had spoken with the Sea Giant executives who had visited the house and insisted on removing his computer and personal papers. Then later that afternoon, Mary's reliable new car inexplicably crashed and caught fire. His voice shook as he spoke of it. Their faces regarded him in compassion

'Where is your mother now?' inquired Iain. 'Is she still down there in England with the bairns?' He leaned forward, his face concerned.

'Yes, and I fear Sea Giant may suspect I might have passed on knowledge of their massive oil discovery to her. If so, then she is at risk. She knows of my survival now, Robin phoned her and I managed a few quick words with her too. She is a very responsible woman and will keep my escape secret. I have to get to the police—but not at local level.' He looked at them. 'Well, that's about it. Now you realise why you must never let anyone know of your assistance to me.' He sat back on the couch, revealing the facts had been mentally exhausting.

'Robin told us little of this—only that you were a good friend in a desperate situation, who needed somewhere safe to hide until you could receive help from the right people. What you have revealed remains between the three of us, Colin,' stated Iain reassuringly. 'How will you know when it's time to make a move?' Colin shook his head.

'Robin said he will contact me.' He stood up. 'Look, please let me help about the croft whilst I am here. I'm handy at most things!' he offered.

'Come out with me on the hill,' suggested Iain, giving him an assessing glance. 'It's a fine place to sort out the mind.' Colin nodded, shrugged on the tan leather jacket Hans Schiffer had gifted and followed him outside. Fiona glanced after them. Poor man, what he had been through, she thought pityingly. To lose his dear wife too—such a bitter fact to come to terms with. But he was only in his late thirties, perhaps would meet someone else one day. None of us knows what the future holds, she thought constructively. Well, there was a hen to be plucked for today's dinner. She went to the outhouse, mind still focused on all Colin had told them. It sounded like something from a horror movie—only it was real and very frightening.

Springy heather tussocks were wet under their feet as they ascended the steep hillside where sheep grazed and lifted questioning heads as they passed, as Iain's red and white collie bounded far in front, and high above skylarks sweetened the morning with thin, reedy song, and curious rabbits took fright at their advance. Iain pointed to a large slab of fallen rock.

'A good spot to take breath,' he said quietly and nothing loth Colin sank down beside him. Far below peat smoke was rising from the croft house chimney, pungent smell blending with the sharp fragrance of the heather while racing past nearby, the shallow brown waters of narrow burn, splashed urgent descent.

'This place is magic,' said Colin slowly. 'It's as though you are entering a different world up here.'

'Just so. There is a sense of timelessness up on the ben. You get a better perspective on the ridiculous rush and bustle of the modern world, and man's obsession to make money at all costs, destroying all that obstructs him. Here on this quiet island of ours, we still retain much of the old ways. Reaching out to neighbours with simple kindness, helping the stranger, and not rejecting God as is the modern way where men acknowledge no authority but their own.' He shot a glance at Colin.

'Do you believe in God, Colin Denton?' The question took him by surprise. He rubbed his chin and struggled to reply.

'Look, I'm no church-going Christian, although my parents brought me up as such—but I do believe. Yet since all that's recently happened, with Jonathon and Kevin's deaths—shock of my dear Mary's murder, I find myself wondering why an all-loving God would allow such cruelty!' The words were forced out passionately. Iain nodded sympathetically. Put a hand on his shoulder, looking him steadily in the eyes.

'At such times, many undergo what is known as the black night of the soul. Something devastating occurs, destroying hopes and dreams—and despair clutches the heart. We need someone to blame—and it may be our Maker. But inevitably time passes bringing healing, new experiences replace the trauma that brought us to this dark and lonely place. We learn to live and love again.' He gave Colin an understanding smile. 'The journey can be hard—a turbulent journey—but you must find the strength to endure and I promise light will flood your life once again—a new dawn.'

Colin heard him in wondering silence. He recognised the quiet wisdom in those sympathetic words. Iain MacLeod was a much deeper man than he had thought. He also spoke as though from personal knowledge.

'You have been there—faced what you described as this dark night of the soul?' he asked.

'Just so. Our only son Alexander, with his wife Morag and their wee two years old daughter Shona, were on holiday on a Greek island. They were booked into a chalet adjoining the hotel. Retired to bed—in the morning were found dead!' He spoke the words carefully, almost analytically.

'What? But how—what happened,' cried Colin aghast.

'Seems the exhaust fumes from a faulty gas installation overcame them as they slept.' He swallowed. 'We went out there—had them brought back and now they lie at rest in the local kirkyard. Fiona and I, well it hit us hard. At one time we found no comfort in the kirk—or each other. Grief can alienate you even from those you dearly love until you accept your loss—hand it to our heavenly father in prayer.'

Colin listened broodingly. So, this man also had faced unutterable pain and loss, and asked that same question why—why? But how do you get past the cold anger—the desire for revenge, he wondered? He stared at Iain.

'My thoughts are in constant turmoil,' he burst out. 'The unrelenting pain of having to accept I will never see Mary again, my children bereft of their mother—all swirls continuously through my brain, combined with a furious need for revenge, and experiencing cold hatred against those who caused such grief. How do I get past this?'

'Not easy—but praying, even when it seems you receive no answer—learning to let go and to let God! Anger and desire for revenge aye make uncomfortable bedfellows. Try to empty your mind.' He stroked his beard and smiled at him. 'While you are with us, come up here and release all this to the wind blowing through the gorse—breath deep the scent of crushed heather—watch the flight of the golden eagle spreading its wings high above as it seeks its eyrie on the summit.' He rose to his feet. 'Let the beauty of this place bring peace to your soul. And always remember you have children who need you, ache for your arms about them. And God give you peace and healing, my friend.' He reached a hand down and pulled Colin up. 'I've work to do in the barn,' he said. 'Here, Glen,' and whistled for his dog. At once his red and white collie appeared from behind a rocky outcrop and sped towards them to nuzzle Iain's hand. The two men descended together in companionable silence, Iain wondering if his words had brought any relief to the troubled figure at his side.

Two days passed, during which Colin began to walk alone on the hill, Iain quietly observing his comings and goings with an approving eye. Then on the morning of the third day, the telephone rang just as Colin was pulling on his jacket. Fiona rubbed floury hands on her apron as she answered it—called to him as he was making towards the door

'Call for you, Colin. Man says he's a friend of your mother's?' He turned hurried back to the kitchen, and took the receiver from her hand.

'Hallo—who is this?' he inquired.

'Name's Lanscombe—Tom Lanscombe. May I ask you to confirm your own name?'

'I'm Colin Denton—I understand you know my mother?' He did not recognise the voice of the speaker.

'I do indeed. My wife Lottie and I have been good friends with Geraldine for a great many years—worked together at one time. She informed us of your situation, details of which have been passed on to the Secret Service. Arrangements are being made to collect you by helicopter in two days' time and be flown down to the village of Willow-Mere in Hampshire. You will be staying at our home, Ivy Cottage, where you will be contacted by those who wish to interview you.' Tom paused, waiting for Colin's response.

'Why Mr Lanscombe—Tom, this is more than kind. Are you sure though? I would not wish to bring any trouble on you or your wife.' His mind was working feverishly. He was aware that sooner or later he would have to leave the peace and security of this croft house, where gradually he was beginning to unwind, even relax somewhat, and think rationally again. If only he could have had a few more weeks—days even. Did Tom sense his reluctance he wondered?

'Colin, you've been through a lot—probably enjoying the quiet beauty of Skye right now. But in order to be finally free of the scoundrels who tried to take your life, and might make another attempt should they realise you've survived, you have to follow through and help the authorities deal with them.'

'Yes, I understand and you're right, of course. I think you said I'll be picked up in two days' time—I'll be ready. And may I say how much I appreciate your offer to put me up in your home?'

'Good. So then, I look forward to meeting you, Colin Denton!'

'Thanks.' he put the phone down, trying to adjust to yet another set of circumstances. Fiona had overheard his words, also noticing his lack of enthusiasm at the news he would be leaving. Well, perhaps even these few days may have brought a degree of healing to his bruised soul. She smiled at her guest.

'So, you will be away soon. We will miss you, Colin Denton. I know how much Iain has liked having you about the place. Perhaps, once you have done whatever is necessary to bring those criminal oilmen to justice, you will return, spend time with us again—your bairns with you!' She lifted the rolling pin and began shaping the dough to cap the chicken pie. 'You will always be welcome here,' she added simply. He watched her busy hands, remembering how often he had observed his Mary at a similar task.

'I will never forget either of you—or this place,' he said quietly and thrusting hands into the pockets of his leather jacket, made for the door, to disguise his emotion. Her thoughtful green gaze followed him, wondering what the future held.

Geraldine heard the news in delight. Lottie had just phoned to explain Colin had made safe arrival on the outskirts of Willow-Mere and was now on his way to Ivy Cottage by car with Tom. Geraldine would be able to speak with her son soon! Hands trembling with relief, she replaced the receiver.

Twins Charles and Melanie were next door at Bramble Cottage now having tea with Anna and little Susan. Thankfully, she would be able to speak to Colin for a few precious minutes, without having to disguise her joy from the children. She longed to give them the wonderful news that their father was alive—could not breathe a word of it yet, not until those rogues at the helm of Sea Giant were arrested and made to face justice! Meanwhile, she must never forget for a single moment just how vulnerable she was here should they decide to pay a visit. She shuddered when she remembered Mary's fate.

Colin climbed into the helicopter that had set down on a relatively flat area outside the barns, lifting a grateful hand in farewell to Iain and Fiona who had walked the short distance to see him off. The kindly couple had made a terrific impact on him during his few day's stay here. As he seated himself in the craft which on its earlier descent had sent sheep nervously scattering, he found his heart beginning to pound furiously, recognised it for the panic attack at being aboard a helicopter once more. He forced himself to breathe slowly and gradually the tension lessened as the pilot exchanged a few casual remarks with him. The rotary blades whirled and within minutes the friendly couple and collie dog below, the stone-built croft house and outbuildings all disappeared from view, as Colin accepted it was time to face the future.

The journey was uneventful. He sat there thinking of his destination and considering what little he knew about Tom Lanscombe, tried to recollect what the man had said in their brief phone conversation. Yes—that he had a wife called Lottie, and that they had known his mother over a long period—had once worked together with her. Why was it then that he had never heard the name Lanscombe before, and how was it that this man had been able to arrange this flight for him and it would seem able to liaise with the secret service?

He sat there idly attempting to recollect his childhood. His mother was often away on business, and when he was very young, they had a live-in housekeeper called Mrs Gregory—he had called her Auntie Greg. She looked after him and his doctor father when his mother disappeared from time to time, cooked splendid meals, and always had a warm smile. Mother liked her too, the little household functioning well in its unconventional way. He had never questioned it or even wondered what work it was that took Geraldine away for weeks at a time. Now he did so.

His thoughts returned to Tom Lanscombe, who had said his wife's name was Lottie. He frowned, Lottie Lanscombe, why did that name sound vaguely familiar? He had certainly never met her. Then his mind made the connection—his dear Mary had loved novels by a writer of this name. Could she be Tom's wife—and a friend of his mother?

His mind moved on to his later childhood—boarding school. The family had left the London house and moved to the small village of Ravensnest, where his father had taken over the practice of a retiring doctor. He fondly remembered his father David now, recalling how popular he had been popular with his patients and always taking part in village life—and how both parents loved their garden.

Mother had eventually given up her long business trips, and Auntie Greg retired. It had been great seeing more of Mother when he was home during school hols, always treasured their long talks together.

Moving on to Uni where he was reading biochemistry, he began to see her with the eyes of an adult and realised his mother had an acutely probing mind. His parents were so different, father, with his quiet wisdom, fun and charm of manner, and mother with her barely suppressed energy and knowledge of world affairs. His father's recent death from a heart attack had devasted her, he had attended the funeral, flown down from Scotland. He had already been married to Mary for eight years, with joy in their twin children. Six years ago, they had moved from their Hampshire home to Grantly, hundreds of miles away when he had joined the staff of Sea Giant. He should have kept in closer contact with his mother, he thought guiltily, must try to rectify this now. He was nearly drowsing off, lulled by the drone of the engine, as all this drifted through his mind.

'We've arrived at your destination!' called the pilot. 'Going to set you down in that field—descending now.' He glanced behind him at his unresponsive passenger, he had tried to chat several times, but given up—the man was seemingly lost in his thoughts. Colin reacted to his words and glanced out of the window as the craft circled and made a perfect landing. He warmly thanked the pilot and got out stiffly, ducking down carefully to avoid the still whirling blades and glanced around the unfamiliar surroundings. On its far side, the meadow was bordered by woods while close to the spot where he was standing the adjacent road was accessed by a farm gate. At this moment the gate opened as a man appeared, and raising a hand in greeting walked towards them.

At the sight of him, the pilot waved and immediately the helicopter rose swiftly back into the sky. Colin stared curiously at the man striding towards him.

'Colin—Colin Denton? I'm Tom Lanscombe,' informed the stranger. Colin gave him a measuring glance, and liked what he saw—the confident dark stare under shaggy eyebrows, an air of authority. He smiled as they exchanged a firm handshake, Tom examining the new arrival, seeking similarities to Geraldine—and noted the man's grey eyes and determined chin. Yes, he was Geraldine's son.

'Glad to meet you, Tom—so grateful for your assistance!' exclaimed Colin warmly.

'It's my pleasure. Your mother is a valued friend. Let's hope we can help to right the terrible wrongs you have suffered. Best not to linger here, let's get into the car—this way!'

The black BMW swung smoothly along the winding road between fields close shaven of corn, banks bright with white cow parsley, pale pink columbine and purple spires of foxglove, while hips and haws were starting to colour in the hedges, late summer preparing to yield to autumn.

Tom reduced speed as they approached the outskirts of a village. 'Here we are! This is Willow-Mere,' informed Tom Lanscombe, nodding at the scattering of pretty cottages with flower-filled gardens, as they proceeded along a high street dominated by an old Norman church. Tom swung the car into the cul de sac between the church and an attractive cottage. Colin got out and stared at what was to be his temporary home, Ivy Cottage. Tom opened the gate, Colin following him along a narrow pathway through a well-tended front garden where roses bloomed when the cottage door opened, and a woman with prematurely white hair framing an attractive face waved a greeting.

'Tom, you found him then! Welcome Colin,' she said easily, extending a hand. 'Come in and make yourself at home.' As he looked into her steady blue eyes, he took an instant liking to Lottie Lanscombe. Yet again, he had been guided into the care of some very special people.

'Mrs Lanscombe, it's so wonderful of you both offering me somewhere to stay,' he said, jerking the words out, a wave of emotion almost overcoming him for brief instant. He was led into a large, cheerful yellow dining kitchen, with an old-fashioned stove, above which a shelf held a collection of brass saucepans. There was a scrubbed pine kitchen table and chairs, while further along set in a window recess, a pine-framed settee was strewn with patchwork cushions. An antique cuckoo clock with a swinging pendulum made distinctive tick. It all looked comfortable and homely.

'Sit down, Colin,' said Tom, pointing to the settee. 'You must feel tired after your journey. We'll show you to your room in a moment, but how about tea or coffee first and Lottie has just baked a fruit cake.' He smiled at his wife. 'I always blame her splendid cooking for my expanding waistline!' he said affectionately and kissed her. Colin seated himself and began to relax as he watched them.

'So, is it to be tea or coffee?' inquired Lottie.

'Oh, coffee—black please, Mrs Lanscombe' he replied. 'And I would love a taste of that cake—it smells wonderful.'

'Make it Lottie— Tom and Lottie, no formalities while you're with us!' She smiled back as she made the point. 'It's a real pleasure to meet our friend Geraldine's son—we were with her a few days ago, visited Rose Cottage and saw your lovely twin children. Young Charles and Melanie are delightful—and what a blessing that they'll soon be reunited with their daddy,' she said quietly.

'You have our deep commiserations on the death of your wife Mary,' put in Tom. 'Do anything we can do to help bring those who killed her to justice! More of that later.' He saw the tiredness on Colin's face.

'Coffee,' said Lottie, pouring from a decanter. 'Sugar?' He shook his head, as he took the hand-painted mug. He sipped it and started to relax, a sense of normality returning. She handed him a wedge of cake—and it reminded him of Mary's baking.

'It's delicious,' he mumbled through a mouthful and saw her pleased smile. 'Listen I have to ask you—but are you the writer? My Mary loves those novels—loved that is,' he added sadly. She nodded modestly in the affirmative as Tom put affectionate hands on her shoulders.

'Yes Colin, my wife is the author—writes children's books too, under a separate name,' he explained. He watched as Colin finished his coffee. 'How about I show you to your bedroom now and you can unpack your belongings.' Colin rose to his feet with a rueful smile.

'Unpacking will take all of five minutes, I'm travelling light!' he said, as he retrieved his small bag, and thanking Lottie for refreshments followed Tom up the steep flight of stairs.

He stared quickly around the charming small bedroom, with a flowered duvet on what promised to be a comfortable bed, saw a well-stocked bookcase, a dressing table, and some unusual lamps on the bedside cabinets and noted a door to a shower room. Now, he glanced curiously out of the window onto the back garden with its fine lawn, and flower beds and boasted a small pool and fountain. A rustic bench invited beneath a spreading apple tree. What a perfect home the Lanscombe's had created for themselves.

'Anything you need just ask,' said Tom quietly. 'Come down when you feel like talking, there's much to discuss.'

'Well, what did you think of our guest?' asked Lottie, as Tom joined her in the kitchen.

'I like him—honest and straightforward!' he pronounced.

'I agree,' said Lottie. 'Quite withdrawn at the moment though, and no wonder considering what he has been through. To have escaped almost certain death from drowning planned by Sea Giant, ending up in Norway with memory loss, only to face the news of his wife's murder when his mind cleared.' She shook her head, blue eyes troubled. 'He is going to need time to adjust to all this.' Tom sank down on his chair and nodded in agreement.

'You're right, Lottie love. I think getting him to talk will help—understandably he's very uptight right now. Importantly though we need as much information as possible to pass on to HQ—I'll ring Charles Latimer and find out when he is likely to arrive and talk matters over!' He looked speculatively at the cake still on the table. She raised a restraining finger.

'No Tom darling, you'll spoil your dinner—steak and kidney pie, followed by fruit trifle and cream,' she added temptingly and he smiled.

'Sounds great, Lottie. Oh—what about Geraldine? Hope all is well at Rose Cottage!'

'I rang Geraldine just before you arrived back, reassured her Colin had arrived safely in Willow-Mere and was on his way here.' She sighed. 'I know she is finding it hard to keep news of their father's survival from the children—must be longing to see him herself.' He nodded.

'She has had her training to sustain her, but until we know for certain that the SG executives responsible for their crimes are in custody, she remains at risk in that remote home, with only one other cottage nearby.' His shaggy brows drew together in thought. 'Thankfully her neighbour is a thoroughly responsible young woman. We can be sure Anna Lindstrom will watch over Geraldine, and then of course, the local police sergeant promised to keep the cottage under surveillance.' He looked up as his phone rang. He glanced at Lottie, 'It's Charles Latimer,' he said. She looked up at him expectantly as he took the brief call.

'Well?'

'He's on his way by copter—wants me to pick him up. Have to go out again!' He smiled. 'Will that steak pie of yours stretch to four of us?' Lottie raised her eyebrows. The question did not need an answer, she was well accustomed to guests arriving unexpectedly.

'We'll put him in the other spare room—I'll get it ready!' and she bustled off. Colin was just coming out of his room when he saw Lottie about to enter an adjacent bedroom.

'Colin! Just preparing for another guest—a close friend and one-time colleague of Tom's. His name is Charles Latimer—he is flying down from London, Tom's on his way to collect him now. Dinner may be a few minutes late!' In a few deft movements, Lottie had the room to her liking. 'There—that will do.' She turned back to Colin who was watching from the doorway and saw the questioning look on his face. 'Charles is MI5,' she said quietly. 'He is coming specifically to see you. You'll like him.'

'I can hardly believe so many wonderful people are prepared to help me.' He drew a deep breath, trying to ignore the fatigue crowding all analytical thought from his mind. He was going to need a very clear head to answer the myriad questions he was bound to be asked. But at least something was going to be done!

For the second time that day, Tom's black BMW drew up by the field gate, as he settled down to watch for the arrival of the helicopter.

He did not have long to wait, heard the heavy whirring sound as the craft approached, descended, and Latimer got out, bending low to avoid the craft's whirling blades. The helicopter took off again immediately, Tom waving from the gate, as the tall, handsome, silver-haired man strode across the grass towards him.

'Thanks for meeting me, Tom!' They shook hands, and within minutes were driving the short distance to Willow-Mere.

'Good journey?' asked Tom. Latimer nodded.

'No problems. So, tell me then Tom, what do you make of Colin Denton?' he inquired.

'Decent type—honest I would say, has shown remarkable courage, appears to be suffering from post-traumatic stress.' And he explained what little he had gleaned so far from Colin. As they turned into the cul de sac between the old church and the Lanscombe's ivy-clad cottage, Charles Latimer glanced at Tom as they both got out.

'This cottage has become a second home to me over the years—so many memories!' he added,' Like that first time Bruce and I met Amber here! How is the refuge going these days?' he asked inquiringly. Tom shrugged and smiled.

'Dream Echo continues to open its doors to the usual nonstop arrival of abused women. Lottie and I spend the greater part of the week helping out there. I'll take you over there tomorrow if you have time to spare,' he suggested.

'Would like to—but guess I have to prioritise this business of Sea Giant. We may need to move quickly if my suspicions are right.' He closed the garden gate as he followed Tom to the front door of Ivy Cottage. Lottie was waiting to greet the MI5 agent who was an old friend, as Tom ushered him inside. He embraced her warmly.

'Lottie—thank you for letting me descend on you today instead of waiting for morning. Oh, have I possibly arrived at the right time for one of your delicious meals?' As they passed the kitchen door he sniffed appreciatively. Lottie laughed, blue eyes looking at him affectionately.

'You have a nose like a bloodhound, Charles! Just ordinary fare, steak and kidney pie, but as always you are so welcome,' she confirmed. 'Tom, why don't you make yourselves comfortable in the sitting room, and pour drinks while I serve up!'

'Where's Denton, dear?' asked Tom.

'Wandering in the garden. I'll call him in, let him know you are back.' She found Colin staring down blankly into the garden pool, where the small fountain gently splashed. At first, he did not look up as she crossed the lawn and called his name.

'Colin—Colin! Tom has just arrived back with Charles—and I'm about to serve dinner now.' He gave her a slightly bewildered glance, quickly seeming to recover his composure.

'I'm sorry, Lottie. I get these flashbacks sometimes—imagine myself back in the water! I'll come in right away.' She looked at him pityingly. Poor man, he certainly needed help, counselling perhaps, and no wonder after all he had endured.

Charles Latimer was quietly observing the man he had flown up from London to meet and had briefly shaken hands with before Lottie summoned them into the dining room, the four of them were now at table enjoying their meal, the pie delicious. There was no doubt that Colin Denton was suffering from stress and thought the MI5 man, whilst also sensing strength and integrity in him, hopefully, would prove a reliable witness. He smiled ruefully as Lottie helped them to a generous serving of fruit trifle and cream.

'Lottie, I always put on pounds after one of your wonderful meals,' he chuckled. He looked across at Colin. 'You certainly won't starve here, my friend!' he informed lightly. They were sitting comfortably in the sitting room now, drinking some excellent Columbian coffee. At last, Lottie got up.

'I'm just going to clear up in the kitchen—do you want to help Tom?' Her husband rose casually to his feet, preparing to follow her.

'Coming, my dear.' Charles looked after them with a smile and turned to glance at Colin.

'I think we have been given privacy to discuss those shocking experiences you have suffered and which are of interest to the secret service whom I am privileged to serve. Are you happy to answer a few questions, Colin Denton?' The younger man met his gaze with a level stare of his own, realising he was speaking to someone of undoubted authority, and whom he could trust. He leaned forward in his armchair and fixed Latimer with level grey eyes.

'Where do we start?' he asked.

'Well firstly, allow me to offer my sincere condolences on the death of your wife Mary. I fully understand you're immersed in grief at this time, but in honour of the woman you loved, have a duty to bring to justice those who caused her death.' He saw Colin flinch slightly but saw from his expression that he was prepared to cooperate fully. After first stiff replies to initial questions, Colin began to open up—and then it was like a dam bursting, as he poured out all that has transpired since he moved his family up North and was employed by Sea Giant.

'So, it was in great part due to your efforts that this new oil field was discovered?' Charles Latimer confirmed. Colin sighed and nodded.

'Yes, you could say that. My work at Uni had focussed on studying the underlying strata of the sea bed, I knew there had to be a vast field of oil and gas in an area I had pinpointed. And exploration proved I was right! At first, I was deeply gratified to have my supposition vindicated.' He paused and gave a wry smile. 'Sea Giant was delighted that my calculations had proved accurate and promised advancement in the company. But you see, it was at this point that I began to seriously study global warming, and the disastrous impact the oil industry was having on climate change. I remember enduring a mental battle with myself as I realised that instead of something to be proud of, the new field I had been instrumental in revealing was likely to inflict untold future damage to the world.'

'Yes, I believe you are right,' said Charles slowly. 'The use of fossil fuels has to be phased out. After all, mankind has many other safe and reliable options—wind and wave power—solar energy and of course hydro-electric power.'

'But none of these offers the huge financial inducements of oil and gas!' said Colin bleakly. 'As I explained, I was now concerned that my own work was propagating global warming. I had to make a choice—continue my well-paid job with undoubted future advancement in an appreciative company—or attempt however ineffectually to persuade the bosses of Sea Giant to forgo opening up the new field. Idiot that I was, I dared to hope that they would understand the damage that going ahead would cause! I made an appointment to speak with the directors, and was flown out to the rig together with a friend of mine who shared my deep worries about the project.' His face hardened, he paused, and Latimer saw the distress in his eyes.

'You need a drink man,' he said quietly and rising went to Tom's brandy decanter and poured a stiff glassful for Colin. 'Get that down,' he instructed, as he lifted a glass to his lips. Colin obeyed, tossing off the fine old brandy with less than respect, whilst inwardly acknowledging its steadying effect as he prepared to describe his near-death experience.

They sat talking there for over an hour, Colin responding to Latimer's detailed questions with directness and honesty. It was a relief to be able to talk freely not only of Sea Giant's murderous effort to kill him but also of Jonathon King, his good friend and colleague who supported his views and had died on the seabed with the pilot Kevin MacDuff. He opened up further now, explaining the mental anguish to which he was subject.

'Sometimes I'm overcome by guilt that I'm still alive, while two decent men died. It was down to my futile efforts to dissuade SG from going ahead with exploration of the new enormous find of oil and gas—knowing it would accelerate global warming that I took the stand I did.' Charles Latimer looked at him sympathetically, this feeling of guilt was a common reaction shown by those who have escaped sudden death when others had perished.

'Colin—you did what your conscience dictated, as any other decent man would. Now, we have spoken of the massive new oil find—but I understand you had another bone to pick with Sea Giant. Their plan to make deals with the Chinese I believe?' He leaned forward seriously as he spoke and watched Colin's face. 'Want to tell me about this?' Colin nodded in the affirmative, meeting his gaze squarely.

'Yes—I was at one of a previous meeting with SG in their office on the rig. It was well before that final occasion when I laid the facts surrounding global warming before them. They were full praise for me that day, I was to receive an appreciable bonus for my work in detecting the new oil find. Even then my mind was confused as I understood the devastating effects climate change could wreak on the world.'

'Go on!'

'Suddenly there was an emergency call on the intercom—a fault had been detected on the rig—the danger of explosion! I was ordered to remain in the office while Lancaster and his executives rushed off to deal with the situation.' He paused and made a grimace. 'Look, I'm not exactly proud of what I did next, for it was out of character.

I'd been left sitting alone at that oval table only a couple of feet from Lancaster's chair. I stood up, and noticed the MD had left his computer switched on. As I looked across at it, the temptation to discover what their plans were for the new oil field overcame scruples. I walked over, sat down and—what I uncovered filled me with shock! A plan for a secret deal with the Chinese, offering details of a secret method of extracting oil from the seabed at a fraction of normal time and cost---the information stolen from a German scientist—this then for the huge cost the new installation would entail. I made a decision, used my webcam,' He shook his head. Latimer's sharp eyes were probing his face at the words.

'Carry on, Colin. What happened next?' he asked quietly.

'I knew the knowledge I had acquired was political dynamite! But had I the right to reveal it to the authorities? It would mean the downfall of Sea Giant—and I would have to admit to my deliberate disloyalty to the company in taking illegal access to that computer. I also realised I'd put myself in immediate danger should they suspect I had obtained knowledge of their plans. I quickly resumed my original place at the table, and opening up a map I had brought with me, pretended to be studying it. I was just in time as they suddenly returned to the office.

Lancaster glanced towards his computer, then at me, seemed satisfied and made a curt derogatory remark about his chief of security panicking too easily, that we should now get some lunch, after which I was to return to the mainland.'

'How much time elapsed between that day and your last meeting on the rig culminating in their attempt on your life?' probed Latimer. Colin frowned considering

'About a month—during which I visited my minister friend Robin MacKinnon. I knew as a clergyman, anything I discussed with him would never be revealed to anyone else. I asked his advice, explaining my gut feeling that I should go to the police with what I had discovered, but constrained by an inherent loyalty to Sea Giant. We discussed the main causes of global warming of which he was already well aware—and as we spoke together, I debated if there was a chance that if I returned to Lancaster and his colleagues and spoke plainly of the imminent danger the world is in of disaster on an epic scale, sea levels rising to cause massive flooding, together with drought and starvation—vast movements of people escaping such conditions, that they might just listen, change their plans!' He jumped to his feet and started to pace restlessly about the room. 'I guess I was mad to even hope that they would. Money is all that matters to these people.'

'What advice did Minister MacKinnon give you?' asked Latimer curiously. Colin sighed.

'That it was worth trying to reason with Sea Giant, to place undisputed data of the causes of global warming before them, ask them to reconsider their plans to develop the field—his thoughts blending with my own. What an idiot I was to imagine they would listen! Yes, and why did I not realise just how ruthless these men were—would not hesitate to exterminate any who obstructed their plans—and also strike out at their loved ones. My Mary is dead because of my actions. I have to live with that!' he said bleakly, lowering his face to hide his distress. Charles Latimer stood up, bent over him, and placed his hands firmly on his shoulders.

'If your Mary were here with us today, she would applaud the decisions you took—continue to take. Thanks to you, we will be able to prevent this corrupt company from giving aid to a foreign power that has no love for our country. We are indebted to you, Colin Denton!'

'Thank you,' said Colin quietly as he regained his composure and experienced a deep sense of relief at being able to hand everything over to this MI5 man to deal with. 'What about my mother—she was part of your secret organisation?' Charles Latimer smiled.

'It is as you probably have guessed Colin! She was once a member of MI5 and worked closely with Tom—retired quite some years before him. Obviously, you must never mention this fact to anyone else.' Colin nodded as he digested information which confirmed the suspicions that evolved in his mind during the long copter flight down from Skye.

'She is an amazing woman,' he said slowly. 'I suppose my father must have been aware of her work?' He saw Latimer's eyes soften.

'David knew and was most supportive,' he replied. 'He was an exceptional human being, as well as a great doctor You have reason to be very proud of both parents!'

'Thank you—I am,' replied Colin huskily. Latimer nodded and continued.

'Now, you asked if your mother is in present danger from Sea Giant. On the face of it, unlikely. Just consider, they met her briefly on that morning following the copter crash, when they so unfeelingly descended on your wife Mary, and in all likelihood would have considered Geraldine as no more than distressed, grieving mother, who lived hundreds of miles from you and your family.'

'So, there is no need to worry?'

'Except that when carefully examining your computer later, they would inevitably have noticed recent activity on it. As you Colin were supposedly at the bottom of the sea—this would indicate usage by either your wife Mary—or your mother.' He looked at Colin sympathetically.

'I am sure in my own mind it was for this reason that Mary was killed,' said Colin bitterly.

'I agree. I am also pretty sure they will have managed to access your empty house, gone over it with a fine toothcomb in an attempt to clarify how much you'd actually gleaned of their illegal activities.' He saw the younger man's face harden.

'Well, there was a folder and some other data,' said Colin slowly. 'I guess they must have found that then.'

'No, my friend. Your mother discovered it before the SG executives arrived at the house. She hid it and when Mary died, bought it back to Rose Cottage and subsequently passed it on to us. At this time SG has no idea that we are aware of their duplicitous activities.' He saw the continuing anxiety on Colin's face. 'The Ravensnest police are keeping Geraldine's cottage under surveillance, and in addition, she has the support of her next-door neighbour, a young woman called Anna Lindstrom whom Tom and Lottie know and trust. She has been informed of the possible danger your mother faces, and is to contact the Lanscombes should anything untoward occur.'

'Anna Lindstrom?' Colin looked puzzled, 'Mother has only one neighbour—a Daphne Pearson who has lived next door at Bramble Cottage, for around ten years.'

'Well, I can only tell you that this Anna Lindstrom is there now! Seems she is good friends with Geraldine. Guess you will meet her one day when you are able to visit your mother.' He paused and looked up as there was a knock, the door opened and Tom and Lottie appeared to stare at them inquiringly.

'Are you talking privately Charles, or may we join you?' asked Tom.

'Colin has been filling me in on his dealings with Sea Giant—just about covered everything now,' replied Latimer. 'I'll return to London early tomorrow. The sooner we can prepare evidence to arrest those SG bastards the better!'

'I still have one question,' put in Colin. 'How much longer must I wait before seeing my mother—and letting my children know I'm alive?' They looked at him, understanding how agonising the additional pressure of remaining apart must be.

'A few more days at the most, if all goes well,' enheartened Latimer reassuringly. 'We cannot take any risk with your mother's safety at this time. If SG has any slightest suspicion that you are still alive, they are capable of using Geraldine—or the kids as pawns. Be patient, Colin Denton and in the meanwhile enjoy your time here with Tom and Lottie!' He rose to his feet. 'I think I'll retire to my room if that's ok—want to contact HQ!' He left them with a quick smile, thoughts already detached from those in the room.

'He is quite a character, isn't he,' said Colin glancing after him. 'I must say I feel much more positive now I've spoken with him.'

'Charles Latimer has been a good friend and colleague for many years,' said Tom. 'I would trust him with my life—have done so in the past! Lottie and I look at him almost as family.' Colin nodded thoughtfully at his words. Then he posed a sudden question.

'He mentioned a woman now living next door to my mother. I didn't know Daphne Pearson had sold Bramble Cottage, although I recollect hearing that she was visiting her son in New Zealand. Do you happen to know what has happened?' It was Lottie who replied.

'Anna Lindstrom is renting the cottage—who knows, she may be in a position to buy it one day. In the meanwhile, it gives her the security she needs at this time to rebuild her life. She is a fine young woman who has experienced a great deal of trauma over recent years. Incidentally, she has a four years old daughter named Susan who has become great friends with your dear little twins Charles and Melanie!' said Lottie with a smile.

Colin noticed the fondness in her voice as she spoke and it made him vaguely curious about his mother's new friends—but his thoughts were focused solely on his mother and the twins, and his desire to see them again. Nevertheless, it was good to know that there was a supportive neighbour on hand should the need arise. Anna Lindstrom—sounded Swedish or Norwegian he thought casually.

'Colin, we'll have to leave you alone for a few hours tomorrow,' said Tom now. 'We are committed to helping out at Dream Echo once we have seen Charles off—his chopper should arrive about ten. We wouldn't normally leave a guest alone, but the refuge is short staffed and Amber needs us.' He looked at Colin apologetically.

'Of course, you must go—and I'll be absolutely fine by myself!' Colin exclaimed and saw the relief on their faces.

'Best not to go outside—we need to keep your presence here a secret for the time being,' instructed Lottie. He nodded agreement and was beginning to feel very weary, his head aching. It had been a long day.

'You have both been wonderfully helpful. Hopefully, I may be able to repay your kindness one day,' he managed. Tom looked at him and saw the tiredness and strain on his face.

'You're not feeling too good by the look of you! Why don't you turn in now, friend Colin?'

'It's this confounded headache—been getting a lot of them since—the helicopter crash. Get nightmares too.'

'I've got something that may help,' said Lottie quietly and disappeared to the kitchen. She returned with a glass of milk. 'Drink that, I've added an ingredient I've used myself—it will help.' He didn't argue, tossed off the milk and with a word of thanks made for the stairs and bed. That night he slept soundly.

Chapter Eight

Geraldine also slept well that night, secure in the knowledge that not only was her son alive but now a mere drive away and would soon see him again, her little grandchildren able to hear the wonderful news that their Daddy had survived, was coming home!

She had already decided that it would be less traumatic if the twins were to remain at Rose Cottage, than for Colin to move them elsewhere. After all, they had only just settled down in their new school—so perhaps Colin could be persuaded to return to what had been his home before his marriage to Mary—or find a home nearby?

Oh, if only she could tell Anna the good news, but had enough self-discipline to realise it was imperative to preserve a sorrowful appearance in the remote chance that an SG operative might be keeping watch in the neighbourhood. It would not be difficult for them to discover her address if they tried—for doubtless, they were suspicious that she had gleaned their secret plans from Colin's computer.

She checked the children were sleeping soundly before seeking her own bed, and sleepily rejoicing at the prospect of seeing Colin, drifted off as soon as her head touched the pillows. She wasn't sure what had wakened her, instinct perhaps, but suddenly she was wide awake and acutely aware of faint movement downstairs. Had one of the children got up and gone down to get a drink? She reached for her dressing gown, and shrugged it over her shoulders, slipping her feet into slippers.

Walking silently, she checked their bedroom first—both were sleeping soundly. She drew in her breath as she heard those sounds again. Someone was moving about downstairs. She returned to her bedroom, grabbed a small spray can from an alcove shelf and seizing an ornamental poker from the fireside, crept to the top of the stairs. She realised the noise was coming from the sitting room, the door slightly ajar. She tiptoed towards it, gently pushed it wider and peered in. There was only one person there, a man dressed in black, head and face hidden under a mask. He was bending over her bureau and had forced the lock.

Geraldine didn't hesitate, her reaction one of fury at this intrusion. In a few swift steps, she was across the room, shouting fiercely as she came. The intruder's automatic reaction was to straighten in shock. Facing her he received pepper spray in his eyes, causing him to drop the papers he was holding and scream in pain. Now Geraldine brought the poker down across his shoulder with all her strength. She must have injured him severely, for he uttered a howl of agony, rushing clumsily past and out into the hall. She heard the bang of the front door as he left the house. She hurried into the hall herself now and relocked the front door, this time slipping the heavy bolts on. She must have neglected to do so earlier, fool that she was!

Reaction now setting in she returned to the sitting room, subsided into a chair, glancing around at discarded papers littering the floor. Who was he? Could it have been a chance burglar? No—undoubtedly it had been Sea Giant. Her ongoing worries had been realised, they had actually penetrated her home. Yes, and might return, she thought grimly. She looked up as she heard voices, and two small faces peered around the door.

'We heard some strange noises, Granny,' exclaimed Charles. He stared at the untidy room, papers all over the floor. 'What has been happening?' he asked.

'I'm afraid we had a clumsy burglar, Charles,' she said lightly. 'I sent him packing, but he made a mess in here.' The small boy looked at her protectively.

'You should have called me!' he said stoutly, as Melanie ran over and held onto the grandmother, her little face worried.

'He might have hurt you, Granny!' she whispered. 'You should ring the police! Suppose he comes back?'

'Oh—I don't think he'll return, Melanie darling. You see I walloped him hard with a poker,' said Geraldine grimly. 'Now you two, back to your beds—we'll tidy up in the morning!' She hugged them both fondly, managing to disguise the trembling of aftershock. 'I'll come up to the bedroom with you—tuck you in!' She did so, bent over them as they closed their eyes, and waited until their even breathing soon announced them asleep.

Ten minutes later she rang the police station, leaving a message for the sergeant with the night duty constable. Then she thought of the Lanscombes, should inform them—but her son might come rushing over here if he heard what had occurred. She couldn't risk this. No! She would contact Tom and Lottie tomorrow and request them not to mention it to Colin. She did not return to her bedroom, but remained in the sitting room instead and sank into her easy chair pulling a warm throw over her. It was extremely unlikely her visitor would reappear tonight, but she was taking no risks. One of Colin's old cricket bats lay on her knees.

She was just drifting into sleep when there was a knock at the door. She was instantly awake, and firmly grasping the bat slipped into the passage and approached the front door.

'Police here,' came a reassuring voice, with a sigh of relief she unbolted the door and recognised the ruddy face and grey hair of the local sergeant. He glanced at the bat she was holding purposefully. He smiled.

'You can put that down, Mrs Denton,' he said calmly.

'Sergeant Evans—thank goodness! The duty constable said you were at home—were off duty! You should have waited until morning,' she exclaimed.

'Johnson rang me, which considering the circumstances was the correct procedure. May I come in?' he asked gently.

'Yes, of course. Guess I'm still a bit shaken. This way.' He followed her into the sitting room, and took a chair facing her, as his eyes sped around the mess of books and papers and a few smashed ornaments on the floor. She nodded.

'Some clearing up to do—thought I'd leave it until morning, stay alert in case the fellow returns. Mind you, I gave him a good wallop with a poker, after using my pepper spray—so he may not be feeling so spry right now!'

'You did what?' He looked at her in concern. 'You could have been killed!' he exclaimed.

'I'm well used to caring for myself,' she said lightly. He shook his head reprovingly as he looked at the silver-haired woman sitting so casually before him in her dressing gown and slippers, trying to imagine the situation she had been faced with.

'Just tell me what happened,' he said, engaging with Geraldine's calm, slightly amused grey stare. She did so, explaining the recent series of events quietly and concisely.

'I am sure in my own mind that the intruder was sent by Sea Giant. I believe he was searching for anything to confirm their suspicions that I'd had access to my missing son Colin's computer and other data revealing certain secret details that would ruin them if handed on to the authorities.' She knew she had to be extremely careful in what she revealed—but remembered Tom Lanscombe had discussed a little of the case to the police sergeant. He nodded. Knew from what Lanscombe had told him that the people threatening this woman were extremely dangerous—had already killed three people and would not hesitate to deal with Geraldine Denton if necessary.

'Can you describe the fellow, Mrs Denton?'

'He was masked—but I noticed he had a tattoo on his right hand—can't be sure, but a dragon I think. Otherwise well, stocky, about five-ten in height.'

'That's very good,' he approved. 'Have you ever worked in the police force, Mrs Denton?'

'Not exactly—but a certain branch of the civil service,' she replied. He stared at her, got her meaning. This whole affair is even more extraordinary than he had realised. Certainly, there was nothing about the quiet woman sitting so serenely in her comfortable armchair to indicate the possibly active and dangerous work she was once involved in. At the same time, those eyes of hers expressed keen intelligence and the way she dealt with the intruder was quite amazing!

'I could stay here until morning if you like, Mrs Denton?'

'Just call me Geraldine—and it's Will, isn't it? No, I'll be fine. I intend to stay down here—don't think I could sleep after the excitement. You go home, get some sleep yourself!' she advised. He saw from her face that she had made up her mind. He rose to his feet.

'I'll return in the morning. Goodnight, Geraldine!' He did not mention that he would spend the rest of the night in his car keeping watch. He had only been there a few minutes when he noticed the door of the neighbouring cottage open and a young woman came out. She stood staring hesitantly as she saw the police vehicle, seemed to come to a decision, and walking along the pathway, approached his car. He wound down the window.

'Sergeant—it's you! Is anything wrong with Geraldine,' she asked apprehensively. 'I woke up a little earlier, thought I heard a noise—but decided I must have been dreaming. Then I heard the sound of your car arriving and wanted to find out what was going on. She gazed at him anxiously. He smiled up at her.

'It's Mrs Lindstrom isn't it?'

'Yes. Look, I'm aware of the danger Geraldine is in, should have come over immediately—will never forgive myself if those devils have harmed her!'

'There was a break-in. The intruder was going through her papers when Mrs Denton who was in bed at the time, heard sounds downstairs. She tells me she confronted the man, sprayed his eyes with pepper spray, and hit him with a poker. He escaped the scene. She then rang the station, who contacted me at home. She is unharmed, trying to get some sleep now. The best thing you can do is to go back to bed yourself, and see her in the morning.'

Anna turned pale at the news and glanced around nervously.

'Does that mean the intruder is still in the area—may come back and try to attack her again?' she demanded uneasily.

'My guess is he is miles away by now. I doubt if he was in any condition to drive with inflamed eyes—no doubt had a colleague waiting for him in a car.'

'Poor Geraldine—she must have had a terrible shock,' said Anna glancing protectively towards Rose Cottage.

'I have the feeling the intruder had a worse shock!' grinned Sergeant. 'Mrs Geraldine Denton is an amazing lady. Goodnight, my dear.' He watched her disappear back into her cottage. It was good that Geraldine had a good friend looking out for her.

Geraldine catnapped in her chair as the minutes slipped by. At six-thirty, she got up and after a quick shower, decided to ring the Lanscombe's before waking the children. It was Lottie who answered the phone and listened in troubled silence to Geraldine's account of her confrontation with the intruder. So, Sea Giant now knew where Colin Denton's mother lived—had dared to break in.

'Please don't tell Colin about this. He will only come rushing down and could possibly be seen by SG! Lottie, how is my son?' she asked anxiously.

'Fine—absolutely fine! Charles Latimer met with him last night—they had a long talk. I must catch Charles now before he leaves for London, tell him what happened to you—his chopper arrives in an hour. It's good to know the police are watching over you, Geraldine.'

'Sergeant Will Evans proved to be extremely helpful! Well, I must get the children up for school. They woke up in the night and saw the state the room was in, so I told them there had been a burglar!'

'Poor little things! Look, my dear, I must go—call you back later!'

Geraldine sighed. When would all this trauma be over? She was about to wake the twins when there was a knock at the door. She opened it and gave a smile of relief to see Anna standing there, Susan at her side, both were still in their night clothes.

'Come in Anna!' she invited, then noticing the police car parked outside the cottage, raised a grateful hand in greeting, realising Sergeant Evans must have kept watch there overnight. He returned her gesture before driving away.

'Why didn't you call me?' demanded Anna blue eyes reproachful. 'What's the use of knowing you are in danger if you won't let me help you?' She followed Geraldine into the sitting room and saw the disorder. 'Sergeant Evans told me you'd dealt with a burglar. We spoke when I woke up in the night and saw his car outside. Thought I heard some noises before that but decided I must have been dreaming. Want to tell me exactly what happened?'

'Look, I must get the twins up first—then we'll breakfast together. Once I've taken them to school I promise we'll have a quiet chat!' Anna frowned but knew there was no use in arguing, besides which Susan was staring around the usually tidy room with a worried look.

'Did you drop all your books and papers,' she asked Geraldine.

'No dear, a bad man came in here and made a mess. I am going to sort it all out later. Do you want to come upstairs with me to wake Charles and Melanie?'

It was over an hour later and Anna had returned home with Susan for them both to get dressed, Geraldine taking the opportunity to restore order to the sitting room. Luckily the twins had accepted that a burglar had been responsible for the break-in, enthusiastically telling Susan about their night's adventure. Although on the surface all was back to normal, Geraldine remained outraged that her home had been violated by Sea Giant, whilst acknowledging it could have been worse. The intruder could have murdered her—worse harmed her grandchildren! Where was he now? She hoped his eyes remained extremely painful, the blow badly damaged his shoulder. Had there been a car with a driver waiting outside for him? He would not have been able to drive himself—barely manage to see. She tried to recall details of that fraught few minutes. No, she'd not heard the sound of a car driving away. So where did he go? Where was he now?

Her thoughts returned to what little the man had been able to achieve. Obviously, he had been looking for documents connected to Colin's work, with any knowledge of Sea Giant's plans. Although he had broken into her bureau he would have found nothing of importance. It only contained details of special times she had shared with her husband David and now tossed contemptuously on the floor. The bookcase had been similarly searched, two precious ornaments on the sideboard damaged. How long had he been in here before she woke up? Suppose one of the children had come down beforehand—it did not bear thinking of.

There—everything was tidy again, and those ornaments could be sent away for repair. She smiled grimly as she thought of her secret hiding place in the attic accessed by a concealed foldaway ladder. Even Colin did not know of it. It was up there that she had hidden the hard drive when faced with the fact that SG might try to break in at some time. Whomever the intruder had been he was gone, disappointed as well as injured!

There was a knock at the door, as Anna returned with her small daughter Susan looking cute in blue jeans and a sweater.

'Please may I play with Marcasite?' the child asked. Geraldine smiled—then bit her lip as she realised she had not seen her beloved cat this morning. It was unusual for he always stalked into the kitchen at breakfast time. She had been so engrossed in restoring order to the place that she hadn't noticed his absence. She looked around and called his name.

'Marcasite—Marcasite, where are you?' she called. He had probably fallen asleep somewhere, and with Susan beside her went from room to room—checked the bedrooms.

'I bet he's in the garden,' suggested Anna. 'I'll go and look. You get his breakfast ready Geraldine.' A few minutes later Anna returned. She had been crying. Geraldine stared at her wondering what had upset her.

'Anna—what's wrong?'

'I think you should sit down Geraldine dear.' She pointed gently towards a kitchen chair.

'But why?' asked Geraldine bewildered. Then she guessed. 'Is it Marcasite—he's hurt?'

'I found him lying in the front flowerbed—and he's dead. Looks as though someone had deliberately hit him on the head. Oh Geraldine, I'm so sorry! But who in their right mind would hurt a little cat!' She put her hand around Geraldine's shoulders as the bewildered woman burst into quick tears.

'Take me to him,' she said quietly. Neither of them noticed Susan's young face registering her shock as she too heard what had happened, glancing in denial from one to the other of them.

'He can't be dead—I love Marcasite,' she burst out. Anna picked her up and held her tight, trying to comfort her and looked awkwardly at Geraldine.

'I'm so sorry—I think I had better take her home. Don't want her to see....!'

'Of course—the front flowerbed you said. I'll deal with things, you go Anna.' She managed to smile at Susan. 'Marcasite was quite an old cat dear, he will be in the pussycat heaven now,' she said softly. She waited until they had gone, steeled herself to go outside, and walked towards the dahlia bed. She stooped over the dead body of her beloved pet, saw the congealed blood on its head and eyes. Someone must have used quite vicious force to have caused such injuries. She lifted him carefully and bore him round the side of the house to the back garden.

It was done, the small grave tenderly marked by a hastily made twig cross, a small bunch of white roses laid beside it. Poor Marcasite—she had really loved the little animal, with his independent spirit and devotion to her. It could only have been last night's intruder who had acted so. But had it been before he broke in—or later as he fled in pain? It was so difficult to come to terms with the reality of sudden death, be it of a beloved family member—or pet.

Back in the kitchen she made herself a strong black coffee and was about to drink it when she noticed Marcasite's feeding dish and water bowl on the floor. She picked them up and rinsed them carefully before sadly stowing them away on the top shelf of the kitchen cupboard. No time now for grieving her cat. She had to face the fact that Sea Giant had broken in here once already, and was likely to try again.

Richard Lancaster lifted the phone on the large, oval black marble table in his oil rig office.

'Yes?'

'It's Bickerton here sir. I am ringing on behalf of Ted Dawson. I drove him to deal with that Denton woman—dropped him off a couple of hundred yards away from the cottage so she wouldn't hear the car draw up.'

'So why isn't he making his report?'

'He's in a bit of a state I'm afraid. He told me the woman caught him as he was searching the living room—crept in, used the spray in his eyes, almost blinded him—then struck him across the shoulder with some sort of weapon. He managed to get away—and staggered back to find the car. He's in quite a bit of pain I'm afraid...!' and his voice petered out as he sensed his employer's silent anger.

'Are you telling me that a small elderly woman managed to disable an experienced operative? Man must be a bloody idiot!'

'Sorry, sir!'

'Well, what did he find out—any material dealing with Sea Giant in the place?'

'Said he discovered nothing of interest in the living room, checked it over carefully, even broke open a fancy desk. Seems he was on the point of going upstairs to search the bedrooms when the Denton woman suddenly appeared and aimed a pepper spray. His eyes are in a right mess, sir!'

'Serve him damn well right for being careless enough to get caught. Tell the fool he's sacked!'

He put the phone down, eyes hard with annoyance. That bloody Denton woman was an enigma. On the one hand, she had merely appeared as a distressed, elderly mother at their only brief meeting, grieving the death of a son with whom she had enjoyed little contact—living hundreds of miles south. Probably computer illiterate too, he'd surmised, certainly a person of no account. But someone had tampered with Colin Denton's computer on the morning following his drowning. Although it was almost definitely Denton's late wife—there was a slight chance Geraldine Denton might have been involved, hence his decision to track her down and search her home. Now, this!

He looked up as Ross Chambers came in.

'Good morning, Richard! Any news from Dawson?' he inquired, settling his portly form in a chair close to Lancaster.

'He blew it—got himself caught by the Denton woman!'

'No! So—what happened?'

'Seems she squirted pepper spray in his eyes and attacked him with some sort of weapon would you believe? Luckily, he escaped— up to that point he'd found nothing of note in the cottage, but we cannot accept this as conclusive. It raises more questions. Why would an elderly woman possess pepper spray or dare to attack a dangerous intruder? Perhaps there is more to Geraldine Denton than earlier apparent.'

'What next then?' Ross Chambers leaned forward and could see the MD was worried.

'I've just got the gut feeling someone has had access to our business plans. There've been planes hovering about—and a mini-sub surfaced uncomfortably close to the rig. All coincidence perhaps—but? What if the Denton female did manage to take some vital information with her when she rushed off with her grandchildren? And if so, what use would she be likely to put it?'

'But the late lamented Colin Denton lacked opportunity to discover anything regarding our secret plans. Yes, he knew the location of the new field—it was down to him that we identified it. But surely he was not aware of anything else?' His hard eyes probed Lancaster's face, saw a slight indecision there.

'Ross—do you remember the day the fire alarm went off—and we all rushed out of the office to deal with the situation?' he asked. The other man nodded.

'Yes, what of it? It was a false alarm, no harm done!' He was frankly puzzled.

'The point is, we left Denton sitting in here at the table. It was only on our return that I realised I'd left my computer on. The thought went through my head that Denton might have been tempted to look at it. I glanced at him, but he seemed to study a map and I dismissed my suspicion. But what if he had indeed seen details of plans involving the deal with the Chinese?'

'Was this the real reason you ordered the helicopter crash? I thought it was merely on account of Denton's intransigence.' Ross Chambers leaned forward, face troubled. 'No wonder you wanted his wife disposed of if you thought he had left any details in their house.' He shook his head. 'Well, we found nothing when we went back the day after her death—the place was searched thoroughly. Of course, she may have had something in her bag when her car crashed—the fire!'

'That's what I've been telling myself too. But the speed with which Geraldine Denton decided to leave Grantley with her grandchildren got me thinking. It took a quick mind. Then there's the fact she didn't leave her address with the minister's wife—strange that. That's why I took steps to discover her whereabouts. Getting Dawson to search her cottage was more to reassure myself I was being overly suspicious, but now?' and he shrugged irritably 'The way she dealt with Dawson suggests she is not some innocent old granny, but well able to look after herself.'

Ross Chambers shrugged, worried but not convinced. He cast his mind back to their brief meeting with Denton's mother when she had appeared inoffensive enough.

'It is not unusual these days for women to keep pepper spray to protect themselves. As for an elderly woman actively attacking a man—well, I'm not so sure! What do you intend to do?' he probed.

'She loves her grandchildren. I'm considering kidnapping the brats, putting pressure on her for their safe return.' Lancaster's eyes hardened as he spoke.

'Bit extreme—might be traced back to us.' Chambers looked anxious. 'Again, there's no real proof at this stage that she holds any evidence of our plans.'

'So, you think we should merely wait until Geraldine Denton decides to hand whatever she has on us over to the police?' said Lancaster disgustedly. Chambers held up a protesting hand. He knew better than to enrage the volatile MD.

'That's not what I meant! Can't help thinking that if she intended to contact the security services, she'd already have done so by now—why wait!' He stood up, walked over to the window, and looked down on the restless waves so far below. 'If only we could ascertain how much she knows! What about bringing Dawson back up here, question him further—perhaps he'll remember seeing something in that cottage that might offer a clue!'

'I told Bickerton to tell him he's fired—man's a loser!' Lancaster joined him, his eyes brightening as he glanced across the vast expanse of surging waters where beneath its depths a great fortune in oil and gas waited to be exploited. The very thought that all their plans could be brought crashing down through the blundering interference of a witless old woman, was insufferable. But how much did Geraldine Denton actually know? If only he could get his hands on her twin grandchildren she'd be forced to be cooperative! The kids were seven years old he recalled—so at school then—and there could only be one in that small village—so possible to have them snatched as they left school after classes. He would trust his instincts in this affair! He was frowning thoughtfully as he returned to his chair. Perhaps he might give Dawson another chance.

Ted Dawson was in his cheap B&B booked at Oak Dene village, mere two miles from the Denton woman's home at neighbouring Ravensnest—wondering about the future. He removed the cold compress from inflamed eyes using his left hand, shoulder too painful to raise his right. He was feeling very sorry for himself, still trying to digest the news that Lancaster had sacked him. If only he could take revenge on that damn woman who had not only caused him so much pain but also cost him his well-paid job. He had only glimpsed the merest quick impression of her as his attacker raised the spray—aimed! Would never forget that angry determined face.

He gave a distorted grin now as he remembered the calling card he had left her with—of the cat! When cautiously approaching the cottage door, the animal had shot from nowhere out of the bushes loudly yowling at him. As he registered it in the dim moonlight, it suddenly leapt at his leg, claws penetrating his trouser. His reaction had been instinctive, as he knocked it off, then bending reached for a heavy rock, and struck the angry feline several vicious blows on the head. On discerning it lying still, obviously dead, he'd picked it up, and slung it into the dim shape of a flowerbed. Luckily no one seemed to have heard anything. Breathing a sigh of relief, he approached the front door again, cautiously used his skeleton key on the lock—and the door yielded, he was in! As he thought back to the incident now, he experienced a cold delight that he had deprived the Denton woman of her pet. His mobile rang as he sat there. Now, who....?

'Bickerton?'

'The boss has had a change of heart and is giving you another chance. A new job—kids this time. The Denton woman has twin grandchildren, a boy and a girl. Lancaster wants them kidnapped and held in a secure place until he manages to pressurise the granny to reveal whatever it is he wants. Interested?'

'You bet. But my vision is still blurry and my shoulder is bad. I'll need a couple of days' rest first. Why don't you come around here and we'll talk?'

'On my way!'

He let Bickerton in. His erstwhile driver looked at him speculatively as he seated himself on the bed. Dawson still looked a right mess—and he wondered if the man would be fit enough to carry out the task Lancaster had ordered. The autocratic MD wouldn't accept a second mistake. Yet another point to be considered—if they were caught, and arrested for conducting kidnap, would inevitably face many years in jail. However, the lucrative reward Sea Giant's MD was offering for snatching the kids was extremely tempting. They were not to harm the children, merely release them safely when the Denton woman played ball with Sea Giant, so need to feel no moral scruples.

Bickerton explained the task they were charged with. Dawson's face brightened as he listened. He looked keenly at the younger man from bloodshot eyes.

'You say we're to snatch the kids as they come out of school. How are we to know what they look like? The fact that they're twins won't help much as they are boy and girl. Need a photo to be sure.'

'We could keep watch outside the Denton woman's cottage, catch sight of them as they leave for school in the morning!' suggested Bickerton. 'Hide and take a few shots of them with a webcam. Be extremely careful not to be seen, for their troublesome grandmother seems a tough cookie. Do you remember the immediate surroundings of her Rose Cottage? We drove past to check it out, the morning before you made your night-time visit—but I don't recall anything much. Refresh my memory.'

'Well let's see,' said Dawson. 'There's another cottage right next door to the Denton place, no houses opposite, just a hedge separating adjacent fields from the lane—the two cottages completely isolated and half a mile from the village.' Bickerton nodded as memory stirred. He had dropped Dawson off in the dark that night, at the point where the lane left the main road—probably less than two hundred yards from the target. He certainly recalled the state Dawson had been in when he staggered back to the car after his aborted mission. It might have been comical, had it not been for the frustration it would inevitably arouse in Lancaster and his mates. This second job they had been given was likely to be more problematical but lucrative, definitely lucrative! He shut his mind to the risks.

They spoke together for a couple of hours. The most important factor was to discover a safe, secure hiding place for the Denton children. Not for one moment did the fact that it would cause terrible new trauma in their young minds, following on from their parents' recent deaths, disturb their consciences. As for Ted Dawson, he was mentally gloating to think of the distress it would inflict on Geraldine Denton.

Anna Lindstrom knocked and waited as Geraldine opened the door, Melanie and Charles standing ready to leave for school, satchels over their shoulders. They had not seemed unduly disturbed by the unsuccessful burglary the night before last, their grandmother deliberately downplaying the incident. But it was still very much in the minds of Geraldine and Anna, neither of whom had slept much last night.

'How are you this morning, Geraldine?' asked Anna, noting the dark shadows under her friend's grey eyes. But when she spoke Geraldine seemed quite sprightly.

'Decided it's no good worrying. I know Sergeant Evans is keeping watch on the cottage at night. Where's little Susan?' she asked, looking behind Anna expectantly. Perhaps the little girl was waiting in the car already.

'Over there—swinging on your front gate! She will wear it out one of these days,' smiled Anna. 'If these two are ready I'll get them into the car!'

'Thank you, Anna dear. Come in for coffee when you get back.' And Geraldine kissed the children, watched as they skipped down the pathway at Anna's side, Susan waving at them from the gate. It was almost as though the two little families had fused into one she thought, and wondered how things would change once Colin was able to return. Hopefully this would soon happen now, when the authorities garnered sufficient evidence to arrest Sea Giant's corrupt executives. But even knowing this to be the case, Geraldine was seized by a strange sense of unease as she closed the door.

'Mummy—I saw some bright flashes from over there!' announced Susan, as she jumped off the gate and pointed at the hawthorn hedge banking the opposite side of the lane. Anna directed a keen glance there, but saw nothing.

'Probably just sunshine glittering on the morning dew, darling! Let's go—now into the car all of you—seat belts on!' She didn't give Susan's words another thought.

The two men on the other side of the hedge looked at each other. Would the involvement of this second woman complicate matters? She was obviously the Denton woman's neighbour and seemed to have a child of her own.

'She's quite a looker! Lives in that next-door cottage then!' said Bickerton

'Wonder if she collects the kids in the afternoon as well as driving them to school,' growled Dawson, frowning.

'What does it matter—we know what both women look like. The plan must be for one of us to distract whichever woman shows up, while the other one gets the kids into the car,' said Bickerton

'Yes, but this afternoon is just to size things up—check times and feasibility. Can't afford any more mistakes,' growled Dawson. Bickerton grinned.

'You mean—you can't! But I agree that today's for surveillance only. Let's get out of here.'

Geraldine put down her coffee cup, lifted the phone, and recognised the number.

'Lottie?' She visualised the caller's face, the rosy cheeks and bright blue eyes.

'I've been worried about you, Geraldine! Any more unwanted activity at the cottage? I still say you would be best to move out for a few days until Latimer and his colleague are ready to act against Sea Giant! You would be absolutely safe at the Dream Echo refuge and Amber says she will give both you and the darling twins the warmest of welcomes!'

'Thanks, but no Lottie. This is my home and no bloody murdering oil magnates are going to drive me out! Sorted that fellow the other night and I doubt if they will try again!' snorted Geraldine. 'I will be quite safe, Sergeant Evans has arranged for one of his men to keep watch after dark and Anna also on alert, most wonderfully supportive.'

'Well, if you are sure, dear! As we agreed, I didn't tell Colin about the intruder. As you said he would doubtless rush over there—and at this stage it's imperative that his survival remains secret.'

'Thanks, Lottie. So difficult not to see him, but I know it's for the best!' sighed Geraldine. Lottie heard her with sympathy, could imagine her frustration.

'Listen, it is always possible other SG employees are watching the cottage. My guess is that they suspect you managed to get your hands on some of Colin's data implicating their plans. They may make another attempt to break in there despite police surveillance, so be very careful.'

'I will! Tell me, how is Colin really dealing with Mary's death?' asked Geraldine quietly. 'I know how devasted he must be, he loved her so very dearly.'

'He remains rather withdrawn, but I'm sure once he sees you again and his beloved children all will dramatically improve. Look, I must go—off to Dream Echo, another admission expected! Ring me if anything happens and take care.'

Geraldine replaced the receiver thoughtfully. For the first time she began to feel deeply curious about the refuge both Tom and Lottie supported so enthusiastically, and of the young woman who owned and ran it—Amber Williams or Marsden, as her married name was. Had it not been for her commitment to her dear young grandchildren, she might have been interested in helping out there herself. It sounded such a much needed, deeply caring project. She remembered Lottie telling her that one in four women worldwide suffered domestic abuse at some time in their lives, and if she needed an example, there was her friend Anna next door who had escaped her dangerous and predatory partner, Malcolm Greer!

Anna watched as Charles and Melanie scrambled out of her grey Nissan and hurried off to join the other youngsters arriving for morning lessons. One of the teachers, Miss Davenport greeted the children as they lined up ready to go in. She nodded across at Anna, glancing at little Susan, who was looking longingly after the twins—next year she would be joining them, thought the teacher with a smile. Anna took a quick decision and walked over to her.

'Good morning, Miss Davenport. May I have a quick word.'

'Of course.'

'It's just to ask you to keep a close eye on the twins. Someone broke in to Mrs Denton's home night before last—police dealing with it. Don't let anyone apart from their grandmother or myself ever collect them from school!' The teacher looked back at her in surprise, but inclined her head in agreement.

'I'll pass it on to the other staff. Don't worry,' and she turned back to the youngsters surging towards the door. As Anna got back into her car she wondered what had prompted her to make the request. It had just been response to a gut feeling and already she was beginning to feel a little foolish. She decided not to mention it to Geraldine who might think she had become overly anxious. Susan looked at her, as they got out of the car.

'Why did that bad man kill Geraldine's cat,' she asked plaintively. 'I loved Marcasite!'

'Sweetheart, sadly there are a few really bad people in this world—sometimes because they are sick in their minds! But always remember there are a great many more wonderfully kind people out there! Now let's go and see Geraldine!'

'Mummy, may I have a kitten?' the child asked as they walked up the pathway.

'Why—I suppose we could think about it,' said Anna slowly. 'Would you really like one?'

'Yes, oh please—please!' Susan's face was bright with excitement. 'I promise I'll look after it.' Her blue eyes were dancing at the prospect.

'Very well. I'll ask Geraldine the best way to get one,' laughed Anna relieved to see Susan looking so happy again. She broached the subject as Geraldine made fresh coffee, and Susan spread her colouring book on the kitchen table and prepared to use her crayons.

'What kind of cat were you thinking of?' asked Geraldine, instantly interested. 'Pedigree or a moggy?'

'Perhaps a grey tabby something like Marcasite?' said Anna gently. Geraldine nodded.

'Yes, I'm sure Susan would love that, I know how fond she was of him. Maybe I will have another cat one day, but not yet. It's too soon—and could never replace Marcasite.' Anna saw the hurt in her eyes, and mentally damned the man who had killed Geraldine's greatly loved pet.

'I suppose the police have not found any trace of the intruder yet?'

'No—nor think they will. Probably miles away by now, nursing his shoulder,' said Geraldine. 'But I have the feeling they will send someone else. I just hope the authorities hurry up and arrest those heading this vile organisation.' Again, she wished she could reveal the wonderful news that her son had survived, would soon be here and for the first time she wondered how Colin would get on with her new neighbour. Surely, he couldn't help but like her.

'So where do I find a kitten?' asked Anna.

'Sometimes local people advertise them at a newsagent, farmers are another possibility. What about asking school parents—sometimes a pet produces a litter! Avoid those who breed them for profit in squalid conditions. The right one will come along, I'm sure of it dear.' Anna could sense her friend's loss was still too raw to discuss it further at this time and changed the subject.

'Shall I collect the twins from school this afternoon—or would you rather go yourself?' Geraldine hesitated. She wanted to keep close eye on the cottage, just in the unlikely case another SG villain should be watching the place, might take advantage of her absence.

'Would you mind getting them, Anna? I would be grateful,' and so it was agreed.

Colin Denton had been left to his own devices, Tom and Lottie away to assist at Dream Echo. He strolled out into the back garden, seated himself on the bench under the apple tree, trying to make plans for an uncertain future. He was now a single parent, would need to find new employment and his past connection with Sea Giant not the finest recommendation. He must also decide where best to bring his children up—Scotland had been their home, but they had apparently settled down well with his mother at Ravensnest. Could he return there to live, buy a house in the village. It would be good to see more of his mother again. As he sat brooding there he suddenly became aware of a stranger coming towards him from the direction of the house. Who was this— and how had he got in? He stood up, looking at him warily.

'Who are you?' he demanded, then noticed the man's dog collar. The visitor smiled at him, and extended a hand.

'My name is Michael Bonnet, Vicar of St Lawrence—that lovely old Norman church you can see over the fence. I am also a close friend of the Lanscombes who told me you would be staying with them—and mentioned a few details of what brought this about. I thought you might like some company?' His eyes were quietly examining the drawn face of the young man, on whom sorrow had left its mark.

'Colin Denton—glad to meet you vicar,' replied Colin. 'I noticed the church as I arrived here. Dominates the village—beautiful old building.'

He was forcing his words out, attempting to make casual conversation whilst wishing the man had not come to disturb him.

'I saw you down here from the gallery window. You should come over and see the church. We get quite a few visitors dropping in you know.'

'Tom and Lottie requested I should not venture out of Ivy Cottage, my visit to be very private. Perhaps another time once my affairs allow it,' he replied brusquely. The vicar showed no sign of hurt at this rejection, merely smiled and pointed at the bench.

'Well then, perhaps I may join you out here for a few moments, Colin?' he said seating himself and after slight hesitation, the other sank down beside him.

'How much have the Lanscombes told you about me?'

'That you have experienced a terrible time, an attack on your life—and also suffered bereavement, your dear wife I understand?' Colin shot a questioning glance at him, sensing the kindness and integrity in the silver haired vicar. Surely the Lanscombes would not have discussed him with this man if they did not fully trust him. He thought of that other man of the church in far off Grantley—Robin MacKinnon. He came to a decision.

Michael Bonnet listened silently as Colin shared those recent traumatic happenings with him, face becoming grave as he realised the extent of all the distressed man sitting next to him had endured. He sat quietly then reached out a hand to Colin, made silent prayer that he might find the words to bring comfort and peace.

'Colin—my heart goes out to you. You have shown extraordinary courage and endurance,' he began—but Colin pulled roughly away and interrupted him harshly.

'If only I hadn't joined Sea Giant, helped them to discover the new oil field, none of this would have happened,' he blurted out. 'My wife would still be alive, as well as two fine men and this continually torments me. All of it my fault—and to think I was so proud of my achievement at first, and look what it led to!' He sprang to his feet and pacing agitatedly back and forth on the damp grass. Michael rose too.

'Colin, calm yourself and answer a question! Mary, the wife you loved so dearly—would she want you to behave so, constantly berating yourself for events for which you bear no culpability—or would she expect you to start looking towards a good future with those innocent children who are now doubly dependent on you?' The calm question stopped Colin in his tracks. He swung back to confront Michael.

'You are accusing me of self-pity?'

'By no means—but grief can lead to distortion of fact if you let it. You have been the victim of evil men whom I hope will soon to be under arrest and charged for their crimes! 'He paused and smiled. 'But through all you've endured I discern a silver thread of something amazing. I refer to the remarkable way in which you have been led to just the right people to help you to recover physically and mentally. Firstly, the wonderful Norwegian family you spoke of who nursed you back to consciousness—then those folks on Skye. They sound an amazing couple—I'd love to meet them one day! Yes, and there's Robin MacKinnon, your minister friend from Grantly.' Colin listened shamefacedly, knew this silver haired vicar was correct.

'I'm sorry, you're quite right, of course. I must now add you to the list—as well as Tom and Lottie and Charles, a friend of theirs with whom I discussed everything last night.!'

'Ah, that would be Charles Latimer! I know him well and esteem him as good friend. It bears out what I what I was saying!' he said quietly.

'I suppose you are angling this all round to the matter of faith? Not sure what I believe now.' Michael watched him sympathetically. He placed his hands on his shoulders.

'Colin, our lives are in the hands of Almighty God, the mysterious Father of all. Sometimes when tragedy strikes we blame Him for not intervening, preventing the pain we suffer. Yet out of the greatest hurt can come healing and eventual good. However hard, just let go of the anger and despair, and trust the One who never ceases to watch over you.' He drew back, raised a hand in blessing. 'I must go—visits to make to those who are housebound. I hope we may meet again soon, Colin Denton!'

Colin watched thoughtfully as the tall figure strode back across the lawn. He had tried not to like his unexpected visitor, but had been drawn to something very special about him. He had also experienced a very strange feeling when Michael reached out and placed hands on his shoulders, as though a heavy weight was lifting. He shrugged, a faint smile touched his lips. Life went on, he had two children needing his care and protection, and a mother whom he had sadly neglected of recent years—and this must change. He couldn't bear to wait much longer to see his family, must make this clear to the Lanscombes. Suddenly for split second he seemed to see image of Mary's face, and she was smiling at him approvingly.

'Mary,' he breathed. 'I know what I must do now!'

Anna slowly drove the last few yards drawing up beside others who had come to collect their children from school. The pupils were pouring out of the main door now, laughing and jostling. Anna glanced at Susan sitting next to her in the front seat.

'Susan dear, just stay here while I get the twins.' The little girl nodded obediently as Anna stepped out of the car, went through the school gate looking around for Charles and Melanie—saw them in an exuberant group of other youngsters, chatting to a tall stranger. She began to hurry over to them when little Melanie saw her and tugged her brother's arm.

'It's Anna!' she cried, 'Come on!' They ran towards her.

'Melanie darling—you too, Charles! Time to go.' She stared curiously at the man who had been talking to them, had never noticed him here before and wondered who he might be. He smiled casually and turned away watching another few students coming out. Anna helped them in the back of the car. 'Who was that man you were speaking to in the playground?' she asked. The children looked at each other.

'I don't know,' replied Charles in surprise. 'One of the parents I suppose.'

'What did he say?' persisted Anna, wondering why she felt slightly uneasy.

'He said he was someone's uncle—her name was Jane I think,' put in Melanie and started to chat with Susan. Anna relaxed, chiding herself for her suspicious attitude towards the stranger. When she handed the twins over to a welcoming Geraldine, she mentioned the incident lightly.

'Guess I'm becoming overprotective of them,' she said, as the twins ran upstairs to change out of their school uniforms and wash. Geraldine smiled at her gratefully.

'Anna, to be honest, I'm still worried Sea Giant may make another break-in, frighten the children—or worse. I'll be so relieved when the SG corrupt bosses are arrested and brought to trial and…!' She bit her tongue, had almost mentioned the wonderful news that Colin was alive, would soon be here. It was so hard to keep quiet. 'You'll stay and eat with us Anna—it's shepherd's pie, plenty for all! I know that Susan likes it.' She glanced fondly at the pretty, little fair-haired girl who had so loved poor Marcasite. She really must help Anna to find a kitten for her young daughter. She was still thinking of Anna and Susan as she lay in bed that night, of how close they had become, so much part of each other's lives. She found herself wondering what Colin would think of them.

The following morning Anna arrived to collect the twins for school, and as she found Geraldine was still reluctant to leave the cottage, also agreed to collect them that afternoon. Her young daughter Susan loved their trips to the school, looking forward to next year when she could join Charles and Melanie there.

Geraldine watched fondly as her young grandchildren skipped down the garden pathway towards Anna's car with all the spontaneous, light hearted behaviour of normal children—so different now from the two bewildered, unhappy youngsters she had brought back from Grantley following the shock of both parents' death. Once those villainous executives running Sea Giant were brought to justice and the children's father could safely return, how different life would be. Nothing could replace the loss of their dear mother—but learning their father was still alive and actually having him back again would bring inestimable joy. She smiled as she imagined that reunion.

Chapter Nine

Dawson grinned his satisfaction as he examined the broken-down shed they had discovered situated in a farm field. It contained a rusty harrow, various scythes and hooks hanging on its walls, probably all left there for years as more work became automated. The place hadn't even been locked, so extremely doubtful anyone would come near it. The two men had noticed it as they drove slowly along the country road. The main farm buildings were quarter of a mile away. It would have to do!

'We need to be able to secure it,' said Bickerton critically. 'There's no key.'

'Yes, there is—look, hanging on that nail!' said Dawson, pointing.

'Let's make sure it works,' advised Bickerton. The lock was stiff after many years of disuse, but the key eventually turned. They exchanged glances of pleasure, and retraced their steps across the field to where they parked their car on a verge.

'Just thought of another problem,' said Bickerton. 'How are we to drag two struggling kids across a field in full daylight in view of any who might come out of that farmhouse?'

'We keep the kids in the car until its dark. Guess we might have to be drug them to make sure they keep quiet. How about crumbling sleeping pills into a couple of chocolate drinks—then hide the kids in the boot of the car until we are ready to move them to the shed,' suggested Dawson, his quick mind coming up with solution.

'Excellent!' agreed Bickerton approvingly.

'Now listen,' said Dawson, 'Your job is to distract whichever of the two women come to collect the kids from school. If it's the young woman we saw yesterday she will likely recognise you, so chat her up while I get the kids into the car.'

'And have you thought how you are going to do that when they will be surrounded by other kids and parents, probably some teachers too around?' asked Bickerton. 'Children are always warned not to go anywhere with strangers!'

'Leave that to me,' returned Dawson confidently.

Geraldine was running her eye down the ads column in the local newspaper, when under the heading 'Pets' she found what she had been looking for. She read it thoughtfully--'Free good homes needed for four adorable kittens.' There was a telephone number. She rang and a woman's voice answered her.

'Good afternoon,' began Geraldine. 'My name is Denton. I saw your ad about the kittens. My next-door neighbour is looking for a kitten for her small daughter. My own precious cat died recently and little Susan was very fond him. Her mother wants to get her a pet of her own.'

'Thank you for your call, Mrs Denton. I met you in the library once. It's Joyce Masters.'

'Yes, of course I remember you! What are the kittens like?'

'Not pedigree or anything like that—but really cute! Bob and I were led to believe that our Patches had already been neutered when we took her on, so their subsequent arrival a surprise. Why don't you bring your neighbours little girl to see them?' and she gave the address.

Geraldine put down the phone and smiled. Perhaps she would take a risk and leave the cottage for a short while. She'd tell Anna that she would collect the twins herself so allowing the young mother to take Susan around to meet Joyce Masters and see the kittens. She opened the cottage door, meaning to catch Anna before she left for school, but was just too late saw the grey Nissan disappearing along the lane. Well, she would follow, perhaps they could visit Joyce and view the kittens together. She locked the cottage door, set off in her beige Ford in pursuit of Anna.

Bickerton parked the black Citroen unobtrusively at the end of the few vehicles already waiting outside the school, and glanced around. Would the Denton woman arrive to pick up the kids herself, or would it be her young neighbour?

'See either of them?' he asked Dawson.

'Yes—look, there's the grey Nissan drawing up.' They watched as Anna stepped out and began walking towards the playground gate. 'Now!' ground Dawson out urgently. Bickerton got out, following behind Anna. He drew level, jostled against her and smiled apologetically.

'Look I'm sorry, wasn't looking where I was going! Didn't hurt you, did I?' Anna stared back at him, recognised him as the stranger she had seen yesterday.

'I'm fine. No harm done,' she said lightly and prepared to walk on. He touched her arm.

'Guess you're here to collect your youngsters—saw you with them when I was waiting for Jane. Doing my avuncular duty while my sister recovers from a sprained ankle. My name's Eric Crawley—and you?'

'Anna Lindstrom. I must collect the twins,' she said, wishing he would go away. There was something about the man that made her feel uneasy. The children were beginning to come out of the school door now, running down the front steps and surging on towards the playground gate. She attempted to take a step forward, but the stranger suddenly pulled her about and smiled down at her appealingly.

'Look—I was intrigued when I saw you yesterday—would like to get to know you better. Would it be possible for us to have a coffee together some time?' he asked continuing to hold her arm. She wrenched angrily away, as the first of the children pushed past them.

'Let me go! I want nothing to do with you!' she snapped. He ignored her words and placed himself in front of her, still smiling down blandly. At this moment another group of children came out of the school door, the twins amongst them. As they looked around for Anna a strange man walked across to them. He smiled, showing twisted front teeth.

'You two are the Denton youngsters?' he confirmed. Charles looked up at him suspiciously, didn't like him instinctively.

'Who are you?' he retorted, taking his sister's hand protectively. The stranger looked at him approvingly.

'Good boy,' he said. 'You should never talk to strangers—unless of course it's someone that your grandmother's friend Anna has sent! Her car broke down, and she rang me and asked if I would drive you home. My name's Arthur—live in one of the new houses at the back of the high street. Car's over there—come along now, I need to get back to my old mother as soon as I get you home. She's in bed.' He took Melanie's other hand, forcing Charles either to come with him or let go of the little girl. 'There's some candy in the car—yes, and chocolate milk-shakes too,' he said persuasively. He tightened his grip on Melanie's hand.

'Let me go!' she cried, as he began to pull her firmly along, while Charles now thoroughly alarmed tried desperately to free her. It only took a few minutes to force the reluctant children out of the school gate, past Anna who was also struggling to get away from Bickerton's advances.

Dawson bundled them into the back of the dusty black Citroen, slammed the door and locked it, jumped into the front seat. He grinned over his shoulder as he glanced back at the playground gate, and to his relief saw Bickerton hurrying towards him. So far it had all gone like clockwork.

Anna's face was red with annoyance as she broke free of the stranger's annoying advances and at last pushing through the gate into the playground, looking around for the twins. As she did so, Miss Davenport came hurrying to meet her.

'Mrs Lindstrom—I just saw a strange man take the twins with him! It was when I was helping a child with nosebleed, and too late to stop them,' she panted. Anna went pale. 'I only had a brief glimpse, stocky, thickset—remembered you had warned me to prevent anyone other than you or their grandmother collect them. I'm so sorry, but it was all so quick!'

'Did he take them on foot—or was there a car waiting?' asked Anna, beginning to tremble in shock.

'They went towards a black car. You've no idea who the man could be?' she faltered.

'No!

'No, but we must call the police at once! Their grandmother will be absolutely distraught,' added Anna grimly. 'Look, I must get my Susan—she's over there in the Nissan, will be getting anxious waiting—I won't be a moment. Ring the police and let the headmistress know!' She ran to the car, helped Susan to scramble out. The child looked at her from troubled eyes.

'Mummy, what's going on? Why did Charles and Melanie go off with that strange man?' she asked. Anna knelt beside her, looked at her anxiously.

'Susan! You saw what happened?'

'Yes. You were speaking to that tall man who was here yesterday,' said Susan. 'Then I saw the twins coming out of the school door. A strange man took their hands. He seemed to be pulling them along. When you got away from the other man who was speaking to you, he hurried after the man with the twins—they got into a black car together and it drove away.' Anna looked down in shock at her daughter's worried young face as the child asked, 'Those men won't hurt Melanie and Charles will they Mummy?'

'Darling, it will all be all right, but I have to speak to the police about this—they will be coming here to the school,' said Anna, as she led Susan across the almost empty playground. And she must also let Geraldine know, she thought.

Geraldine had been on her way to the school, when she slowed down outside the local book shop, remembered she had ordered an illustrated book of fables for Charles and Melanie. She went in, paid for it and chatted for a moment with the proprietor, and returned to the car. She should still be in good time to catch Anna—or meet up with her as she collected the twins, she thought, but frowned as she glanced at her watch, it was later than she had thought.

She was just driving off along the street when a black car sped past, going through the village at a reckless speed. She glanced at it disappear in her rear mirror. Idiots, she thought. She arrived at the school now, to see the playground was almost empty—but Anna's Nissan was still parked outside the playground gate. Perhaps Anna had stayed behind to speak with the teacher. As she got out of her Ford, she heard the sound of a siren and saw the police car speeding towards her. And suddenly Geraldine felt a cold fear grip her heart, guessed instinctively, something terrible must have happened to the children. She ran into the school building, calling Anna's name. The office door was opened and she saw Anna with Susan beside her, speaking with Mrs Walters the Head Mistress, and Miss Davenport—but no sign of the twins.

'What's happened?' she demanded through stiff lips. 'Where are the twins?'

'Geraldine, it's so awful—they've been snatched!' cried Anna, shakily. 'I was distracted for a few minutes by a man who tried to detain me. I'm so very sorry.' Even as Geraldine was receiving the news, two police entered behind her and overheard the exchange. One of them Sergeant Will Evans looked sympathetically at Geraldine. Poor woman—how would she cope with this new disaster if it proved to be a case of kidnap! Then everyone was talking at once. Sergeant Evans held up his hand for silence.

'Who saw the kidnapper's car?' asked the sergeant, glancing from Anna to the staff.

'I got a quick glimpse,' said Miss Davenport. 'A black saloon, didn't see what make. It was all so quick—I was helping a child with nosebleed.'

'Yes, it was a black car!' put in Susan's small clear voice. 'I was in our car waiting for Mummy. A bad man was dragging Charles and Melanie along. He pushed them inside his car. There was another man speaking to my Mummy—then he rushed over and got in the car too. They drove away!'

'I think I may have seen them too,' exclaimed Geraldine in a low voice and explained about the black car that had sped past her. 'It was being driven dangerously fast,' she added. Anna looked at her in distress. If only she had been more alert.

'I can only believe that this same stranger I mentioned yesterday was party to what has happened. He must have been watching, making plans for today. Oh Geraldine, I'm so dreadfully sorry!' She was beginning to sob in frustration, Geraldine however had managed to regain her self-control. This was no time for panic. Sergeant Will Evans shot her a quick glance.

'This car you saw, Mrs Denton—I don't suppose you caught the registration number?' he asked hopefully. She was about to shake her head, when a strange flash of memory brought the scene back into consciousness and Sergeant Evans looked at her in astonishment, repeating the number she quietly gave.

'That's remarkable, if you've got it right!' He made a call. Minutes later he gave a satisfied smile. 'A black Citroen! It's registered to a fellow called Bickerton whose employers are the oil company Sea Giant!' Geraldine went cold as she heard his words.

'Dear Heavens—no!' she gasped. Although already convinced they were culpable for this outrage, as well as for her recent break-in, it was still hard to have it confirmed. Sea Giant had already taken the lives of two innocent men and her daughter-in-law Mary, and almost killed Colin. Were her dear little grandchildren now to be added to the list? Then logic took over. After the abortive break-in at her cottage, the twins had been kidnapped for one reason only—to put pressure on her to reveal all she knew about SG's plans.

'We have to find that car then,' said Constable Dale Roberts, 'You'd have had no idea where it was going, Mrs Denton?' She shook her head, trying to ignore her pounding heartbeat.

'Heading back the way I'd come, so out of the village—but there are several turnoffs aren't there, lanes leading off into farmland, as well the one that runs past my cottage. But if they kept to the main road—they could be in the next village along by now.'

'Hazelford, four miles away,' said the Roberts, glancing at the sergeant. 'Should we get over there, Serge?'

'Got the feeling they will hide the kids somewhere nearer than that,' retorted Sergeant Evans. 'They must be aware we'll be involved, and roads watched.' He looked at the two troubled school teachers listening quietly to the conversation. 'I think you ladies should close afternoon school as usual now,' he said addressing them with a calm smile. 'Ask that you do not discuss what you've heard with anyone else.' They gave quiet agreement, as he then shepherded Geraldine, Anna and Susan out of the school, across the playground and onto the road.

'I advise you both get straight home,' he said, then looking at Geraldine, 'The kidnappers will undoubtedly make contact very soon with their demands.' Within minutes they were making the short return drive, the police car closely behind. Anna held Susan's hand and waited as Geraldine unlocked Rose Cottage door. entering behind her, followed by the police officers.

'I will remain here with you, need to listen in to any phone calls you receive,' instructed the Sergeant but Geraldine shook her head decisively.

'No Will—Anna will stay here with me. You'd be better employed trying track the abductors down. I promise to let you know immediately they contact me.' He saw her determined face and reluctantly nodded his agreement.

'In that case, I'll phone policewoman Julie Bird to come over and stay with you, she's a good dependable officer, and will be most supportive.'

Dawson glanced behind him to the Citroen's back seat, where two small figures were sitting in frightened silence, the boy holding his sister's hand protectively. So far all had gone to plan, and he gave a short chuckle, and turned his head to regard the man next to him.

'Well Bickerton—stage one successfully carried out. Now to find somewhere safe to park until dusk. Have to get off this road in case the police are on lookout!'

'What about opening one of those field gates, and parking behind a hedge!'

'Good thinking!' Dawson braked as they approached the next gate. Bickerton got out and opened it, closing it as Dawson carefully angled the car parallel below the bushy hawthorn hedge.

'There're some cows over there,' announced Bickerton, pointing uneasily at a black and white herd, as he got back in.

'They won't hurt us! Relax,' said Dawson loftily. Now the car had come to a standstill, Charles looked towards their captors apprehensively.

'We want to go home!' he called out in his most determined voice. 'Granny will be worrying about us—and we're hungry!'

'You'll shut up if you know what's good for you!' snapped Dawson, but Bickerton poked him in the side, and gave him a meaningful grin.

'You said you'd something for the kids to drink, didn't you? And what about those chocolate milkshakes—that will keep them quiet!' Dawson nodded, got his meaning, groped under the dashboard and produced two cartons and a bag of sweets. He tossed them behind him.

'Get that inside you, kids! Nothing bad will happen to you if you behave—if not...!' he added threateningly, and saw the little girl shrink back against her brother.

Charles looked at the milkshakes. He had always been told never to take anything from strangers, but he was hungry and thirsty. He handed a milkshake to Melanie.

'It's ok, Melanie,' he whispered. They began to gulp the thick creamy liquid down—and minutes later their heads drooped, as they fell into a drugged sleep. The men exchanged satisfied glances. It was an easy job to lift them out and place them in the boot of the car.

'We'll wait two or three hours,' said Dawson. Did you bring sandwiches?'

'No, sausage rolls—got them here. And there's beer.'

Young Danny Mills noticed the black car parked over by the hedge as he came to collect the cows for milking. What was it doing there— probably belonged to townspeople on holiday many such were neglectful in closing gates behind them. He decided to mention it to his father. He was going to approach and ask their business, but the cows were restless and he shepherded them through the gate into the adjoining field and across to the milking shed set amongst barns close to the farmhouse.

'Dad—saw a strange car parked in the low meadow,' he informed his bluff faced father, who looked back at him in interest.

'What kind of car, Danny lad?' he asked keenly. 'The police have alerted everyone in the area—they're on the lookout for a black saloon.'

'I couldn't see much from where I was,' explained the lad. 'It was parked on the far side of the field under the hedge, alongside the road.' He thought back, 'Yes, it was definitely black,' he volunteered.

'Good lad,' said Farmer Mills. 'I'll be with you in a jiffy—get the beasts into the stalls.' He pulled his mobile phone from his pocket, made a quick phone call.

Dawson and Bickerton were relaxing in their car, after consuming their bagful of cold sausage rolls, washed down by a couple of cans of beer.

'Those cows have disappeared,' said Bickerton, staring across the field in. Dawson nodded.

'Yes—saw a lad driving them through that gate on the other side of the field a few minutes ago,' he said casually. Bickerton glanced at him in alarm.

'Do you suppose he noticed the car?'

'No idea. Who cares! It wouldn't have meant anything to him,' said Dawson complacently. Bickerton frowned uneasily, threw the empty cans and paper bag out of the window, and glared at him reprovingly.

'Depending on whether anyone actually saw you get the kids into the car, and may possibly have given a description to the police, there may be an alert—they could be looking for us.'

'One black car is much like another to most people,' said Dawson. 'Look, if you're seriously worried that the lad may report seeing us— we'll move. That hiding place we have chosen for the kids is only about a couple of miles away. We may as well drive over there now. Hopefully find a nearby field to park the Citroen until dark. Let's go.'

Sergeant Evans received the call with satisfaction—and turned the police car about. On arrival at the field gate Farmer Mills had described, both he and his fellow officer leapt out and approaching the gate, glanced over it hopefully. But no black car stood there. Evans breathed a sigh of frustration, but opened the gate nevertheless and glanced around. He saw deep, muddy tyre marks on the wet grass where the car had reversed.

'Look at this, Serge!' cried the constable pointing to the empty beer cans and crumpled paper bag he had spotted as he bent and handed them over. Sergeant Evans opened the bag, saw the crumbs, noticed a receipt, glanced at it and nodded.

'These sausage rolls were purchased in the village earlier this afternoon—'Ford's Bakery', he exclaimed with satisfaction. He made a call on his mobile.

'Is that you Mrs Davidson—Sergeant Evans here. I believe you sold six sausage rolls this afternoon. Do you recall the person who made the purchase?'

'Sold a lot of sausage rolls today, Sergeant. But there was a man who bought six—I remember him because he also bought two cartons of chocolate milkshake. Thickset man, had a strange tattoo on his hand—a dragon I think.'

'You have been most helpful, Mrs Davidson—many thanks!' There was excitement in his eyes as he looked at Roberts. 'A dragon tattoo—Geraldine Denton noticed one on the hand of the man who broke into her cottage! Now the same devil has her grandchildren. Can't wait to get my hands on him and the other bloke—Bickerton!' Constable Roberts nodded vigorous agreement, and was about to reply when he noticed something else in the long grass!'

'What's this then—milkshake cartons!' he picked them up, they weren't quite empty and some of the chocolate ran over his hand. 'Look Serge!'

'Bag them, Roberts—they must have given them to the kids. Now where the hell have they taken them?' He rubbed his chin. 'My guess is they plan to stay in the area, hence their brief break here.'

'So which way have they have they gone now?' Roberts puzzled.

'Somewhere remote—certainly not in the village. I've the feeling they were waiting until dark, otherwise why bother wasting time in this field. That farm-lad appearing must have prompted them to scarper.'

Geraldine was doing her best to remain calm as Anna offered her a fresh cup of tea which again she left untouched, too tense even to drink. Anna studied her from worried blue eyes, knowing that apart from offering her presence, there was little she could do to help—and retreated to the kitchen where Susan was busy with her colouring book. It was an hour now since they had returned to the cottage, to be joined by P C Julie Bird, the supportive young woman who was sitting by the phone.

'If only the kidnappers would make contact!' Geraldine burst out in frustration.

'They will soon, I'm sure of it,' said Julie. 'Try not to worry, we will get your grandchildren safely back, I promise you.' Geraldine forced an anxious smile, knew the policewoman was making a promise perhaps unable of fulfilment. At least she had rung Lottie Lanscombe who was going to let Tom know. But what they could do so many long miles away? She had exacted a promise from Lottie not to inform Colin of his children's kidnap. Under no circumstances must her son appear here and risk being seen by these vile employees of Sea Giant.

Dawson and Bickerton sat tensely in the car waiting for dusk. They had parked in another field in similar to that they had recently vacated, and again behind a hedge. They were now less than half a mile from the derelict farm shed where they planned to leave the children. Bickerton got out of the car to stretch his legs and on sudden thought opened the boot to check on the children, looked down on them in satisfaction. They were still sleeping. That medication must have been strong! It was getting darker. He checked his watch, and glancing upwards noticed the heavy clouds gathering in the sky above. It looked as though it was going to belt down with rain anytime soon. Good, less likely for anyone to be around. He returned to Dawson, taking his ease in the front seat.

'Time to move the kids, Dawson! Brats still fast asleep, should be easy to carry.'

Dawson was instantly alert. Grabbing a couple of plaid rugs brought in readiness, he joined Bickerton by the open boot. As he did so, the first drops of rain began to fall.

'You can just about see the shed over there,' said Bickerton. 'Ready?' He bent as he spoke and lifted the still form of the little fair-haired girl in his arms.

'Put this over her,' instructed Dawson, tossing a rug at him. He watched as Bickerton arranged it around the girl, stepping back to allow Dawson access to the second child. Dawson checked Charles was still asleep, then scooped him up similarly covering him.

'Right—let's go,' he said. They started across the stubbled hay meadow denuded of its summer grass and wild flowers, the rain splashing down on them now, quickly soaking through their own clothes and the plaids covering the children. They proceeded with greater caution as they approached the shed. They could see lights going on in the farmhouse about quarter of a mile further on, but no one was around.

The shed smelt sour and mouldy inside as they tossed the children carelessly down in a corner.

'Pity the rugs got wet,' said Bickerton.

'They're lucky to have them,' replied Dawson callously. 'Look—I've brought biscuits and orange drinks in case they get hungry when they wake. See that hook in the roof, I suggest we secure them to that, so they can't get to the door—we've only lightly tied their hands, they should be able to move to eat to eat. Help me—a cord round their waists so, and up there on the hook. There, that should do!'

'Suppose they call for help?'

'Who will hear them? Why would anyone come near this tumbledown shed—stop worrying. Our next step is to contact the Denton woman. She'll be frantic by now—bitch!' added Dawson with a satisfied smile.

'What if the police listen in to your call? She's bound to have notified them!'

'I know what I'm doing. You stick to your driving,' said Dawson loftily

'Huh! You didn't do so well last time you were dealing with the woman. She doesn't sound like your average pensioner!' declared Bickerton lightly, then drew back as he saw the sudden fury on Dawson's face—the fellow obviously had a short fuse. 'Best get out of here before they wake,' he said nervously and edged towards the door. Dawson glowered but nodded. He knew he should ring Lancaster first before contacting Geraldine Denton but wanted opportunity to prove his quick thinking and reliability. He turned the rusty key in the lock, pocketing it as they left.

Tom Lanscombe listened in troubled silence as Lottie caught up with him in Dream Echo's grounds, where he was bending over a bed of brilliant red and gold cactus dahlias.

'You say the twins have been kidnapped in broad daylight? How could this happen!' he exclaimed, drawing heavy brows together in shock. He put an arm about his wife's shoulders as he saw the distress in her blue eyes. 'Lottie dear, I'll ring Charles Latimer with the news, then drive straight to Ravensnest and see what help I can give Geraldine.'

'What about Colin?' she questioned, 'Part of me thinks he should be told—but Geraldine said not to!' He frowned as he considered the situation.

'Then I think we have to trust her judgement in this, my love. I'll get back to the cottage and grab a bag—will tell Colin I've been called away on business. If you hear any more from Geraldine in the meanwhile, phone me.' He paused as he saw a slim figure in a navy trouser suit approaching, her chestnut hair ruffled by the light breeze.

'Lottie—so this is where you are. May I take you away from Tom—another woman on the way! Apparently, she's deeply traumatised, broken ribs and facial injuries. Two small children coming with her.' Amber turned unusual golden-brown eyes on Lottie, their arresting shade reflected in her name. It was she who owned and ran this secret women's refuge with the help of a few devoted people, Lottie and Tom amongst them.

'I'll come at once,' said Lottie quickly, but Amber sensed her friend's agitation.

'Is something wrong?' she asked. Lottie nodded.

'Yes, Amber. You remember our telling you about Colin Denton whom we're caring for at Ivy cottage? We've just heard his twin children were kidnapped this afternoon and almost certainly on the instructions of that corrupt oil company, Sea Giant!' she blurted.

'But that's dreadful!' cried Amber, her lovely face troubled. 'His children were in the care of their grand-mother, right? Poor woman! I take it the police are involved.'

'I'm off to Ravensnest to see what help I can offer,' said Tom. 'Lottie—don't forget to phone me with any news!' and he turned swiftly away. Amber took Lottie's hand and held it reassuringly.

'I pray they will be rescued soon and restored safely home,' she said quietly. 'Come inside now and have a coffee. You've had a shock.'

'Geraldine Denton was a close colleague and good friend of ours a few years ago when Tom was in MI5,' explained Lottie. 'She doesn't want Colin informed about the situation—his own life still in danger if they find out he survived the helicopter crash. I'm going to find it difficult to behave naturally in front of him when I get back to Ivy Cottage,' and she bit her lip. Amber squeezed her hand understandingly.

'What dangerous devils those Sea Giant officials are! I remember only too well my husband's near death at the hands of another similarly corrupt organisation—Oleumgeldt, when he attempted to expose them through his work as an investigative journalist.' Her eyes blazed as she recollected those events.

'You're right Amber, both companies driven by greed and totally unscrupulous! What you went through for over a year in believing your Robert was dead, quite unimaginable,' sympathised Lottie. Amber smiled and looked at older woman reassuringly.

'More importantly my dear husband is alive and well and helping to run Dream Echo—while many of Oleumgeldt's corrupt officials either languishing in prison—or dead! I'm sure that the evil lot operating Sea Giant will meet a like fate!' she declared firmly and Lottie nodded, raised an answering smile.

'Hopefully Tom and others will find the children and take them safe home to Geraldine. He's about to ring Charles Latimer, seek his advice,' she added, but her eyes betrayed ongoing worry as she walked back towards the refuge with Amber, attempting to re-channel her thoughts towards the latest abused woman about to enter their gates.

Dawson was still debating whether to proceed with the enterprise on his own. Should he phone the Denton woman personally, applying pressure to make her reveal whatever secret matter she was privy to and thus causing Sea Giant to resort to their present drastic action? It must be of supreme importance for them to have resorted to ordering her grandchildren's kidnapping. Perhaps if he had such details in his own possession, then…?

'Have you contacted Lancaster yet?' asked Bickerton. 'We need to get fresh instructions!'

'Your job is to drive and assist—I take all necessary decisions,' replied Dawson grandly.

'If you muck this job up, then it's curtains for any other work for Sea Giant!' said Bickerton uneasily, but after a glance at Dawson's dark expression desisted from questioning him further.

Geraldine glanced out of the window. It was dark now. Where were her precious little grandchildren? Had they been hurt—certainly they must be terrified. Anna sitting opposite on the couch with Susan read her thoughts and reached a hand out to her.

'It will be alright, I'm sure of it,' she said softly. She looked at policewoman. 'Julie, it's getting dark, almost seven. Surely we should hear from the kidnappers soon?'

'I'm surprised we haven't so far,' replied the officer. 'Sergeant Evans just texted me—he's on his way back here.'

'Did he say if he has discovered any clues?' Geraldine began urgently when at that moment there was a sudden knock at the door.

'That must be the sergeant now,' said Julie. 'I'll let him in Mrs Denton.' But when she opened the door it was to face a man she'd once met briefly at the station when he had spoken with Sergeant Evans—she tried hard to remember his name as he smiled at her.

'It's Tom Lanscombe, officer—a close friend of Geraldine Denton. May I come in?'

'Of course, sir,' and she locked the door after him. 'You know what has happened?'

'Yes. Any news of the kidnapper yet? Have they made contact?' he inquired as he followed her through to the sitting room, she shook her head.

'No. Sergeant Evans is on his way back here now—he's been out searching for the twins. Poor little things must be terrified,' she said quietly and drew back as Geraldine saw the ex MI5 man and jumped to her feet. He drew her into his arms, and stroked her hair soothingly.

'Geraldine dear, so terribly sorry to hear the worrying news. Lottie sends all her love, would have come with me but they are rushed off their feet at the refuge.' He paused. 'As you wished I haven't told Colin what has happened. When he saw me packing a bag I said I had a business meeting and would be away for a day or so, but that Lottie would be back with him soon.'

'Colin is all right?' she asked anxiously.

'Yes, my dear. Now just fill me in with all that you know so far.' He turned his glance on Anna. 'Glad you are here, Anna.' She smiled back at him.

'I'll make coffee. Would you like a sandwich?' she asked. You've had a long drive.'

'Coffee would be good, Anna. Hallo there young Susan,' and he smiled at Anna's small daughter, then turned his full attention back on Geraldine. 'Tell me everything from the beginning,' he instructed and hearing his familiar calm voice, Geraldine relaxed slightly. He listened attentively to her account, asking quick questions as she proceeded.

'So, we have a description of the kidnapper, and details of the getaway car—not a bad start,' he approved, and paused as there was another knock at the door. 'I'll go,' he said. and minutes later returned chatting with Sergeant Evans and Constable Roberts.

'I'm certainly glad to see you, Mr Lanscombe,' the sergeant was saying. 'How right you were when you alerted us of possible attacks on Mrs Denton. As you may be aware she fought off an intruder a few nights ago—then today this fresh assault on her family.' He sank down on the settee, as Roberts took an upright chair.

'What have you discovered about the kidnappers so far?' demanded Tom crisply.

'One of them has been described as stocky and having a dragon tattoo on his hand, which identifies him as the same man who broke in here that night and whom Mrs Denton forced out with her pepper spray and a good walloping! We don't know his name yet, but his colleague is a man named Bickerton and an employee of Sea Giant!' He saw the excitement in Tom's eyes.

'So, a definite direct link to Sea Giant! Well done. Now any clue as to where they've taken the children?' he asked urgently.

'We tracked their earlier movements to a field just outside the village where they made a brief stay.' He gave details of the few items they had discovered on the grass where the car had been parked.

'You still have the milkshake cartons?' asked Tom.

'Yes, nothing out of the ordinary, bought in the village together with some sausage rolls. My thought is the drinks were for the kids—the men had been drinking beer, found the cans.'

'I would suggest any residue left in the cartons is checked for drugs,' said Tom and saw Geraldine stiffen at the suggestion. He smiled at her reassuringly. 'They would have wanted to keep the twins quiet, so some sort of tranquiliser used.' He returned his attention on Evans. 'Any clue as to where they may be now?' The Sergeant shook his head.

'No, but my thought is possibly an old barn or a derelict cottage. Something of that sort,' he volunteered and caught Tom's approving stare.

'And do you have a list of such properties,' Tom pursued.

'I've already checked the only two derelict cottages I know of—drew a blank. I've also phoned around farms asking them to check any neglected barns, again no joy. Will drive around again at daybreak.' He shook his head. 'I am surprised they haven't already phoned Mrs Denton with their demands.'

'Yes, it's strange,' agreed Tom thoughtfully. 'Possibly waiting instruction from their bosses.' He turned his eyes on Anna sitting with Susan on her lap, the child falling asleep.

'Look Anna, why don't you take your little girl home for the night. I will be here with Geraldine and so will Policewoman Bird!' He glanced at the sergeant. 'You agree,' he asked courteously.

'Good idea,' advised Evans, 'Get some sleep, then you'll be fresh to come over again in the morning.' Anna nodded. She was already worried about the stress the situation was having on Susan, but she looked questioningly at Geraldine, who forced a smile.

'You've been wonderful Anna. See you in the morning,' she said. As Anna left the room the phone rang. Geraldine looked at it apprehensively then snatched it up.

'Yes?'

'Is that Mrs Geraldine Denton?'

'It is.'

'Then no need to tell you what this call is about. We have the kids. If you want to see them back alive I suggest you cooperate with our demands.' Dawson's voice came over clearly on speaker phone as Tom and the police exchanged glances. Tom placed his hand on Geraldine's shoulder.

'I understand,' she replied quietly. 'Who are you—and what do you want? I'm far from rich but if the sum you intend to ask is realistic I'll do my best to raise it!'

'Very kind of you Geraldine,' came the sneering reply. 'But as you will be aware, this is about far more than financial ransom. You have certain documents and information which must not be allowed to fall into the wrong hands—you will turn all such over to me.'

'Exactly what documents are you referring to?' she asked. 'Please be explicit—I want my grandchildren back as soon as possible.' It seemed her calm voice infuriated the caller. She heard him swearing. When he spoke again, his voice full of suspicion.

'Have you got the police in there with you? I hope not, for if you involve them your grandkids will die—and not pleasantly.' Her face went white at his words, she glanced at Tom for guidance.

'Naturally I reported their kidnap to the police. They called earlier to ask questions, but they've gone and I'm alone. Look, I'm desperate to get the children back—I beg you not to hurt them! I'm just a very ordinary, elderly grandmother. I don't understand any of this—so please just tell me what documents you are talking about?' He gave a sadistic laugh.

'My heart bleeds! You damn well know!'

'No, I don't! So just explain these illusionary documents to me! To what do they refer?' Her knuckles were white with tension. She felt on the point of screaming, but knew she had to remain calm. This man she was speaking to and who had the lives of little Melanie and Charles in his hands was possibly that same intruder she had so recently dealt with. If so he would already know she was no gentle inoffensive pensioner.

'Shall we just say the oil industry—Sea Giant!' he barked in frustration. Sergeant Evans smiled satisfaction, the conversation being recorded, as Tom whispered to Geraldine to keep the man talking.

'My son worked for them before he died,' she said with a catch in her voice. 'What have they to do with me?'

'That is for you to figure out when you hand over the information I require. You have ten minutes to consider the matter Mrs Denton. If you do not accede to my demands, you will never see your grandkids again!' The call ended.

Dawson was both angry and uncertain as he tossed his mobile phone on the bed. None of this was going as he had planned. He had grudgingly admitted to himself Bickerton was right and he should contact Sea Giant to give a progress report and ask for further instructions. After some thought he had indeed made several calls to Sea Giant HQ on the number that normally would have connected him with Lancaster—but there had been no answer! Why was that? Having ordered the kids kidnapping surely SG would be only too eager to learn how all was going? He had made one last futile call, then decided to use his initiative and handle the situation himself.

'Bloody bitch!' he exclaimed wrathfully now as he strode back and forth about his dingy room in the cheap boarding house. She was well aware of what he needed, and obviously in a position to expose some dodgy dealings at SG. How she had acquired this was of no relevance to him, the power such knowledge would provide all that mattered.

Geraldine looked up anxiously at Tom Lanscombe, her heart pounding.

'What now?' She was trying so hard to remain calm. 'Any chance of establishing where the call came from?' He nodded, a smile breaking on his face as he listened in on his own phone.

'It's almost local—boarding house in Oak Dene hamlet, two miles away. We could go over there now, arrest the fellow. But he might decide not to cooperate—refuse to reveal where the twins are hidden! Better perhaps to watch his movements when he leaves the hotel—follow him.'

'What about the other kidnapper, Bickerton?' asked Sergeant Evans. 'We need to know if he is there as well.'

'Good Point. He is obviously working hand in glove with Geraldine's caller whose name MI5 have established as Ted Dawson—the dragon tattoo helped identify him.'

'So, we are to leave my poor grandchildren shut up somewhere in the dark and feeling absolutely terrified!' flashed Geraldine.' Tom placed a sympathetic hand on her shoulder.

'Try to remain calm, my dear. As I've said, if we arrest him now, he could refuse to reveal where he has hidden the children from sheer cussedness. Remember, he already has reason to revenge himself on you for defeating his plans when he broke in here. A man of his type doesn't take easily to being overcome by a woman.' Geraldine clenched her hands together, realising the logic in Tom's words—but how could they just sit here and do nothing! She tried to deal with the situation with the same detachment as when involved as a member of the secret service. Something occurred to her now.

'Tom—I do not believe Dawson is party to Sea Giant's secret plans—just merest pawn in their game, to be tossed aside once he has fulfilled his orders. That's why he was demanding I hand over documents involving SG, without being able to specify what they were. He was fishing, attempting to obtain secret material with which to pressurise—blackmail his employers.' Tom smiled at her approvingly—this was the woman he remembered from their previous work together a few years back.

'Exactly! When he calls back, you must offer him what he asks for. Leave it to me—I'll prepare something that will fool him. Hurry now—let me have your computer.'

She did so and watched his agile fingers produce plans for an apparent secret oil deal to be made with China, using names of prominent Chinese officials and demands for a huge sum of money. It certainly looked authentic enough to convince Dawson, who would never have viewed anything comparable. She smiled excitedly.

'This should serve, Tom! Now, once I mention I've found a document mentioning illegal deals with a foreign company, he will demand I hand it over, but doubt if he would agree to come here, ask me to meet him elsewhere.' Tom nodded agreement, drawing shaggy brows together in thought. Under no circumstances must Geraldine be exposed to this ruthless chancer.

'No doubt he suspects a police presence here, despite your previous assurance to the contrary. But you daren't risk meeting him away from the cottage—he's obviously dangerous and quite ruthless. Already guilty of kidnapping the twins, he'll not give a second thought to disposing of you once he has the document!'

'It's a risk I must take!' she stated firmly.

Sergeant Evans who had been attentively following their conversation, was astounded at the speed with which Tom had invented his fake document. As for Geraldine, she had changed in amazing way from distraught grandmother to the cool decisive individual making plans with this ex MI5 agent. But however courageous she must not be allowed to deal with the man Dawson on her own. He cleared his throat and holding up a hand for attention.

'Surely the safest procedure is to arrest Dawson—Bickerton too if he is at the same B&B hotel. Once charged with kidnap and threats to the children's lives, he'll know he faces a long stretch in prison. Under these circumstances, I believe he will buckle and volunteer the twin's whereabouts in hope we will go easier on him,' stated Evans. They turned and stared at him, had almost overlooked his presence.

'Yes, that makes sense, Evans—but what if he refuses to reveal where he has hidden the children? Left imprisoned and unattended they could die. It's a stark choice!' said Tom grimly, as Geraldine flinched. The brief silence that followed was broken by Tom's phone. He glanced at it, walked to the side of the room.

'Charles?'

'Tom—splendid news for you! We've arrested Lancaster and four of his immediate colleagues—being flown down to Paddington Green for interrogation. Tell Geraldine she can relax!'

'That's terrific! What made you move so quickly?' exclaimed Tom in delight.

'Obtained irrefutable information confirming proposed illegal deal with China! Sea Giant bosses face extensive prison sentences. We owe Colin Denton a huge debt of gratitude for bringing this to our notice.' Charles Latimer's voice expressed his enthusiasm.

'Is it OK to tell Colin about arrest?'

'Yes, but obviously he must not discuss it with any others apart from yourself, Lottie and Geraldine at this time. Any sign of the kidnapped children yet?' Tom filled him in on Dawson's call and attempt to force

Geraldine to reveal any documents she had acquired pertaining to Sea Giant.

'My feeling is he's fishing—wants to obtain details with which he can put pressure on SG. He's to phone back here any time soon. We know where he is—tracked him to a rundown hotel couple of miles away.' He explained dilemma, if they arrested Dawson he might refuse to reveal the twins hiding place, with devasting effect on the children. They spoke for another few seconds. As the call ended, Tom realised all eyes in the room were anxiously trained on him. He was about to speak when Geraldine's phone rang. She bit her lip as she glanced at Tom, no decision yet made as how to proceed with Dawson.

'I'm waiting for your answer,' came the harsh voice. 'The documents?' His voice came clearly across the speaker phone as Tom and Evans exchanged glances. She thought desperately.

'I have been searching through some papers my late daughter-in-law left with me. Wonder if one of them is what you are anxious to get your hands on. As far as I can make out it deals with a secret deal to be made by Sea Giant with some Chinese officials.' She heard a cry of satisfaction from the caller.

'Yes! That is exactly what I need in exchange for the safe return of your grandkids!'

'Good! Well here is what I propose. You collect the twins from wherever you have hidden them and bring them here. I'll then hand over the document as soon as they are safely home with me.'

'I make all decisions—not you!' he snarled angrily.

'That depends on how much you want to get your hands on this document,' she forced herself to reply coolly.'

'Or how greatly you value your grandkids lives!'

'We both know what we individually want.'

'Yes—and I don't wish to risk a police reception on arrival at your cottage!'

'I told you I am alone!'

'Huh! Now you're wasting both our time! Meet me at the crossroads going west out of the village. Hand over the document and once I've checked it, in return will give you the key to unlock the kids shed.' He was so excited he no longer cared about revenge on this stupid female, only the sheer joy of getting hold of information to give him power over Lancaster.

'Very well, I'll leave now,' she replied.

'Good. Any sign of police and the kids die! Remember that. But I'm sure you will be sensible Geraldine!' He smiled as he called off, then locking his door, hurried downstairs, out to his car.

Sergeant Evans whistled softly as he stared at the determined woman preparing to risk her life to rescue her grandchildren. Who would have thought that this quiet silver haired widow was capable of such courage? He exchanged a glance with policewoman Julie Bird, wondering if he should try to dissuade Geraldine from taking such risk.

'Where's your printer, Geraldine? You'll need that fake document to offer Dawson,' advised Tom. 'Now this is how we will arrange things. I'll hide in the boot of your car which he certainly won't expect. I am well armed, so promise you will be safe.' He patted his pocket. She didn't hesitate, grabbed her jacket and waited impatiently as he printed out the paper, while Sergeant Evans looked on deeply concerned. Surely it was his duty to deal with this situation, and not allow Geraldine to put herself in danger and however competent Tom Lanscombe was, how could he condone the use of firearms? He was about to intervene when there was a knock at the door. They all glanced at each other.

'It may be Anna returning to check all is well,' said Geraldine. 'I'll let her in before we go.' As she hurried into the passage, Tom folded the document, put it into an envelope and started to follow her. He watched her open the front door, heard her cry of joy—saw her enveloped in a man's arms—the arms of her son, Colin Denton! He stared in astonishment.

'Colin—my darling son! At last—at last!'

'I couldn't wait any longer, Mum!' He hugged her to him and as they embraced, both had tears in their eyes, Geraldine clinging to him, trying to reassure herself she wasn't dreaming. Then reality took over. How did he happen to be here now? Tom said he had not been told about the children. She must go—rescue little Charles and Melanie. She drew back, trembling still from emotion—and at this point Colin glimpsed a man standing behind her.

'Tom Lanscombe! What are you doing here?' he asked in bewilderment. Tom stared back at him as he tried to frame an answer, knew that only the truth would serve.

'I could ask you the same question, Colin! You were supposed to remain at Ivy Cottage. Things have been transpiring that I was unable to discuss with you earlier. But since you are here it is only right you should be told. Your children have been kidnapped by an employee of Sea Giant!' He saw the shock spread across Colin's face at his words, followed by great wave of anger. But when he spoke his voice was urgent but controlled.

'Tell me!'

'The kidnapper's a man called Dawson,' put in his mother. 'Tom and I on our way to meet with him in attempt to get the children back. He's demanding a document he believes I possess showing Sea Giant's plans to make an illegal deal with China. Tom has prepared a fake document I intend to hand over, in exchange for return of the twins. They were kidnapped this afternoon, Colin. Police have been searching hard, but no success so far—then the phone call. Look, I must go darling. You cannot come with us, if he sees you he will panic and…'

'Give me that paper—I'll deal with him,' said Colin grimly. 'If he has dared to injure a hair of their heads I'll kill him!' He turned to Tom. 'As for you, Tom, how could you have withheld this from me?' Tom stared at the angry man in front of him, sympathising with his outrage, but knowing time was too short to discuss things now.

'Time to go over that later! Your mother and I must leave. I'm going to conceal myself in the car boot—got this,' and he patted his revolver, 'Once Dawson hands over the key and details of a shed where he has concealed the little ones, I'll arrest him. Listen every minute is vital if you want your children back safely.'

'I am their father—insist on coming!'

'While you two are arguing he'll arrive at the meeting place and sees I'm not there he will drive off again!' cried Geraldine in exasperation. 'Listen Colin, get in the back of the car, lie down low and I'll cover you with a car rug. Now let's go!'

Dawson frowned in annoyance as the minutes ticked past. The Denton female should have been here by now. He began to feel uneasy. Suppose she had alerted the police instead? Then he heard the sound of a car approaching and smiled in relief as it slowed down and a woman stepped out. Yes, it was her. He opened his car door got out and faced her after checking there were no other cars in the vicinity.

'You took your time—you have the document?' and he held out his hand eagerly.

'I have. First of all, I need the key and details of where that shed is.' He thrust his hand impatiently into his pocket, and withdrew a clumsy-looking key. He handed it to her. 'Now!' he said, 'Give me that document!' Geraldine stared at him levelly.

'I need to know where the shed is,' she repeated.

'Field at Farringdon Farm, about a quarter of a mile from the farmhouse. Should be easy to find. Now—the document!' He watched as she withdrew an envelope from her shoulder bag, and held it out to him. He ripped it open, and held it nearer the car light. It certainly appeared to be authentic, and he grinned. That grin turned to sudden shocked surprise as a man leapt out of her beige Ford and sprang at him. He lost balance, stumbled, fell—found himself pinned down by the shoulders, the eyes of his attacker glaring down at him in cold fury.

'Who in blazes are you?' he blustered, whilst directing a malevolent glance towards Geraldine. The reply his assailant made baffled him.

'Colin Denton—father of the children you have dared lay hands on! If they have been harmed in any way, you are a dead man!' Dawson looked at him in bewilderment.

'Denton—the man who drowned in that helicopter crash? Impossible!' But as he stared into the implacable face of the man threatening him, he realised the fellow's features bore a similarity to the Denton woman.

'Yes, Ted Dawson—this is my son, and as you see very much alive!' Geraldine confirmed calmly 'Your employers also will be equally amazed I imagine—their fine plans suffering total collapse!'

'You will accompany us to release my children,' Colin ground out. 'On your feet, bastard!'

Despite his shock, Dawson's mind was working. If what he had just heard was true he had to escape—or face the full rigours of the law. With desperate strength, he brought his knee up into Colin's groin. The suddenness of the pain made Colin relax his hold on his shoulders and Dawson rolled free and struggled to his feet. But the enraged father shot up, ignoring his pain to face Dawson. He raised a fist, grey eyes blazing.

'Hold on there, Denton! We need the fellow in one piece,' came a calm voice. Tom Lanscombe had quietly let himself out of the car boot and approached training his revolver at Dawson's head. 'You there, Dawson—you are under arrest!' and as the kidnapper stared helplessly around, he heard the armed stranger pronounce the customary formalities—saw him holding something in his free hand.

'Tie him up, Colin,' instructed Tom, tossing a length of cord found in the boot. 'Hands behind your back, Dawson. Attempt to escape and it will be my delight to fire!' He watched as Colin secured Dawson's wrists, was not gentle and the man swore in protest. 'Into the Ford with him now—the back.' He then gestured to Geraldine.

'Geraldine—get the keys out of Dawson's car. We'll hand them over to Evans later.' She did so, and pocketed them. 'Good. Now let's drive to this Farringdon Farm, find the shed, and release young Charles and Melanie.'

'Yes—and hurry—please hurry!' she implored impatiently. 'I'll drive—know the way!'

It was dark in the musty shed and Little Melanie Denton was sobbing quietly as her twin brother attempted to comfort her. They could hear strange rustling sounds—mice or rats thought Charles. He had tried in vain to rip the rope about their waists from the hook in the roof of the shed.

'It will be all right, Melanie. Don't cry—try to be strong! Granny will find us—get the police and they will arrest those two crooks!'

'Why did those men do this to us? Is it to do with Mummy and Daddy being dead?' Her sobs had quietened as she tried to understand all that had happened.

'I think they want to force Granny to give them something important. Remember that break-in Melanie?' he asked.

'Yes! When granny chased the burglar away. One of the men who brought us here had sore, red eyes. Granny said she had sprayed something in the burglar's eyes that night.'

'So, the same one,' replied Charles, glad that his sister was calmer now. 'The other man is a crook too.'

'I'm frightened. Suppose those horrible men just leave us here and nobody finds us?' she whispered plaintively. Charles still trying vainly to jerk the rope securing them free of the hook, was about to reply, when he thought he heard something faintly—voices!

'Hush Melanie, listen—it's people talking outside.' Both stiffened in fright as they heard the sound of a key turning in the lock, and the door suddenly opened, fresh night air drifting in. The children blinked as a torch was played over them—then their grandmother was beside them smiling and crying at the same time as she knelt and hugged them to her. Now a man stooped over them, cutting their bonds with a penknife—and although they couldn't see his face clearly, they knew him.

'Daddy?' whispered Charles. It couldn't be, he thought fearfully. 'Are you a ghost?' he asked forcing out the words as Melanie drew back trembling in shock.

'No—I'm no ghost, Charles. Here just feel my hand—and you too, Melanie darling. Don't be afraid. I'm real! Some wicked men tried to kill me—but I escaped from that helicopter and was rescued from the sea by kind fishermen.'

'You are quite safe now children,' said another familiar voice, as Tom Lanscombe bent over them. 'Come on—let's get you out of here!' He lifted Charles, as Colin scooped his daughter into his arms, Geraldine walked between the two men, beginning to relax from the tension she had endured for so long. They were safe, her beloved grandchildren were safe—and her son was back after so many desperate weeks. It was all like a wonderful dream. They reached the Ford which she had driven over the grassy field and parked immediately outside the shed.

'Where is Dawson?' she cried, seeing the backseat empty. Tom grinned.

'I persuaded him to take my earlier place in the boot—it's safely locked! Knew we would need space for the youngsters. After all, they would not have been happy to see him! Look, I'll drive, Geraldine. You sit in the back with Colin and the twins.'

'What about that other villain—Bickerton?' asked Geraldine.

'Rang Sergeant Evans—his two officers are driving over to the hotel to arrest the fellow. Leave the clearing up to me, Geraldine! You concentrate on your family now. It's all over, my dear!' Back at last in Rose Cottage, Colin and his mother glanced lovingly at each other as they bent over beds where the exhausted children had fallen asleep. Then they stole quietly out and made their way downstairs. Tom was waiting for them.

'I'll be off soon—chopper on the way here to take Dawson and Bickerton to Paddington Green for interrogation together with Sea Giant! An armed officer coming along too. Will see you in a few days.' They nodded, too tired to ask questions—but wonderfully happy.

Chapter Ten

Colin awoke early, it was only 6 am. He glanced slowly around this familiar bedroom he had once shared with his dear wife Mary when visiting his mother, and a lump came into his throat. If only he had not moved to Scotland, become involved with the oil industry. But you cannot go back in life, only forward learning from the mistakes of the past. He got up quietly, careful not to wake his mother or the twins. He could still hardly believe he was actually here at last—that this was no dream. He showered and dressed, while mentally reviewing the events of the previous evening. Tom had left, would be in London now with the two kidnappers. He felt nothing but gratitude for the amazing help he had received from the ex MI5 man—and from Lottie. Such a wonderful couple!

He walked slowly downstairs—needed a coffee. He opened the kitchen door eyes widening in astonishment as he saw a strange young woman pouring boiling water into the coffee decanter, and a small girl sitting at the table reading a book.

'Who are you?' he demanded in astonishment. She turned, and almost dropped the kettle as an expression of fright spread across her attractive face. She raised a hand and pointed at him.

'No, you cannot be real,' she murmured. He stared lifting a quizzical brow.

'I assure you I am! And more to the point, why are you in my mother's kitchen?'

'Geraldine is your mother? Then I don't understand. I know her son Colin is dead,' she said shakily. 'Yet you look just like his photograph.'

'I think we had better start again,' he said gently. 'Now please put that kettle down before you do yourself a damage!' She did so and sank down in a chair next to the little fair-haired girl. He examined her troubled face. She really was rather lovely, and had the most astonishing blue eyes. 'May I ask your name?' he inquired curiously.

'I'm Anna Lindstrom—and this is my daughter Susan. We live next door in Bramble Cottage!' She drew in her breath and posed a question of her own. 'So, who exactly are you? I know Geraldine has been mourning Colin's death for weeks—are you a relative?'

'Anna, you said? Well Anna, I am indeed Colin Denton and amazingly survived a helicopter crash meant to kill me. I was rescued from the sea by some kindly Norwegian fishermen, taken to Norway suffering amnesia due to hurts received by impact when the craft came down. My mother was only made aware of my survival a short while ago—but because some very dangerous individuals were involved in the matter, the security service thought it wiser that she should keep the news private.'

'So, you are Colin Denton? Oh, what wonderful news for Geraldine and the twins! I wish she could have trusted me to keep her secret.' He saw the slight hurt on her face. 'But the important thing is that you're alive!' she continued.

'When mother mentioned she had a special new neighbour, I instinctively thought it would probably be someone of her previous neighbour's age! I'm delighted to find I was mistaken. So, this little girl is your daughter?' and he glanced at the fair-haired child whose eyes were as blue as her mother's.

'Yes, this is Susan. She loves playing with your children.' She took Susan's hand. 'Susan darling, this gentleman's name is Colin—he is Charles and Melanie's daddy.'

'No Mummy—their daddy is dead,' corrected Susan, her small face puzzled.

'Lots of people thought I was dead, Susan,' said Colin gently. 'They had tried to hurt me—but I escaped.' She trained her blue gaze on him earnestly, trying to understand.

'They must have been very bad people. My daddy was bad too—I mean!' and she bit her lip as Anna shot her a warning look. 'Sorry Mummy,' she murmured, 'I didn't mean to say it.' But Anna forced a smile, and bending slipped a reassuring arm about her.

'It's all right, darling. Look, I think we should go home now. The twins will want to have some special quiet time with their daddy.' Susan nodded and closed her book and before Colin could remonstrate Anna hurried her out of the kitchen. He heard the sound of the front door closing. He stood there hesitating, then shrugged and poured himself a mug of the coffee the girl had made. Obviously, this Anna Lindstrom had problems of her own which understandably she didn't wish to share with a stranger.

Back in Bramble Cottage, Anna was sitting broodingly in one of the deep brown velvet armchairs in the comfortable living room. Susan climbed onto one of its wide arms and touched her mother's face for attention.

'Are you cross with me because I spoke about Daddy?' she asked, her young face troubled. Anna came out of her reverie and smiled ruefully.

'No, Susan darling. I understand it's hard remembering not to speak of the past. It's only for our safety it has to be so. But what a wonderful surprise to meet the twins' daddy and find he is still alive. Just think how happy they must be!' She glanced tenderly at Susan, who smiled relieved.

'He looked a nice man, Mummy,' she said. 'Will he take Melanie and Charles away now?' Anna heard the worry in her voice and held her close.

'Darling I don't know. Let's hope he will stay next door with Geraldine and the children. You would like that wouldn't you?' she confirmed gently.

'Yes! Please, please will you ask Geraldine to ask him to stay?' she asked. Anna laughed.

'It's not really for me to interfere in any way. But I'm sure Geraldine will do her best to persuade him. She loves her grandchildren,' she said reassuringly. 'Now why don't you take your modelling clay onto the kitchen table and make another of your beautiful little cats!' Susan nodded and ran off to comply, leaving Anna still sitting there thinking of recent events.

It had been fairly late last night when Anna thought she heard a noise below and peered out of her bedroom window. To her amazement she could dimly see Geraldine followed by two men each carrying a child, hurrying up the pathway next door and disappearing into Rose cottage! How wonderful, she thought. They had managed to rescue little Charles and Melanie! She couldn't make out faces in the dark, but one of the men must be Tom Lanscombe the other possibly Sergeant Evans. She was tempted to return to Rose Cottage and congratulate Geraldine on the children's safety, but it would mean rousing Susan who was sleeping, completely exhausted after all the day's upsetting incidents. She decided to postpone her visit until the next morning to discover exactly what had happened!

She had wakened Susan early and after a hasty breakfast made their way to Geraldine's cottage. Using the spare key, she slipped in quietly leading Susan through to the kitchen. No one was around yet. She realised Geraldine and the twins were probably still sleeping after all the trauma. Perhaps she should go home and return later, but hesitated as she heard a sound upstairs. It decided her. She would prepare coffee for Geraldine. She put the kettle on and reached for the decanter. The sight of the stranger had astonished her. Even now it was hard to comprehend that Colin Denton was alive, had survived the helicopter crash.

She was trying to analyse her feelings about his arrival. She liked him instinctively, but found Susan's suggestion that he might take the twins away disturbing—she was extremely fond of the little seven-year-olds and knew that Susan was also. Their presence next door had proved beneficial in boosting her young daughter's confidence in their new home. Then recently problems had started when Susan was forced to face the death of Geraldine's pet cat Marcasite—next the frightening abduction of the twins now thankfully rescued, followed by the new possibility of change should Colin take them away from the village.

Geraldine opened her grandchildren's bedroom cautiously, not wanting to wake them if they were still asleep. She glanced at the two little heads resting peacefully on their down pillows and murmured a prayer of thanks to Almighty God for preserving their lives. She could hardly believe that all danger was now over, Sea Giant's corrupt executives arrested and under investigation in London, Dawson and Bickerton to join them there at Paddington Green. She turned as a quiet whisper reached her and saw Colin smiling at her.

'They're still asleep?' he confirmed softly. She nodded, but as though sensing their presence little Melanie stirred and opened her eyes. She looked about her fearfully at first as the memory of being bound and helpless in that dark and musty shed flooded back into her consciousness. She uttered a soft scream which woke her brother Charles. He sat up abruptly and slipped out of bed and reached out to her comfortingly.

'It's all right, Melanie. I'm here,' he said. Then his eyes registered his granny standing at the doorway—and behind her the father he had mourned as dead. It was difficult to sort out in his mind all that had happened yesterday, being incarcerated for hours in that horrible shed and being scared no one would ever find them. Then he remembered his father and Tom miraculously appearing and releasing them from the cords securing them to that hook in the roof. It had seemed like a dream seeing his father there—how could it be when he had died in the sea? Was he a ghost—then Tom had lifted him and his sister Melanie was in his father's arms—and Granny was there smiling with tears in her eyes.

'Granny,' he called now as she hurried to him and held him close, and his father sat on a confused Melanie's bed and soothed her.

'Daddy—is our Mummy really dead,' asked Melanie now. The little girl having witnessed one miracle was hoping for another. Her father shook his head sadly.

'Yes, my darling. Mummy is in heaven and will be so happy that both of you are safe. I promise nothing bad will ever happen to you again!' He turned to Charles. 'One day I will try to explain all that's been happening. The important thing now is that the bad people who caused so much hurt to our family are now under arrest in London. They will assuredly go to prison for many years.'

'Granny walloped one of them and sprayed pepper spray in his eyes,' said Charles looking proudly at Geraldine.

'He was a burglar, Daddy,' explained Melanie. She looked up at him anxiously. 'You're not going back to work to work on that oilrig, are you?' He stroked her hair gently.

'No, my darling, not ever again!' he said, his voice choked. Geraldine looked at him compassionately.

'Colin, the children need to shower—were too exhausted last night for a proper wash and then we'll all have breakfast.' At her practical words, the children made obediently for the bathroom. 'They will be all right—but you must be patient, Colin darling,' she added.

'I met your neighbour Anna Lindstrom this morning,' informed Colin, as Geraldine stirred the porridge. 'Found her here in the kitchen earlier with her daughter Susan. She had a shock when she saw me!'

'Anna was here? Why didn't you tell me before!' exclaimed Geraldine. 'Did you tell her who you are?' He nodded thoughtfully.

'Actually, she recognised me from my photo—took some convincing that I was real at first. She is to come back later. She's an attractive girl,' he added. Geraldine shot a look at him. It was an encouraging sign that he was noticing such matters. Hopefully one day in the months ahead he would no longer be blinkered by grief. Anna—Colin? She was smiling as she poured the porridge into earthenware bowls and the children came in, damp hair tousled.

'We're hungry, Granny,' they intoned together.

'Good—there's grilled bacon and scrambled eggs to follow,' she assured them. 'Now sit down next to your Daddy.' As they did so, Colin looked at her curiously. This was not the mother he remembered from his own sometimes fraught childhood, often disappearing on business for weeks at a time, when he was left in the care of the housekeeper. Geraldine Denton had changed in some indefinable way from the woman he now knew to have been a dedicated member of the secret service, into this deeply caring Grandmother. The dedicated way she had taken care of his children was unbelievably kind and he sensed the strong bond that now existed between Charles and Melanie and his mother.

He had been contemplating buying a small house somewhere here in the south and bringing the children up himself, but watching the interplay around the table began to question the plan. Would it be possible for the four of them to become a regular family unit? He wondered what Mary would have thought, remembering how fond she had been of Geraldine. He glanced at Geraldine as she buttered extra toast for the twins. Had he not survived the helicopter crash, she would have taken permanent care of her orphaned grandchildren.

The phone rang and she handed him the toast as she hurried off.

'It was Tom Lanscombe,' she said as she returned. 'Dawson and Bickerton will definitely remain in police custody until their trial—and the Sea Giant contingent still undergoing interrogation. Tom says they face many years in jail. It really is all over as far as we are concerned Colin!' She realised the twins too had been following her words.

'Those bad men who tried to kill our Daddy are going to prison?' confirmed Charles.

'Yes dear—and they will be away for many years,' replied Geraldine. 'And so also will the horrible men who kidnapped both of you. There's nothing to be afraid of anymore!' Melanie jumped to her feet and clapped her hands in delight and looked at her father.

'Does that mean we can just go on staying here with Granny—and you will be here too?' Challenged thus he was about to prevaricate wishing to put off the decision until he had more time to consider, but he saw the pleading look on the children's faces and hopeful expression in his mother's eyes.

'Well, I will have to discuss it with Granny to see if she approves—but as far as I'm concerned, then yes—I would like it if we were all to live here at Rose Cottage!' The smile on his mother's face was reward enough for this decision as well as the shouts of delight from the twins. Everything was happening rather fast he thought, but knew he had made the right choice. He would have to find work around here although that might prove difficult in such a small village in a rural area—but where there was a will there was a way.

Back at Ivy cottage Tom and Lottie Lanscombe were talking quietly. It was evening and Tom had not long returned from London having helped deliver Dawson and Bickerton to the authorities there. Lottie had just served him a delicious meal of chicken in white sauce, with fruit dumplings to follow and now they were relaxing in the sitting room as he gave details of the last few hours. He pulled her head onto his shoulder, as they sat there.

'I rang Geraldine this morning before I left for home—she was delighted that Dawson and Bickerton are safely in custody down there and as far as the Denton family are concerned all danger is now definitely over.'

'Poor woman, what she has endured over the last couple of days!' exclaimed Lottie.

'She was marvellous when we were dealing with Dawson—had lost none of her previous expertise in dealing with such dangerous scum. Her son was good too.' He paused, 'I've been thinking about him, Lottie. What did you truly make of Colin Denton?' he inquired. She raised her head and looked at him.

'I believe he is still suffering from stress but possesses a quick mind together with a steely determination. Why do you ask, Tom?' she questioned curiously. He smiled.

'I wondered if Latimer might recruit him into the service. He is of proven courage, doesn't panic easily and will be looking for employment once he has had time to readjust to a changed life. What do you think, Lottie?'

'A good idea. But whether he will want to leave his children so soon after the family have endured so much trauma is debatable. On the other hand, Geraldine adores the twins, and since she is now widowed the little twins have given a new focus to her life. Colin must know they will be safe with his mother,' She gave Tom a quick kiss and sat thinking for a moment. 'My advice is this—run the idea past Charles Latimer first, then just make a light suggestion about joining the firm to Colin. Give him time to come to terms with Mary's death before making any decision on the future.' He patted her hand approvingly.

'You are right as usual. Well ok, I will sound Charles out—and take it from there. Denton will probably need a few weeks to reassure his children about all that's happened. I know he is safely back with them—but they have also lost their mother. And of course, it will be good for Geraldine to have her son with her—she's been through a lot as well!' he added soberly.

'Yes—I'm pleased we are back in touch with Geraldine. Such a shame she lost her husband, he was a fine man as well as a great doctor. By the way, how did that new arrival settle into Dream Echo? I remember Amber mentioning her just as I was about to leave for Ravenscroft.' Lottie shook her head.

'Badly hurt—rib fractures and bad facial bruising and not speaking so far, still traumatised. Her children are beginning to respond to kindness, but goodness knows what scenes they witnessed recently of their father's brutality.' They continued to discuss the work at the women's refuge, the main focus of their lives these days, until Tom yawned.

'Bed now I think,' he said. 'It's been a long twenty-four hours!'

Anna Lindstrom walked hesitantly along the pathway to Geraldine's cottage, Susan skipping happily at her side. She didn't use her key this time but knocked. To her relief, it was Geraldine who answered and beckoned them in.

'I'm delighted and the twins are safely home!' cried Anna. 'Also, that your son Colin is alive! I don't know if he mentioned it but I met him earlier this morning.'

'Yes—he told me, dear.'

'Listen, I heard noises last night, peered from the bedroom window and could just make you out down there, together with two men carrying the twins! I would have come over straight away to offer my congratulations, but didn't want to wake Susan.'

Geraldine gave her an affectionate hug and explained all that had happened after Anna had left last night. As she rapidly poured out the basic facts, she realised Anna's eyes held a brooding look and uncomfortably guessed the reason why. 'I should have told you about Colin before. Forgive me for that—but you see I was advised not to breathe a word to anyone.' Anna inclined her head understandingly.

'It's fine, Geraldine. I realise you had to be careful—but you could have trusted me you know.' Her face revealed the hurt she was attempting to conceal. Geraldine sighed. It had all been so difficult. She tried to reach out to the girl.

'Colin will probably want to tell you all he's experienced since escaping from the helicopter that was meant to be his tomb—some incredible adventures. More recently he has been staying at their home with Tom and Lottie. I had no idea he was about to arrive yesterday, but oh, what joy it was to hold him in my arms—and then the sheer relief of recovering little Charles and Melanie!' Sensing a softening in Anna she took her hand gently. 'I hope you will include Colin in the friendship we share,' she said simply.

'I agree with that!' broke in a deep voice. They hadn't noticed the sitting room door open. Colin smiled at them. He had already gleaned from his mother just how supportive her new neighbour had been and was glad to see her again. He noticed Susan watching them solemnly at Anna's side. 'Hallo, again Susan, would you like to play with the twins?'

'Yes please!' the child replied eagerly. He stood back as she ran past him and they heard the sound of children's excited voices. Colin smiled at Anna.

'They say children are remarkably resilient,' he said quietly. 'Unbelievably Charles and Melanie appear almost back to normal—on the surface at least, despite enduring the shock of kidnap. Seeing your little girl may be just what they need right now.'

Anna smiled thoughtfully as she glanced after her daughter, remembering Susan's deep anxiety following their escape from Malcolm Greer, the child's constant worry that he might find them. She also recalled the many weeks during which Geraldine had dealt with her grandchildren's grief at their parent's death with all her quiet wisdom and kindness. Now just as Charles and Melanie were beginning to enjoy some stability again, they were having to deal with sudden new conflicting emotions—the joy of finding their father was still alive, mixed with all the trauma of their kidnap, with the cruelties perpetrated on them by those swine Dawson and Bickerton. She looked at Colin.

'You may find their sleep will be disturbed at times—possibly note other little signs of insecurity. Continuity is important, their grandmother's presence and yours—school. With love and patience, all will be well.' She blushed under his curious gaze.

'I feel you speak from experience,' he observed quietly. He turned to Geraldine. 'Mum, I disturbed Anna when she was preparing coffee earlier this morning—and talking of coffee, why don't we make some now!'

'Let's check all is well with the children first,' she replied, sliding the sitting room door open. They peered in and saw Susan bending over Melanie's wrist, before turning to Charles.

'Is your wrist sore too?' she asked him in concern.

'Not so bad now—Granny put some salve on it,' the boy replied lightly. 'The men tied us up—ankles as well as wrists and a rope around our waists.'

'It was very scary there in the dark,' whispered Melanie. 'I was frightened We could hear rustling noises and it was so cold.'

Colin bit his lip as he heard his children's voices. Susan was speaking again.

'Why are some men so bad?' she asked, small face puzzled. 'Why do they hurt people?' Charles frowned as he fought for a reply. He shook his head.

'I'm not sure Susan—perhaps they are just cruel inside. Some want to steal other people's things, or want power over them. But don't you worry, I'll not let anyone hurt you—or Melanie,' he said protectively.

'My daddy was bad,' said Susan. 'I'm not supposed to talk about him—he used to hurt mummy!' The children looked round as they heard a cry from the door and saw Anna standing there. Susan lowered her head, knew she should not have told her friends about this secret. The twin's grandmother put an arm around Anna, as Colin glanced sympathetically at the young mother.

'Let's get that coffee,' said Geraldine quickly, drawing Anna away towards the kitchen. Sitting around the table now, Anna sipped her coffee and wondered if she should make any comment to Colin on Susan's revelation he had overheard. Although he had made no allusion to the child's uncompromising statement about her father, if they were to be in regular contact it would obviously place a question mark in Colin's mind. She came to a decision.

'Colin—we have only just met. Ordinarily I would never discuss personal matters in such circumstance—but I know you heard what my little girl said. Geraldine already knows that I recently escaped from an abusive relationship, at which time it became necessary to change our names! The man concerned is a powerful individual whom I fear. He'd snatch Susan if given the chance—and undoubtedly wreak his vengeance on me.' She saw Colin's grey eyes darken at her statement, looking inquiringly from Anna to his mother.

'Surely the police should be involved in this? Anna—I'm so very sorry you've been enduring such worry whilst supporting my mother through all our ongoing trauma. Now you have honoured me with your confidence, believe this—I will personally do all in my power to deal with the skunk who has been terrorising you!' Anna murmured her thanks as Geraldine looked at him approvingly. She leaned across the table

'Tom Lanscombe said that the police are investigating the man's business affairs, suspect people trafficking! He's a real brute and thank goodness Anna managed to get safely away!' She looked caringly at the girl, pleased at Colin's protective attitude towards her. He smiled at his mother and as he reached to a plate of chocolate biscuits, the years suddenly seemed to melt away. He realised instinctively that this was where he wanted to be—with his mother and beloved children with the added bonus of this interesting neighbour. Mary would have liked her, he thought. Even now it was so hard to realise he would never see his dear wife again in this world—would have to be both father and mother to their beloved twins.

'I think I will take a walk in the garden,' he said abruptly. Geraldine looked after him. In the short time since he had arrived, there had been no real time to talk—for him to unburden himself of the deep grief he was still experiencing. Her anger towards Sea Giant surged through her mind. Their cruelty had torn her son's family apart. She thought of little Susan's question to Charles asking, 'Why are some men so cruel—why do they hurt people?' Her young grandson had been correct in his answer as he explained they were bad inside, wanted other people's possessions—and power. At seven years old Charles was unusually perceptive.

'He will be alright,' said Anna softly. 'I think your son Colin is a fine man.'

'He is. Right now, he is grieving his Mary's death—they loved each other dearly. Healing takes time,' Geraldine sighed.

'Being with his children will help,' said Anna. 'Has he any plans for the future?'

'He has decided to stay here at Rose Cottage! I'm so relieved he is isn't going to move the children away,' Geraldine confided and saw an answering smile on Anna's face.

Colin walked slowly about his mother's garden. It was as beautiful as he remembered it, roses dying back a little now with the approach of autumn and dahlia's and chrysanthemums coming into bloom. He wandered casually around the flower beds—then he saw it, the little wooden cross with the name Marcasite, a faded bunch of white roses lying beside it. Why of course, that was the name of her beloved cat. Surely the tabby hadn't been that old? Poor Mum, she must have been devastated! He returned to the house, found Geraldine still talking with Anna.

'Mum—I saw the little cross—Marcasite? You must miss him!' he said gently.

'Dawson killed him the night he broke in here,' she explained. 'Anna found Marcasite lying dead outside, his head badly battered.' He saw the pain on her face. 'The twins were very upset as was little Susan. I was on my way to choose a kitten for Anna's little girl when the kidnap took place.'

'We could still do that,' said Anna, 'What about getting one for you as well—if it's not too early?' she added hesitantly. Geraldine smiled.

'It might be good for Charles and Melanie. I'll ring Joyce Masters now and see if she has any kittens left—how about it, Anna?' she checked. Anna nodded enthusiastically.

'Great idea,' she exclaimed, then glanced at Colin. 'Do you like cats, Colin?' she asked. He lifted an eyebrow.

'Never really thought about it. Always got on well with Mum's Marcasite. I guess I could get used to having one around.'

Two hours later, Geraldine and Anna were back from Joyce Master's noisy, welcoming household carrying a cardboard box containing two indignant, small loudly protesting felines. Colin looked up as they came in and glanced inquiringly at the box as they set it down on the sitting room floor.

'You were successful then?'

'Yes dear—two lovely little kittens! Why don't you get the children?' suggested Geraldine. Once informed a surprise awaited them, the three youngsters came rushing in. There was no need to tell them what it was as they heard the shrill, urgent meows emerging from the box. Charles knelt beside it opening the lid, then as Melanie and Susan joined him he lifted out the first of the kittens.

'That one is yours, Susan,' informed Anna smiling at her excited small daughter. Charles looked admiringly at the kitten before handing it over to Susan. It was tabby with a white bib and paws. Susan held it to her tenderly. Charles meanwhile lifted out the second kitten and inspected it. He glanced inquiringly at Geraldine, the kitten's resemblance to Marcasite was remarkable.

'This one is for you, my dears—it's a boy,' his grandmother said quietly. 'Oh, and Susan's kitten is a girl.' There were cries of delight from the children and Colin smiled approvingly at his mother.

The arrival of their kitten proved a welcome distraction to Charles and Melanie, with the mental scars left by their recent kidnap seemingly replaced by their day to day fascination with this tiny creature determined to wreak mischievous havoc with his adventurous antics. They had named him Pyrites. Anna noticed similar contentment in young Susan the little girl delighted with Patches as she called her kitten.

Since Colin's arrival at Rose Cottage, Anna had deliberately cut back on her frequent visits to Geraldine, not wanting to intrude upon the ongoing healing and reunification taking place there. At the same time, she had felt herself strangely attracted to her friend's handsome son. He had endured so much—his dear wife's death, murdered by those vile Sea Giant operatives—his own close escape from a watery tomb, his whole life disrupted, followed by their attack on Geraldine and his children. She felt enormous sympathy for Colin Denton, found herself wondering what the future held for him?

'When may I play with Charles and Melanie again?' asked Susan, as she watched Patches lapping milk from a saucer.

'Soon—but they need to spend some quiet time with their Daddy, my dear,' she replied.

'I miss them!' complained Susan, blue eyes fixed pleadingly on her mother. Anna ruffled the little girl's fair curls and smiled.

'Tomorrow then!' she promised

Geraldine opened the door to them and beckoned them in. It was raining and had been all morning, a fine drenching rain. Anna handed over their waterproofs, and Geraldine smiled to see Susan was clutching her kitten.

'How is Patches getting on, Susan?' she asked.

'I really love her—but she is quite naughty you know,' replied the child. 'She keeps trying to climb up the curtains and sometimes she scratches me—but I don't think she means to.' She looked around inquiringly. 'Where are Charles and Melanie?'

'Their Daddy is reading a story to them—why don't you join them in the sitting room, Susan?' She smiled at Anna as Susan ran off still firmly holding the kitten. 'I'm glad to see she has bonded so well with Patches!'

'Absolutely adores the little creature,' returned Anna. 'How about Pyrites?'

'The twins love him. He reminds me of my Marcasite as a kitten.' She stared at Anna. 'So why have we not seen much of you recently?'

'Thought you needed some peace and quiet with Colin. How is he doing?' she asked. Geraldine smiled as they entered the kitchen and sat down at the table.

'I believe his stress is lessening now—and the children overjoyed to have their daddy back. He is beginning to think of the future, definitely going to stay here in the cottage and find work of some description. But, right now he needs time to relax!' She glanced at Anna. 'He appears quite interested in our new neighbour.'

'He certainly was surprised when he came across me in here, the other day!' She looked at Geraldine. 'The death of his wife Mary must have been the most terrible shock. But at least the twins can rejoice that their father is safe. It's such a relief that those corrupt people at Sea Giant's HQ are under arrest and will be out of the way for many years!' Her blue eyes flashed as she spoke. Geraldine nodded in agreement.

'The law will take its due course with them! But you have been brilliant through all this, Anna! I will never forget he wonderful support you gave me when things were at their darkest.' She reached out a hand, took one of Anna's. 'I truly hope you will decide to remain permanently at Bramble Cottage,' she probed softly. Anna smiled.

'Geraldine, I never had the joy of knowing a mother, mine died at my birth—but I have begun to feel a caring and closeness between us that means more than I can express. I have no wish to move away from Bramble Cottage—and those I now consider my new family!'

'Anna, that's a lovely way of putting it! You have become very dear to me also. So, you really will stay?'

'Yes. I feel safe here—little Susan is happy—and I treasure our friendship! All good reasons to remain!' Anna replied. 'I admit I felt very anxious at first in case Malcolm Greer should track me down, but as the weeks have safely passed I've begun to relax and now rarely think of the man who caused me so much grief!' Geraldine smiled back at her sympathetically.

'According to Tom Lanscombe he is under police investigation for people trafficking. I imagine if brought to trial and convicted, Malcolm Greer faces a substantial period behind bars!' she said reassuringly. It was at that moment that her cell-phone rang. She glanced at it. 'Why—believe it or not, it's Tom—how strange just as we were talking about him!'

As Geraldine took the call, Anna saw her face light up with pleasure.

'You will be very welcome, Tom—and so will Charles! When do you expect to get here? Early afternoon—no that's fine. Look forward to seeing you both then!' and she slipped the phone back in her pocket.

'Tom is driving over here?' confirmed Anna.

'Yes dear—and bringing Charles Latimer. I had better let Colin know, and must plan dinner. You will be here of course with Susan—so that will be five adults and three children!'

'If you're sure, then I'll help you with the cooking later,' replied Anna, whilst wondering the cause for this unexpected visit by Tom and his MI5 friend.

'We had better tell Colin—come along,' said Geraldine. They found him in the sitting room, seated on the couch, a twin on either side of him, while Susan perched on a stool as she looked up at him earnestly. He was reading from an illustrated book of fairy tales, his young listeners completely engrossed. He smiled at his mother and shot Anna a welcoming glance as he was given the news of the impending visit.

'Be glad to see Tom again—and Latimer. Any idea why they are coming Mum?'

'No—probably just checking that we've recovered from recent events!' she guessed. 'I'm off to prepare the spare bedroom in case they decide on an overnight stay!' she added. Anna made to follow her, but Geraldine shook her head.

'You stay with Colin and the youngsters,' she said and saw by Colin's face that he approved the suggestion. Perhaps Anna might prove the perfect companion for her son as he came to terms with Mary's loss—a friendship that might one day blossom into something stronger.

Lottie Lanscombe gently stroked the hand of the frightened little girl whose badly bruised face the hospital doctor had recently examined to ascertain there was no fracture to the cheekbone. Her father had lashed out at the child when she tried to intervene as he was savagely beating his wife. Mother and daughter had just arrived at Dream Echo and Lottie was at Amber's side as the lovely young woman who had founded this women's refuge welcomed yet another abused woman. The welfare officer who had driven them here was scathing in her assessment of Lisl's violent husband Claude Strang, now in police custody. Hopefully, he would be denied bail and when he came to trial for domestic violence, be handed a substantial sentence.

Amber studied the notes swiftly. Lisl was Austrian, had married Claude Strang eight years ago, during which period she had received hospital treatment for a variety of supposed accidental mishaps. The staff had questioned her feeble accounts—walking into an open cupboard door, a fall downstairs—a slip on a wet floor. But this time a neighbour had heard her cries and called the police who had caught Strang in action, arrested him, calling for an ambulance to take a badly injured Lisl and small daughter to hospital. Lisl had at last broken down and confirmed the abuse.

Amber handed the notes to Lottie, who glanced at the listed injuries the hospital had diagnosed and treated—they included three broken ribs, dislocated shoulder now reduced, facial injuries including torn ear, badly cut lip and bruised temple. She shook her head. No matter how many new arrivals presented here she would never get over the shock of seeing what cruelty some men perpetrated on their wives. She glanced down at Lisl's little daughter, five years old, with blond curls like her mother and frightened blue eyes. Her name was Heidi.

They helped the badly injured woman upstairs to the comfort of one of the welcoming bedrooms, little Heidi following behind. At last she was in bed. She had not spoken since she arrived, but her eyes expressed her gratitude. Experience told them she was still deep in shock. A smaller bed had been placed next to Lisl's for Heidi. Amber held a glass to Lisl's lips as the injured woman struggled to swallow her medication—and soon fell asleep.

Heidi looked at the two strange, kind women who had been helping her mother, wondering what was going to happen next. Lottie smiled down at her.

'Come with me, little one,' she said softly. 'We will leave your mummy to sleep. She may need to stay in bed for a few days to get better. So, what about you Heidi? Is your cheek very sore?' She noticed that Heidi stiffened at mention of her own injury, touching her face with exploring finger.

'It is still hurting. My Daddy was very angry,' she whispered. 'He hurt Mummy and wouldn't stop. Will he find us here?' She looked around anxiously. Lottie exchanged a glance with Amber.

'No, Heidi dear, your father will not be able to come here. It is a secret place where people who have been hurt come to feel safe and get better.' She saw the quick relief in the child's eyes. 'There are some other children staying here you know. Would you like to meet them?' At first Heidi shook her head nervously, but after a few more encouraging words from Lottie allowed herself to be led downstairs into the playroom. Here she was met by a tall, dark haired woman in red shirt, bright yellow scarf and jeans who greeted her gently and introduced her to a small group of young children, playing with a toy garage. Lottie stood watching until she was sure Heidi was comfortable in her new surroundings and smiled gratefully at Amber's artist mother who was one of Dream Echo's founding members.

'This is little Heidi, Gwenda dear—poor little thing is badly traumatised. I have to go, Tom is going to be away for a day or two and I want to see him off!' Gwenda Williams smiled back reassuringly at Lottie who was one of her dearest friends and fellow workers at Dream Echo.

I'll make sure Heidi settles down well. Leave her to me Lottie and all my best wishes to Tom! Where is Amber by the way?'

'I left her studying the admission notes of this little girl's mother, Lisl Strang. Yet another case of severe domestic violence ongoing for many years, and thankfully now ended!' she snorted, and after a last tender glance at little Heidi, she slipped quietly away. She drove back to Ivy Cottage to find a familiar car parked in the cul de sac, and recognised it as Charles Latimer's. He had arrived early. She found the two men sitting in the kitchen in urgent discussion. They rose to their feet as she came in and Tom gave her a quick kiss, before Charles added his embrace.

'Wasn't sure if you would be able to get away when you said there was a new admission at the refuge,' said Tom. 'How did it go?' Lottie gave him a brief account, realising as she did so, that it mirrored countless other such reports she had given him. The size of the problem of domestic violence was enormous, their valiant efforts at Dream Echo a mere fleabite in a worldwide situation where one on four women suffered domestic violence at some time in their lives—and this was a conservative estimate.

After providing a quick lunch for the three of Lottie glanced curiously at Charles Latimer, Toms treasured friend and onetime colleague before his retirement in that special secret work in which she also had been involved. She knew how much her husband still missed his position in MI5, although the challenges presented by Dream Echo helped to fill the gap. Charles had remained a dear friend, as had his work partner the late Paul Trent before he tragically lost his life at the hands of a terrorist a few years back.

'I take it since you are both going to see Geraldine Denton, that the real reason is to sound out her son Colin. Don't you think it is still rather soon while he is still grieving his wife Mary—and helping his twin children come to terms with the future?' Lottie glanced from one to the other of the men. It was Charles who replied.

'Two days ago, we suffered a casualty in the firm. Young Leonard Owen who had been working closely with me since his training, was on his way to the office when he came across a terrorist wielding a machete and a sword at the entrance to that new store at Victoria. Several people were lying wounded on the pavement. Leonard was unarmed, but he didn't hesitate. Spectators say that he flew at the man and a violent struggle ensued. The terrorist fell unconscious, but not before he had swung the machete at Leonard's thigh severing a major artery. He bled out before anyone realised what was happening.' Latimer's voice demonstrated his distress.

'Oh Charles—such a terrible, terrible thing to happen! That poor courageous young man. I read an account of the incident in my daily paper. They named the terrorist and spoke highly of the brave man who had lost his own life saving that of others. I had no idea he might possibly be part of the service—or connected with you!'

'These things happen,' Tom put in quietly. 'Charles rang me explaining matters. He remembered we had previously discussed the suggestion of Colin Denton. joining the firm at some stage. Since Charles already knows Colin and his background and feels comfortable at the idea of working with him should he agree, now would seem to be the time to discuss it with him.' He looked at Charles. 'I hope he agrees. Personally, I think he would be an asset to the firm. He has a cool head and has demonstrated his courage.'

Lottie frowned slightly as she glanced from one to the other of them. Had they for one moment thought of Geraldine whose only son had just been restored to her after mourning his death—or of his twin children still coming to terms with the loss of their dear mother, but rejoicing that their father had survived the helicopter crash designed to murder him? Men! As she stared at them she realised she could not intervene in any way. Perhaps this was what the future held in store for her friend's son. After all, the firm was a family—composed of a small, diverse group of individuals possessing certain unique qualities of courage and devotion, capable of laying down their lives if required to protect the country to which they owed allegiance.

'Give my love to Geraldine—and Anna. I suppose you need to leave soon and I must get back to Dream Echo.'

Lottie was thoughtful as she drove back to the refuge. Usually she accepted Tom's decisions without question if for no better reason that they normally coincided with her own. But she was not comfortable with this plan to enrol Colin Denton into the firm when he had barely had time to readjust to all he had recently endured. Of course, he could always refuse the invitation, she told herself, and dismissed the problem from her mind.

It was early evening when a car drew up outside Rose Cottage and the two long limbed men stepped out. Geraldine opened the door to her friends and onetime colleagues.

'Tom—Charles! Welcome!' she cried as they embraced. 'Come through—Colin and Anna are in the living room with the children.'

'Making music by the sound of it,' exclaimed Tom. 'Who is that playing?'

'Anna. Come along.' They found Anna seated at the upright piano, surrounded by the three children, Colin leaning over the back of a chair, listening to her rendering of the Pastoral. It was a delightful scene and the two men glanced at each other doubtfully. Were they justified in removing this man from the healing presence of his mother and children—and the companionship of the lovely blonde-haired woman at the piano? But he could always return home at the end of each engagement.

'We need him,' said Latimer quietly and Tom nodded.

A few hours later after Geraldine had served a delicious dinner, Anna said regretful goodnight as she took little Susan home to bed. It was obvious the two guests had come to speak privately with Colin—and she wondered why? Perhaps it was because he would be required as a witness for the prosecution when Sea Giant's trial commenced. Yes, that must be it. But it had been such a happy evening and so wonderful to feel almost one of the family.

Geraldine also realised that Tom and Charles had not come merely to reassure themselves that all was well in the aftermath of the twins' kidnap. Glancing back as she led the youngsters upstairs to wash before bed, she noticed that the two men drawing their chairs closer to Colin's and an uneasy presentiment crossed her mind. Did they want to involve Colin in the firm? Oh no. Surely not—her heart pounded uncomfortably. It was Charles Latimer who took the initiative and raised the subject with the young man.

'Well Colin, I wonder if you've had time to consider the future yet? I can only guess at the happiness you're experiencing, reunited with your delightful young son and daughter and your mother. You mentioned over dinner that you've decided to make your home here so I imagine you will soon be making plans jobwise?' He leaned forward companionably. Colin nodded.

'Yes. I believe what the children need now is continuity with their schooling and that special relationship they have developed with my mother. To move them at this stage would be far too disruptive—and I'm enjoying getting to know my mother in a way I never did before—knowing her history makes it easier to understand her frequent absences during my childhood!' He looked at Latimer to see if he understood—saw he did.

'Yes—of course. Your mother was highly esteemed in MI5. It is very specialised work and as you would expect, very few people invited to enrol in the secret service. They have to be of a high calibre, trustworthy, courageous and with quick minds. Colin Denton—I believe that you are one such. I've come here today specifically to ask if you will consider joining us.' An expression of astonishment crossed Colin's face, his brows knitting together incredulously. There was a moment's silence.

'Are you serious?' he demanded.

'Absolutely I do assure you. Tom agrees with me that you will prove a fitting candidate. So, what do you say? The fact that the children enjoy a warm and loving home here with your mother means you need feel no anxiety about their welfare when away. Actually, since your previous occupation in the oil industry made short separations necessary, hopefully the twins will accept this new situation without problem.' He studied Colin's face expectantly, watched as he sprang to his feet and walked over to the window, to stand staring into the dusk. At last he turned and spoke, grey eyes troubled.

'My first reaction was to refuse your offer! I am only just coming to terms with my wife's death, and my children need the comfort of my presence. You are right in saying I need to seek employment—but certainly have never considered the future you offer! Charles, there must be many others better suited, men or women without responsibilities.' He returned to his chair and glanced from Latimer to Tom. 'Why me?' It was Tom who answered, staring at Colin reflectively and reaching a hand out to him.

'You more than fit the requirements—and both Charles and I like and trust you! As for responsibilities holding you back, you have only to look at your mother and the way she successfully balanced a very happy marriage to your father and raising you.' He paused. 'Then again, Lottie and I have always enjoyed a very fine marriage and brought up a loving family. I admit there are risks attendant on such occupation, but you have proved yourself well able to deal with emergencies.' He smiled. 'I promise you will never have time to be bored.' He turned to Latimer. 'Anything you want to add Charles? After all, I'm officially retired now. He will be working with you!'

'You would of course go through a rigorous training first,' put in Latimer quickly, 'But I'm certainly looking for a new working partner.' He gave Colin a straight look. 'It may be that you would prefer a more conventional occupation, running a small business perhaps—or something in the city, commuting each day, cricket on the village green at weekends?' he suggested casually. Colin stared back at him, as the boredom of such a future unfolded before him.

'I must be mad—but I accept your offer!' he exclaimed and saw approval in the eyes of both men.

'You will never regret it,' replied Latimer. 'I will be in touch when I have spoken with colleagues to arrange time and place for formalities. But for now, my hearty congratulations Colin Denton!' He held out his hand and Colin grasped it firmly. It was at this moment that Geraldine came back in, overheard those last words—and knew instinctively what had transpired. She felt a moments dismay quickly displaced by pride in her son. She looked questioningly at Charles Latimer.

'Am I right in guessing that you have just invited my son to join the firm, and that he has agreed?' she asked directly, grey eyes slightly troubled as she probed his face. He looked back at her uncomfortably. Perhaps in all courtesy he should have discussed it with her first as an ex-colleague. But Colin was a grown man, able to make his own decisions. He smiled innocently.

'If he proves as fine an agent as his mother before him, we'll all be well pleased! Look, I spoke it over with Tom who has spent more time with Colin than I have—and he approves the idea. Should have mentioned to you first, apologise!'

Thoughts raced through Geraldine's mind as she sank down on the couch. Yes, undoubtedly Colin would be exposed to danger from time to time, and the work would demand absences from home—but at least this way the children would be able to remain here at Rose Cottage. There again, Colin would be working with good friends who would guide him along the way. She looked across at him.

'I'm proud of your decision, dear. You are quite sure though, it's not well—too soon?' He came over, stooped over her planting a reassuring kiss on her forehead.

'It's almost as though it was meant to be! But will you be able to care for Charles and Melanie long term when I'm called away? It's a big commitment at a time when you should be enjoying your retirement Mum?' She didn't hesitate.

'It will give me a new lease of life in having my beloved grandchildren here—combined with the happiness of seeing more of you, my darling!' At her words, Tom exchanged a smile with Latimer. All had gone extremely well—MI5 had gained a new recruit!

'One question,' put in Geraldine suddenly. 'What about Anna Lindstrom? Is she to know about Colin's future employment?'

'I know she would prove completely trustworthy,' said Colin decisively. But Latimer shook his head. There were certain facts and disciplines Colin must learn, starting now.

'You may tell her you are seeking employment in the Civil Service—but no more than that. It is not only your own life you must safeguard from now on—but that of your future colleagues. Do I have your promise?' He searched Colin's face, sensed the protest about to spring from his lips, then Colin bowed his head slightly—nodded agreement. He had passed the first test. Geraldine smiled at his reaction.

'If Anna wonders about the purpose of our friend's visit today, I suggest you say it was to discuss the evidence you'll be required to give at the eventual trial of those villains heading Sea Giant!' she advised gently.

'Yes, of course,' he replied. He shook his head reflectively. 'What an extraordinary day this has been. None of this seems quite real yet.' He rubbed his chin soberly.

'Oh, it soon will,' chuckled Tom Lanscombe. 'Can't wait to tell Lottie!' He glanced at Geraldine. 'How about playing us something soothing on your piano, Geraldine? As I remember you are quite a musician.'

She rose to do so, and as the notes of a snatch of Fingal's Cave floated hauntingly around the room, her three listeners noticeably relaxed.

Chapter Eleven

Malcolm Greer tossed notification of this latest consignment of women onto the pile of unanswered correspondence littering the desk. It had all been going wonderfully well until something had caused the police to start probing his affairs! Everything had started to fall apart from the day that his beautiful golden-haired partner Erika Nicholson and little daughter Trudy had mysteriously disappeared! According to his servant Hassan, a strange car had driven up to Enderslie House and before anyone could prevent it, Erika and the child had dived into the shabby vehicle, the driver speeding swiftly away!

He swore under his breath now, thoughts returning malevolently to the woman whom he had surrounded with every luxury but had betrayed him by her outrageous escape. He had desperately tried to find the girl and his small daughter but to no avail! He who could mastermind the arrival and dispersal of so many desperate women from Eastern Europe, tempted by the promise of well-paid domestic jobs in this country only to find themselves forced into prostitution, had found himself helpless to find the one woman he esteemed.

That first day he had lambasted Hassan with his tongue, then ordered his man of business Dalton to employ the finest private detectives to discover Erika's whereabouts, but all to no avail! She had completely disappeared. It was as though the earth had swallowed her up! He had searched the house for clues—realised she had taken nothing with her. All the expensive jewellery he had bought her remained in that velvet lined tortoiseshell box on her dressing table—and her fine evening gowns, stylish suits and furs in the wardrobe. She really had departed with only the clothes she stood up in—incredible behaviour!

So how had her escape been arranged when denied access to a mobile phone, never allowed out on her own? He had asked himself this repeatably over the last few weeks. Then other matters had arisen to disturb his mind. He had a visit from two hard faced men in grey suits, who had questioned him as to his business dealings. To his dismay found they had gleaned information on his people trafficking, which he of course hotly denied. So far, they seemed to have discovered nothing conclusive, but he had the uneasy feeling that they would not tamely give up. Surely his carefully contrived smokescreen as a respected property developer must be accepted.

A sudden thought occurred to him now. Was it possible that Erika's disappearance had in some way provoked this interest in his financial affairs? But how—she had no slightest idea of the true source of his wealth. But where was she now and who had aided her in her escape. He swore viciously under his breath. He had already had all hospitals and nursing homes in the area checked to see if she had found employment but with no success. It was a mystery.

He stared moodily around his well-appointed study, where like all else in Enderslie House everything was the best money could buy. If only he could get Erika out of his mind! He sent his luxurious black leather swivel chair spinning savagely backwards, strode over to the window and stood surveying the perfectly manicured grounds. Surely any woman would have been proud to call this place her home? Then again, he was a good-looking man he flattered himself, on whose arm she could enter the finest restaurant or theatre with every confidence.

Perhaps he had been slightly overbearing in his manner towards her at times—raised his hand when she had shown less than complete obedience—but a woman was her husband's chattel was she not, to be treated as he thought fit. Only Erika had not been his wife, had refused to marry him! He rang the bell and Hassan entered quietly and looked at him expectantly.

'You rang, sir?' His dark eyes were respectful as he scanned his employer's face, recognising signs that another intense outburst of irritability was about to explode on his head. As he did so he cursed memory of the blond-haired woman whose abrupt departure a few weeks ago had caused so much disruption in this usually well-ordered household.

'Ring Frank Dalton—tell him to drive over here immediately!' Greer growled. Hassan bowed and retired. If only they could find that wretched woman and her brat, hopefully all would go back to normal. Either that, or perhaps his master could find another woman to delight him. Sadly, none of those who had made recent overnight stays at the house, had ever been invited to return.

Malcolm Greer's mood had not improved when Dalton arrived in his discreet black Ford to be shown into the study by Hassan. He glanced at the lawyer imperiously from behind his desk, signing to him to be seated.

'Almost two months have passed since I asked you to engage private investigators to track down Erika and my daughter. Have you any news for me?' he inquired curtly. Dalton shook his head.

'Nothing as yet I fear. But a suggestion was put forward that perhaps she might have made her way to a women's refuge?' he remarked tentatively. Greer raised his dark arched eyebrows questioningly.

'A women's refuge—what exactly is that?' he inquired, leaning forward intently. Dalton stared back at him, and licked his lips awkwardly. 'Well man—explain!' demanded Greer.

'Why Mr Greer—it is a term referring to certain sanctuaries set up to help abused women, and where they may stay until they recover, and make new lives for themselves.' He drew back apprehensively as he glimpsed the fury in Greer's dark eyes.

'You dare to suggest that I abused Erika?' Greer sprang to his feet and furiously pushing his heavy desk away from him. Dalton had never seen him so angry.

'Of course, not—but such places offer refuge to variety of women, some wishing to leave shall we say a—somewhat dominant partner.' He readjusted his spectacles over his pale blue eyes and watching Greer nervously, deeply regretting he had uttered the suggestion. He saw the dark red flush staining Greer's face and neck flare fiercely, then start to recede.

'So—are there any of these so-called refuges in our area, Dalton?' asked Greer directly.

'Their location is always kept secret for obvious reasons,' replied Dalton. 'It was only merest suggestion, sir. I had no wish to cause offence.' Malcolm Greer glared at him in exasperation. This idea however outrageous did at least offer slight gleam of hope.'

'You will discover the addresses of all such institutions within a hundred miles radius!' he snapped brusquely. 'That is an order!' Dalton rose to his feet, returned Greer's stare.

'But not possible to fulfil, I fear. As I've stated, the location of these refuges is kept a close secret. Now if there is nothing else this morning Mr Greer, then I have another client to see.' He bowed hastily and made for the door. Greer was a generous employer, but there was only so much discourtesy a man could accept even from a man as powerful as this.

Greer looked after him in frustration. He had been tempted to fire Dalton, only refrained because he was usually so damned good at his job. His thoughts rioted as he paced restlessly about the study. Was Dalton's suggestion the answer to Erika's disappearance—that she had actually sought safety in a refuge? If so, did her action label him as—an abuser? He was appalled to think of the reaction of his important friends should it come to their ears! Just let him get his hands on the woman and she would learn what abuse was!

So how was he going to discover the whereabouts of these refuges, since Dalton was proving less than helpful. A grim, knowing smile tightened his lips. What was the name of that corrupt plain clothes cop who had been useful in the past—O'Sullivan, that was it! A phone call, and an arrangement made to meet with the cop at the Stag hotel at nearby Lynchester. Greer smiled as he drove his car, the fine new Bentley replacing his BMW, along the quiet country road. He had the feeling that at long last he was on the verge of finding Erika Nicolson and their small daughter.

'Well Mr Greer, how can I be of assistance today?' asked the officer, as he tossed back the fine whisky appreciatively from where they sat in a quiet corner of the hotel bar. Greer told him and O'Sullivan restrained his surprise. So, his woman had left him and possibly fled to a refuge! Strange, he would not have taken Greer as an abuser, always appeared as the perfect gentleman. But nothing really surprised him these days, and obviously there was money in this for him if he helped find the beautiful golden-haired partner whom Greer prized so dearly.

'There is only one refuge I've heard tell of—and it's not far from where you live. If I reveal the address you must swear not to say who informed you. Agreed?' He pocketed the envelope Greer slipped across the table to him, gave him the information. Greer listened incredulously. The refuge it seemed was at a farmhouse owned by a fellow called Roddy Forester and his wife Norah, and situated only a few miles from Enderslie House. He was filled with a sense of rage that Erika might have been living almost on his doorstep and probably laughing at him all this time! He thanked O'Sullivan, rose and left.

He drove furiously on his return journey, only slowing as a narrow farm lane adjoining the road came in sight. He turned the car carefully along its bumpy track. A red-haired woman dressed casually in jeans and loose sweater and leading a rough coated pony looked up as the Bentley drew up in the courtyard. She pacified the startled pony and frowned. They were not expecting any new inmates today, nor would any social worker appear in a car of this magnificence. She stared uneasily at the man who stepped out of the vehicle and stalked over to her.

'Mrs Forester—Norah Forester?' he inquired curtly. Norah drew herself up and returned his stare, forcing a calm smile.

'Yes, I'm Norah Forester—and who are you?' she demanded, trying not to reveal the apprehension that seized her mind. Had it happened at last—someone had betrayed the true function of their farmhouse as a women's refuge? This man with his hard, dark eyes, was he the partner of one of those desperate women who had dared to make the break from a life of misery and abuse? As she looked at him intently memory surfaced of a recent shopping trip into Lynchester, where her husband Roddy had pointed this man out as the owner of Enderslie House, and from whom they had facilitated the escape of his abused partner Erika and her young daughter. She had only had a brief glimpse of the man that day as he came out of an exclusive jewellery shop and got into his car—this car.

'I am Malcolm Greer. I believe you have my partner Erika staying with you?' He would try the courteous approach first he thought. Norah returned his stare blankly.

'I cannot think why you imagine the lady you mention is here. I give you my word that you are mistaken,' she replied calmly. 'I'm sorry you have had a wasted journey. Good day to you, Mr Greer.' She turned her attention back on the pony, hoping the man would accept her rebuttal and leave. He did not, but strode nearer and laid a fiercely restraining hand on her arm. As though sensing the hostility in the stranger's manner, the pony reared bringing one of its hooves down heavily on Greer's foot. He uttered a cry of pain and outrage, released his grasp. Norah glared at him indignantly.

'I'm sorry if Charlie Boy hurt you, Mr Greer—but you have only yourself to blame. You should never startle a horse.' She rubbed her arm where his pincer like grip had left marks. 'Please leave,' she instructed.

'Not until I've had a look inside this house of yours to check Erika is not here!' Then before she could anticipate his move he leapt up the steps to the farmhouse door, pushed it open and entered. It was all so quick. Leaving the pony with a softly quieting word, she rushed after Greer, at the same time putting a whistle to her lips, its three shrill notes echoing both inside and outside the house. Roddy Forester heard its piercing sound as he was returning home in his tractor. He swore and increased his speed—drew the red tractor up beside the strange limousine, saw the pony standing nervously in front of the house. He switched off the engine, was up the steps and into his home within seconds, calling out his wife's name.

'Norah—Norah—where are you?' he cried. The sound of raised voices drew him to the back of the house—that secluded area where their guests having safely escaped from abusive relationships now enjoyed security and anonymity. Here he found his wife attempting to prevent a tall arrogant figure whom he instantly recognised as Malcolm Greer from entering the room where a group of women were chatting, heads bent over their sewing.

'Roddy! Thank goodness,' cried Norah in relief, as her husband strode forward and seized Greer by the shoulder. 'This man who appears to be suffering from some mental affliction, has forced his way in and is threatening our women's sewing group!'

'Let go, you oaf!' Greer shouted, struggling to free himself, but the strong hand the angry farmer clamped down on his shoulder pressing on a nerve, now grasped him ever more securely.

'Norah—ring the police station. Have them send someone over here to arrest this intruder,' Roddy requested. Norah did so, as the women looked nervously towards Greer. On the arrival of each new woman here, they were advised that should the worst ever happen and an abusive man track his partner down and burst into the refuge, that all should pretend to be part of a local sewing group. Norah's urgent whistle had alerted the ten women presently sheltering at the refuge to take immediate action.

As Greer looked angrily around the assorted women staring at him, eyes lifted calmly from the sewing in their laps, he registered the fact that what Norah had said could be true—this really was some sort of women's sewing club.

'Ok—sorry! Let me go,' he said to Roddy, his voice quieter. 'Maybe I have made a mistake and if so I do sincerely apologise. I was told this was a women's refuge, thought a woman to whom I am deeply devoted might be here.' Roddy heard the uncertainty in Greer's voice, and relaxed his grip slightly.

'And why should this lady have been seeking a refuge? Had you been abusing the unfortunate woman?' he asked coldly. 'If so I can only wish her well whoever she is. As for you, the police are on their way now and you will have to explain why you broke into our home terrorising my wife and her guests.'

'Please, tell the police it was a mistake and you'll never hear from me again,' pleaded Greer.

'Just let the fellow go, dear,' broke in Norah contemptuously. 'He said his name is Greer. He is obviously suffering from some kind of mental illness.' Her heart was pounding as she spoke but none would have guessed it.

'If you are right, Norah, the police will see he is offered the right kind of help,' her husband replied firmly. He smiled at the women sitting nervously around the room. 'I'm sorry this fellow has disturbed your sewing club. Please, just carry on ladies. Norah, love—perhaps you could deal with the pony. Charlie Boy is wandering about out in the courtyard, and may panic when the police car arrives. I'll look after this low life meanwhile—take him through to the kitchen.' He increased the pressure on Greer's shoulder once more, propelled him out of the room.

The two officers who had arrived in answer to Norah's call for help, regarded Malcolm Greer curiously. He was a well-known figure in Lynchester, known to be of a secretive nature, an extremely wealthy property developer, and owned Enderslie House. It seemed extraordinary that he had forced himself into the Forester's farmhouse, disturbing their guests—and also laid hands on Norah Forester, to be rightly restrained by her husband Roddy. Sergeant Hugh Thomas cautioned Greer, as accompanying officer P C Jill Lyon, watched the man's face, saw the arrogance mixed with unease at the situation he found himself in.

'So, Mr Greer—what have you to say for yourself?' demanded the sergeant. 'Have you an explanation for your behaviour? What brought you here today—have you previously enjoyed acquaintance with the Foresters?' Greer shook his head. He realised what an awkward position he had placed himself in by recklessly forcing his way into the house—would have to come up with some plausible excuse—but what? He plumped for the truth.

'I wish to deeply apologise for my actions. You see sergeant, my partner Erika Nicolson left me a few weeks ago taking our young daughter. I have been desperate for news of her, but unable to find any clue as to her whereabouts. Then someone mentioned women's refuges to me—that perhaps Erika for whatever strange reason might have entered one of these places. I was told by an impeccable source that this farmhouse was one of these refuges. Accordingly, I came here today and asked Mrs Forester with all courtesy if Erika was staying here. I fear I did not believe her when she denied it.'

'Why did you not believe her, sir?' the police sergeant demanded.

'Because the source of my information on what he assured me was the true purpose of this farmhouse, is one of your own people. I refer to officer O'Sullivan.' That would throw the cat amongst the pigeons he thought grimly. He had no slightest compunction in revealing the bent coppers identity despite his promise to conceal it. The two officers glanced at each other.

'You will accompany us to the station for further questioning, Mr Greer.'

Three hours later he was back home again in Enderslie House, waited on by an impassive Hassan. He had endured a gruelling interrogation by the police as to why Erika had disappeared from his prestigious mansion house—and why had he considered it possible she might have sought place in a women's refuge? Surely that could only mean that he had been abusing the lady—and if that were so he had much explaining to do now.

'Look—if you charge me over my intrusion into the Forester's farmhouse, I'll be forced to publicly name the officer who gave me relevant information to its supposed true function. If news of an officer accepting money for information on the location of such a place should come to light, I presume it would not exactly enhance the reputation of the police force. Up to you, of course!' he had said blandly. And now he was free and back home, but had been cautioned never to set foot on the Forester's property again.

He threw himself down in his comfortable tan leather, recliner armchair and scowled as he considered the situation. Possibly O'Sullivan had given him the faulty information in good faith—someone must have noted the collection of women visiting the farmhouse and come to the wrong conclusion. But that didn't mean that Erika had not fled to one of these genuine so-called women's refuges. His task now was to investigate all such places! But there again—how to go about it?

As he sat there he revisited in his mind every detail of what had occurred at the Forester's farmhouse. Those women he had seen with their heads bowed over their needlework, had seemed genuine enough. He wondered idly why they would have taken the trouble to drive all the way from Lynchester rather than use a facility within the town. But they could not have driven there today he realised now. There had been no vehicle in the courtyard other than his own! They could of course have rented a minibus, a possible arrangement made to collect them later. That might be it!

He rose restlessly to his feet, poured a whisky, tossed it off. Had he just been taken for a fool by the Foresters? Were they really running a refuge? He swore and hurled his empty glass across the room. He knew he could not risk another visit there, the police had warned it would mean immediate arrest, and he certainly did not want to draw any unnecessary attention to himself at this time, when his business affairs were under official scrutiny. But he was determined to find Erika, would do so whatever the cost. But where was she, damn her!

The Foresters sat quietly in their kitchen that evening. They had been lucky this time and happily those women under their charge who had recently escaped a nightmare of abuse, were recovering from the shock of facing the angry individual who had forced his way in seeking his partner. Each one of those women realised uneasily that Greer could well have been their own abuser. The ruse of pretending to be a women's sewing group had worked—this time.

'I think we should contact social services—they need to know how narrowly the refuge escaped exposure today,' said Norah decisively. Roddy reached out a hand and stroked hers comfortingly.

'We knew when we started the refuge, that we would always be vulnerable to a situation such we experienced today. But look at it this way Norah love—our plans for such contingency worked!' His wife gave a tired smile. She had spent the last few hours reassuring the women under their protection that the intruder who had been removed by the police had been informed he would face immediate arrest if he dared show his face there again.

'But what made him think this was a refuge?' one of the women had asked anxiously.

'Betty I just don't know, dear. Rumours spread, people gossip—but what actually made that man Greer suspect this to be a refuge is a mystery. Someone must have put the idea in his head, I guess. But this refuge like others across the country is only known to a branch of social services and a few members of the police force. We just need to put what happened today behind us Betty—look to the future!' The young mother she was addressing nodded and forced a smile, the once vivid scar across her lovely face, dealt by a husband's open razor now less noticeable these days. Betty and her small son Stephen had been with them a month now, would soon be moving on.

It was knowledge of the many women in similar plight to Betty, that initially impelled the Foresters to open their home as a refuge. Roddy spent most of his working day running the farm, but always ready to collect another abused woman should the need arise, while Norah received wonderful help and support in running the refuge from Roddy's mother Connie who lived with them but had been away today visiting an elderly aunt—had missed the drama.

'Listen—that's the front door—Mum's back!' exclaimed Roddy rising.

'I'll make tea. She will need a cup when she hears what happened today,' smiled Norah, as almost at once the kitchen door opened and Connie bustled in, a warm smile on her rosy face, as she sank down in a chair.

'How was your Aunt,' asked Norah, lifting the kettle.

'Not bad really, considering her age. Still able to remember details of her childhood and full of gossip about the neighbours. What kind of a day have you both had? Quiet I suppose!' She stared as the couple burst out laughing. 'Well—are you going to tell me what the joke is?' she demanded. They did so and her eyes were grave as she listened.

'Does this mean that the man Greer could come back again or spread rumours about the refuge around the district?'

'We can only hope not. The police have warned him against any such action, so we can only hope! But we go on regardless!' said Roddy firmly and Norah smiled agreement as she poured tea.

Malcolm Greer spent the next few days researching what little information he could glean about women's refuges on the internet. He read about their function, scanty funding—that one in four women suffered domestic abuse during their lifetime. Abuse? Surely a man had a perfect right to expect certain standards from the woman he maintained, make his displeasure known if his partner defied him. It was the way of the world, always had been. But if these places existed, then where were they—and how did a frightened, confused woman find one?

He tried to recollect faces of the women he had briefly noticed in the Forester's farmhouse. Erika had not been amongst them, that was certain. But there again, if she had indeed sought refuge there, would surely not have remained so near to Enderslie House for any length of time. No, she would have moved on to another refuge. Was there a list of such places? And who helped these disloyal women who left their protectors? Social workers—professional busy bodies interfering in the lives of others. How would Erika have found opportunity to meet with a social worker, watched closely as she had been at all times.

Damn it, he raged, how had she arranged to escape the house with little Trudy without money and leaving nearly all her jewellery behind? His mind in turmoil he reached for the decanter, pouring yet another generous measure of whisky. Greer was heavily drunk when he staggered upstairs to bed late that night.

Morning dawned, he flinched as he swung his legs over the bed, assailed by a ferocious headache, swallowed a couple of painkillers, and dispensed with breakfast. But his mind had cleared. He realised the way to find which of the many refuges Erika had fled, could only to be discovered through the auspices of the social services. It was unlikely that any relevant social worker would disclose Erika's location to the partner she had accused of abusing her. But surely social workers must have offices—keep private records of those to whom they offered their assistance?

So where would he get the address of the Lynchester branch? He rang the bell, Hassan appeared. He gave an order and sat back to wait. Suddenly the phone rang. It was the lawyer Dalton. He smiled, no doubt the man would be full of apologies for his recent unhelpful attitude! But his smile faded at what he heard. The latest assignment of women trafficked from Eastern Europe had been intercepted. None of their minders had so far revealed details of the man who master minded the organisation, but when men are facing long prison sentences they may snatch at promises by the authorities to go easy on them in exchange for information. Dalton advised Greer that he must be prepared for the worst—and further, Dalton was personally unable to accept further work from Mr Greer. He had to protect himself.

Greer tossed the phone across the room and swore. Thoughts of Erika receded in his brain. when faced with this new worry! When the hard-faced individuals from the home-office had called on him recently, it had been obvious that they had suspicions of his involvement in people trafficking—but no definite link at that stage. But now—with those escorting the latest batch of women under arrest?

The women in their charge also undergoing interrogation although the latter would know little of any relevance. He started to sweat as he realised fate was closing in on him.

When Hassan knocked, entered and handed him a slip of paper with the details of the social workers office at Lynchester, he merely nodded absently, glanced at it carelessly. The name of the woman running the office was Beth Ellis. She also dealt personally with cases of domestic abuse. He frowned. Had Erika met with this Ellis woman? If so when—how? It was hard trying to juggle with two devasting problems simultaneously. The more immediate matter had to be his business dealings with the gang procuring young women from Eastern Europe, his own master minding the organisation on the verge of coming to light.

As to Erika, he would find the woman soon, be revenged for the humiliation her disappearance had inflicted on him. Perhaps a start could be made in the meanwhile, the social workers office searched for clues. He imagined there must be a filing cabinet there with details of the whereabouts of abused women in these so-called refuges. His eyes hardened as he summoned Hassan, and gave specific order.

He relaxed slightly. Now to devise a method to disassociate himself officially from the present European fiasco. It would not be easy—and acknowledged that if not successful could face many years of imprisonment. People traffickers received very heavy penalties. Had he been a fool taking such risk all these years? But look at the luxury and splendid lifestyle he had enjoyed and hopefully would continue to after the dust had settled.

Back in Bramble cottage, Anna Lindstrom rarely thought of the life she had fled two months ago kept under the rigid control of Malcolm Greer, and constant scrutiny by Hassan and Nanny Beecham and the elderly housekeeper Moira Banks and other staff. She had so completely accepted her new identity, she no longer felt herself to be Erika Nicolson, just as Susan had accepted she was no longer called Trudy. She felt happy and secure in her new home enjoying the kindly support of her neighbour Geraldine Denton. She had never known a mother's love, hers dying in giving birth—now increasingly Geraldine was taking position of adoptive mother to her, Susan and Geraldine's twin grandchildren behaving as family.

She acknowledged life had changed slightly with the advent of Colin Denton at his mother's Rose Cottage, reunited there with twin children who had grieved his supposed death for so many weeks. Anna had not wanted to intrude during the family's healing process—but Colin made it obvious that he was not averse to her visits to his mother realising how close the two women had become, as had Susan with twins Charles and Melanie.

After the recent visit by Tom Lanscombe and Charles Latimer Anna sensed a slight difference in Colin. It wasn't just the suppressed grief he was working his way through, but a new detachment she realised, was polite and considerate as before, but his thoughts seemed elsewhere during her visits. She mentioned it to Geraldine today as the children played with their kittens. Susan had brought Patches to play with Pyrites, and now the antics of the small cats swinging precariously on the curtains they were attempting to climb were so comical the youngsters collapsed in laughter.

'Geraldine—is something troubling Colin? He seems different somehow—not distant exactly, but detached?' She looked at Geraldine questioningly.

'Perhaps he is concerned with the forth coming trial of the villains from Sea Giant and the evidence he will have to give. It won't be easy, bringing back up all the horrors he suffered at their hands—in especial the murder of his dear Mary. He is also considering a job in the civil service, says he will need a steady income to support his children.' She smiled at Anna, wishing she could tell her the truth, that Colin was to join the Secret Service, but Charles Latimer had suggested it was kept secret.

'Does it mean he'll have to move away from Rose Cottage?' asked Anna in dismay.

'Well, he may have to spend some time away, but this will always be his home. It's good that you are getting on well with my son, Anna,' she said quietly. 'I know he enjoys your company, my dear.'

She turned her head at a distressed meow from one of the kittens. Its claws had almost lost hold on the curtain it was climbing and Geraldine ran across to its rescue, glancing ruefully at the snags caused in the fabric. She handed the small struggling kitten to Charles and sighed. The once immaculate sitting room looked like a bear garden these days she thought whimsically—but the sight of the happy children more than compensated. She bent down starting to gather up the ebony chessmen the children had knocked from the chess table in their play. Anna stooped to help her.

It was then that the phone rang. Geraldine picked it up.

'Hallo?'

'Would that be Mrs Geraldine Denton,' a strange voice inquired. 'This is the

'Global News.' We understand your son Colin Denton is staying there, would like to speak with him.'

'About what exactly?' she asked brusquely.

'Why the forthcoming trial of the Sea Giant executives. We have been informed that he is to give vital evidence against them, wish to come down and interview him.'

'I'm sorry but I do not think my son would wish to speak with the media,' she said curtly.

'Surely that is for him to decide! May I speak to him please?' She about to make another refusal when the door opened and Colin appeared, saw the frustration on her face as she held the phone. He looked at her inquiringly.

'Everything alright?' he asked. Muting the phone, told him. 'Let me have it,' he said.

'Colin Denton here. I understand you have spoken to my mother suggesting an interview with regard to matters pertaining to Sea Giant. Thank you for your interest but it will not be possible!'

'We could offer you a good sum for an exclusive, Mr Denton,' pursued the caller.

'Money doesn't come into this. Thank you for your interest, but I will not be granting interviews with your paper or any other. Good day to you!' He put the phone down and glanced at Geraldine, his eyes troubled.

'How did they know I was to be called as a witness do you suppose? As far as I know the fact that I survived the helicopter crash hasn't been officially announced yet' He threw himself down on the deep settee, his face expressing unease. 'Damn it, where did the bloody paper get their information from?' then realising Anna was listening he forced a smile. 'Sorry about that outburst,' he apologised.

'I think we need to let Tom know,' said Geraldine quietly. He nodded soberly.

'You're right. I'll call him from my room, the children are quite vocal in here!' he said lightly, glancing fondly at the youngsters absorbed in play with the two kittens. He rose and left the room. Anna was about to make a remark to Geraldine, but instinct restrained her. She knew that the older woman was worried about him, and hopefully would discuss it in her own time.

Colin sat on his bed listening to Tom's calm advice on his mobile, as they discussed the call from 'Global News'.

'But how did they know I'm still alive?' he asked in exasperation.

'These things come out despite our best efforts,' came Tom's reassuring voice. 'Be watchful in the meanwhile—the press may not abide by your refusal to speak with them. Just be wary—say nothing. I'll contact Charles, he needs to know. In the meanwhile, don't worry.' Colin shrugged as he got up from the bed, walked over to the window and stared out at the garden, the flower beds ablaze with white, bronze, and gold chrysanthemums, late yellow roses, Michaelmas daisies and others he did not recognise. He remembered how much his father had enjoyed the garden spending happy hours with his mother who had created this delightful haven.

As he stood there he realised how much his mother must have missed his father, dealing with her grief alone in the cottage that had proved such peaceful retirement home for the couple. But she hadn't allowed that grief to shatter her life as he had almost done in similar situation with Mary's death. No, life goes on, and is what you make it. Suddenly the children ran across the lawn below him and as he heard their excited young voices he felt as though a curtain lifted in his mind. He ran downstairs, joined them out in the garden and Geraldine smiled as she saw him tossing them in his arms to screams of laughter.

'I think he is going to be just fine now,' she exclaimed softly to Anna, wishing she was free to share Colin's new career with the girl. 'The future is going to be bright for all of us!'

The following morning Colin stood at the gate watching Geraldine helping the children into the car for the short drive to school, and waived as they set off. He turned to go back into the cottage when he was hailed by a young woman in a red jump suit, and carrying a large black leather satchel, who seemed to appear from nowhere.

'Mr Denton—Colin Denton?' she inquired as she opened the gate and approached him boldly. 'Name's Katy Richards—Global News! Just need a few minutes of your time, sir!' He stared at her in outrage.

'I made my decision clear to the person who phoned me from your office yesterday—the answer remains no to any interview. I'm sorry you've had a wasted journey Miss Richards!' Colin's voice was calm but his expression displayed his displeasure. The woman's smile did not fade as she continued to close the distance between them.

'Oh, come now—you are going to be bombarded by members of the press once the court case starts! Giving me an exclusive will prevent all that.' She beamed a seductive smile at him from lips as red as her jump suit, dark eyes watching him closely.

'You are trespassing, Miss Richards. I must ask you to leave,' he said stiffly. It was at this moment that Anna appeared at the gate with little Susan. She stared at the reporter curiously as Susan ran forward along the pathway and took Colin's hand. He smiled at the little girl, lifted her up in his arms.

'Hallo there, Susan. You have just missed my mother and the twins.' He beckoned to Anna. 'Come in both of you—this lady is just leaving!' He glared pointedly at the reporter. Anna glanced at the woman as she joined Colin at the front door, placing a hand on his arm.

'Who was that, Colin?' she inquired, turning her face towards him. Neither of them noticed the reporter take those three quick shots on her phone cam before slipping out of the gate.

Katy Richards grinned satisfaction. This was perfect—Colin Denton caught with mystery woman and child. Was he having an affair two months after his wife's death? It wasn't the story she had come for but it would do she thought with amused satisfaction. She turned on her red high heeled shoes, hurried to the car she had parked at the bend of the road—drove off. She wondered briefly who the beautiful blonde with her cute child had been. Well, so long as their readers also wondered, her trip had been worthwhile.

Hassan picked the papers up and carried them through to the dining room for Greer to peruse after breakfast. As he put them down, a photograph on the front page of a tabloid caught his eye. He gasped—it couldn't be! He picked it up and carried it across to the window. Greer saw him standing there as he stalked in casually and seated himself at table, as by clockwork the maid appeared with coffee on a silver tray. Hassan turned back still holding the paper.

'Good morning, sir. I think there is something you need to see,' he said quietly, handing him the copy of Global News. There was no need to draw his attention to the photograph, Greer's eyes widened as he snatched the paper closer, then read the caption.

"Colin Denton reported dead in copter crash in North Sea, seen alive weeks later and according to confidential sources preparing to give evidence at trial of Sea Giant executives. Who is beautiful woman seen comforting Denton whose own wife died in mysterious car crash the day after his reported death."

He read it through a couple of times, staring searchingly at Erika's face and that of his small daughter held in the arms of this complete stranger, Colin Denton! There was no slightest doubt in his mind that it was Erika and Trudy. She was looking amazingly happy, animated. Well, that would soon change he thought grimly.

'Hassan—contact this paper, see if you can get details of Denton's address. There is no mention of it here. Oh, and find out any details of this mentioned helicopter crash.' Hassan bowed, delighted to have been instrumental in bringing the difficult matter to Greer's attention.

'Anything else, sir?'

'Yes, endeavour to discover what you can about the forthcoming trial of those Sea Giant executives. Big oil company, due to make a packet with the new reported find. There's some sort of mystery here. I need to discover how Erika is involved in it!' He waived Hassan away. 'Don't waste time, man!' He was smiling grimly as his breakfast was served. He had found her and before long she would be back here where she belonged—and oh, she would learn her lesson! No need now to break into the social workers office to search for details of any possible women's refuge now—that plan cancelled. She was obviously living openly with this Denton fellow. He could easily be disposed of.

Geraldine's phone rang as she was pulling her dressing gown on. It was Lottie and she smiled as she heard her friends voice.

'This is an early call Lottie dear, lovely surprise!' she said warmly.

'Geraldine—you need to alert Anna that there's a photograph of her standing next to Colin in today's Global News! How did it come to be taken?'

'What's that!' Geraldine sank down on the bed, her face bewildered. 'Are you sure?'

'I wouldn't joke about such a thing. Listen, there's a caption mentioning Colin. I'll read it out to you.' Geraldine's face blanched as she tried to take it in. 'Well, how did the reporter manage to get the photo of them both?' asked Lottie.

'I think I know. When I returned from driving the twins to school yesterday morning, Colin told me a woman reporter from Global News had arrived in my absence demanding an interview—this, despite Colin's refusal to speak with the paper on the previous day. Apparently, Anna arrived with Susan as the reporter was leaving. He said nothing about a photo!'

'She must have taken it without his permission. MI5 hadn't really wanted news of Colin's survival to become public knowledge until the onset of the trial. But it's Anna we must be concerned about. If the man Greer sees her photograph she is in danger. You had better warn her at once.'

'You're right! We must get Anna and Susan away from here immediately!' Geraldine's face was taut with dismay. 'I'll tell Colin, then dash next door to Bramble Cottage. Where can she go though, poor girl?' asked Geraldine anxiously.

'Why back to Dream Echo! Tom is driving over to collect mum and child as we speak, should be there within the hour. But your Colin could be in danger too. Greer will guess he has knowledge of Anna's whereabouts, put pressure on him. He's a ruthless individual. Tell Colin to take great care.'

Geraldine didn't stop for more, put the phone down hastily, pulled on a skirt and sweater and ran to knock on Colin's door. He looked up sleepily as she came in, then recognising the worry on her face jumped out of bed.

'Mum! What's wrong?'

'That reporter who came here yesterday managed to take a photograph of Anna standing next to you, her little girl in your arms.

The blurb in the paper makes play of the fact that you survived the helicopter crash and suggests Anna is—well, they mention Mary's recent death!'

'But that's outrageous! I didn't see the blasted woman take any photograph, and how dare she makes such suggestions!' His face was rigid with anger.

'Colin—the greatest problem is that Anna's dangerous ex-partner, Malcolm Greer may see the paper—recognise Anna and come here after her. Lottie rang me just now, suggests the best plan is for Anna to return to Dream Echo for a few weeks. Hopefully the police will soon have enough evidence to arrest Greer for people trafficking and he'll be put away for a long while!'

'Why can't Anna just stay where she is? If Greer shows his face anywhere near her he will have me to deal with!' said Colin forcefully. Geraldine shook her head decisively.

'No Colin. He has many people working for him and this place is very isolated. We cannot risk any harm coming to Anna or Susan. Tom Lanscombe is on his way over to collect and get them safe away—and I'm on my way next door to alert Anna to what has happened and help her pack a few essentials.' She turned for the door.

'No, wait!' he began. But she merely called after her that he should get the children up and give them breakfast. He looked after her in exasperation, dressed and called the twins.

Anna opened the door to Geraldine and stared at her in surprise.

'Geraldine!'

'Sorry to be such an early caller—but something has happened. May I come in!' Five minutes later Anna was trying to calm the thoughts rioting through her brain. Geraldine had repeated Lottie's account of the photograph and suggestive article. It had happened, she realised, her carefully contrived new identity of little use now her picture was there in the Global News for all to see! She thought back to the attractive woman in the red jump suit and high heels who was turning away as she arrived with Susan. How had the reporter taken her shot of them?

'So, you must see Anna, the safest path for you right now is to return to Dream Echo for a short time. Tom is on his way over. Just get ready, pack a bag and tell Susan you are going on an exciting adventure.'

'Does Colin know?' asked Anna quietly,

'Yes—as you can guess he wants you to stay. If it was just Greer himself we had to worry about I might have agreed—but from what you have told me of the man, he employs some very dangerous people.

We can't risk his getting his hands on your little girl!' She saw the flash of fear in Anna's eyes at this.

'I'll get Susan dressed. Would you get some cereal ready for her whilst I pack?' She attempted to control her anxiety—knew she had to be extremely calm. Geraldine smiled at her reassuringly.

'Everything is going to be all right, Anna dear. We know that Greer will soon be arrested, and prosecuted for his crimes. Those poor women brought into this country illegally are treated abominably poor things! People like Greer who make a fortune out of the desperation of others deserve no pity. Now make haste!'

'What about the kitten?'

'I'll look after little Patches until you are back. The twins will take great care of her.'

Two hours later, Colin sat glowering out of the window, frustrated that the young woman he had come to admire for her charm and honesty had been forced to leave so precipitately because of their friendship. If he could get his hands on that woman reporter, he would give her a piece of his mind. How dared she throw aspersions on them in such a manner? It was also unfortunate that Sea Giant would now be aware that he had not perished as planned deep down on the sea bed. But there was little they could do now under arrest and awaiting trial.

Geraldine looked at him sympathetically as she came into the kitchen. Just an hour ago they had waved goodbye to Anna and Susan as Tom Lanscombe drove them away. She had just come back from Bramble Cottage where since then she had been gathering all of Anna's private belongings together, so that if any of Greer's employees should break in there, they would find no trace of the lovely young woman and her little daughter. She sank down in a chair, exhausted by all her early morning activities.

'None of this should have happened!' burst out Colin. 'That reporter should be sacked for the chaos she has created. How long do you think Anna will have to be away?' Geraldine sighed, understanding his frustration but knowing they had taken the only sensible step to protect Anna. He glanced at her face, saw the weariness and felt remorse for his attitude.

'Sorry about that, Mum! You relax dearest, and I'll make coffee. It's just that after all our family have suffered at Sea Giant's hands, to now find Anna also facing possible danger is difficult to come to terms with.'

'She is an intelligent woman and very brave,' replied Geraldine. 'She will soon be back again—and it's not as though she is going to an unknown destination. Tom and Lottie say Dream Echo is a very special place, and the young lady who runs it, Amber Marsden, is an amazing person.'

'I'll miss her—I mean the twins will miss her—and Susan,' he exclaimed correcting himself, as he lifted the kettle.

'Well, in the meanwhile, we have another small guest—little Patches! Life should be interesting with two energetic kittens rampaging about the cottage,' smiled Geraldine. She looked at her son curiously. Was he taking more than a friendly interest in lovely Anna Lindstrom? No—it was far too soon after dear Mary's death. But in the future?

'It was good to see Tom,' said Colin now. 'Shame he couldn't have stayed longer after his long drive here. I will always remember the kindness both he and Lottie showed me when I stayed at their cottage. So many kind people have crossed my path this year. It was the vicar of the church next to the Lanscombe's cottage who made me realise it.' Geraldine looked up.

'Would that be Michael Bonnet, vicar of St Lawrence Church? I met him years ago when staying with the Lanscombes—a fine man of God,' Geraldine stated simply. He glanced at her questioningly, wondering now about those secret years she had spent in MI5. Perhaps one day she would open up to him. He had noticed the speed and efficiency with which she had organised Anna's departure this morning—recognised the steel beneath the outward appearance of an innocuous elderly lady. She had been a respected member of the secret organisation he was about to join and as he thought about this, had a sense of pride in his mother.

'Yes, Bonnet—that was his name. We spoke at some length and his words have stayed with me.' She looked at Colin curiously, and was tempted to question him, but knew instinctively that this was not the time. If only she had tried to get closer to her son before he met Mary—but so much had been going on in her life, particularly during his childhood years when she had so often been absent. She turned and sighed. Had she disregarded something infinitely precious in exchange for what—the excitement and dangers offered by membership of MI5?

'Perhaps I should have been a stay-at-home mother,' she exclaimed inconsequently. He looked at her and raised an eyebrow.

'I don't exactly see you as that,' he said frankly. 'You would have been bored to tears!' He put an arm around her slim shoulders. 'I could never have wished for a better mother,' he added and knew he meant it. She glanced up at him gratefully.

'It helps to hear you say so, Colin. Both our lives have been embroiled in the doings of wicked unscrupulous individuals—as has Anna's also. It is of her we must think now. It's just so cruel that she should be exposed to further hurt at that man Greer's hands.

Hopefully, he will be arrested soon—but in the meanwhile, we must be prepared in case he arrives here in search of Anna, or sends his unpleasant employees.' Her grey eyes stared broodingly towards the window. 'We need to keep a careful eye on the twins,' she suggested baldly.

'What's that—the twins? What make you think they might be at any risk?' His face hardened at the thought.

'Because when individuals of his sort want to put pressure on people, they often resort to threatening those dear to them—as with Sea Giants' recent kidnapping of your children, Colin!' He glanced at her startled.

'If he comes anywhere near Charles and Melanie I'll kill him!' He raised his fists as he spoke and Geraldine placed a soothing hand on his arm.

'All this is merely looking at the worst picture. We do not even know if Greer has seen that photograph in the Global News. The trouble is the other papers will jump on the story in the next day or two—and when the court case starts you will find yourself headline news—until another story appears.' She looked at him sympathetically. He scowled.

'I hadn't considered any possible publicity. Surely it will hurt my joining MI5?' he exclaimed doubtfully.

'I doubt it. Your appearance can be changed if necessary, a new identity. Now let's be practical. I'll collect the children from school this afternoon. They will have to be told that Anna and Susan have gone to stay with friends for a short time. I'm hoping the fact we are caring for Susan's kitten will reassure them that they'll be back soon.'

'Perhaps I should be the one doing the school run?' suggested Colin. 'Now that picture has appeared in the press, there's little use in hiding away here. You speak with the teachers today, tell them I will be coming in future.' He looked protectively at his mother. 'Whenever I'm away keep the doors locked—promise?' She nodded.

'I'll take every care. But you know if Greer asks around the village, any number of people will tell him that Anna has made her home next door. We will have to plead ignorance if asked about her private life by Greer or any of his associates.' Her mind was trying to encompass all eventualities as she reached out for the coffee he offered her.

'At least we got Anna safely away,' she breathed as she sipped it.

'Yes—so now we just wait I guess!' he replied heavily.

'Actually, there is someone I ought to inform about Anna—Sergeant Evans! I'll ring him now—let him know that Anna is safe away, but that we may have a future visit from Greer!' He listened reflectively, had a high opinion of the local police sergeant.

'Evans is a good man. Can't do any harm to have him in the picture.' As his mother made the call, Colin glowered as he sat there contemplating what he would like to do to the man who had caused so much distress to their delightful neighbour. Hopefully, Greer would be arrested and face many years in jail!

Anna Lindstrom was doing her best to reassure her small daughter that they would soon be returning home to Bramble Cottage. She looked around the attractive bedroom painted in pale primrose yellow, at the flowered curtains and duvet cover in soft pastel shades, the bowl of white and gold chrysanthemums on the bedside table and a baby doll placed on the small, comfortable foldaway bed for Susan.

Amber had greeted them kindly, glad that this was one arrival that did not need an urgent call on the local doctor to advise on the severe injuries with which new admissions so often presented. Normally she would not have allocated one of their few spare places for a guest who had previously left them to start a new life. But Anna's circumstances were such that she needed the safety and anonymity of the refuge until her abusive ex-partner had been dealt with. It was the first time that a woman rehomed by Dream Echo had been forced to return.

'Why do we have to stay here again?' asked Susan fretfully. 'I want to be back in our cottage! I want Melanie and Charles—and my kitten!' Her blue eyes so like her mother's, held a rebellious look. 'When can we go home, Mummy?'

'When it's safe to do so! Susan darling, there's a chance that your father may discover our home and come after us. Someone put a photograph of us visiting the Dentons in a newspaper. We can't be sure he will see it—but it's possible.' She felt uncomfortable at letting her know, but on balance thought it better to be truthful so that Susan would be cooperative. She saw a flash of fear in the child's eyes.

'Will he try to make us go back to Enderslie House, Mummy? That would be terrible—please don't let it happen! It was so scary there—and I didn't like that horrid Nanny.' Anna put her arms around the little girl and held her close.

'Don't worry, Susan. I'll make sure we are both safe, even if it means remaining here for a while. There will be other children for you to play with, and Tom and Lottie are often here and you like that nice lady Amber.' She kissed her and watched as Susan seemed to accept matters and started to explore their room. Thank goodness children were so adaptable, she thought.

The next day Anna slipped back into the familiar routine of Dream Echo, although she felt far removed now from the frightened, deeply anxious individual who had arrived there months earlier, transferred from the first refuge where she had briefly stayed run by Roddy and

Norah Forester—but all too close to Enderslie House. Nevertheless, the sudden wrench from the normality of her home at Bramble Cottage and the everyday support of her kindly neighbour Geraldine Denton was a shock.

She was walking in the grounds at the back of the old mansion house, with Susan skipping in front of her, making for the children's play area. She smiled as she saw the confidence with which Susan started to climb the steps, whooshing down with screams of delight. What an amazing difference had been wrought in the child by that relatively short period away from the malign influence of Malcolm Greer. He must never be allowed to get his hands on either of them again!

'Anna—Anna!' She turned around as she heard her name called and saw Amber approaching, Tom Lanscombe at her side. She smiled back at them, thinking how very unusual it was for someone as young and beautiful as Amber to have shown such generosity and initiative in turning her once formal mansion house into the amazing refuge she had named Dream Echo, which had already transformed the lives of countless abused women referred by social services.

'Amber—good morning!' she called happily, her smile fading slightly as she saw the grave look on both their faces. 'Is something wrong?' she cried quickly, glancing from one to the other of them.

'Hopefully not,' replied Amber gently. 'But the fact is, Tom just informed me that your abusive ex-partner has visited Forester's refuge in the hope that he would find you. He actually laid hands on Norah— but her husband Roddy appeared on the scene and dealt with him. Police were called. He was cautioned with immediate arrest should he go anywhere near the refuge again. The Foresters managed to persuade him that the ladies he had seen when he burst into the farmhouse were a visiting women's sewing group and seems he accepted this.' She paused now and looked sympathetically at Anna. 'The problem is that Greer is now convinced that you have sought safety in a refuge. So far, we have been extremely fortunate in that no one has ever penetrated Dream Echo's secret.'

'The village locals believe Amber is running a residential artist commune here,' Tom broke in. 'It speaks for the excellent security system we operate that no one has ever questioned this assumption. The present problem is that it has come to light that it was a corrupt police officer who helped Greer identify the Forester's farmhouse as a refuge. He has been sacked of course—warned he faces years in prison if he reveals the location of any other refuges—but?' and his face expressed his concern.

'What that police officer did was shocking!' exclaimed Anna hotly. 'Whatever made him do it, Tom—and why was he not jailed for such a terrible betrayal of trust!' Even as she asked she began to guess at the answer. His answer confirmed it.

'He was paid by Greer for the information. If he were put on public trial it would focus the attention of many other dangerous abusers on the establishment of women's refuges.' He shook his head and glanced at Amber. 'We thought it best to alert you that when Greer realises you are no longer at Ravensnest as he'll discover if he goes there, may then suspect you have sought shelter in a refuge. Hopefully, it is doubtful he would ever come to hear of Dream Echo, very few are aware of its existence.' He looked protectively at Anna.

'Amber—do you want me to leave?' asked Anna suddenly, staring into the unusual golden-brown eyes of the lovely girl who ran the refuge.

'Under no circumstances, Anna! You are as much under our protection here as any other of our guests. Tom just wanted you to be aware that Greer has begun to search out the location of refuges. But we cannot know at this stage whether he actually saw your photograph in the Global News.' She smiled encouragingly. 'The important thing is you are safe here, Anna!'

'Thank you, Amber. I am deeply grateful for your help. Let me know if there is anything I can do to help any other of the women seeking shelter here,' replied Anna.

'I will take you up on that!' said Amber. Tom listened approvingly.

'Hopefully, the police will soon have sufficient evidence to arrest the fellow for people trafficking. It's a very serious crime, Anna. The impact it has on the innocent lives caught in his evil web is indescribable. We'll get him soon and you'll be able to return to your cottage!'

Chapter Twelve

Malcolm Greer looked at the coded email he'd just received with satisfaction. Twenty young women landed at Dover—not the original batch who had been intercepted recently, these were from Latvia. Their minders were escorting them to a lodge in the woods to be processed and then dispatched to their new owners, who would pay generously for the permanent services of the women. Some would serve as unpaid domestic servants, working all hours and beaten if their work did not satisfy their owners—others would be sold on to brothels, imprisoned with no slightest chance of escape.

As he reread the email, Greer's earlier satisfaction was diluted, somewhat, as he recognised how damning it would be if this latest consignment of women should be discovered by the authorities. Of course, there was no reason why things should go wrong, but considering the way that earlier assignment of females had been intercepted in Eastern Europe, their minders arrested, it made the fact that this new batch of arrivals that had just passed through customs in this country might have aroused suspicion. He knew that the police liaised with their counterparts in the EU and that his affairs were under investigation.

This must be the last consignment for the foreseeable future! He had more than enough money to live in luxury for the next many years. He would miss the excitement of his illegal activities, but a man had to know when to put the brakes on! He sent a cryptic reply to the email, dissociating himself from further involvement. There—it was done. There would be others who would gladly take on his lucrative business.

Now to make a trip to the village where Erika was apparently having an affair with the man about to give evidence in the forthcoming trial of the executives of that major oil exploration company Sea Giant. How had Erika who had led a secluded life at Enderslie House, never coming into contact with any other than his invited guests, met this Colin Denton? He had made an inquiry at Global News and spoken to the woman reporter who had taken that photograph. She had not been able to furnish him with any details of the connection between Erika and Denton, but at least he now knew the name of the village—and Denton's address.

He sat brooding as he considered the situation. He would have to proceed with caution. It seemed that Denton had made a miraculous escape from a helicopter crash, and was going to bring evidence of corruption against Sea Giant's director and close associates. No doubt he would be looked at as some sort of hero. It would therefore not be wise to come against the man directly. He would order a watch kept over Denton's house. He did not know yet whether Erika was living openly with Denton or had a home close by. He must arrange for her abduction and that of his daughter, but it must be when she was away from Denton. He could not risk drawing attention to himself at this stage when he was under investigation by the police. He rang for Hassan and gave orders.

Hassan's face was inscrutable as Greer made his intentions known. He felt no slightest pang of remorse that he was to facilitate the return of the lovely young woman who had made a desperate escape from the master who dominated his own life and was completely unscrupulous in his treatment of others. As far as Hassan was concerned, Erika had held a privileged position in the household, pampered with the finest clothes and jewels, and obviously would be greatly envied by most other women. Why she had mysteriously fled from Greer made no sense—certainly, it had caused him a tongue lashing from his furious master.

'I know just the right person to send to this Ravensnest,' he said quietly. 'I think it better that I do not show myself there openly, Erika would recognise me. Leave the matter to me, sir and I promise you the lady will soon be back where she belongs.'

The middle-aged woman wearing glasses, mousey hair worn short with a fringe and her dumpy figure in a tweed suit, drew her car up in the unremarkable village to which she had been dispatched. This was Ravensnest at last. Edna Black was being well paid to track down the beautiful young woman in the photograph. She withdrew it from her bag now and studied it. This Erika Nicolson had dark blonde hair framing an oval face, vivid blue eyes, determined mouth over a dimpled chin. She should be easy to identify. She drove on and parked outside a newsagent. The owner looked up as she came in, not one of the locals.

'Good morning,' he said, smiling politely.

'Hallo—do you have a copy of the Global News?' she inquired. He produced the paper from a stand and placed it on the counter before her.

'Anything else today, madam?'

'Well—some information if you would be so kind. I am looking for this young woman,' and she handed him the photo and looked at him hopefully. He glanced at it recognised Anna Lindstrom's attractive face and stared curiously at his customer.

'Why do you want her?' he asked bluntly. He liked Anna and her small daughter and there was something about this stranger that repelled him.

'Oh—I have some good news for her,' replied Edna Black. 'Do you know where I'll find her?' she gave him a gushing smile that didn't reach her hard eyes.

'Sorry, I can't help. We get many people in and out. Hope you're successful in your search.' Edna recognised the man's decision not to talk and gave a nonchalant shrug as she pocketed Erika's photo, paid for her paper and left.

He looked after her. Together with many others in the village had seen Anna's picture in the paper with the suggestive caption. It had been intriguing to learn that Geraldine Denton's son Colin had survived that helicopter crash and was to give evidence against some high officials of a famous oil exploration company. But to suggest that the delightful young mother who was now Geraldine's close friend, was involved with a man she barely knew was tripe! He snorted as Edna's car drew away.

Edna slowed down as she saw an elderly woman walking her dog. She lowered the window and called to her.

'I wonder, can you direct me to the Denton's house?' she asked. The woman looked across at her whilst trying to restrain her energetic Jack Russell.

'You mean Geraldine Denton's cottage—the widow of the late Dr Denton? Wonderful doctor he was, we all miss him. Rose Cottage is on that narrow side road as you come out of the village. You can't miss it—only two cottages there, Geraldine's and Anna Lindstrom's—a young woman who lives next door at Bramble Cottage.' She gave into the impatient dog's sharp tug on the lead and hurried on.

Edna drew her breath in satisfaction. This was becoming much easier than she had dared hope. She now knew Erika Nicolson's new identity and the fact that the girl lived next door to Colin Denton's mother. Perhaps more had been read into that photo shot than it warranted. Now to find Bramble cottage, to get an actual glimpse of Erika. Her car shot forward. She sighed satisfaction as she reached the two cottages standing remote from the rest of the village.

She drove past slowly, glancing at the names on the gates—Bramble Cottage and Rose Cottage. She drove on, wondering what to do next. She needed to get physical sight of Erika now known as Anna, to confirm it truly was the girl she had been engaged to find. Then there was also a child she remembered—Trudy. Probably had a change of name as well as her mother. She braked, drew in on the bank and sat considering the situation. As she did so she noticed movement in her right-wing mirror. A man and woman were coming out of Rose Cottage gate accompanied by two lively children. She watched as they all climbed into a beige car.

They did not drive away at once and she had the feeling they had observed her car parked only thirty yards away. She bit her lip. Should she drive off? Before she could make her decision, the beige car reversed and drove towards her. It drew level and stopped. A good-looking man put his head out of the window and called to her. She opened her own and smiled.

'Are you lost or in difficulties?' he asked, examining Edna carefully, and was not impressed by what he saw. The woman staring back at Colin possessed shrewd, hard eyes behind her spectacles, and now a sixth sense warned him she was trouble. Edna Black thought quickly—possibly have to risk a half-truth.

'No, I'm not lost—just curious about a story I saw in a newspaper. You are Colin Denton are you not?' He drew his brows heavily together. Had not expected such blatant curiosity. Geraldine placed a restraining hand on his arm, as she leaned forward fixing her own grey gaze on this self-proclaimed nosey parker.

'What is that to you?' asked Colin coldly. 'Are you a member of the press?'

'Most definitely not,' replied Edna forcing a repentant smile. 'Just an incurable romantic! The sight of a truly brave man in that photograph with the lovely woman he loves, just so touching. I suppose I just wanted the opportunity to see you both for myself!' She hoped it didn't sound too implausible. 'I would dearly like to see—meet your lady friend.'

'That will not be possible I'm afraid. The lady you allude to is merely a pleasant neighbour a friend of my mother's! Apart from this she has gone to stay with friends for a few weeks.'

'What my son says is correct,' called Geraldine, speaking for the first time. 'The young lady is a dear friend of mine, whom Colin met only a few days ago. Why that reporter made those ridiculous statements in 'Global News' I have no idea.'

'Oh—that's disappointing,' Edna jerked out, not knowing whether to believe them or not. 'So, Anna has gone away you say?' She realised her mistake as soon as the words left her lips.

'How did you know her name,' asked Colin immediately. 'It was not mentioned in the paper?'

'I asked in the village,' she said defensively but knew she was making matters worse. 'I'm sorry to have disturbed you—I must go!' The car leapt away. Colin looked at Geraldine.

'Who the hell was she?' he asked. 'That nonsense about being a romantic—hard as nails or I miss my mark! Why was she so interested in Anna?' Geraldine shook her head nodding warningly towards the twins on the back seat. Colin had almost forgotten their presence.

'Was she a bad woman?' asked Charles now. Both he and his sister had overheard the short conversation, and looked inquiringly at the adults.

'I didn't like her,' added Melanie. 'Why did she want to know about Anna?'

'We don't know,' their father replied. He looked at them reassuringly. 'Just forget her children—she's gone now. But listen, if any other strangers should ask you about Anna. just don't answer them and tell Granny or me!' They nodded solemnly. Events of the last few months had matured them he realised, and looking back at their concerned young faces he felt a deep regret that it was so. That delightful innocence of childhood they had enjoyed before the attempt on his own life and their dear mother's death—then combined with the recent shock of kidnap, all this had left emotional scars.

'Anna is scared of Susan's father,' said Melanie now, her grey eyes so like his own fixed anxiously on his face. 'Susan is frightened of him too. Is that why they have gone away, Daddy?'

'You won't let that bad man hurt them, will you!' said Charles, slipping a protective arm around his sister. Colin glanced fondly at them.

'You have my word, darlings!' he promised and they relaxed, started chatting together. He turned to face his mother in frustration. 'Children should not have to deal with any of this!' he growled. 'If that fellow Greer comes anywhere near Anna and Susan he'll have me to deal with!' She smiled at him reassuringly.

'Don't worry, Colin—they are both safe now. But I can't help wondering if that strange woman we just encountered could have been sent by Greer! He probably wouldn't want to come here personally until he was sure our Anna really is his ex-partner. Photographs can be deceptive!' He nodded, he had also considered this possibility.

'Can we go to the shops now!' cried Melanie. Her grandmother usually took them to the bookshop on Saturdays and she looked pleadingly at the grownups who were still talking. Colin laughed, the tension vanished as he reversed and they sped off to the village.

Edna Black checked that the Dentons were not following her, slammed on her brakes and sat wondering what to do next. The Denton family had been preparing to drive into the village before coming to investigate her. She reversed and drove back carefully. No car was parked outside Rose Cottage. They had obviously driven on into Ravensnest.

She pulled up outside the neighbouring Bramble Cottage, slipped out of the car and made her way up the pathway to the front door. Colin Denton had stated that Anna had gone away for a few weeks. Could this be true? At least she could check it out now. She rang the bell. No answer, so she walked around to the back of the cottage, no one in the garden, but she noticed a few toys lying around. She tried the back door—locked. She picked up a heavy stone and smashed a downstairs window, threw her jacket over the broken jagged glass before climbing carefully in.

She knew she had to be quick, the Dentons might come back at any time. She hurried exploringly from room to room, finding no trace of the owners. It made little sense. If a woman decides to visit friends for a few weeks, she certainly would not clear her home of all normal features—there were no photographs, and the wardrobe and dressing chests were empty. She opened a desk—no papers. The cottage had been thoroughly emptied of anything that would identify the owner. If Anna Lindstrom was Erika Nicolson, no proof of it was to be found in this cottage—nor trace of her small daughter, apart from those few toys in the garden. Nothing else!

She muttered a curse and climbed carefully out of the window— hurried back to her parked car and drove swiftly away, bypassing the village. She could only hope that the man Hassan would pay what he had promised. She could not offer definite proof that the woman he sought was the girl pictured in the newspaper—but at least she knew her name, not Erika but Anna. And whoever the normal occupant of Bramble Cottage was, she had for whatever reason stripped all personal traces from her home before making an apparent visit to friends. This was not normal—only a person with something to hide would behave so. The more she thought about it, the more she became certain in her own mind that the illusive Anna really must be Malcolm Greer's missing partner.

Hassan paid Edna—not the full amount he had guaranteed for definite identification of the girl photographed with Colin Denton as being Erika Nicolson, but enough to send her away reasonably satisfied with her remuneration. He went in search of his master and gave him the information such as it was.

Malcolm Greer scowled in frustration. He had no doubt in his mind that the mysterious occupant of Bramble cottage was his missing Erika. He muttered her new name under his breath. Anna Lindstrom. Erika had Norwegian ancestors he remembered. Yes, it fitted the pattern. So where was she now? She would have needed help to find another safe haven at such short notice—he was sure she had seen that photograph in the Global News, and realised he would have recognised her—would come after her.

Whom could Erika have reached out to for assistance? He went over the notes Hassan had left with him made by that female private detective he had engaged, Edna Black. He read it over again. The Denton's had been most protective over Anna as they called her. He thought about them for a moment. The mother, Geraldine Denton was an older woman and she it was who had apparently befriended Erika and his little Trudy. Her son Colin seemingly only met Erika recently, despite the suggestive caption placed next to the photograph by that reporter, unlikely then that any relationship could have developed between them. So that meant that any help Erika had been given to move away so quickly must have been offered by Geraldine. But there again, where had she been before moving to Bramble cottage?

He swore vehemently as he struggled to make sense of matters. Then light dawned, his original suspicion that she had sought out one of those secret women's refuges coming back into focus. She had probably contacted that refuge again—fled to it before he could track her down. He studied Edna's report again. Every slightest personal item had been removed from the cottage and that surely indicated that she did not intend to return. He was no better off now than before seeing that photograph in the Global News.

He reread Edna's report one final time. She mentioned two children seen in the back of the Denton's car—a boy and a girl, looked like twins. So, Denton must be the father, he thought. Gradually he began to consider the implication of this. Denton had disappeared for many weeks following his remarkable escape from that helicopter crash—pronounced dead. His wife had apparently died at almost the same time. This meant that the children's grandmother Geraldine Denton must have cared for them. He began to see the picture. Erika had moved into the next-door cottage with little Trudy—no doubt a friendship developing between the three children. How much had she revealed to Geraldine?

Colin Denton was to give evidence against the powerful top executives of Sea Giant in their forthcoming trial. What if anything had been Colin's own position in Sea Giant's company? Could any of this impinge on the association of Erika with the Dentons? He swore again, the more he tried to understand the situation the more blurred it became. No—forget the Dentons! He had to discover the address of the Women's refuge that had opened its doors to Erika two months ago, and to which she had in all likelihood fled once again. But suppose Erika had taken the Dentons into her confidence regarding her past—and were they aware of her new address?

His mobile rang—it was Frank Dalton! Now why—after all, his former solicitor had declined working any further for him.

'Dalton?'

'Believe you should be aware that the police received a tip off. They've arrested that latest consignment of women who arrived at Dover and those in charge of them. Considered I should let you know in case you need to make any urgent plans.' Before Greer could question him, Dalton rang off. Greer sat before his desk in shock, thoughts of Erika receding into the far recesses of his brain. He pushed his expensive leather swivel chair aside, jumped up from the desk and made his way almost unthinkingly along the passageway towards his opulent drawing room. As he entered, his gaze swung around the magnificent antique furniture, the priceless pictures and ornaments—walked to the window and stared out across the manicured lawns where gardeners were bending over the immaculate flower beds. Wherever he looked everything was of the finest quality, the best money could buy. As he stood there calmly acknowledged that all had been paid for by the rich rewards of his work in people trafficking. But no thought of the misery he had brought to hundreds of women disturbed his conscience, only the terrible thought that all this might be torn away from him—this beautiful mansion house replaced by prison walls.

Everything had started to go wrong from about the time Erika had left him! Could she have drawn the attention of the authorities to him? Was she behind all of this? But Erika had not known any details of his business affairs, had accepted that his wealth was the result of his work as a property developer. But now again and again the thought assailed him that Erika was the cause of his present woes. Whatever else happened, he would find and be revenged on her!

'Hassan—Hassan!'

'Here, master.' His dark-skinned attendant appeared as from nowhere and took in the agitated appearance of the man he served and admired. Hassan bowed, and waited.

'Hassan—the latest consignment of women has been discovered by the authorities together with their keepers—all arrested. Do you think it possible that Erika Nicolson is involved in this most recent disaster?' Hassan stared at him, had never seen Greer in such an agitated state before.

'No sir. I consider it unlikely Miss Nicholson is to blame. She lacked any knowledge whatsoever of your secret affairs. Not that this makes her abandonment of you and her privileged position in your household any the better in my estimation.' It was quite a long statement by Hassan and Greer stared at him. This was one man at least whom he knew he could depend on.

'Nevertheless Hassan, I wish her tracked down—brought back!'

'I regret that Edna Black was not able to more specific in her investigation. But at least you are now aware of Miss Nicolson's new name—and where she has been living.'

'But where is she now? I need to know—to contact her. I believe there is some connection between Erika, and the interest the police are showing in my affairs. I know I can trust you to track her down for me. It is vital!' There was an unusual agitation in Greer's voice.

'I will do my best, sir, that I promise!' Hassan bowed inscrutably, withdrew at an impatient gesture of Greer's hand. How would he able to keep that promise he thought. Was Greer right in suspecting Erika of being responsible for the police closing in on him? What about the Dentons—what had Erika told them about her past with his master? This man Colin Denton who was going to give evidence at the Sea Giant trial—had he any connection with the police other than as a witness and if so—what? He sighed knowing that he had to come up quickly with answers to satisfy Greer. Perhaps watch had to be made on Colin Denton's movements. If he knew Erika's whereabouts he might let something slip. Then there was Denton's mother and what about the children? Was it possible that little Trudy may have mentioned her mother's plans to them—Edna had suggested the youngsters might be twins and slightly older than Trudy. He certainly could not use Edna again, the Dentons would recognise her instantly. He needed a new investigator, someone who would be good with children. A young woman came to mind—Jane Wilson.

Tom Lanscombe listened intently to the call as Colin explained his meeting with the strange woman who had made pretence of wanting to meet Anna—of knowing her name although it had not been mentioned in the newspaper caption. Like Colin, he did not believe the story that the stranger claimed to be a romantic who just wanted to meet the couple in the photograph. So, who was she—and who had sent her?

'Sounds as though she works for Greer.'

'Just what I thought—but there's more! The twins were in the garden and kicked a ball over the fence onto Anna's lawn. Charles climbed over to retrieve it—came back very worried. One of Anna's back windows was broken. Charles wanted to reassure me that their ball had not caused the damage.'

'Go on!'

'I went around there. The window was smashed right enough, glass littering the sitting room floor—someone had definitely been inside. Noticed a shred of beige material caught on jagged edge of the broken glass window. I suspect that the woman we spoke to must have doubled back and managed to check Anna's cottage over. It made me feel coldly angry I can tell you!'

'I'll pass this information on to Charles. Take great care of Geraldine and the twins in case any other unpleasant types show up.' Tom replaced the receiver and looked at Lottie. Her blue eyes looked troubled as he explained what had happened.

'I suppose there can be no doubt that Greer is behind this? What an evil bastard he is,' she said angrily. 'Why can he not accept that Anna has a perfect right to her own life! The man's just a cruel bully and like so many similar offenders has no conscience. Thank Goodness Anna and her little girl are safe at Dream Echo. There is no way in which he can find her there!' She slapped the dough she was needing on her pastry board.

'One thing this has proved—young Colin has a quick mind and will be a true asset to the team. But I'm concerned for Geraldine and the children once he has to leave for London and the trial! Wonder if I should spend a few days down there at Rose Cottage, just to be on the safe side.'

'Do you think Greer will have pressure put on Geraldine to disclose Anna's whereabouts?'

'I think it is possible, dearest. From what Anna has told us he is not a normal human being but has a warped nature. All this borne out by the fact that he is heavily involved in people trafficking—and this takes a particularly vile and cruel individual.'

'Why don't they arrest him then? That would sort out young Anna's problem as well serving Greer his rich deserts!' snorted Lottie. He bent over and kissed her.

'From what Charles told me, they have almost got enough evidence to make an iron-clad case against him now. A group of frightened women from Easter Europe brought illegally into the country were discovered in a disused building a few miles from Dover. They have been arrested, as have the men guarding them. All are being interrogated now. The women are ignorant of those master-minding the business, were promised good domestic jobs on their arrival.' Tom drew his heavy eyebrows together in disgust. 'Such a bloody awful business. They were all designed for the sex industry!'

'I hope they put that man Greer away for a good long time,' snapped Lottie. 'Those poor women! To think that such a lovely person as Anna was in the power of the brute!'

'Well, her problems with him will soon be over—but in the meanwhile I need to phone Charles!' He left Lottie busy with her pastry and went into his study.

The conversation he had with Latimer left him troubled. None of the men guarding the frightened tearful women discovered in the dilapidated building in the woods had named Greer as being behind the organisation. True once they realised the length of the prison sentences they were likely to receive sank in, they might become more forthcoming—but as Charles explained, promises had been made to the guards that their families would be well looked after if the men were caught and subsequently imprisoned. They also had a sort of perverse loyalty to those they served in the evil business.

'No immediate arrest to be made on Greer then? That's a damned nuisance, Charles!' exclaimed Tom in frustration. 'With Colin soon to leave for the trial in London, I'm concerned for Geraldine and the children,' he explained. 'Wonder if I should spend a few days at Rose cottage.'

'Sounds a good idea, Tom! If any of the arrested guards speak eventually, I'll let you know.' He paused. 'Since Greer is determined to continue in his search for Anna, and knowing the character of the man, it would do no harm to keep watch over Geraldine and the twins. Her cottage is remote from the village and she has already endured so much trauma at the hands of those corrupt representatives of Sea Giant—as have those poor children. What they must have gone through during their kidnap!'

'I'll go then. At least there's no way in which Greer can discover Dream Echo!'

'No one has so far—and I'm sure it will remain that way. Your security there is a credit to you Tom—and to that wonderful young woman Amber who runs it with her husband and their team. Oh, the trial is set to start this coming Wednesday'

'That's settled then—when Colin is called to London for the trial, I'll move into Rose Cottage with Geraldine and the twins. Lottie can always contact me if there should be any problems at Dream Echo.' The call finished he joined Lottie in the kitchen. She looked up as she closed the oven door.

'You spoke with Charles?' she inquired and listened as he related the discussion. 'Good, I'm relieved you're going to Rose Cottage, Tom. I was worried at the idea of Geraldine being left alone there with little Charles and Melanie, with that reprobate Greer in the offing!'

'Hopefully Greer will soon be under lock and key,' he growled. 'In the meanwhile, he had better not cause any problems for our friend Geraldine.'

Hassan glanced at his watch. The dark green Saab was parked outside Lynchester Museum—his usual meeting place with those he employed on Greer's behalf. He saw the young woman approaching, casually swinging her red suede bag. He beckoned her to get in the car. She did so and listened to his instructions. Jane Wilson looked at Hassan curiously. She had worked successfully for him before, knew he could be relied on to pay generously for jobs that needed a special expertise. With her attractive heart shaped face framed by silver blond curls, straight forward green stare, she displayed a false air of innocence.

'Let me get this straight, Mr Hassan. You want me to win the confidence of seven years old twins, Charles and Melanie Denton and discover what they know of the present address of a woman called Anna Lindstrom and her little daughter. Is that it?' she asked crisply.

'Yes, my dear. This woman Anna normally resides at Bramble Cottage which is immediately next door to Rose Cottage where these twins live with their father Colin Denton and his mother Geraldine Denton. All you need to know is that Anna and her child have disappeared—and are known to have been close friends with the Dentons.' Hassan spoke concisely, not wanting to reveal more than he needed to.

'I take it that you are unable to inquire Anna's whereabouts from the Dentons yourself for some reason?' she said quietly. 'Forgive me, but would this Colin Denton be the same man recently mentioned in the Global News—pictured together with a lovely woman? I remember reading that he is to give evidence at a trial of some executives from a well-known oil and gas exploration company. Is his friend the Anna you need to trace?' She spoke in business like tones, watching him shrewdly. He nodded.

'Correct. Just persuade the Denton children to give you Anna's present address and you will receive a substantial reward. Oh, and here is donation towards travelling expenses etc. Don't let me down, Jane.' He handed her an envelope. She smiled, slipped it in her red suede bag, got out and strolled away. Hassan looked after her. It was to be hoped she would be as diligent as usual.

It was six on Tuesday morning. Colin had already breakfasted with Geraldine. Now he was making sure he had packed all necessary for his London trip. He closed his bag. It would be good to get the trial behind him, see those who had murdered his dear Mary and two colleagues, and attempted to kill him, as well as ordering the kidnap of his children, eventually face justice. He knew he had nothing to fear from them now, but still felt uneasy at leaving his mother and the twins alone here in this remote cottage. The strange woman they had encountered last Saturday blatantly seeking information on Anna had been disturbing—the realisation that she had subsequently broken into Anna's cottage extremely worrying. He had no doubt that her abusive ex-partner Greer was behind it. Well at least she would not have found any clue as to Anna's present abode at Dream Echo!

'Colin—Colin,' called Geraldine as she came into the room where he was checking all needful relevant documents his briefcase. He looked up with a smile.

'What is it, Mum?' he asked.

'Phone call from Tom Lanscombe! He is driving down here, means to stay until you are back again. He was about to leave as he rang. I told him it wasn't necessary, but he was adamant and to be honest dear, I'll be glad of his presence. With Greer still at liberty and determined to find Anna I don't want to encounter any more strangers sniffing around.'

He smiled at her. This was good news, now he could relax and concentrate on the case. He had great respect for Tom and his wife Lottie and knew they had been his mother's close friends and colleagues during her time in the secret service. So strange that he was about to engage in similar future career.

'Bless Tom!' he said approvingly. 'Must say I have been uneasy since that weird female appeared last Saturday! Good idea of yours to strip Bramble cottage of all Anna's personal belongings when she left—the woman would have found nothing of any help in her search.' He frowned. 'If only that wretched reporter from Global News had not taken that photograph!' Geraldine touched his cheek affectionately, her grey eyes gentle.

'Well, we can't go backwards in life—only forward with courage. That same courage you have been showing, Colin dear.' He took her in his arms and kissed her wordlessly. She smiled as he turned back to his briefcase

'You have you finished packing?' She glanced towards his suitcase. He nodded.

'Yes—all ready to go. Are the kiddies up yet?'

'In the kitchen playing with the kittens. Never a dull moment these days,' she laughed. 'I should make their breakfast now, then drive them to school.'

'I'll go through to them—say goodbye. Just remember, Mum, any problems whatsoever just ring me—and I'll return immediately. Must say I feel much happier that Tom will be here!'

Ten minutes later Geraldine stood on the steps waving goodbye, her young grandchildren at her side. As the car disappeared the twins faces dropped.

'Daddy will come back again, Granny,' asked Melanie, her face worried, as Charles too looked at her anxiously.

'Oh yes, my darlings! Remember I explained he has to give evidence against those wicked men from Sea Giant. Once the trial is over your Daddy will be back,' she promised. Melanie looked at her solemnly.

'But will he stay here always, or go away again like he did when we lived in Scotland?' Geraldine put her arms about them, knew she had to be completely truthful.

'I can only say, that your father may have to make business trips in the future which will mean being away from home for a week or two—but he will always return to us!'

'And will Anna and Susan come back?' Charles demanded. 'We really miss them, Granny!' She looked at them fondly.

'Yes, I know you do—just be patient. They'll be home soon.'

'Susan says her Mummy is frightened of her Daddy—that he is a bad man,' said Melanie now. 'Is that why they have gone away?' Geraldine evaded the question.

'They are just visiting friends—so stop worrying. Now some good news! Tom is coming to spend a few days with us. So, come inside and have breakfast—we're running late.'

She dropped them off at school, watching them run happily up the school steps, then smiled at a parent trying to comfort a reluctant small girl. Luckily the twins loved school. She returned to the car. She barely noticed the young woman standing unobtrusively outside the school gates. She drove away. She would just have time to tidy the cottage before Tom arrived.

Jane Wilson stared after the beige Ford. She turned away thoughtfully. Yes, that was definitely Geraldine Denton and this likely her usual routine, dropping the kids off in the morning and collecting them at end of the school day. So how was she to get a chance to speak alone with the fair-haired twins whom at least she could now identify. It was going to be difficult—but the reward it would gain her should she extract the information Hassan wanted make all worthwhile. An older woman standing outside the gates and about to leave looked at Jane curiously.

'Haven't seen you here before?' she said.

'Oh—just wondering how good the school is. I'm thinking of moving into Ravensnest,' Jane invented.

'Well it's a good village, we look out for each other. As for the school, wonderful teachers. I can thoroughly recommend it Mrs...?' she glanced inquiringly at Jane.

'Oh—I'm not married,' said Jane. 'My name's Mary Jones. My mother is looking after my little Jenny. Thank you for the information. So then, school starts at 9am—and closes at 4pm?' she checked casually. The middle-aged woman smiled at her. The girl was certainly doing her homework, looked a pleasant enough young thing.

'Well, half past three for the two lower classes,' she volunteered. 'The whole school are going on a nature walk later this morning. Thought

I'd come along and see if the teachers need any help shepherding them.' Jane seized on the information.

'Perhaps I could come along too—get the feel of the school,' she said tentatively.

'I suppose it would be alright—we leave at about 11. See you here later then, Mary. Oh, and by the way, my name is Clara Richards.' With a quick nod, she walked off briskly towards her car as Jane looked after her with satisfied smile.

About a dozen mothers had arrived outside the school to offer their assistance on the planned nature walk. Jane waited until the children came pouring out of the gates, forming into a double line as they proceeded along the village street flanked by teachers and volunteer parents—then joined the procession unobtrusively at Clara's side. They turned into a country lane, walked a few hundred yards, stopping outside a gate leading onto the local common where wild flowers nodded amongst breeze ruffled grasses, and thick clumps of brambles and alder trees banked a babbling stream, the scene backed by a coppice of mature oaks and beeches showing the first pale gold of autumn. It looked idyllic, but as the children filed through the gate Jane had eyes only for the Denton twins, easily recognised by their blond hair and similarity of features.

'That's my Joanna over here!' said Clara fondly, as she pointed to a solemn faced little girl with pigtails. 'What happens next is that the children fan out, and try to find any small wild life they come across. It can be anything from beetles and butterflies to frogs and newts.' She paused as the children started off in excited small groups, some of them making for the banks of the stream. 'Oh, excuse me a moment!' She pointed to where little Joanna had slipped into the stream and hurried to her daughter's rescue. Jane sighed relief, and strolled across to the Denton twins who were watching in amusement.

'I hope your little friend hasn't hurt herself,' said Jane lightly, as she stood next to Charles and Melanie. They glanced up at her questioningly, did not recognise the attractive woman wearing a grey suit smiling down at them. 'That's young Joanna, isn't it,' continued Jane. 'I'm a friend of Joanna's Mummy. I'm here with Clara to see what the school is like in action. I'm thinking of sending my little girl here when we move to Ravensnest, you see.'

The twins looked at each other, knew they shouldn't speak to strangers—but if this lady was a friend of Mrs Richards.

'Don't worry, Joanie will be alright—the water is only a few inches deep,' said Charles scornfully as they watched the child scramble up the bank with her mother's help.

'She'll just have a wet tunic,' added Melanie. 'I expect her mummy will take her home.'

'Is Joanie your best friend?' asked Jane.

'No, not particularly,' replied Charles. 'I expect you will want to go and help Mrs Richards with Joanie,' he added pointedly. But the strange lady ignored the suggestion. She bent down and carefully eased a ladybird onto her wrist.

'This is called a ladybird isn't it? I remember finding them in my garden when I was small.'

'Our friend Susan likes ladybirds,' exclaimed Melanie artlessly.

'Susan? Is she in your class?' asked Jane.

'No, she lives next door to us with her Mummy,' explained Melanie, as Charles frowned warningly, but Melanie didn't see and continued. 'We're sad because Anna has taken Susan away and we miss her!'.

'Oh, I'm sorry to hear that,' sympathised Jane. 'Have they gone far?'

'I don't know,' replied Melanie. 'But I expect it is because Susan has a bad daddy and they are scared of him.'

'Melanie! Remember what Granny said!' exclaimed Charles putting a hand on his sister's arm. She gave a gasp of dismay at his words.

'Oh, I didn't mean to,' she said tears springing to her eyes. She looked uncertainly at Jane now, realising how careless her words had been.

'We must go,' she said as taking Charles hand they both turned and walked briskly away to join a group around one of the teachers.

'Damn!' muttered Jane. Well, at least she had established that Anna had fled to escape an abusive partner—and that her child's name was Susan. It was also obvious that the children's grandmother was alert to their being questioned about her neighbour's disappearance. She had no doubt in her own mind that Geraldine Denton was party to the knowledge of Anna's present whereabouts.

As she walked away from the school party, retracing her steps back to the layby where she had left her car, she was deep in thought. She knew that the children's father Colin Denton would be on his way to London for the opening of the Sea Giant trial, which meant Geraldine and the twins would be alone at Rose Cottage. She had already driven past their home earlier, knew it was remote from the village and Bramble Cottage empty. Could she dare a break in? She needed to know where Anna and her daughter were hiding! No one else in this miserable little village could supply her with the information—only Geraldine.

She thought back to her sighting of Geraldine this morning when the woman had dropped her grandchildren off at school. She had given the impression of being alert, in good health, and had driven away with assurance—so apparently not some frail, elderly person to be easily subdued by threats, should such be necessary to extract the information Jane needed. She briefly considered breaking into the cottage by night, scaring Geraldine out of her wits in hope that she would reveal Anna's present address. But instinct told her this would not work with the sprightly grandmother.

So how could she trace Anna? She could not come up with an answer right now. It was obvious that the twins had been instructed not to disclose any information about Anna or her child Susan, but interesting that the Denton twins were aware of the fear in which both mother and daughter held Malcolm Greer. She drove back to her B&B to consider her options.

Tom Lanscombe arrived about an hour after Geraldine's return from school, during which she managed to tidy the cottage up after Colin's early departure. He greeted her fondly, watched as she made coffee in the kitchen, then took the tray and followed her into the sitting room and sank down on the couch, chuckling as he watched her trying to prevent two lively kittens leaping up the curtains.

'I see you have double trouble there,' he laughed.

'One is Susan's,' she explained lifting both down patiently and offering a toy mouse as distraction. 'Tom, I really do appreciate your coming. But won't they miss you at the refuge?' He stared at her, saw the tiredness behind her usual confident smile, remembered she had endured a great deal of stress recently.

'Geraldine, all will go on smoothly as ever at Dream Echo, that I promise you. They have a good staff there, plus Amber's husband Robert Marsden who is as hot on security as I am! Look my dear, I was concerned when Colin rang with news a strange woman arrived here asking questions—had then broken into Bramble Cottage. It's seems fairly obvious that she was employed by Greer—also that the fellow will be aware that Colin is away in London now, and that you are here alone with the twins. Lottie was all for my coming, just as a precaution of course.' She poured coffee, he accepted his cup and a slice of ginger cake.

'Thank you, Geraldine. Now tell me, how are the twins getting on now? They must miss Anna and their little friend Susan—and it probably doesn't help that their father has had to leave at this time?' he said gently. She nodded.

'They went off to school happily enough this morning, but they're uneasy at Colin's departure after so wonderfully getting him back in their lives again —and you're right, they miss Anna and Susan. Oh, I do hope the police have enough evidence to arrest that man Greer soon! He has caused so much hurt—must be completely without conscience!'

'The nets of justice are about to bring him down any time now. Luckily we have Anna and her little girl safely away from his revenge—but we must be aware he will not give up trying to find her while he remains at liberty.' They continued to chat until Geraldine disappeared into the kitchen to prepare lunch.

Tom walked over to the window and peered out, was about to turn away when he saw a car draw up, as a woman put her head out of the window to stare at his own parked car. He took his phone-cam from his pocket, took a quick shot of her. As he did so, she started to drive away—he managed to catch her car registration number. He must be getting paranoid he told himself, as he replaced the phone in his pocket. The girl could have stopped for many reasons—one could be that she had lost her way. But almost instinctively he made a call to a familiar department. The car was registered to a Jane Wilson, who lived in Lynchester! And that was where Greer lived!

He slipped out into the garden, walked to the gate and looked along the road—but the car had disappeared. He returned inside, unpacked his tablet from his bag, and tapped the woman's name on search. He swore under his breath at what he saw. Jane Wilson was a private investigator! It appeared that Greer had sent a second woman to track down Anna and the child. He went through to the kitchen to give the news to Geraldine. She bit her lip as she listened, her immediate thoughts for Anna and Susan, with deep relief that they were safe at Dream Echo. She looked seriously at Tom.

'I'm relieved that you are here,' she said simply. 'Not that I cannot cope on my own, but I have the children to think of! I simply don't want Charles and Melanie to endure any more disturbance in their lives. Do you think this Jane Wilson will come back?' He frowned thoughtfully.

'It would be strange if she didn't, having driven so far to get here. I believe she saw my car and realised you have a visitor. Forewarned is forearmed—now we know who she is, will be ready for Miss Wilson whenever she shows up again.' Geraldine inclined her head in agreement., then her eyes narrowed in thought.

'Listen, Tom, do you really think she will come back while that car of yours is parked outside? You need to move it.'

'But where to?'

'What about leaving the BMW in the field opposite. You can access it by a gate in the hedge about a hundred yards on. It will be completely safe there and completely hidden from the road,' she suggested. He liked the idea.

'Good thinking—may as well do it now.' Ten minutes later he was back and watched Geraldine prepare a late lunch, chicken salad followed by a raspberry mouse. She glanced at him as he complimented her on the meal.

'I don't pretend to be a wonderful cook like Lottie, but promise you won't starve while you are here,' she stated. They chatted together reminiscing on their time together in MI5. At last she checked her watch, realised it was almost three pm.

'This is where I must leave you for a short while and collect the twins from school. They come out at half past three. Better we are not seen together in case the Wilson woman is hovering around. There are plenty books on those shelves, David was a great reader—or there's music! I will be back within the hour.'

She drove her beige Ford towards the village, wondering how Colin was getting on in London. At least all the devastating trauma the family had sustained at the hands of Sea Giant would eventually become mere bitter memory—a happier future beckon. Was it possible that there would be a place for Anna in Colin's future she wondered. But before that could happen Malcolm Greer had to be dealt with, his demented obsession in tracking down Anna and little Susan finally come to an end. She drew up outside the school and stepped briskly out of the car. Her eyes swept over the assorted parents waiting at the gates for their offspring as she approached—and her gaze hovered on the slim figure of a girl wearing a silver-grey trouser suit—studied her face. Surely it couldn't be..? She tried to recall the photograph Tom had shared with her earlier of the woman who had drawn up outside Rose Cottage and disappeared when she saw Tom's car. Surely the girl wouldn't dare come openly to the school? But then she could not know Tom had traced her identity. What was it she wanted with the twins, for there could be no other reason than wanting to question the children about Anna!

'Hallo there, Mrs Denton.' She looked round as a plain faced, good natured woman she knew slightly called to her. 'It's Clara Richards—we met at the school concert!'

'Why, of course. You have a little daughter—Joanna?'

'Yes, you have a good memory! This is my third trip to the school today—I went on that nature walk this morning. It was fun—at least it was until Joanna slipped into the stream on the common. Had to take her home and change her wet clothes and then take her back! Be glad of a sit down tonight.' She realised Geraldine's attention had strayed to the girl in the grey suit. 'Do you know her?' she asked, jerking her head towards Jane Wilson.

'No. Don't recognise her as one of the usual parents,' said Geraldine.

'She's not—yet. She spoke to me this morning, asked a lot of questions about the school. Is going to move to the village and said she has a child. Strange really—she insisted on coming along when I mentioned the nature walk. Then when Joanna had her small accident I looked for her but she had disappeared. Without a word too.'

'Sounds a strange person,' said Geraldine lightly. 'Look—the children are coming out now.' They smiled at each other, and drew closer to the school gates. Geraldine glanced back at Jane Wilson, caught her staring fixedly in her direction. Then the youngsters came pouring out of the school door and racing across the playground to their waiting parents. The twins spotted Geraldine and ran towards her and as they did so she thought Melanie looked slightly troubled and wondered why.

'How did the nature walk go, my darlings?' asked Geraldine. It was Charles who answered enthusiastically.

'It was marvellous Granny! We found some beetles and a frog and..' he stopped and pointed in front of him. 'There's that woman again Melanie! The one who asked all those questions!' Melanie gave a cry of protest and looked down uncomfortably. Geraldine turned and looked straight at Jane Wilson, who hesitated and then came forward.

'Good afternoon,' she said to Geraldine. 'Are they your children then? I met them this morning of that nature walk. My name is Mary Jones. I hope to be moving to the village with my daughter and have been taking a look at the school.'

'Really. Then no doubt we will see more of each other,' said Geraldine. 'Well, I must get my grandchildren home—so excuse me.'

'Perhaps we could meet for a cup of coffee?' said Jane Wilson. 'I would certainly like to see more of these two delightful children—they are twins I take it?' Geraldine merely took the children's hands and stared coldly at the woman.

'That will not be possible I'm afraid. Goodbye er Mrs Jones!' she said firmly, and as Jane Wilson looked after her in frustration, she escorted the twins to the Ford and drove off. Once they left school behind the twins visibly relaxed. Geraldine watched their faces in her mirror as she drove. Soon they were approaching the cottage.

'I'm glad the nature walk went so well. Do you want to tell me about it?' she called over her shoulder. Charles looked at Melanie. He took her hand and nodded his head.

'I did something bad, granny,' said Melanie. 'That lady asked me some questions and I told her about missing Anna and Susan—that they had gone away, were scared because Susan's daddy was a bad man. She asked where they had gone—and I said I didn't know. I'm sorry Granny—I just forgot you had said we mustn't speak about them.' Geraldine braked as they drew up, parked and helped them out. She put her arms about Melanie.

'Listen sweetheart, you made a small mistake and I know you will be extra careful in future. You see, there are some bad people in this world who pretend to be kind, but can cause a lot of trouble. I think that lady was one of those. Just don't speak to her ever again!'

'I won't I promise,' said Melanie determinedly. Geraldine kissed her and turned to Charles. 'I know you'll take care too,' she said hugging him. 'Now listen children, we have a visitor—it's Tom Lanscombe. Remember I told you he is going to stay with us for a few days.'

'Oh, that's great!' cried Charles and ran in front of her to the blue cottage door. It was opened by Tom who greeted them with a smile—then looked inquiringly at Geraldine.

'Everything all right?' he asked. She shook her head slightly but did not comment. Time enough to speak of it later.

Chapter Thirteen

The twins were now in bed, all thoughts of the strange woman dismissed from their
thoughts as Geraldine told them a story, then said prayers with them and slipped
quietly out. She found it difficult to hide the annoyance she still felt that Jane Wilson had dared to interrogate the twins. She joined Tom in the living room.

'So—what happened?' he demanded, his dark eyes watching her curiously. 'It's obvious something upset you?' She sank down in her chair and told him. He swore. 'She actually invited herself on the school outing to the common—and tried to get information out of the twins? Were there no teachers keeping an eye on things?' His bushy eyebrows almost met across his forehead.

'Yes, and in addition tried to make conversation with me outside the school, actually had the gall to ask me out for coffee!' she snapped. 'It's plain she is quite desperate to find out where Anna and Susan are staying. Luckily the twins had no slightest idea. She told one of the mothers that she intends to move into the village with her child, hence the interest in the school. She's clever and devious.'

'Do you consider she is capable of trying to possibly abduct the twins?' he asked now. She looked back at him in shock.

'No,' she said slowly, her face troubled. 'What would it gain her?' she asked.

'She might hold them hostage for information about Anna. But for that she would need an accomplice, and she appears to be working alone. But I don't need to tell you to keep a watchful eye on the twins at all times.'

'Perhaps she will just give up—return to Lynchester,' said Geraldine hopefully. 'I'm just so tired, Tom. It's been one worry after another.' She looked up as the phone rang. It was Colin. The trial was due to start officially tomorrow. Charles Latimer was with him and they were discussing the evidence Colin was to give. He asked fondly after the twins, was told they were asleep—but Geraldine made no mention of the day's occurrences. Then Tom spoke with him, wishing him luck for the morning.

Jane Wilson sat frowning in the impersonal bedroom of her B&B. She had checked out the registration number on the BMW she had seen parked outside Rose Cottage that morning. It belonged to a Thomas Lanscombe whose address was in a village many miles away, one she didn't know. It was called Willow-Mere. So, what would have brought him to that lonely cottage in Ravensnest? It was a puzzle, especially as she knew that Colin Denton would now be in London for the Sea Giant trial.

She had intended trying to break into Rose Cottage when the Denton woman and the kids were sleep—take a quick look around in case she should be lucky enough to find trace of Anna's address. It would be a long shot of course—but one she dared not take if Lanscombe was still there.

She took a decision, got into her car and drove the short distance out of the village to where the two isolated cottages stood. She turned off her car lights as she approached. There was only one vehicle parked outside Rose Cottage and it was Geraldine Denton's beige Ford!

She gave a sigh of satisfaction. With the stranger definitely gone it should be possible to break in once the cottage was in darkness and the household asleep. As she stared at the cottage, someone appeared at one of the upstairs windows, closed the curtains. But it wasn't Geraldine Denton she saw, but a man. She gasped in surprise. Now who—the car she had noticed outside this morning and which she knew belonged to a Tom Lanscombe had disappeared—and the woman's son supposed to be in London.

She frowned as she considered the situation. It would be far too risky to attempt to get into the cottage tonight with a stranger present. And there again, how did he get there without a car? But to have come this close to discovering the details she sought about Anna and not to pursue the matter was unthinkable. She swore under her breath—then an idea dawned.

As Jane got out of the car and approached the cottage she realised the wind had got up blowing with quite strong gusts. She opened the gate, then crouching almost double raced lightly up the pathway and found herself facing the front door. There were windows looking out on the front to both the right and the left. With the curtains drawn it was impossible to guess which room was occupied. She turned to the right and put her ear up against the window, could detect no slightest sound. She retraced her steps and bending low pressed her ear against the window of the opposite room. Yes! She could hear voices.

She placed her sensitive camphone against the glass, switched it on to record whilst listening at the same time. A man's voice. He seemed to be talking about a woman called Lottie and the work they did at a place with a strange name—Dream Echo? Now a woman was speaking, she recognised Geraldine's voice. What was that she said—about the wonderful work of the refuge? She drew in her breath—heard the word Willow-Mere. That was where Tom Lanscombe lived—so was he in there now with Geraldine Denton? If so where was his car? He must have parked it somewhere to disguise his presence. But from whom—unless he guessed that she was likely to appear?

She had learned enough—must get away from here in case discovered. She turned and didn't realise how very close she was to the thick, bushy tresses of the climbing roses cladding the cottage walls. Her grey linen jacket caught, and as she struggled became more closely entangled with the invasive creeper with its sharp prickles. One caught by a gust of wind lashed against her face—she was unable to suppress a cry of pain as she broke free. Tom looked at Geraldine.

'Did you here that? Someone's out there!' He leapt to his feet, and ran to the front door, Geraldine behind him. They were just in time to see a shadowy figure running down the pathway and slamming the gate. They set off in pursuit, only to hear the sound of a car drawing away.

'I'll get my car keys!' cried Geraldine. Tom shook his head.

'I fear whoever it was, will be long gone, my dear. But who the hell could it have been? Surely that Wilson woman would not have had the nerve to risk it?' But as they looked at each other, realised this must have been what happened.

'Do you have a torch?' asked Tom urgently. 'Want to see if the intruder left any trace behind.' Geraldine handed him the heavy flashlight she kept just inside the front door, followed him round to flower bed outside the sitting room window. He flashed it on the ground, saw the imprint of a woman's shoe—raised the beam of light to the window where the wind was still tossing a loose branch of the climbing rose bush back and forth. He saw something caught there, carefully removed a small fragment of cloth from its thorns.

'Let me see that' cried Geraldine and he handed it to her. They returned inside—sank down in the living room facing each other. Geraldine spoke.

'Tom—I believe this came from the grey suit Jane Wilson was wearing this afternoon.' She held the tiny piece of material out before her. 'She must have been listening to us talking. What were we speaking about last, do you remember?'

'I mentioned Dream Echo—and the work of the refuge! We also spoke of Anna's presence there.' His face was grim. 'I could shoot myself for revealing a secret that has been so carefully kept since it opened. We have to catch that girl before she can disclose what she overheard. I'm going off to get my car—useless to hide my presence here now!' Geraldine stared at him, her eyes worried.

'But Tom, we don't know which way she has gone! My guess is that she's been staying at a B&B in the village—but now she's got what she came for and is probably on her way back to Lynchester to hand the information over to Malcolm Greer.'

'Had an idea. I'll see if we can have her car stopped—have her detained by the police,' said Tom. 'I must pass it before Latimer first, need his authority. We have details of her car and her photograph!' He pulled out his phone and spoke a few urgent words, face slightly relaxing afterwards. 'Charles is right on to it. Said I should stay here. The police at Willow-Mere will be instructed to keep a close watch over Dream Echo—and Amber informed of possible intrusion.' He still looked upset and Geraldine glanced at him sympathetically.

'I think we both need a drink,' she said quietly.

'Make mine a brandy,' he said.

Jane Wilson had only driven about sixty miles when she heard a police siren—had passed a parked police car a few minutes before. She gave a quick glance out of the side mirror, saw it signalling to her to stop. Damn! It must be her lights, she thought. She braked and waited. The police car drew up next to her, an officer stepped out and tapped on the window. She wound it down.

'May I see your driving licence and insurance, madam,' he said.

'Why—what's wrong?' she asked. He continued to hold his hand out. 'Oh, very well!' She forced a smile she handed him the documents.

'Thank you. Kindly step out of the car, madam.' She stared at him uneasily. His fellow officer was standing by his side now. She obeyed uneasily.

'What's all this about?' she demanded.

'Miss Wilson, you are under arrest—are accused of trespass with malicious intent. Anything that you say……..!' She barely registered his words, stared at him in shock. The handcuffs bruised her wrists and as she sat in the back of the police car she began to feel very frightened.

Amber Marsden listened intently to what the police sergeant had to say. It wouldn't be the first time that there had been a security scare and she knew how unbelievably fortunate they had been so far in keeping Dream Echo's secret. There was always a chance that some enraged abusive partner might discover them, attempt to break in, but their security was extremely good and for this she had the expertise of Tom Lanscombe to thank for his ongoing help and support.

'So, the young woman who has accessed information about on Dream Echo's true function has now been arrested. That's a relief! But what if she has already passed on details to others—on the phone perhaps?' Her unusual topaz gold eyes looked at him steadily. They were friends of long standing, Sergeant Jack Shackleton in long term engagement to her personal assistant Susan.

'I can only pass on what I've heard so far, Amber. This is just to warn you to be extra vigilant.' She placed a grateful hand on his arm. 'I'll get Robert—make sure we are on high alert. I wish Tom were here. Thank you, Jack!' He smiled at her as he got back in his car. She watched it disappear along the long driveway, then closed the front door. Anna—she must tell Anna that a slim chance existed that Greer now knew her whereabouts and warn her husband Robert to clamp down on security.

Jane Wilson sat miserably in the police cell, wondering what was in store. They had taken her cell phone—would see that she had contacted Hassan with a text message, explaining that she was on her way with details of where Anna was hiding—had mentioned the word Dream Echo, but not given its address. She had wanted to make sure he gave her the promised reward before explaining the refuge was at Willow-Mere.

Charles Latimer was already in possession of details the Ashton police had established so far. He stared at the name Hassan—knew he was Greer's right hand man, the Wilson woman obviously engaged by him on his employer's behalf. Jane Wilson must be encouraged to talk. He ordered that the female private investigator be driven to London.

Malcolm Greer had retired for the night when he heard a discreet knock at the bedroom door. He looked inquiringly at Hassan, beckoned him to the bedside.

'Well?' he said.

'I've had a text message from the woman we sent to investigate what information the Denton family might possess on Erika's present location. She's on her way to us now—mentions a place called Dream Echo.' He fixed his dark eyes respectively on Greer. 'Have you ever heard of it I wonder?' Greer snorted in disgust.

'Dream Echo? Surely no town or village could possibly have such a fantastic name! The woman is playing games with you.' He gestured dismissal, but Hassan remained standing there. 'Well—what more?' he snapped.

'Could it possibly be the name of a women's refuge?' suggested Hassan. At that Greer became alert, his eyes narrowed. He swung his legs out of the bed and faced Hassan

'That at least sounds more plausible. Have you checked it out on the net?'

'Yes. There's a large mansion of that name in a village called Willow-Mere. It is supposed to be an artists' commune. But what if that is just a blind as to its real purpose, sir?' Greer nodded slowly. If it was possible Hassan was correct—then Erika would very possibly be back in his power very soon. The thought of it brought a feverish flush to his face and neck, in surge of anger and frustrated desire.

'Get onto the matter immediately Hassan! You say the woman you employed to spy on the Dentons supplied this information and is on her way here?'

'Yes, sir.' Hassan gave an inscrutable smile. 'I'll have her brought to you as soon as she arrives—that probably means the morning now.'

Morning dawned wetly, rain splashing down the windows of Enderslie Mansion and gathering in deep puddles on the gravelled courtyard. Malcolm Greer rose early, had not slept well, lain tossing and turning all night, imagining the revenge he would take on Erika once under his control again. He stared out at the immaculate gardens in exasperation, swearing at the relentless rain. Why did this Jane Wilson not come?

Hassan sent another text message to Jane, which received no reply. What had happened to the girl? He had used her before, knew her to be determined and reliable. For the first time he began to feel uneasy. What if she had been involved in a motoring accident—or there again was it possible she had fallen foul of the law, been arrested? If so would she talk.

Greer summoned him to his office and saw from Hassan's troubled eyes that the man was deeply worried. He stared at him inquiringly from his black leather swivel chair.

'Have you heard from the Wilson woman? Surely she should be here by now?' he asked irritably as he downed a whisky. Hassan shook his head regretfully.

'Alas no—and I must admit to some misgivings, sir! It is totally out of character for her not to keep an appointment—especially one in which she would expect to receive a good remuneration for her work. I am concerned in case her activities in obtaining the information have been discovered.' He waited for the storm to break and it did. Greer sprang furiously to his feet.

'The police you mean! Do you think she will talk?' he demanded. Hassan spread his hands out helplessly, how could he answer. Greer vented an angry tirade on his head. Hassan tried to find words to calm him.

'At this time, we can only hope there is some other reason for her non-arrival. But in the meanwhile, we could perhaps explore that place at Willow-Mere—Dream Echo?' He saw the distraction work as Greer paused and stood considering the idea. He walked over to a wall map and found the place he sought, stabbed it with his finger. He nodded.

'Very well. We will wait until mid-day, and if your woman has not contacted us by then, we'll drive to Willow-Mere and make inquiries about this Dream Echo! The journey should take only a couple of hours at most!' Hassan shook his head with a placating smile.

'Do you think it wise to go yourself?' he said quietly, showing genuine concern for the man he served and esteemed, yet in return treated him with such scant respect. 'With that awkward people trafficking matter hanging in the air, better perhaps to keep a low profile, sir?' Greer exploded.

'You dare to interfere in my decisions? I have said we will go and that's final! This is the first real clue to Erika's hiding place—and I'm going to find the bitch!' Hassan bowed and withdrew. There was no arguing with his master when he was in one of his dark moods. But where was Jane Wilson?

Tom Lanscombe was also up early that morning and rang Lottie at Ivy cottage before she left for Dream Echo. He recounted the events of the previous evening, found that Amber had already been informed and the refuge on alert.

'I feel such a fool for allowing myself to be overheard speaking of Dream Echo,' he said ruefully, but Lottie quickly put an end to his self-reproach.

'Don't be an idiot, Tom!' she said firmly. 'You were speaking privately with Geraldine, in the privacy of her home. How could either of you possibly expect that young woman to be hiding beneath the window. She probably didn't hear much and anyway she is under arrest now!' She knew how damaging to his self-esteem this episode must have been. He had driven to Rose Cottage to take care of Geraldine and the twins while Colin was in London for the trial, only for this to happen.

'I've spoken to Charles this morning—he intends to interrogate Jane Wilson personally later this morning. The problem is that the girl had already texted Greer's assistant, Hassan, mentioning Dream Echo. I have the unpleasant feeling that Greer will attempt to access the refuge—and I'm torn. I want to remain here to watch over Geraldine and the children, but feel my real place is at Dream Echo to oversee security there.' Lottie heard the uncertainty in his voice.

'Listen, Tom darling, Jane Wilson is the second woman that Greer's sent to Geraldine's home to investigate Anna's whereabouts—and there is nothing to stop him sending yet another! The man is an evil bastard, and partly deranged in my estimation.'

'Yes Lottie—but now Greer is aware of Dream Echo's existence, he has no further need of further investigation here in the Denton's home.' She knew he was right, but still felt uneasy at the idea of Geraldine being alone there with the twins.

'What does Geraldine say?'

'That she will be fine if I leave.'

'Then I suppose it's alright,' she said. 'Must admit I feel slightly anxious at the possibility of Malcolm Greer's likely advent.' He detected her uneasiness.

'That settles it. I'll contact Sergeant Will Evans at the local station. I'm sure he will agree to keep watch over Geraldine and the twins. Maybe that young PC Bird could stay here for a day or two. I'll get on to it now, Lottie love. See you soon!'

Geraldine glanced after Tom's BMW as it disappeared on the long trip back to Dream Echo. She had already driven the twins to school, and now stood at the door with Sergeant Evans at her side together with Julie Bird, the caring young PC who had been so supportive at the time of the twins' kidnap. They had arrived immediately after Tom contacted them, explained he had to leave, needed to be sure they would keep an eye on Geraldine and the twins.

'As I told Mr Lanscombe, you should have contacted me last night. We might have stopped that Jane Wilson before she got as far as she did—out of our area.' Geraldine looked up at his bluff ruddy face with a repentant smile.

'I know Will—sorry. But Tom's first thought was for the safety of Anna and her little daughter and for others at the Dream Echo refuge. He got in touch with an ex colleague at MI5 on whose instructions the woman was arrested, is now in London where she is to be interrogated. You may not be aware of it, but Anna's ex-partner is a very dangerous man and deeply involved in people trafficking. Women brought to this country on the promise of well-paid domestic posts—but forced into prostitution, sex slaves.' The sergeant stared at her in amazement.

'That lovely lass Anna was involved with this villain?' He was plainly astonished.

'She was kept under duress together with little Susan—managed to escape at last, sought safety in a nearby refuge, but it was thought to be too close to her abuser's mansion house. She was moved on to Dream Echo. Tom is involved in security there, his wife Lottie helps out there too.'

'There need to be many more refuges,' broke in Julie Bird. 'At least people are talking about abuse now—and not before time!' Her eyes flashed as she spoke.

'You're quite right, Julie,' replied Geraldine and glanced back at Evans.

'We were discussing Dream Echo last night when we heard a noise—became aware Jane Wilson was hiding outside the window. Tom had mentioned the name of the refuge as we sat talking—we knew she must have heard. Just the most enormous bad luck! If Jane told Greer the name of the refuge then not only Anna but all others seeking safety there might be at risk. So far, the true function of what appears to be merely a remote old mansion house, has never been exposed.'

'Thank you for bringing me into the picture,' said the sergeant. 'Now Mr Lanscombe suggested that Julie might stay with you for a time, at least until Greer is dealt with. Are you happy with the idea?' he asked gently. She looked tired he thought and no wonder with all she had endured over the last months. It was deplorable she should have this new worry when her son was away in London giving evidence at the trial of the Sea Giant executives, when she should be able to relax with that murdering lot out of the way.

'If you can spare Julie, I'll be delighted to have her with me,' exclaimed Geraldine. 'Did you know that Jane Wilson had managed to join the school's nature walk to the common—used the opportunity to interrogate little Melanie about Anna. It has left me anxious about the twins even when they are at school.' The police sergeant exchanged an amazed glance with his young WPC. In this quiet village where nothing out of the way ever occurred, to find a family targeted again, by a second offender, was quite extraordinary.

'I'll have a word with the head mistress,' he said. 'I would appreciate it if you would keep me informed of any developments at that refuge—Dream Echo!'

Malcolm Greer sat beside Hassan who was driving the maroon Saab. It had been decided not to take his usual magnificent Bentley so as not to draw any unnecessary attention to themselves. Greer was frowning in frustration as a tractor drew out of a field gate just ahead and commenced to drive slowly in front along the narrow country road.

'Make the fool move,' snapped Greer, but the thickset driver did not even turn his head when the Saab's horn tooted loudly and persistently.

'Pass him!'

'Too narrow, sir.' As Hassan spoke another car sped past them from the opposite direction enforcing his words. He felt uneasy with Greer in one of his difficult moods, could feel his master's rising tension. Finally, the tractor turned into a side lane and they were off again. At last after another twenty miles they saw a signpost for Willow-Mere and the village came into view. Hassan cut his speed and the two men glanced curiously about them as they entered what appeared to be the main street, dominated by the tower of an old Norman church.

They were passing a chemist shop now. Greer instructed Hassan to stop.

'Go in there and buy some plasters or paracetamol—anything. Then ask where Dream Echo is situated.' He sat there waiting impatiently until Hassan returned.

'Well?'

'The pharmacist said it is on the outskirts of the village—we need to drive on a bit. Apparently, it's a private residence owned by a young couple Robert and Amber Marsden—and the place is said to be an artist's commune. Amber Marsden's mother, Gwenda Williams, is a famous artist it seems.' He saw Greer's face darken at the news. Had they really driven all this way to find nothing but a collection of crazy artists at journey's end?

'I've heard of Gwenda Williams,' he said disconsolately. 'Her work is much sought after!' and he swore in frustration. But Hassan persisted.

'It could still be a refuge—the story of an artists' commune put about to retain the secrecy of its true status as a women's refuge?' Hassan hoped his suggestion might prove to be the truth, for he did not fancy a fruitless drive back with Greer in his present foul mood.

'Very well. We'll go and find out for ourselves!' Greer instructed and the maroon Saab moved off again. A quarter of a mile on the gates of Dream Echo came into view. Hassan braked and turned into the driveway, did not notice the police car parked just inside a lane to the left where it converged with the main road. He drove carefully, as Greer stared curiously ahead and drew in his breath as an imposing mansion came into view. He was not sure what he had expected—a somewhat dilapidated property perhaps. But the building before him appeared in excellent condition—and he was very thoughtful as Hassan helped him out of the car.

'Look sir, up there—CCTV.' He followed Hassan's gaze. Certainly, he employed a similar security device for Enderslie House for obvious reasons, but why should a remote country mansion have need of it. He motioned Hassan to remain by the side of the car as he mounted the front steps. He rang—and waited. His first thought on seeing Amber Marsden was that she was extremely lovely. Chestnut hair framed an oval face, her mouth had a slightly fuller lower lip above dimpled chin, but it was intelligent eyes of an unusual golden brown that struck him—an amber shade actually he decided, hence her name. She was dressed in well-cut trouser suit of navy cashmere, ruffled white silk shirt open at the neck, string of fine pearls about her throat.

'Good afternoon,' he began courteously. 'This is Dream Echo I believe?'

'It is. How may I help you?' she said and he noticed the slight hauteur in her voice.

'I—well, I have reason to believe a dear friend of mine may be staying here,' he said announced tentatively. She raised an inquiring eyebrow.

'Your friend is an artist—Mr..?'

'Oh—Sharpe. I'm Rodney Sharpe,' he invented. 'May I ask the name of someone so lovely?'

'Amber Marsden—I'm sure my husband will be pleased by your compliment, Mr Sharpe! Now who is this friend of yours?' Her voice was cool, dispassionate.

'Perhaps you might invite me in? Easier so to explain matters,' he said carefully.

She looked as though she would refuse, then stood back and led him along a deeply carpeted passageway into a large reception room. All was beautifully furnished in exquisite taste, with comfortable chairs and couches, fine pictures, tall ferns in ceramic pots at the windows. Anything less resembling a refuge for runaway women impossible to imagine. The woman seated herself and signed he should do likewise.

'Now Mr Sharpe—what is it that you found difficult to discuss outside?' she inquired. He looked around uncomfortably. Either this woman was a consummate actress or he had made a dismal mistake. But this was Dream Echo—the name Hassan's agent had supplied and there did not appear to be another of that name anywhere else. He took a gamble.

'The name of the lady I am looking for is Erika Nicolson—but she sometimes uses the name of Anna Lindstrom,' he said, watching Amber's face for the slightest change of expression—saw none.

'Ah, she is the artist to whom you were referring?' asked Amber. 'Well, I'm sorry to disappoint you Mr Sharpe, but I have never heard of your friend. As you may know, we do indeed run a small community of artists here, my mother much involved in the project. I am sorry you have had a fruitless journey.' She rose to her feet, glanced towards the door. He was about to leave, but a sixth sense that all was not be as it seemed gave him pause. What had he to lose by confronting her. Besides he did not like her cool, almost haughty attitude. He placed his hands on his hips, fixed her with darkly, arrogant glare.

'Look—I'll be frank with you! I've had it on good authority that Dream Echo is in fact a women's refuge! Do you deny it? I believe my Erika is here and demand to see her!'

Amber stared back at him in astonishment.

'You are either joking or deranged!' she said. She pressed a bell and an attractive, neatly dressed woman appeared.

'Susan—this gentleman is just leaving. Please escort him to the door,' she instructed.

'You don't get rid of me so easily. Why not show me around the place and if Erika is really not here—prove it.' He knew he was going too far, but could not restrain his rising fury. It was the first time a woman had treated him with less than respect and Greer did not like it. He strode past the woman called Susan to the sitting room door and before they could prevent him he started along the passageway, opening and slamming the first two doors he came to. At that moment two men descending from the main wide staircase appeared in front of him.

'What the devil is going on here!' demanded the younger of the two, planting himself before Greer. 'Who are you and what are you doing in my house?' Greer tried to evade him, but the second man, grey haired with strong features, shot out a hand and grasped him by the shoulder.

'Call the police, Robert,' he barked. 'Tell them we have caught a housebreaker!'

'Let me go, damn you! I'm here to find my partner Erika—know she is here!' shouted Greer furiously as Robert Marsden produced his cell phone. Greer panicked, broke away from Tom Lanscombe, and ran for the front door. He was out before they could stop him. Hassan who had been patiently waiting outside, saw him, and immediately opened the Saab door, flinging himself in the driving seat next to Greer. Robert Marsden and Tom appeared in the doorway in time to see the maroon car speeding away along the driveway, Tom noting the number. They swore and turned as Amber came to join them.

'It was Greer, wasn't it?' she confirmed. 'I thought I had disarmed his suspicions at first, then he became extremely angry, was determined to search the house. What happens now? Can he be arrested for trespass?' Her face was a little pale and Robert slipped an arm about her.

'Sweetheart, I'm so sorry you had to go through that!' he consoled her, as Amber's personal assistant Susan Mears put in a word of her own.

'Amber was absolutely wonderful,' she exclaimed. 'Really put him in his place. He was obviously used to getting his own way with women—would say he's a very dangerous individual.' Tom Lanscombe smiled at her.

'It isn't the first time Amber's been called on to deal with an angry, suspicious abuser! Dream Echo could not have a more valiant defender. As for Greer, hopefully he will soon be under arrest for people trafficking—face a heavy jail sentence if found guilty.'

'But surely he should be arrested for his behaviour here today!' exclaimed Amber hotly. Tom shook his head slowly.

'I do not agree. You see Amber, his case is bound to receive massive coverage in the media. Surely the last thing we need is for Dream Echo to be widely mentioned as a place suspected of being a refuge?' She listened intently and inclined her head in agreement.

'You're right, Tom. But are you sure he will have to face those major charges soon? Suppose he tries to come back in the meanwhile?' Tom frowned as he considered her words.

'A police car was positioned to supposedly watch over comings and goings along the entrance to Dream Echo. I'm surprised they didn't intercept Greer's car.' He drew his heavy brows together in disapproval. Robert intervened.

'Perhaps they were given details of Greer's normal car—didn't recognise the maroon Saab as belonging to him. He's wealthy, may have several cars,' suggested Robert.

'Fair enough,' retorted Tom. 'When he attempted to break into the Forester's refuge, it was reported he drove a Bentley. But every vehicle should have been checked. We need to have that Saab tracked to ensure he leaves the neighbourhood.' Amber smiled at him gratefully.

'Well at least he has gone! And Tom—I can only thank you for your foresight in warning of his possible appearance here. So far, we have been so lucky in keeping our secret at Dream Echo. It's three years since we opened our doors to abused women and little short of a miracle that we have not been exposed, despite several close shaves!' and she held her hand out to Tom Lanscombe who together with his wife Lottie had from the very beginning had helped organise the massive alterations necessary to turn the original austere old mansion house into the welcoming refuge that had already helped so many terrified, abused women into safe and happy new future.

With the front of the house giving appearance of a normal, delightful residence, the back of the building had been transformed into a marvellously comfortable refuge, with huge sitting room and dining room, well equipped kitchen and attractive, beautifully appointed bedrooms on the two upper floors. No expense had been spared, and the women who came to stay both enjoyed and respected their surroundings. Then there were the grounds, landscaped gardens and a children's playground.

Tom looked at her fondly. He had great respect for Amber and her dedicated team of helpers. To combine all of this with being mother of a fine little son and daughter was quite an achievement.

'How is Anna doing?' he asked her now as they entered the tranquillity of her front sitting room. 'Does she know Greer suspects she may be here at Dream Echo?'

'Yes—I told her. Seemed right to do so. She is understandably very scared of Greer and having met him I see why. There is something hard and very evil about him.' she said quietly. 'It's dreadful to think he had Anna under his control for four years—used the child as a hostage for her obedience!'

'He has to be a horrible piece of work to have made his fortune out of people trafficking!' Robert shook his head in disgust. 'Well I for one would like a coffee now!' Susan heard him and slipped out to prepare a tray. When she returned with the coffee they were discussing the risk of Greer's making a second appearance at Dream Echo during the night hours. But surely, he just wouldn't dare, thought Susan Mears dismissively. In any case her police sergeant fiancé would be on alert. However obnoxious, Greer was only one man against those protecting Dream Echo!

Colin Denton had listened studiously to the opening trial statements by prosecution and defence with intense interest. It seemed almost unreal to see these men who had caused his dearest Mary's murder, ordered his own death and that of his colleague and their pilot without the slightest qualm. Then there was the kidnap of his twin children. Their faces when they saw Colin had survived had been almost comical, he thought savagely. Let them try to deny their evil actions, much good it would do them with the evidence he was prepared to give!

He decided to give his mother a ring.

'Mum—is that you?'

'Colin, darling! How is it all going there?' He relaxed as he heard her familiar voice, a little huskier these days than when she was younger he thought.

'Trial has opened—nothing of any note happening yet. Can't wait to give my evidence. I hope the bastards get life!' he stated. 'Tell me, how are the twins? I miss them already and can't wait to get back.' He thought he noticed a slight hesitation as she replied.

'They're both fine, darling, and being as good as gold.'

'And Anna—any news from her?' he asked lightly.

'Not since she left for Dream Echo. But that will be for security reasons. She will be completely safe there, so don't worry.' Again, he thought he detected hesitation in her voice.

'Something has happened, hasn't it?' he demanded. 'What is it?' And Geraldine gave in to his demand—gave brief explanation of all that had transpired. He listened incredulously. 'So that fellow Greer sent two separate women there to discover where Anna had gone?'

'Yes. The second one as I told you is under arrest—but not before she had sent a text to Hassan, Greer's trusted attendant, mentioning Dream Echo.' Colin swore.

'So, Greer now knows where Anna is?'

'I've only just heard from Tom Lanscombe—Greer has already been to Dream Echo today asking for Anna. Seems Amber the woman who runs it stuck to their usual story—that the old mansion houses an artists' commune. Tom says the man wasn't convinced, tried to force his way around the place in search for Anna, but Tom and Robert Marsden intercepted him—he's gone now. Police are watching over

Dream Echo in case the fellow attempts to return, so all should be well.'

'If I find Greer he'll wish he'd never been born!' growled Colin angrily.

'With any luck, he will be under arrest very soon—police are waiting for final details of his involvement in people trafficking—he's believed to be masterminding a huge organisation, hence his wealth and power. Hopefully, he will soon join those Sea Giant villains in jail!'

'I should ring Tom!

'No—just wait. You concentrate on Sea Giant. Anna has plenty of experienced people looking after her.' He heard the authoritative note in her voice and it calmed him.

'The twins though—I hope they weren't scared by that woman, what did you call her—Jane?'

'I've told them not to answer anyone asking questions about Anna and little Susan. They are very sensible for such young children, you should be proud of them, dear!'

'Believe me, I am!' he replied fervently. 'Now you look after yourself, Mum. I don't like to think of you alone with Charles and Melanie in such an isolated spot. Shame Tom had to leave, although I appreciate why.' She gave a light chuckle.

'If only you had any idea of my past! Perhaps one day I'll tell you, but for now, have no concern about me—quite unnecessary I assure you.' He stared down at the phone as the call ended, questioning himself on why he should feel so concerned about Anna. After all, he barely knew the girl—yet strangely it felt as though he had always known her. He shook his head. Too much had been happening over these last months. For a moment he wished himself back on that magical island of Skye again with that kindly couple, Iain and Fiona MacLeod. He had glimpsed a peace there, a different way of life. He sighed—one day perhaps! But for now, he had his family to protect—as well as Anna Lindstrom and her little daughter Susan.

Hassan consulted a map. They had drawn into a layby in a wooded area about ten miles west of Dream Echo. He glanced at Greer. Had his master had time enough to decide on their next move? Greer had not spoken since he had rushed out of that imposing-looking mansion that they suspected housed a women's refuge. As he bent his eyes over the map Hassan cast a quick sideways glance at the sombre face of the man beside him. He had never known Greer so uptight before in all the years he had worked for him, as time and again he wished Erika Nicolson had never come into his life.

Still, Greer had not spoken so Hassan risked questioning him.

'What was your impression of the place, sir—could it really be the refuge we sought? I noticed that woman you spoke to when we arrived. She seemed like one of the gentry—not what you would expect.' Greer looked at him irritably.

'She's a stuck-up bitch,' he said. 'Seemed very plausible and the interior of the house is well furnished. A great deal of money must have been spent on it. But something told me that what I saw was a mere façade. I tried to examine the rest of the place, began looking in other rooms before she could prevent it. Then two men intervened, one was the woman's husband, the other fellow older, hard-faced, with an air of authority. They were about to call the police when I decided to get out of there. But I'm not satisfied! We're going back, Hassan!'

'Is that wise when they will have alerted the police—the building may be watched. And then there's that CCTV! If our car appears on camera they will certainly recognise it!' He waited for a storm to break on his head, but Greer barely acknowledged his words.

'We are going back,' he repeated in icy tones. Perhaps for the first time, Hassan began to question Greer's sanity. Much as he revered his master, he did not want to face the prospect of arrest if they were caught trespassing on private property. Surely Greer could see the danger of returning when he had already been threatened with the police? But such was his conditioning to obey Greer's every command that he lowered his head, waited for instructions.

'You are right about this car,' said Greer suddenly. 'We need another vehicle—something innocuous. We passed a garage with second-hand cars for sale. Take me back there.'

Half an hour later Greer was in the driving seat of a black Ford, Hassan left behind in the maroon Saab to wait for Greer's return. He had pleaded to be allowed to go with him but to no avail. He could only sit anxiously wondering what the outcome of this whole crazy episode would be. Suppose Greer was arrested, what then? How was he know what was transpiring a few miles away at that mysterious mansion Dream Echo?

Amber found the young woman sitting in the comfortable communal sitting room with little Susan, reading to her from a book of fairy tales. She didn't want to speak in front of the child. Noticing two other young children playing with a toy robot dog she pointed at it.

'Why don't you help them with the dog, Susan! Tell them to stroke its head and talk to it and it will bark and wag its tail!' she said. Susan sprang up and glanced at Anna who nodded her to do so.

'What is it, Amber?' she asked.

'Malcolm Greer was here this afternoon!' She explained what had transpired.

'Will he be back?' She saw a flash of anxiety on Anna's usually calm face, took her hand, looking steadily into her blue eyes.

'If he does the police will be waiting for him—so don't worry! For what it's worth I thought there was something particularly evil—calculating about Greer.'

'He needs to control all around him—he's not normal,' she said with a shudder.

'Anna dear, I'm so glad you've escaped the brute. In this work, we encounter details of many violent and mentally unstable men. Very occasionally a suspicious abuser makes it to the door—and the story of an artist's commune sends them sheepishly away. No one yet has penetrated the secret of Dream Echo! I've no intention of breaking our record!' she stated.

'I guess I'm so scared he might try to snatch little Susan—Trudy as he knows her.'

'Put your mind at rest. All of us will be on full alert over the next few days. Tom says the authorities are closing in on Greer with regard to his people trafficking. Waiting for one of his operatives in this vile trade to break down under interrogation and name him officially as the mastermind of the evil organisation.' Anna's face remained troubled.

'I find it incredible I lived with him for so long without the slightest suspicion of the business he was involved in. It makes me feel sick to think that fashionable gowns and expensive jewellery he insisted on my wearing to impress his guests, were bought through the enforced prostitution of those poor women!' She blinked angry tears from her eyes.

'Believe me, he will soon be facing life in a prison cell! In the meanwhile, I have a proposition for you. With your compassion and nursing training, you could be a great asset to the team here at Dream Echo. Think about it, Anna. No need for a decision right now. I've watched how you interact with the other women here—as have Connie and Lottie.' Amber rose to her feet and smiled at an astonished Anna, before making her way to her office to speak with Tom who was currently checking the CCTV coverage.

It was over three hours since Malcolm Greer had taken hurried departure in the maroon Saab. Since then there had been no report of the vehicle in the vicinity of the refuge. Tom and Robert had their heads bowed over the tv screen checking for any sign of movement around the house. It was nearing dusk now and the automatic outside lighting was now switched on.

Greer approached the gates of Dream Echo in his second-hand black Ford, a determined glint in his eyes. He was about to turn into the driveway when instinct made him glance to the junction of a minor road opposite the gates. A police car was parked there. He swore and drove past and did not stop for about a hundred yards when he drew into a layby.

Why would the police have the old mansion house under surveillance unless it really was a women's refuge and not some odd collection of artists? Of course, that snobbish bitch who owned the place might have been telling the truth, but his gut feeling was that she was protecting a motley crew of dysfunctional women who had fled their husbands and homes. Well, somehow or other he was going to discover the truth of the matter.

He left the parked car and looked at the thick hedge bordering a field that stretched back to Dream Echo's gates. He noticed a slight gap in the bushes, forced his way through and scrambled into the grassy meadow beyond. He thought for a moment. He would be too exposed if he tried to cross the field diagonally but instead would need to skirt the field on this side of the hedge and once it joined the Dream Echo's entrance, proceed at right angles parallel with the long driveway.

He was almost there now and could see the upper storeys of the mansion crowned with tall chimneys rising above the thick surrounding hedge beneath which he was sheltering. He remembered the CCTV mounted on Dream Echo's walls, there must be a blind spot somewhere. He hadn't come all this way to leave without Erika and his daughter, they were inside there, he just knew it! But he must wait until it was dark. He settled down on the damp grass beneath the hedge. Before long he began to feel cold and realised he was hungry.

He began to think logically for the first time since he arrived there. Always supposing he managed to gain entrance to the house and discover Erika and Trudy—how without transport would he get them away from the house and back to his car parked half a mile away? It would be almost impossible to drag a struggling woman that distance, more so encumbered by a small child.

Suddenly through a small gap in the hedge, he glimpsed the dazzle of car lights approaching, He got up stiffly, and thrust his body through the hawthorn hedge, ripping his jacket as he did so. He moved cautiously through the screen of closely packed trees and bushes that formed a barrier to the front courtyard. He saw a woman get out of the car and run up the front steps of the house. The door opened and she was admitted by Amber Marsden's assistant she had addressed as Susan. He realised the woman had not locked the car, so was not planning to stay long.

Could this be the answer—if he could manage to find Erika and the child, get them out and into that car they could be away in no time! But it was a huge house and she could be in any of its many rooms—and there were three floors! It seemed a formidable task and he almost weakened in his determination to kidnap the beautiful golden-haired woman who had obsessed with him for the last few years and take his revenge for her rejection of him.

It was nine pm. Amber sat talking happily with her mother Gwenda Williams who had just arrived back from a trip to London to discuss the inclusion of her paintings in a major art exhibition at the Geddes Centre. Amber listened with a smile about her lips, Gwenda's enthusiasm for her work lightening the underlying tension caused by Greer's intrusion of a few hours ago. Gwenda leaned forward watching Amber intuitively as she twirled a strand of her long dark hair between her fingers. With her scarlet trews, gold shirt, and jacket of magenta velvet, she presented a colourful presence in the tranquil sitting room.

'So, what's wrong then, Amber darling?' she inquired. 'Another seriously abused woman arrived in my absence? Can I help—open up child!' Amber did so, brought her up to date with Greer's earlier appearance, and concern that he might return.'

'Greer's an evil devil,' said Amber. 'He's definitely dangerous and in my opinion, unhinged!'

'Well my darling, it won't be the first time we have had to deal with such a creature,' cried Gwenda in her soft Welsh accent. 'Remember Sadique Khan? Surely this man cannot be worse than that monster!' She saw Amber's lips tighten at this, and wished she hadn't mentioned the name of the vicious terrorist who had almost killed Amber just over three years ago,

There had been other incidents at Dream Echo, but all were efficiently dealt with by their small dedicated staff who lived from day to day in the knowledge that at any time they could be faced by an angry, abusive ex-partner demanding to see the woman who had dared to leave him and sought refuge there. It was nothing short of a miracle Dream Echo's secret had never been revealed—the presently held view in the village that the refuge housed a strange artists' commune, providing a perfect shield from its true purpose.

'How is Anna Lindstrom dealing with the knowledge Greer suspects her presence here?' asked Gwenda now.

'Concerned of course, but she's a very courageous young woman,' replied Amber. 'I suggested she might like a future position on the staff here. Her nursing experience plus the fact that she has had to deal with abuse on a personal level would prove such a useful combination.'

'When I spoke to her recently, Anna mentioned Colin Denton very warmly.' Gwenda glanced casually at her daughter. 'You don't think there might be a budding romance in the offing? If so she may not wish to leave her next-door neighbour!' But Amber shook her head.

'Colin lost his wife in a terrible car accident less than three months ago—believes it to be murder and down to those masterminding Sea Giant. I can't see he will be ready for another relationship yet.' She smiled at Gwenda. 'Mummy, you must be hungry after that long drive. Let's go the kitchen, see if dinner is ready yet!'

Tom looked up from his careful watch on the CCTV monitor as Lottie came in. She was carrying a tray—placed it on the desk next to him.

'Brought you your dinner, Tom! Robert said he would come and relieve you, but I said he would be better with Amber—and Gwenda's back from London.'

'Yes—saw her car arrive out front not long ago.' He glanced back at the large monitor screen showing different areas on all sides of the building. Was that a slight movement to the left side of the house adjoining the driveway and banked by the shrubby area in front of the hedge dividing the grounds from the meadow beyond? He stared, then relaxed. Must have been the lower branches of one of the trees caught by the evening breeze. Still watching the monitor, he lifted the lid covering the plate and sniffed its contents appreciatively.

'Yes, it's steak and kidney pudding. Eat it before it gets cold Tom. I'll watch the monitor while you do,' she said practically. He glanced back at her tenderly.

'But what about yours, Lottie love?'

'I've already had it. Here—change places with me.'

He did so, taking the other leather swivel chair swiftly demolishing his meal and smiling thanks to Lottie. At this moment Robert put his head around the door and both looked up. Neither could guess in that short few seconds, Malcolm Greer risked a quick dash from the screening trees and bushes and now crouched immediately beneath a side window. Had he been seen? His gaze swung anxiously around and saw no sign he had been detected, no alarm shattering the silence. The next step was to find access to this refuge where Erika was hiding herself and the child. Soon they would be in his power once more.

He glanced upwards and realised one of the cameras was trained precisely in his direction, swivelling in slow arc. He flung himself flat on the ground—had to discover a way in before he was detected. He heard a sound that appeared to come from the back of the house. He began crawling around from his position on the left side of the building around to the rear where floodlights had been switched on illuminating the exterior walls and extensive grounds that lay beyond.

He thought he heard the sound of laughter coming from inside—women's laughter. Was Erika one of those indulging in such merriment? Well soon she'd have little to laugh about, he vowed. He glanced up at the windows, all were in darkness, curtained. Then the back door opened and two men came out. One he recognised as Robert Marsden—the other the fellow who had also intercepted him on his earlier attempt that day. He was lying flat on the ground, his back pressed hard against the house wall, knew he might be spotted at any moment.

'I don't know what you think, Tom,' he heard Robert say, as they stared out across the floodlit grounds, 'but I doubt if the fellow will show up again—but if he does we're ready for him. He struck me as an arrogant bastard—definitely unbalanced.'

'Well, no sign of him—all seems perfectly quiet out here,' said Tom Lanscombe. 'But you can't be too careful. Hopefully, he'll be under arrest any time now.
Charles Latimer, one of the men employed to guard those poor trafficked women has been singing a merry tune!' Robert listened to this statement in satisfaction.

'That's great news, Tom! So, the bastard will soon be in a prison cell. Let's get back inside—you must return to surveillance duty in the office, relieve Lottie!'

Chapter Fourteen

Greer could hardly believe his luck—had been unseen although mere few yards away. Who was that man Charles Latimer they mentioned? He must be involved with the police at a high level, to be a party to details of the people trafficking case. He swore under his breath. So why would a high-ranking police officer be interested in those running a refuge for a few feckless females? The thought he was likely to be arrested shortly did not disturb him overmuch, the police simply wouldn't find him. He had no intention of remaining in England and would move to one of his properties in Europe.

But first he had to extract Erika and Trudy from this foul refuge despite its extraordinary security system. But how to get in unobserved? He threw logic to the winds, crawled to the door which Marsden and his friend had just slammed—rose to his feet and cautiously tried the door catch. He had expected it to be locked, but to his amazement it yielded. He couldn't restrain his excitement as he eased the door slightly ajar. All that CCTV—and they didn't even lock the door! He drew in his breath—opened it further—found himself in a small lobby! Looking urgently around he saw a half open door to the right, voices coming from inside it—he glanced in, saw four people, three men whom he recognised, and a woman with white hair. He had to take a chance. He slipped past the door and along the passage way stretching ahead.

He was sweating as he found himself peering in what appeared to be a very long, comfortably furnished reception room. A small group of women were seated close together at one end, two busily knitting, the others watching the large wall mounted TV. His eyes sped over them in disappointment. Erika was not here. So, where was she? There must be bedrooms. That was it. She must have retired early.

He crept up the stairs and swore as he reached the landing, saw the long passageways leading off on both sides—many doors. Was Erika behind one of these? How could he risk opening one door after another in an attempt to discover her? As he stood there torn with indecision, one of the doors opened and a young woman in a white fleece dressing gown emerged. She saw him—and screamed. Quick as a flash he was at her side, clamped a hand over her mouth, edging her back into the room.

'Not a word or it will be your last,' he whispered coldly. She nodded, eyes expressing her terror. He released his hold and drew a gun from his pocket.

'What is your name?' he asked.

'Mildred,' she whispered between dry lips. 'What do you want?'

'Information. Give it to me and you live—otherwise, and his finger touched the trigger suggestively. The girl—she appeared to be in her teens, looked at him pleadingly.

'Please don't hurt me.' She was visibly trembling. They had been warned that a disturbed individual might attempt to break in, but that the police were watching over the refuge.

'I need to know where I will find Erika Nicolson,' he said. He saw the blank look in her eyes. Of course—Erika was using an assumed name here. 'She is also known as Anna Lindstrom,' he added. This time he noticed recognition of the name.

'Why do you want Anna,' she whispered, glancing desperately towards the door.

'That is no concern of yours, Mildred,' he said coldly. 'Where is she?' This time he thrust the gun against her chest.

'The second door along.' She jerked out fearfully. He nodded, dealt her a quick blow to the side of her head with the gun—she collapsed.

Anna was seated on a chair between her own bed and the smaller bed where little Susan was already sleeping quietly. She looked up as the door was suddenly thrown open and saw Malcolm Greer framed in the doorway. She opened her mouth to scream—then as her eyes focussed on the gun he was pointing at her forehead, she forced herself to be calm.

'What are you doing here?' she demanded icily.

'What do you think, Erika! I have come to take you—and our daughter, back home. He looked at the sleeping child possessively. 'Now you will wake Trudy, and put a jacket on her. It will be chilly outside. You will need your own coat too.'

'I refuse to go with you, Malcolm! You cannot make me leave. One scream and security will be here—the police are watching the place!' He looked at her sneeringly, did she really think he would mildly disappear after tracking her down. But he sensed a change in Erika—she no longer feared him! That would soon be sorted, he thought grimly.

'The coats—now!' he instructed. It was at this moment that Susan awoke abruptly, caught sight of her father, sat up in bed and stared at him from terrified eyes!

'No—no-no! Go away,' she screamed and before he could react she was out of her bed and dived out of the door, yelling at the top of her young voice. Greer looked after her furiously.

'I see you have poisoned our daughter's mind against me, Erika. You will be sorry for it I promise you!' He rushed out into the passageway and caught up with the fleeing child in three long strides, stifling her screams with his hand.

'There is nothing to be frightened of Trudy. Mummy and Daddy are taking you home.' He carried her back into the bedroom, closing the door as on hearing the screams, the occupant of the neighbouring room came out to investigate.

'What's going on?' she called. There was no answer. 'Anna—was that Susan I heard?' she questioned as she banged on the door. Greer glared at Erika—placed the gun at Susan's forehead.

'You will tell that woman nothing is wrong,' he said. She saw the wild look on his eyes, stared in horror at the gun, and opened the door. She slipped out into the corridor trying hard to present appearance of apparent calm as she smiled at her neighbour.

'Ah—there you are Anna! What's wrong with little Susan?' inquired the woman looking at her anxiously.

'She had a bad dream—it happens sometimes you know,' said Anna. 'She will be alright now, but thank you for taking time to check Laura! I'm sorry you were disturbed.' She turned back into the bedroom. Greer lowered the gun, smiled at the trembling child, whilst eyeing Anna in cold amusement.

'I see that you are already beginning to obey me again, Erika. Good. As for you Trudy, you will behave—or I might have to hurt Mummy and you wouldn't want that, would you.' She stared back at him from frightened blue eyes. 'Now—the coats, Erika. And I am going to need directions to get out of this house unseen. If you do anything to draw attention to us I will not hesitate to use this!' and brandished the gun threateningly.

'How did you get in?' asked Anna,

'By the back door. A couple of men stepped outside to survey the grounds—and actually forgot to lock the door as they re-entered! Some security!' he grinned. 'I want to reach the front of the house. Now—get the child dressed.' She did as she was bid, helping the trembling little girl into a denim jacket, then pulling a similar one over her pale blue sweater. He nodded approval.

'Come,' he instructed, lifting his protesting small daughter in his arms, as he opened the door, checking the corridor was empty. Anna had no option but to follow him. Her thoughts were in turmoil. Her instinct was to scream for help, but didn't dare, for she sensed a change in Greer. He was not only displaying his usual arrogance, but showing evidence of being mentally unstable, paranoid. The fact that he had actually held a gun to his own child's head was proof enough of this, and she had to protect little Susan whatever it cost.

'Which way?' he demanded as they descended the flight of stairs. Before them lay the door to the communal living room—further along were two offices, one Amber's administration office, the second the security office where the CCTV monitor was watched round the clock.

'I do not wish to go that way. How do we get to the front of the house from here?' whispered Greer harshly. Anna looked at him helplessly.

'There is only one door connecting the front of the house from the refuge, It is always kept locked—only Amber, her husband and members of the staff have keys. It is not possible for you to access it, and that's the truth.' He stared at her face, recognised she was not attempting to deceive him. So now what? Even if he managed to get them out of the back door without being detected, once outside they would be picked up on the CCTV.

'Then we risk it,' he hissed. 'Remember—one scream out of you and you will mourn your daughter.' He plunged ahead, hurried past first one and then the second office doors, reached the lobby and clutching Susan closely to him, tried the outer door. He lifted the catch, recognising the type of lock turned it twice and it yielded.

'Come Erika!' he instructed—as with face taut with anxiety Anna followed behind him. 'Now—run!' he called, starting off in front of her, as almost immediately an alarm bell shattered the evening air. He ran faster, Anna despairingly in his wake, were round the side of the house now, making for the front courtyard.

'In the car!' and he pointed to Gwenda Williams red Toyota parked beneath the front entrance steps. 'Get in,' he barked as the alarm shrilled into the night. Lights were going on at many of the windows now, curtains pulled aside. He jerked the back door open, placing the child on the seat, didn't stop to strap her in but slammed the door, next shoving Anna violently down into the front seat, and finally flinging himself into the driving seat. He smiled triumphantly. The fool woman who had arrived in this about an hour ago, had not locked her vehicle, but obligingly left the keys in the ignition. He reversed as several people came rushing round the side of the house in hot pursuit. He sighed relief—they were off!

The officers in the police car heard the alarm even before Tom Lanscombe rang through with news that Greer had kidnapped Anna and her little girl. They were about to start down the driveway when they saw Gwenda's familiar red Toyota speeding towards them, saw a man driving, and a woman seated beside him. They didn't recognise the man and barely saw the woman automatically taking her for the famous artist who was Amber's mother as the car shot past them. The police car tore down the driveway towards Dream Echo as Malcolm Greer laughed gleefully as he drove the short distance to the black Ford he had parked in the layby. He slammed on the Toyota's brakes, leapt out and opened the rear door first, snatched the child out, clutching her close, as he beckoned Anna to get out. As he guessed on seeing their daughter in his arms she obeyed immediately,

'Now—into this other car,' he snapped. 'Quickly woman—in—in!' Within less than a couple of minutes they were off again, leaving Gwenda's red Toyota in the layby.

Hassan looked up as the black car approached. As it drew up he saw Greer with Erika seated beside him. He had done it then! Hassan's face expressed relief, as he climbed stiffly out of the maroon Saab in which he'd been anxiously waiting for the last few hours.

'Master—congratulations!' he exclaimed in delighted tones, and watching as Greer stepped out of the Ford, pulling Anna out beside him.

'Get my daughter out,' instructed Greer, pointing to the small shape on the back seat. Hassan did so, handling the frightened little girl with rough kindliness. She was after all his master's child, and as such to be treated with care.

'We return to Enderslie House?' he inquired. But Greer shook his head.

'No Hassan—to that private airport you know of.'

'Our destination, sir?'

'The Netherlands –I have good friends there. The police will be after me here, Hassan, so I will relieve them of my presence!'

'What about passports, sir?' Hassan inquired practically. Greer smiled, smacked the breast pocket of his leather jacket.

'I have them all here, brought them just in case I was successful, yours, mine and fakes for the woman and child, they're good, no-one will question them. I've plenty money too, have already transferred most of my funds abroad!' He smiled triumphantly. 'Now I want you on the back seat with the child. I'll drive, with Erika beside me in the front. Hurry now, Hassan. The next hour is vital!'

'Why not continue to use that Ford sir—less recognisable.' But Greer shook his head dismissively.

'We may need to use speed—I don't trust that heap of rubbish!' he stated impatiently. Hassan nodded understanding.

'Oh—I changed the car's number plates while you were away, sir.'

'You did?' and Greer nodded approvingly, 'Well thought of! No doubt the original would have been recorded at Dream Echo earlier, the police informed.' He watched as Hassan placed the traumatised child in the back of the maroon Saab, barely noting she was very pale.

'Please, let me sit next to Susan—she doesn't look well,' pleaded Anna now, speaking for the first time since their arrival in the remote country lane. His face darkened as she referred to their daughter by this new assumed name. How dare she! He glared at her.

'You heard my instructions. Hassan will sit beside—Trudy!' and he put heavy emphasis on the name. She bit her lip understanding her mistake. But why should the name offend him when he had been prepared to shoot the child an hour ago? She recognised he wasn't thinking rationally, was out of his mind—and very dangerous. Then she found herself thrust down roughly on the front seat by Greer, knew she was helpless at this time—that it was safer not to inflame him further. She shot an encouraging glance behind at her little girl, but there was no response in her eyes. Oh, if only Colin Denton were here. Thought of his calm, strong face flitted on her inner vision. Colin—and Geraldine.

Greer was seated by her side now and she tensed as the car started up and she tried to concentrate. An airport he had said—destination the Netherlands. This was what lay in front of her unless she could prevent it—but how? He gave her a mocking smile as he increased their speed. Anna turned her head coldly away from him, transfixed with the helplessness of her situation, as she closed her eyes now—and prayed. As she did so, the tension holding her body rigid seemed to relax, felt another was guiding her actions.

Tom and Robert stared at each other stiffly, trying to come to terms with what had happened. Not only had Greer managed to penetrate Dream Echo, kidnapping Anna and Susan—but as they now discovered had also severely injured one of the women in their care. They lifted the unconscious body carefully onto her bed. Mildred Johnson was still alive, but a huge bruise swelling on her temple told its own story. One of Amber's senior helpers, Connie, an experienced nurse, bent over the teenage girl, who now showed signs of returning consciousness.

'Mildred—Mildred? There—there, my dear—you are safe now,' said Connie gently. She turned to Amber who had just come in, Lottie at her side, and staring down in dismay at their injured guest. 'I think she should be alright, but I'd like the doctor to have a look at her head,' she said softly. Amber nodded.

'I'll ring him right away,' she said.

'Let me,' said Lottie and did so. 'He's on his way, Amber!'

'Good—thanks Lottie! Now then, let's work out how this happened!' she looked interrogatively at Tom and her husband Robert. 'How did that swine get in when the place is covered by CCTV?' she demanded. It was Tom who answered shamefacedly.

'Amber, I'm so sorry. Can only think that when Robert and I went out of the back door to make a quick inspection outside, leaving Lottie to watch the monitor, that on our return just minutes later we neglected to lock the back door! I have tried to analyse my actions and have no recollection of turning that blasted lock! How I could have been so lax is disgraceful, I have no excuse—but consider it's the only way Greer could have accessed the building. To have done so in that incredibly short timespan can only mean he was already close to the door when we went outside. Why we didn't see him is more than I can fathom.' Amber looked at Tom's miserable face and touched his arm comfortingly

'Tom dear, it could have happened to any of us! Besides we have always known something of the sort was inevitable at some stage and it's not the first time we've had to deal with a predator! What's important, is to catch Greer and bring Anna and her little one safely back!' she was watching Mildred's white face as she spoke.

'Yes—but let's be clear, it's my fault as well as Tom's you know,' put in Robert ruefully. 'I should have checked that door too, Amber!' She nodded and gave him a warm forgiving smile, before turning all her attention on the injured girl.

'Do you feel well enough to answer a few questions, Mildred dear?' The girl whispered a quiet assent, as Amber sat beside her, taking her hand comfortingly. 'Can you tell me who hurt you?'

'It was a stranger. I was coming out of my bedroom when I saw him' She started to tremble. Amber patted her hand gently.

'Can you go on, Mildred?'

'He grabbed me—pushed me back in the room. He had a gun—I was terrified. He demanded to know where Anna was. I didn't want to, but I told him—was just so scared. Next, he lifted the gun—there was a bad pain and everything went black. I don't know what happened after that.' She looked up at Amber miserably. 'Did he get Anna and her little girl?' she asked.

'Yes dear. But you had no slightest option but to tell him where she was—so never blame yourself! There are a lot of police looking for them right now.' She got up glanced at Connie.

'Perhaps she should have a painkiller for her headache?'

'Would really like to wait for the doctor,' she looked doubtfully at the girl's face. 'Well, a paracetamol will take the edge off her pain, poor child.' Suddenly another person erupted into the room and looked around her questioningly. Amber recognised her as Laura, who had the room immediately adjoining Anna's.

'What's going on?' the woman asked, casting a troubled look at the injured girl lying on the bed. She noticed the huge bruise on the girl's forehead. 'What's happened to young Mildred then?' she said aghast. Tom Lanscombe led her aside, explaining briefly what had occurred. Laura's broad, lined, middle-aged face contorted with shock. She put a hand to her mouth as realisation dawned.

'Must have been before I heard little Susan screaming outside in the passage. I came out but no one was there. Anna must have taken her back in the bedroom. I called out to Anna, asking what was wrong with Susan. She said the child had had a bad dream. Naturally I believed her.' Tom listened intently.

'But you didn't hear Mildred call out when she saw the intruder?' Laura shook her head.

'No. I was listening to a soap on TV. Only heard little Susan scream because it seemed to come from right outside my door,' she exclaimed her face mortified.

'Laura, I'd appreciate it if you didn't tell the other women about this yet. We don't want a panic!' said Tom. She nodded.

'Just tell me if there is anything I can do to help! You've all been so wonderful here. I hope the police catch that brute soon and bang him up in jail!' she snorted.

'Perhaps we should let Mildred have some peace,' Connie suggested firmly. They all nodded, Lottie putting her arm about her husband's waist drawing him out of the room, while Robert escorted Laura back to her own bedroom.

'Tom, do you think we should let Geraldine know what has happened,' asked Lottie. He frowned, inclined his head.

'Yes—you go ahead, my dear. I'm about to ring Charles—leave it up to him if he tells Colin Denton. Then the police must be informed about Greer's assault on Mildred Johnson. Poor girl—she escapes brutality at the hands of her violent father for this to happen to her!'

'It's alright, I'll speak with the police, Tom,' said Amber, 'I have questions of my own for them. Then I must get back to my mother. I left her in the studio furious with herself for leaving her keys in her car—she'll be even more distressed when she learns what Greer has done to Mildred!'

'The greatest importance is that no whisper of this gets out to the village,' said Robert quietly. 'As it is, with police cars coming and going some busybody may become curious.' He saw Amber's shattered face, and drew her into his arms. 'Try not to worry my darling. Anna will be safe, I just know it—and that sweet little daughter of hers.'

Charles Latimer took the phone-call in shock. It was incredible that Greer had actually returned to the refuge, managed to kidnap his ex-partner and her child. That he had also almost killed another woman in the process even more devastating.

'What I find difficult to understand is why the police didn't intercept the car Greer was escaping in. You said it was a red Toyota, that belongs to Gwenda Williams?' He wanted to be sure he had his facts straight.

'That's correct. They saw a man seated in front with a woman—took it to be Gwenda at a quick glance. Don't forget it was dark, and the car by in a flash. I've just been told that the Toyota has been found a mere hundred yards or so from the entrance to Dream Echo.'

'Meaning of course that they changed cars! Either Greer left a car parked there in readiness—or phoned that fellow Hassan to bring the maroon Saab he used on his earlier visit!' suggested Latimer.

'No to the second idea—the police are on lookout for the Saab—have the number! Definitely no sign of it,' Tom explained.

'So then, Greer is driving an unknown vehicle, on his way to who knows where? Back to Enderslie House?' Latimer scowled as he considered Greer's options. 'He is bound to realise, he'll be arrested on sight if he returns there with Anna and the child. Then again, he must be also be aware his people trafficking business is now exposed and he faces arrest over that in the very near future.'

'So, he may try to leave the country then? What other choice does he have!' said Tom.

'We'll have a watch kept on all airports for possible sighting of Greer, Anna and the child. But there are a few private airports over which we have less jurisdiction.'

'Which would be the nearest for him to make for?' asked Tom.

'Two come to mind—"Sky's the Limit" and "Up and Away" My bet is on the last. It's about two hours' drive from the refuge. I'll take the copter—with any luck be there before they arrive. To be on the safe side, we'll also send a car to the other airport. Wish I could take you with me Tom—sadly time doesn't allow. Phone me at once if you have any fresh news.'

Colin Denton was settling down to watch TV in his hotel bedroom, but was feeling restless. His phone rang—it was his mother. He smiled as he heard her voice.

'Mum—everything alright with you?' he asked.

'I've had a very disturbing call from Lottie Lanscombe. Listen Colin dear, Greer has kidnapped Anna and Susan from Dream Echo. He managed to get in past security and drove off before anyone could stop him. The police are searching everywhere—and I'm so worried about Anna and the little girl!' He heard her words in shocked horror. Anna had told him of her fear of Greer, explained how traumatic those years had been under his constant control. He felt a surge of anger.

'Have the police any idea where he's taking them?'

'Well he could go back to his mansion, Enderslie House, but the police will be bound to check there, and I don't know what other properties he owns. Well there is a flat above a jeweller's shop in Lynchester, but that is also know to the police, so unlikely.' He heard the distress in Geraldine's voice and knew there was little he could do to help here in faraway London. He could fly up to be with his mother, but would prefer to do something practical to find Anna himself. The very thought of her exposed to Greer's cruelty made his blood boil.

'Let me think for a moment,' he said.

'I've another call coming through, Colin. Better take it in case there is some news. I'll call back.' He sat there and stared down at the phone, mind in a turmoil. Minutes later the phone rang again. It wasn't Geraldine, but Charles Latimer. He listened intently to what Latimer had to say.

'Yes—I'll be delighted to go with you Charles! Where do we meet?' Within a few minutes he was ready, recognised Charles distinctive silver hair and authoritative posture, where the MI5 man stood waiting at the desk in Hotel reception.

'Rather thought you might like to come,' he said with a quick smile. 'This way, we've no time to lose if we're to catch the bastard!' Quarter of an hour later they were airborne During the flight Charles Latimer revealed what they knew so far of Greer's actions that day. Colin listened in increasing anger. He exploded into a blistering diatribe against Greer. Latimer sitting next to him, viewed Colin with raised eyebrows.

'You have personal feelings for Anna Lindstrom?' he inquired calmly. Colin was suddenly quiet, and hesitated before replying. What were his feelings for the beautiful, golden haired woman, with her intense blue eyes and wistful smile. As a widower of a few months he should not have the slightest interest in her, but knew as he sat there analysing his deepest emotions that he did in fact care very greatly for Anna. If not love, then he acknowledged experiencing a deep attraction to the young mother.

'I care for her—cannot say more than that at this time. Only know I will kill Greer with my own hands if he hurts her!' he replied simply. Latimer looked at him. If Denton was to act as his official assistant once he had undergone training, he must be sure the younger man could be relied on to remain stable in all circumstances, their very lives could depend on it.

'Very well. Just remember you are to act under my instructions if we are lucky enough to intercept Greer before he attempts to leave the country! No false heroics.'

'You have my word,' replied Colin, his emotions once more under control. Latimer sat back satisfied. He started to discuss the Sea Giant trial with Colin.

'Just thought, I'm supposed to be on standby to be called,' said Colin suddenly. 'Will I be in trouble for missing my witness slot?'

'Have no worries. I'll see the right people are informed,' replied Latimer, and Colin stared back at him, wondering how much power this handsome silver haired man sitting beside him exercised. For the first time, the actuality of working closely with Charles Latimer touched a spark of pride within him. To have been chosen was indeed an honour he acknowledged. The pilot called back to them, only twenty minutes now from the airport.

Malcolm Greer shot a look at the woman sitting so rigidly beside him in the car.

She seemed devoid of all emotion now, merely staring listlessly ahead. He had expected hysterics, tears or an outburst of anger, but Erika showed none of these. Good! She had accepted the situation.

'How is Trudy?' he called to Hassan, turning his head to glance at the back seat.

'She is sleeping, sir,' came the reassuring reply. Greer smiled, hands tightening on the driving wheel he leaned forward and increased their speed. All was going so very well. Once at the airport his troubles would be over. It was then that the unexpected happened! He took another acute bend on the minor, winding road through dense woodland along which they were swiftly progressing, when a young roe deer leapt down the bank in front of them. Greer tried to brake—to avoid the creature, but struck it full on. The car swerved to the right, hit the bank. catapulted and landed on its side!

Anna was the first to react, glancing at the man seated next to her saw blood running down his forehead, he was either unconscious or stunned. She was shaking, her shoulder seemed badly wrenched, rib cage aching, but ignoring discomfort, she unbuckled her seat belt and turned anxiously behind her. Susan was staring in front of her, eyes wide with shock. As for Hassan —one look at his face was enough to see he was dead! From his position she realised he must have thrown himself partly across Susan to protect her from the oncoming impact.

She struggled to force the car door open. She had to get Susan out before Greer regained consciousness. It seemed an age before she managed it—saw the car had glanced off a stunted tree. Steam was coming from under the bonnet. She wasted no time but opened the rear door, and called softly to her traumatised daughter.

'Susan—are you hurt dear?'

'I don't think so,' faltered Susan, trying to free herself from the weight of Hassan's body, as Anna reached in towards her. 'Why doesn't Mr Hassan move?' Anna didn't answer but stretched in effort to reach her.

'Give me your hand, darling—and I'll help you out.' When she had Susan safe in her arms she uttered a trembling sigh of relief and held the little body close.

'Now, we must be quick Susan. We need to get away from the car!' She cast a quick glance at Greer's inert body in the front—noticed to her dismay he appeared to be coming to, eyes opening. She didn't wait for more—but frantically stumbled off between the trees clutching Susan in her arms whilst trying hard to ignore the throbbing pain in her shoulder. She could barely discern where she was going in the fading twilight, the few gaps between the trees merely letting in last traces of the bruised sunset.

After about two hundred yards, the pain in her shoulder becoming intolerable, she lowered Susan to the ground, sat beside her easing the child's head onto her lap and seeing how white the little girl was looked desperately around. As she slipped her hands into the pockets of her denim jacket looking for a handkerchief to wipe Susan's tear stained face, her fingers engaged with her mobile phone! She pulled it out, had not realised she had it with her. Would it be possible to get a signal in this remote place?

Where was she? All she knew was that they had been making for an unknown private airport and had taken a minor road in case Greer's maroon Saab was recognised, had not seen other cars for many miles. She dialled a 999—as she feared there was no signal.

Perhaps it might make a difference if she were on higher ground— she looked around, flashed the light of the phone in front of her. They appeared to be situated at the bottom of a steep rise, but with the trees massed so closely together it was hard to judge how much height she would gain if she clambered to the summit with Susan. But to do so, would mean that she would be further away from the road and any possible rescue.

'Mummy—is Daddy going to come after us,' called Susan now, looking around apprehensively. 'It's getting quite dark, and I'm very frightened of him—please don't let him catch us!'

'Don't worry my darling, I'll keep you safe,' replied Anna, but knew how vulnerable they were if Greer recovered sufficiently to follow them. The car must be quite a way behind them now and he wouldn't know which direction they had taken. Her shoulder was extremely painful, and she wondered how she would manage to carry Susan up the wooded hillside above them.

'Susan—do you think you can walk now—if we don't go too fast?' The child nodded.

'Yes, of course I can walk—and run too!' she affirmed. 'Let's go Mummy in case he finds us!' The fear had left her small face now, blue eyes determined as they both rose and Anna took her hand.

'I've got my mobile with me—need to get somewhere higher to get a signal.' They started off again, Anna finding the going was easier without the child's weight. Both were panting when at last Anna paused, noticing a small clearing ahead. She smiled down at Susan. 'Can you manage to go just a little further,' she asked.

'Yes, but I'm tired,' the child replied. Anna took her hand again and they struggled on. They reached the clearing and Susan sank down exhausted and watching as her mother lifted her mobile. Anna was near tears when she realised there was still no signal. She looked about her in despair. She stared at a towering oak tree a few yards away. Suppose she managed climb into the crotch about twenty feet up—try for a signal up there?

Susan watched anxiously as her mother attempted to climb the ancient tree, saw her fall back twice, unable to get a secure foothold on the trunk, each jolt to her damaged shoulder excruciatingly painful. At the third attempt Anna made it, sat clinging on to the solid cleft branch she had reached before steeling herself to advance higher.

She struggled upwards. This should give sufficient height! She braced herself against a swaying, solid branch—looked around, flashing the thin light from the phone, found that she had reached the summit of the wooded hillside. Glancing down ahead she saw to her relief an area of rough pasture land with a large farmhouse surrounded by outbuildings She raised the phone again, but as she did so, heard the sound of a violent explosion! Swinging her head towards the source of the noise still vibrating through the trees, saw flames rising from what she judged was the direction of the upturned maroon Saab from which she had made her escape.

As her mind registered the shock, she wondered whether Greer had managed to get out of the car before the explosion? She had realised that Hassan was dead when she managed to extricate Susan, with Greer unconscious. Had he died back there in those orange flames plainly to be seen snaking upwards—or was he somewhere nearby, seeking dire vengeance on her and possession of their child? She forced herself to think logically. She had to summon help. Her fingers moved as she sent a text to Tom Lanscombe and another to Amber explaining briefly what had happened and describing the minor road they had taken, the heavily forested area in which they had crashed—her escape, and that the car was now apparently in flames.

There was no immediate answer to either and with a sigh of frustration Anna started to awkwardly descend the tree. She fell the last six feet. The jolt received to her shoulder almost caused her to faint.

'Mummy—Mummy! Are you all right,' came her daughter's anxious young voice as Susan knelt beside her mother.

'Yes, Susan darling, but I've hurt my shoulder a bit. We have to get away from here fast now. Did you hear that explosion?'

'A big bang—yes I did. What was it?' asked the child glancing around fearfully.

'I'm guessing it was the car. Petrol could have been leaking—perhaps a spark ignited it'

'Was my father still inside it?' asked Susan trying to take it in.

'Sweetheart I just don't know—maybe. There again he may be looking for us right now. Listen, just a few yards ahead all these trees come to an end. Just fields then, and I've seen a farmhouse in the distance. We have to get there and ask for help.' Susan nodded, held her hand out to help her mother up. Both gave last apprehensive backwards glance before leaving the forests covering screen, and commencing to tramp down through the rough, tussocky pastureland.

They could glimpse lights on in the farmhouse—Anna judged it must be about five hundred yards away still. Susan was straggling behind her slightly, the little girl almost at the end of her endurance. It was then that they heard the sound—a harsh voice shouting behind them.

'Stop! Stop or I'll shoot!' Anna went cold as she recognised the voice—Greer!

She swung about, could just about make out his figure in the near dark. Susan let out a terrified scream! Anna swung her up into her arms, gasping as the pain in her shoulder intensified, and started running down the slope towards the farmhouse—but it was still some distance away, Greer gaining on her.

Suddenly he let off a shot. She guessed it was more to frighten than kill her, did not turn her head but increased her speed—and prayed. It was now that the farmhouse door opened. Bright light streamed out illumining several people who appeared in the doorway and were staring towards her.

'Help!' she screamed. 'Help—he's trying to murder me!' A voice called back to her.

'Don't worry lass—we're coming!' She could just make out the shapes of three men running towards her now. Casting a desperate look behind her, she saw Greer was standing motionless. Then a shot passed within inches of her head. On instinct she dropped to the ground, covering Susan with her body. If he thought she was dead he might not shoot again. She could hear the rapidly approaching rescuers uttering shouts of outrage. Then she heard another sound—it became louder—a tremendous roaring noise dulling out all else as a helicopter loomed overhead, began descending.

Colin Denton ran in front of Latimer as both emerged from the chopper—he stooped anxiously over the woman's body, almost too scared to look—then she opened her eyes and uttered a soft cry as she recognised him. She was visibly trembling, and still shielding Susan.

'Anna dear—it's Colin! Charles Latimer is here too. You're safe now!'

'Colin—oh, thank God' she murmured.

'She's alive!' he called to Charles Latimer, as the silver haired special agent bent beside him, glancing down keenly at Anna in turn.

'Where is Greer, Anna?' asked Latimer. She responded to the urgency in his tones. She sat up, cradling Susan in her arms, and trying to speak coherently.

'Behind me—he has a gun, tried to kill me just now—shot almost got me.'

'We'll get him. Can you stand, Anna?' asked Latimer.

'Here, let me help you,' put in Colin, reaching for Susan, and lifting the traumatised little girl up gently as Latimer eased Anna to her feet. He saw the pain on her face.

'You're hurt?'

'My shoulder—it happened in the car crash. I think something's broken,' she admitted, was going to say more but the rescue party from the farmhouse were arriving on the scene, panting heavily as they skirted the helicopter and commencing to fire questions.

'What's been going on then—and who was that devil shooting at you—which way did he go?' demanded a grey-haired man with bushy beard, as the two younger men at his side, one carrying a shotgun, looked on questioningly.

'Thank you for coming to help me,' replied Anna, forcing a smile at the bluff-faced farmer. 'My attacker seems to have made it back to the woods.'

'You alright though, young woman,' the farmer inquired urgently as he glanced at Anna and the small girl beside her, and relaxed as she reassured him.

'Right—and who are you a lot,' he challenged, staring at Colin and Latimer. '

'We're affiliated to the police—are going after him now,' stated Latimer. 'Your name, sir?'

'Bill Trentham—these are my sons Pete and Andy. It's my land you are on. Look, if you like I'll take the lass down to the farmhouse. She needs to lie down by the look of her. You go after that murdering swine—my boys will go with you!'

Latimer hesitated, glanced at Colin who was equally impatient to go after Greer, some precious minutes lost already. It was a long walk for Anna to the farmhouse—the helicopter surely a better option. He made the point and Trentham nodded agreement.

'Very well, sir. In that case the three of us will come along of you. We know every inch of the woods. Can't wait to get my hands on the vermin who tried to kill a mother and her child!' His face was grim as he glanced towards the trees.

'He is armed—dangerous!' put in Colin.

'Well—my Pete has a shotgun. No arguments—we're with you! Best get the lass into that chopper of yours.' Colin nodded, put his arm about Anna as he led her quickly over to the helicopter, Latimer carrying Susan. The pilot Bob Preston who had been watching, helped his new passengers aboard, closed the door. Anna sank down on a seat as the man placed she little girl gently beside her. It was hard to realise she was safe now, so amazing that Colin and Charles Latimer had come to her assistance in such unusual fashion. She looked up at the pilot as he offered her coffee from a thermos flask, then produced a small carton of fruit juice for Susan.

'Always best to be prepared on these flights,' he said. He saw her wince as she reached for the coffee. 'You are in pain?' he asked.

'My shoulder—think it's fractured, but oh, just so wonderful to be safe! How did you find me?' she asked.

'You sent a text to Colin Denton. We were on our way to a private airport they imagined Greer might be making for. It was nothing short of a miracle that we were so close when you texted Colin.' He shook his head. 'Incredible coincidence!' She nodded, but as she did so she remembered that desperate prayer she had made.

'It was no coincidence,' she murmured. He looked at her, puzzled. She was probably not thinking clearly and no wonder after all she had been through.

'Look—I've got a couple of paracetamol capsules here. Should take the edge off your discomfort.' Anna thanked him, swallowed them gratefully. He smiled down at Susan.

'How are you little lady?' he asked gently. She didn't answer him, but closed her eyes falling asleep as he took the juice carton from her fingers. Anna eased the small head onto her good arm. Now all they could do was to wait.

Malcolm Greer had watched Anna drop, mind in a daze as he realised he had killed her. It was over—he was revenged. Perhaps he should collect the child, his daughter Trudy. But did he really want to be burdened with the brat at this time? He heard shouting coming from the farmhouse, saw the figures starting out towards him. He hesitated, then heard the sound of the helicopter. Saw it start to descend. How in hell had the authorities known where to come? He swore savagely and started back towards the darkness of the forest. He cast a final glance behind him, saw two men clamber out of the helicopter and walk towards the spot where Anna had fallen.

He had to get away fast now—would be arrested for murder if caught. Once back within the dark anonymity of the forest he started to relax a little. Trying to find him in this wilderness would be like looking for a needle in a haystack! But he needed to get away from this area. He had plenty of money as well as his passport in his inner jacket pocket. Money got you most things in this world, he thought grimly.

Damn shame about the car! He would also miss Hassan, not that he had felt any particular liking for his late devoted servant, but the man had been useful. He could still make out a red glow where the remains of both car and Hassan still smouldered. If they came searching for him, it would doubtless be in that direction. He must get closer to the road, make progress along the bank immediately above it, hopefully see the lights of an oncoming car and thumb a lift. He was tired but started forwards with a dogged tenacity, making his way downwards between the trees. Then he heard it—shouts coming from close behind! Must be those bloody men from the helicopter—but the voices seemed to be coming from either side of him, and sounded he realised as though more than the original two men were involved. He pulled the pistol out of his pocket—reloaded, would use this without any qualm if necessary.

Colin Denton was coldly angry as he hurried between the trees at Latimer's side, and swore as he caught his foot on a looped tree root. The fact that Anna had escaped death by a few inches at the hand of her demented ex-partner had shocked him to his core. The world would be well rid of Malcolm Greer.

'Remember Denton, we are here to implement the law—not for revenge,' said Latimer now, as though sensing the younger man's thoughts. 'It is vitally important we take him alive, and that he goes though the due process of the law. He has information about a huge people trafficking organisation across borders in Europe. We need to identify all of its ringleaders!' Colin heard him, the words penetrating his mind as he panted by Latimer's side.

'I know, Charles. But he would have killed Anna as casually as one swats a fly! I hate his guts!' he ground out. 'And how are we going to find him amongst all these endless trees?'

'By trying to think as he does. Hear our farmer friends shouting over there? He will guess there are quite a few of us looking for him. Too dangerous just to hide—will realise that once dawn breaks he will be easier to spot. My guess is he will make for the road—try to get a lift.'

'So how will we know which part of the road he'll make for?'

'Colin, my friend, that's where your intuition will come in. It's a sixth sense you develop in this work and at times it can save your life!' Latimer clapped a hand on his back as they paused for breath for an instance. He called across to Bill Trentham and his sons.

'Quiet for a moment my friends—and listen.' They did so, straining their ears for any slightest sound. Colin touched Latimer's arm, pointed to the right. Latimer nodded. He had heard it too, a slight crash ahead.

'Sounds to me as though the swine tripped over,' he whispered. 'We must be close behind him now. Remember Denton, he is armed, has nothing to lose.'

Greer had indeed lost his footing, fallen a few feet, bruised his elbow. He swore, struggled to his feet, no harm done he thought in relief. Then he realised he could no longer hear the shouts of his pursuers. Why not? They certainly would not have given up so soon. Then he guessed—they were listening. He strained his eyes in front of him—could just make out the road below him. With fresh energy born of desperation he stumbled down the last few yards, was on the tarmacked road. Glancing in both directions—saw it, a small van coming towards him. He jumped in front of it waving his arms. To his relief it slowed down—stopped beside him. An elderly man put his head out of the window.

'What's wrong, mate?' he called.

'Crashed my car—need to get into town. Will you give me a lift—I can pay for it?'

'Saw a burned-out car just back there! Hard luck friend. Jump in then.' The elderly driver waited as his unexpected passenger got in next to him.

'Name's Ed Parsons,' he said, and glanced at Greer inquiringly.

'Oh—Henry Warren!' invented Greer. 'Shall we go then!' The driver smiled.

'Can see why you don't want to hang around in this deserted place. Good luck I was passing, eh! Here we go then!' Greer sighed relief as Parsons drove off—he was safe now!

Colin and Latimer had arrived just in time to see Greer climb into the van on the road below them and watched in frustration as it disappeared.

'Damnation!' swore Latimer angrily. 'I couldn't even get the number—too dark.' He bit his lip. 'White van—not much to go on!'

'Of all the foul luck—when we were so close!' cried Colin hotly, then both looked round as the farmer and his sons joined them.

'We heard the sound of a car. He got away then?' confirmed Bill Trentham seeing their disappointed faces.

'Yes—a white van!' responded Latimer, scowling as he realised the danger Greer could still present. Trentham smiled and glanced at his sons.

'Ah—that will be Ed Parsons van then, won't it, lads! He is often out this way of an evening—visits his daughter Beth back there in her cottage. He lives in Little Monkton about ten miles on. More of a village than a town.' Latimer's face brightened at the news.

'We need to get back to the helicopter right away. Perhaps you could guide us back, Mr Trentham?'

The pilot saw them coming—leaned out, looked at them questioningly He saw their grim faces, they hadn't caught the fellow Greer then.

'Everything alright here, Bob?' asked Latimer, as they climbed aboard.

'Yes, sir! Anna and the child have fallen asleep. She was in quite a bit of pain—gave her some tablets,' the pilot explained. Colin stooped over the girl looking down at her with compassion. He suddenly knew how devastated he would have been had Greer's bullet reached its intended target.

'Charles, will it be safe bringing them along,' he asked now, keeping his voice low so as not to disturb Anna. Latimer glanced at Anna analytically. They could leave the mother and child with the farming family, but was loathe to let them out of his sight.

'They come with us!' he replied crisply. He turned to the pilot. 'We may leave them in your care Bob, once we reach Little Monkton.' He seated himself, gesturing Colin to do likewise. 'Right—let's go then!' They took off, leaving the Trentham father and sons standing bemused, and staring up at the disappearing lights of the helicopter. What an extraordinary evening.

Geraldine was listening in shock to Lottie Lanscombe voice on the phone, trying to take in the horrifying news that Anna and Susan had been kidnapped by Greer—there had been a car crash—Anna and Susan had got away, hiding in the woods, fearful Greer would find them.

'How did you know this, Lottie?'

'Anna texted Amber to let her know they're safe for now—texted Tom as well. Listen Geraldine—that man Greer is completely unbalanced and extremely dangerous. He actually broke into Dream Echo, almost killed one of the residents, and got away with Anna and the child. Since then Tom has just heard from your son. Colin is with Charles Latimer right now, they've taken a helicopter and have found

Anna and the little one. They're now in pursuit of Greer. Just thought you ought to know as Colin in involved.

'Thanks, Lottie. How is the woman Greer attacked?'

'Received a savage blow to the head poor girl—but will recover.'

'Let me know if there is any more news.'

'Will do—must go.' Lottie rang off, and Geraldine put the phone down. So what Anna had feared had happened. She could only imagine the sheer horror she must have experienced at being in Greer's hands again. At least she was safely in the care of Colin and Charles at the present time. Where would they leave her since in the process of tracking Greer down? Surely, they wouldn't take the young mother and child with them—expose her to more danger from Greer? And how about her son Colin—suppose he should suffer an attack from Greer when attempting to arrest the thug? Little Charles and Melanie were only just getting over the trauma of losing their dear mother—while experiencing relief that the father they had mourned as dead was wonderfully alive. But if anything were to happen to Colin now!

She was feeling very troubled as she stole quietly upstairs to check on the twins, and found them sleeping peacefully. She returned to the living room. Oh, if only her husband David was still alive. She stared at his photograph, sat down, and sighed. Then as she always did when in trouble of any kind, closed her eyes and prayed—felt a peace afterwards, sat there quietly waiting for more news.

Ed Parsons jerked his head towards the signpost his van headlights illumined. We're almost at Little Monkton now, pal. My house is just off the high street—but we're coming to an all-night garage any moment now. Would you rather I let you off there? You could rent another car perhaps? What do you say then?' He glanced at the brooding figure beside him. There was something about his passenger that made him feel uneasy, would be glad to be rid of him.

'A garage? Not a bad idea,' agreed Greer. 'Yes—just stop there then. What do I owe you for the ride?' He thought it a good idea to leave on good terms with the man.

'Pleasure to help you, my friend,' said Parsons. 'Look—see that's the garage lights ahead!' He swung the van into the courtyard and waited as Greer stepped out. He didn't stop to see the outcome of the man's conversation with the mechanic who came out of the office but drove swiftly away. Greer turned his head, saw him go and muffled a curse.

'Look, my car broke down. I badly need transport. Have you a car I can rent?' he asked the mechanic, who scratched his balding head as he surveyed this late-night customer.

'The boss has gone home. Can't do that without his permission, sir!'

'What about selling me a car then? I see you have a couple marked for sale over there!' persisted Greer. 'Look—I can pay cash as it happens!'

'Well, I'll show them to you then.' He led Greer over to the two vehicles. Neither were of the standard he would normally have contemplated owning. He looked at the black Volvo. It would do.

'I'll take this one. How much?' he asked brusquely.

'Two grand—and cheap at the price,' returned the mechanic. 'Come into the office and I'll sort the paperwork.

Less than ten minutes had passed and Greer was on the road again, with a full tank of petrol, he had also bought a map. But where was he to go to? For the first time he realised how much he missed Hassan who had always smoothed his path in whatever difficulties arose. It was all Erika's fault, he thought perversely. Had she not left him in the first place, none of his subsequent actions in tracking her down at that refuge would have been necessary—Hassan still be alive. Erika! Well at least she was dead, and would fill his dreams no more.

But where to go now? He couldn't risk the airport at this time. The authorities would doubtless be on the lookout there—guess that was where he had been bound when he had crashed the car back there in the woods. So where then? He couldn't return to Enderslie House, no doubt would be arrested on sight. The same went for his flat above the jewellers. He urgently needed somewhere to stay—keep his head down for a while, then hopefully the police would think he had already left the country. A sudden wild idea came into his head. His eyes darkened. It was risky—but surely, they'd never suspect he would dare venture there!

He drew in at a layby, opened the map, he must be about here—his finger traced the distance from his present position to the junction with another secondary road ahead. Now where exactly was Ravensnest? That fellow Colin Denton was apparently away in London to give evidence at the Sea Giant trial. That left an elderly woman and two young children. He grinned. Well, Geraldine Denton was about to have a visitor. He put the map down, started off.

As he drove on, his thoughts darted back to all information Hassan had passed on to him garnered from his efficient woman agent. There had been a second woman too—that Jane Wilson. She it was who had sent that text mentioning Dream Echo—had supposedly been on her way to give a fuller report, but strangely never turned up. All under the bridge now—Erika finally found and dealt with. For a brief instance he thought of his small daughter, Trudy. He had been mildly fond of the child, but she had shown her distaste for her father when they had met again at Dream Echo. Obviously, Erika had turned her against him—so did he want the responsibility of a rebellious, unloving child at a time when he had to make his escape to the continent. He casually dismissed Trudy from his thoughts. The fact that with her mother dead she would be alone in the world did not trouble him in the slightest.

Greer knew he was tiring—it was a couple of hours from dawn and still about ten miles to Ravensnest. He realised he would need all his wits about him in what lay ahead, the previous long stress filled hours having taken their toll. He drew the car up on the low bank bordering the winding country road, transferred to the back seat, and disporting his limbs as best he could to sleep.

The noise of a tractor going past wakened him. He sat up stretched and rubbing stiff legs as he looked around. He glanced down at his watch—six thirty. Damn, the Denton woman would probably be up by now. Getting the children's breakfast. He felt desperately hungry himself—the sooner he arrived at that cottage the better! He remembered that Erika had been living at a Bramble Cottage—the Dentons next door. He rubbed his rough chin, missed his razor. He returned to the driving seat, was off.

Geraldine was towelling herself dry after a quick shower. Now to get the twin's up. Then the phone rang—to her delight and astonishment she recognised Anna's voice!

'Just a quick call, Geraldine.' In a brief few words Anna explained what had happened, that Greer had shot at her, that she had dropped down pretending to be dead—Colin and Charles Latimer descending in the helicopter—and with help from neighbouring farmers had pursued Greer who had got away. Geraldine listened intently, trying to understand Anna's urgent words.

'So where is Greer now?'

'The men had almost caught up with him in the woods but he managed back down onto the road—thumbed a lift! Listen—he got away in a white van identified as belonging to a friend of the farmers. They went to the man's home. He had dropped Greer off at a garage where he hoped to buy a car. I'm with Colin and Charles now. Geraldine, I cannot go back to Dream Echo. My being there caused a lot of problems.'

'Lottie phoned me—said one of the abused women was attacked by Greer. She received a blow to the head but is expected to recover.'

'You can see why I hesitate to return to Dream Echo. Amber was all kindness, such a wonderful woman, but I feel so guilty my affairs may have exposed the anonymity of the refuge. What I'm trying to say is— how would it be if I were to return to Bramble Cottage?'

'You say Greer left you for dead?'

'Yes. We now know he purchased a second-hand car for cash at the garage. It's a black Volvo. The police are on alert for it now. He'll be unable to get far—but I won't feel really safe until he is under lock and key!'

'Well. If he believes you to be dead there's nothing to draw him here—I see no reason why you shouldn't come home! Can't wait to see you and dear little Susan. What a traumatic time you have both undergone.'

'If you will feel comfortable having me back there, I'll tell Colin and Charles of my decision. Obviously, I can't remain with them as they plan how best to find Greer. Geraldine, I'm just longing to see you again—and the twins.'

'Ring me when you know what time you will arrive. Must go dear—have to get the twins breakfast and do the school run!' She was smiling happily as she put the phone down. Soon all would be back to normal.

Chapter Fifteen

It was almost seven as Greer drove through the small village of Ravensnest and took the side road that led to the two isolated cottages, one of which had housed the woman he had sought for so many months and was now dead at his hand—and next-door Rose Cottage, where Geraldine Denton lived with her twin grandchildren. It was perfect that the woman's son Colin was away in London, called to give evidence in the Sea Giant trial. Hopefully he would be away a few weeks.

Where to park the black Volvo? It must be well hidden but not too far away from the cottage in case needed to make a quick getaway. He drove slowly past the two secluded homes, noticed the curtains were open at Rose Cottage. The woman and youngsters would be up now he thought as he continued on glancing around for somewhere safe to leave the car, saw nothing. He reversed—had remembered seeing a gate back there. Ah, this was it. He drew up as he saw the farm gate set between high hedges. He got out, opened the gate. He stared across the meadow with its short-cropped grass—a hay meadow so probably not much used at this time. He drove the car through the gate, pocketed the key and retraced the distance he had come past the cottage, peering through small gaps in the hedge every so often until he was almost opposite the house he sought.

He was barely able to squeeze through the slight gap in the hedge, swore as the hawthorn caught at his trouser leg. This was going to be the trickiest part of his plan—managing to get close to the place without being seen from the windows. He stared at the two cottages—the first, Bramble Cottage was now empty. He would get into what had been Erika's garden, and access the Denton home from the back.

He had made it, was now in the back garden of Bramble Cottage, just a fence separating it from that of Rose Cottage. He peered over the fence. No movement in either the garden or back door of the Denton home. At that moment the door opened and a small boy let two kittens into the garden. He crouched down, daring a quick glance every so often, saw the cats relieve themselves in a flower bed and return to the cottage door. The same small boy picked them up and took them back indoors. Had the boy locked the door? Well, he would soon know the answer!

He climbed over the low fence and with a few swift strides reached the cottage door. He turned the handle cautiously. Hah—not locked! He was in a passageway, heard the sound of voices coming from a half open doorway. He peered in, saw a distinguished looking, silver haired woman, serving porridge from a red saucepan, and placing three bowls on the kitchen table.

'Come along you two!' she called to the small boy and girl bending over the frisky kittens. 'You can play with them later!' Greer's mouth watered as he looked at the porridge—it was many hours since he had last eaten. He took a chance, strode into the room and produced his gun. Geraldine uttered a shout of outrage as she registered the stranger brandishing a revolver, while the children screamed!

'I advise you to be quiet if you wish to live,' said Greer coldly. He stared at the twins, gesturing to the chairs at the kitchen table. 'Sit!' he instructed. They did so, faces scared. 'Now you,' he called to Geraldine. 'I will not hesitate to use this if you do not obey!'

'Who are you?' she challenged him. 'If you are looking for valuables you have come to the wrong place I'm afraid.' He detected the calm authority in her voice, realised this woman would not easily be cowed. This must be dealt with immediately. He walked slowly towards the table, gestured at the two frightened youngsters seated there. He pointed his gun in their direction.

'You will sit, woman—or I kill one of these children. Which shall it be—the boy or the girl?' She watched him, her mind racing. She knew instinctively this was no bravado—the stranger meant it. But who was he—and why was he here? For one blind moment she wondered if he was attached to Sea Giant—dismissed the thought as impossible. Then who? She stared at his face, remembered Anna's description of Malcolm Greer—and she knew. But why was he here? Seemingly he believed Anna to be dead.

She sank down on one of the chairs. He nodded coldly acknowledging her obedience.

'Hand me one of those bowls,' he instructed. Geraldine did so, offering her own. She watched as he took an empty chair, started to gulp down the porridge whilst holding the gun.

'Perhaps I may cook the children's eggs and bacon now—some for you too since you appear hungry?' she said quietly. He stared at her face, wondering at the lack of fear she was displaying. But the notion of his captive cooking for him struck him as humorous.

'Do so,' he said harshly. 'If you make any bad move then one of these will die!' Geraldine inclined her head, and cast a swift reassuring glance at the children. There was silence in the kitchen now, apart from the sizzling of bacon in the frying pan, and sound of eggs being cracked. The twins started to eat their porridge as the man with the gun looked at them broodingly.

'What are your names?' he inquired. It was Charles who answered.

'I am Charles and this is my sister Melanie. Who are you and why are you here?' he demanded calmly. Greer uttered a harsh laugh.

'So, you have spunk, boy! My name's no concern of yours—all you need to know is that it's my intention to stay in this house for a few days. If you behave yourselves you've nothing to fear—otherwise!' and he brandished the gun.

'Are you hiding from someone?' asked Melanie now, turning questioning grey eyes on him.

'Silence girl—you will speak when spoken to!' he growled. Geraldine swung around from the frying-pan. She sent a warning glance at the twins.

'Quiet children,' she said. Minutes later she served up the eggs and bacon and placed a plate of buttered toast on the table. Greer wolfed his down—then pushed his plate back with a satisfied smile. If the woman continued to behave in this way, then he had indeed chosen well in coming here.

'You should eat too,' he said to her, nor was it any kindness that prompted the order, but he needed her to keep strong in the days ahead, was going to need her compliance. She took some toast, spread it with marmalade, made herself eat. Greer had no idea of the turmoil surging through Geraldine's head as she sat there with apparent composure. Anna was coming back today—how to warn the young mother to stay away. She needed her phone, had left the mobile in her dressing gown pocket.

'What now?' she asked Greer now. 'I have to drive the children to school?'

'That will not be possible. They stay here, nor are any of you to go outside the house—understand!' His hard, dark eyes swept over her menacingly.

'Very well. Children, you will study at home instead,' she said serenely. 'You have your text books in your satchels—perhaps you could study history this morning, remember how we were discussing that history often repeats itself!' The twins caught the slight emphasis in her words and groped for the meaning. Just then one of the kittens that had been hiding under the table approached Greer and attempted to climb up his trouser leg. With an exclamation of annoyance, he brushed the small creature off roughly, as it squealed dismay at such treatment.

'Don't you hurt Susan's kitten,' cried Melanie hotly. 'Her Mummy Anna will be very upset with you!' Greer looked contemptuously at the fair-haired child with her direct grey eyes. She was talking of Erika and Trudy. He gave a sneering laugh at Melanie's words.

'Anna will not be upset with anyone now—she is dead!' he announced cruelly and then wished he had kept silent. There was an appalled silence from the children, while Geraldine stared at him questioningly.

'How would you know anything about our friend Anna—unless you are the man who has been pursuing her for these last months? And what makes you think she is dead?' she asked. Greer could have cursed his inadvertent remark but could not withdraw it.

'My identity is no concern of yours,' he said icily. 'But I happen to know that Erika Nicolson, known to you as Anna Lindstrom is indeed dead. We will not discuss it further.' Geraldine forced an expression of realistic shock on her face, while the twins whom had not been informed of Anna's kidnap and subsequent events heard his words in deep distress.

'Anna can't be dead!' sobbed Melanie now breaking down, as Charles slipped a comforting arm about his sister, his face expressing his horror at the news.

'What about Susan?' he asked Greer directly.

'I've no idea,' replied Greer casually. 'Now we will make plans for all that is to happen over the next few days. Do you children have mobile phones?' Melanie nodded in affirmative, too deeply shaken by the stranger's revelation of Anna's death to think clearly.

'Give them to me,' he instructed, handling his gun threateningly as he glanced from one to the other of the youngsters. Melanie slipped her hand not her pocket and produced hers, as Charles reluctantly offered his. Greer pocketed them.

'Good! Now, Mrs Denton, I will have yours if you please!'

'I lost it a few days ago, haven't replaced it yet. I have my landline meanwhile.' He stared at her, wondering if she was lying.

'So, your son Colin—he contacts you on your landline?'

'Yes. What do you know of Colin?' she demanded. He shrugged.

'What many will have gleaned from the papers—that he is to give vital evidence at the trial of the directors of Sea Giant!' He glanced at Melanie who seemed the most likely to answer honestly. 'Tell me girl, when do you expect your father to return?' he asked. Melanie shook her head, still overwhelmed with grief at the news of Anna's death.

'I don't know. Some bad men tried to kill our Daddy—and we thought he was dead, but he escaped. He came back to us again, but now he's had to go to London. I hope he comes back soon!' she sobbed. He listened in satisfaction. The woman might lie, but he believed the child was truthful.

'Very well. Now there are two doors to the cottage are there not? Both are to be kept locked and I want the keys.' He stared at Geraldine. 'Now!' he instructed. Geraldine hesitated, knew that to refuse would only inflame him. She walked over to the kitchen door where she had hung her shoulder-bag on a hook. She opened it and withdrew her keyring, handed it to him. He smiled, took it. 'And now I will have the bag,' he added. This time she almost balked at his request, but glancing at the two frightened children knew she had no option but to obey. He pointed to the chair. 'Sit,' he said and she did so, biting her lip in frustration as he examined the contents of her bag, thankful that her mobile phone was upstairs in her dressing gown pocket. He withdrew her wallet, took out her visa debit card.

'What is the security number,' he demanded.

'I am not prepared to divulge that,' she snapped. He pointed the revolver at the terrified Melanie's forehead.

'I think you may wish to change your mind, but if not...!' He saw the frustration in her eyes, as he put his finger on the trigger.

'It's 4267 damn you!' He grinned, delighted to have dented her composure. He continued to delve into her bag, but found nothing of further interest. He tossed it across the table to her.

'I'm thirsty,' he said now. 'You will make coffee.' Geraldine rose to her feet, the children watching her from white faces as she went about the simple task.

He drank the coffee appreciatively. It was as good as that which Hassan normally brought him—only Hassan would no longer attend this duty or any other, was dead—and all was the fault of Erika!' His anger rose again. He glared at Geraldine who had poured herself a mug of coffee. How was she able to suppress the fear she must certainly be feeling? However better so, he privately acknowledged. At least she was sensible enough to obey his demands.

'I need to go to the bathroom,' said Geraldine now. 'I will only be a few moments.' He hesitated at her request, realised that it was reasonable enough but nevertheless harbouring suspicion of the woman.

'Very well—but I am sure the wellbeing of your grandchildren will prevent any stupidity,' he said now. 'Where is the bathroom?'

'Upstairs. Please do not scare the children while I go—I will be quick!' she said anxiously, and slipped out of the kitchen.

'You two—come with me,' said Greer to the twins. 'I wish to check all outer doors are locked.' They got to their feet and followed him as first he checked the front door and saw the bolts were in place—then the back door by which he had entered. Good, all was secure.

Geraldine locked the bathroom door, snatched the phone from her dressing gown pocket and sent a quick text to Colin informing him of Greer's presence—he should warn Anna not to come, then sent a text to Tom Lanscombe. She did not dare stop for more, looked around for somewhere safe to hide the mobile. The pot plant in the corner. She pushed it down, a little soil covering it. It would have to do. She flushed the toilet before leaving.

She descended the stairs in time to see Greer ushering the twins into the sitting room and it jarred her to see this foul creature entering the room once so special to her husband David and herself. She steeled herself to be calm, knew that she must be careful not to aggravate him in any way. Greer stared around curiously, noticed the photographs on her mantlepiece.

'Your husband?' he inquired staring at David's smiling face. She nodded, not trusting herself to reply. 'And this one—your son Colin and his wife and these two?'

'Our Mummy is dead,' whispered Melanie. 'We miss her very much!'

'How did she die?' he asked casually. It was Charles who replied stiffly.

'In a car crash—we believe her car was tampered with by Sea Giant—that it was murder!' he asserted quietly. 'It is why Granny brought us to live here.' Greer stared at him, wondering at the maturity in the child's account. He would have liked a son of his own. True Erika had given him a daughter—and Trudy had been delightful at first—until Erika had poisoned her mind against him. Bah—why did he need children! Perhaps there would be another woman in his life in the future, and then? He banished the thought, must concentrate. He had to remain in complete control of the three individuals in this room.

His eyes rested on the chess set. This must be Geraldine's—so a quick mind no doubt, but let her play him for a fool and she would suffer a final checkmate!

'Children, why don't you settle down and read,' instructed Geraldine now, gesturing to the book case. They looked at her and obediently chose an illustrated book of fairy tales and seated themselves on the settee, heads bent over it together. Greer smiled. The woman was obviously making decision to cooperate. This was good. As for the solemn faced youngsters, they seemed well behaved and easily biddable. All was going well and he sank down to plan his next move, throwing himself down heavily, legs thrust out before him.

He was not to know he had chosen the late David Denton's chair, nor would have cared. But Geraldine found fresh fury rising in her mind at his effrontery, mixed with anxiety for Anna. Perhaps she should have texted the girl instead of Colin, but then since Anna was under her son's care right now, it had seemed better to give warning that way, alerting them jointly of the danger.

Charles Latimer and Colin rose early that morning. They had snatched a few hours' sleep at a nearby guesthouse on the outskirts of Little Monkton after admitting that they had lost Greer's trail for the immediate future. Hopefully the police would track down the black Saab he had purchased at the garage. Anna had been completely exhausted as had little Susan when they reached the guesthouse which was only a few minutes' walk away from the meadow where they had left the helicopter Their small party could have rested in the helicopter, but in the end decided to leave the pilot Bob Preston there, whilst they saw to the comfort of mother and child. Tomorrow they would resume their search for Greer.

When she awoke Anna winced, found she was still experiencing a lot of pain from her shoulder, wondered if she should find a hospital, get an x-ray. No, it would have to wait. She knew her presence was bound to restrict Colin and Latimer's activities, as they sought to arrest Greer. Just where was he now? She shuddered as she thought of him—facing the reality that he had attempted to kill her. Susan stirred beside her, rubbed her eyes, smiled as she saw her mother, then memory returned and an expression of fear crossed her young face.

'Are we safe from Daddy here,' she asked anxiously after giving her mother a kiss. 'I just wish we could go home to Bramble Cottage and see Geraldine and the twins!'

It was those words that prompted Anna to ring Geraldine, bringing her up to date with events and expressing a wish to return to the cottage. Susan watched her mother from the bed as she made the call and save a smile of delight as she heard Anna's plans to return to their home.

'I know it's early darling, but we must make a start. The men will probably be up already and that poor pilot Bob will be tired after spending the night in the helicopter back in that field!'

The elderly landlady prepared breakfast for her guests. She was still dressed in her pink housecoat and slippers, pondering it was hardly worth going their having gone to bed, only to rise so early. Strange people—no luggage with them. But guests were not frequent and those who came to be treasured. She noticed the flicker of pain on Anna's face, looked at her in concern.

'Have you hurt yourself, my dear?' she asked solicitously, as she placed an offering of sausages, tomatoes, eggs and bacon to the young woman, and a smaller helping to the pretty child beside her. Anna looked up with a smile.

'Well—I had a fall, twisted my shoulder badly. Must see a doctor when I get home!' The men looked up as she spoke, had heard her mention her shoulder yesterday but not realised she was badly hurt. Latimer remembered the pilot explaining he had offered her painkillers, he glanced at Colin.

'We had better find a doctor for you, Anna,' exclaimed Colin remorsefully.

'Perhaps I can help there,' said the landlady who had been listening. 'My second cousin John Harris is a doctor—practices here in Little Monkton. Shall I give him a ring?'

Half an hour later Anna was seated in the landlady's front room, facing a grey-haired doctor's inquiring dark eyes.

'Everything I say must be in strict confidence doctor,' she began. The man smiled.

'That goes without saying, my dear,' and he waited. He heard with increasing concern the story of her abduction from a refuge by a man who had previously held her in his power for years, until she escaped with her young daughter. He listened to her account of the car crash in which she had sustained her injury—desperately running through a forest to escape before he regained consciousness, climbing a tree to obtain a phone signal, falling the last few feet down causing further pain to her shoulder. Then the wild run with her child over rough ground, as her pursuer fired at her—and she dropped pretending death.

Doctor Harris shook his head. A physician hears many stories from patients—but this was extraordinary in the extreme. He reached out a calming hand to her.

'You have endured so much, Miss Lindstrom—are a very courageous woman. From all you have revealed I suggest you require many weeks of quiet, the mind needs healing as well as the body. Now let me look at your shoulder which I suspect is dislocated. What followed after examination was uncomfortable as he took her wrist and extended her arm—and she felt the jolt as the bone returned to its socket.

'You did well,' he approved. 'Now I am going to put your arm in a sling. You will need pain relief for a few days—must not lift anything heavy—in fact take life easy if that is possible!' She smiled at him gratefully.

'I shall take your advice—and thank you for your kindness in coming to help me so early in the morning!' She returned to the men, who were patiently waiting. Susan jumped to her feet as Anna came into the room and stared to see her mother's arm in a sling.

'Has the doctor made it better, Mummy?' she asked. Anna smiled.

'It feels much more comfortable, but still aches a bit.' She looked at Colin and Latimer, realising she must tell them of her plans to return to Bramble Cottage. She did so now and saw their troubled faces.

'What's wrong? You are both going to be very busy tracking Greer down, and with my arm in a sling I would only slow you down. Then besides this, I feel truly exhausted, and know my little girl is too. Greer believes me to be dead—nothing to take him anywhere near Bramble

Cottage, so the safest place I could choose. When I rang Geraldine earlier she seemed happy with my decision.' The altercation between them that followed left the men frustrated as Anna held firm to her plan.

'And how do you propose to reach Ravenscroft from Little Monkton?' demanded Charles Latimer.' We could drop you off there in the helicopter I guess—but?' She shook her head.

'No, Charles! Catching Greer has to be your priority. I shall take a taxi. Whatever the cost it will be worth it. Perhaps we could find an automat first—I need to draw out some cash.'

'You will be extremely careful, won't you Anna dear,' said Colin. He felt uneasy about her decision to return to the cottage, but on the plus side, his mother would be able to look after her, and he would soon be returning to Rose Cottage once his very necessary evidence was given at the Sea Giant trial.

'I'll pay for the taxi—expenses,' put in Latimer quietly. He also thought that Anna and the child would be safe with Geraldine. Those two isolated cottages would be the last place where Greer would turn up, believing Anna to be dead. Nothing to take him there—indeed he might already have left the country by plane or ferry—slipped past customs on a forged passport. He was secretly relieved that the young mother and child would no longer be his immediate concern.

'Tell mother I'll be back there soon as I can,' said Colin. He looked at Anna protectively. Why did he have a sixth sense she still remained in danger? Surely getting her right away from this area and safe under his mother's care was the best solution at this time.

Charles Latimer watched Colin giving Anna a goodbye hug as she got into the prepaid taxi. Yes, something was possibly developing between these two he thought, despite Colin still grieving his late wife Mary's death. Well providing it did not interfere with the very special work he had agreed to take up, it was no bad thing. He liked Colin, his new colleague possessed integrity and was of proven courage. The taxi drew away from the guest house as the men waved. Time to return to the chopper and their weary pilot—but first he must call the police, see if there had been any sighting of Greer in that black Volvo!

An hour and a half later the taxi drew up outside Bramble Cottage and Susan waited impatiently while her mother gave the driver a generous tip as he opened the door and helped her out, her sling making the process awkward. She glanced across at Rose Cottage wondering why Geraldine had not opened her door to greet her. Well, she was possibly in the kitchen. She hesitated—decided to go into her own home first and relax, see Geraldine a little later.

'Come along Susan darling!'

'Can't we go to Rose Cottage and see Geraldine—and I want my kitten!' exclaimed the little girl eagerly.

'We will go next door once we have had a little rest—my shoulder is still quite sore you know.' Susan looked at her in concern. She had forgotten that her mother had been badly hurt and walked obediently up the pathway as Anna unlocked the front door, thankful she had hidden a spare key under a flower pot. As she went in she heard the sound of the taxi drawing away.

Someone else heard the sound too—coming back into the sitting room, Greer glanced out of the front window but saw nothing, must have been a passing car he thought casually. He decided he would examine the back of the house again. He already had a good idea of the cottage layout. Sitting room and dining room were in the front facing onto the road—the kitchen was situated at the back as was a small study and there was also a conservatory, all looking out onto the back garden. There was no garage and Geraldine's beige Ford was parked outside the garden gate on the grass verge at the roadside.

He was about to order Geraldine to accompany him back to the kitchen when suddenly the phone rang. She gave a quick glance down at the caller's number, then looked up uncertainly, waiting for Greer to respond.

'Shall I answer it?' she inquired quietly. He nodded.

'Do so—put it on speaker! And just remember one wrong word and one of these will die!' and he jerked his head towards the twins sitting together on the settee, trying to concentrate on their illustrated book.

'This is the school Mrs Denton—Mrs Walters speaking. Miss Davenport informed me the twins have not arrived today?'

'I'm sorry Mrs Walters—I had meant to ring. Charles and Melanie seem to be going down with the same bug they had back in August. I have not called Doctor Evans as I did last time—hopefully they should be well again in a couple of days!' There was moments silence before the head mistress replied courteously.

'Yes—I remember the time you mentioned. Please tell them I hope they feel better very soon.' The teacher rang off and Geraldine replaced the receiver and glanced at Greer, who was smiling at her performance.

'Good! I can see that you are showing the wisdom to cooperate,' he said approvingly.

Colin Denton was waiting on the grass as Latimer climbed aboard the chopper before him. He glanced at his phone, went cold when he read his mother's text message informing him that Greer was in her home. He was to tell Anna, and warn her not to return to Bramble cottage!' He glanced urgently at his watch—8 am. Anna would not reach her cottage for at least another hour.

'Charles—something terrible has happened,' he called, and Latimer turned about hearing the shock and urgency in the younger man's voice, noticed the phone he held in his hand.

'What is it?' His dark eyes studied Colin's anxious face as he descended. In answer, Colin proffered the phone with its stark message. He read it, face registering his anger. 'We must call Anna—only hope she'll be able to get a signal in the taxi. Whatever happens, she must not be allowed to return to either of the cottages. I'm sorry your mother is having to deal with the situation Colin—but she's a strong woman.' He could see that Colin was trying to remain calm, the present situation severely testing with his two children as well as his mother in danger. He watched as Colin called Anna's mobile number—there was no answer. Perhaps she had muted it—he sent an urgent text message as Latimer stood quietly beside him. They both waited—but there was no reply to his urgent warning.

It could be that her battery is flat,' said Latimer. 'If this is so we need to find another way of warning her to keep away from both cottages.'

'I felt distinctively uneasy that she was so determined to return—gut feeling all was not well!' admitted Colin, his brows drawn anxiously together. 'Should we notify Sergeant Evans at the local Ravensnest police station?'

'Yes, but can't risk a police car arriving outside Rose Cottage—must warn Evans to keep a low profile. Greer may panic if he realises we are on to him, is armed remember and with so many serious charges against him has nothing to lose by inflicting further mayhem.'

'Don't you think I realise that!' exclaimed Colin hotly. 'The twins are still fragile after all they have been through—and now this devil has them in his power! Then my mother! Yes, she's strong Charles—but she must be so very careful with someone as unbalanced as Greer. We have to get there—deal with the bastard.'

'Then we fly. Wait a sec—my phone! Tom Lanscombe—I must take this.' Colin listened in as they heard Tom's voice explaining the text he had received from Geraldine. Latimer cut him off. 'Tom, we already know! She texted Colin as well—and we're about to take the chopper there. Tried to contact Anna to warn her not to go near the place—but she's on her way there in a taxi right now, not answering her mobile.' Tom's reply was immediate

'Divert, pick me up from the usual place! It will delay you ten minutes at most and an extra pair of hands is no bad thing!' Latimer hesitated. Although every second counted, they should still have plenty of time to prevent Anna from arriving at Ravensnest.

'Ok, Tom—you drive over there right away then—on our way to collect you!'

Fifteen minutes later with Tom now aboard, the pilot hovered above the road to Ravensnest. They had no slightest idea that the taxi they were seeking to intercept had already arrived at Bramble cottage and deposited its passengers there, was now on the return journey. The driver had driven fast, taking slightly less than an hour for the trip, not the estimated hour and a half.

The pilot flew low, as Latimer, Colin and Tom Lanscombe kept careful watch on the road below them—but seeing no sign of a taxi. Colin frowned anxiously as they drew ever nearer to Ravensnest.

'Are you sure the driver estimated an hour and a half for the journey?' asked Colin uneasily. 'It is possible he overestimated the time to enhance his payment?' Latimer turned a troubled face towards him.

'If you're right in your suspicion—it's just possible Anna has already arrived at Bramble Cottage.' His voice was grim, blaming himself for the time wasted in collecting Tom. She could be in Greer's hands right now.

At the village school, Headmistress Mrs Walters put the phone down, a puzzled look on her face. She tried to remember the exact words Geraldine Denton had used during their brief conversation.

What had the children's grandmother meant by saying the twins had the same bug they had suffered back in August—mentioned Doctor Evans? There was no such doctor in Ravensnest as Geraldine would have been well aware—but there was a Sergeant Evans at the local constabulary who had been so caring when the twins had been kidnapped last August. Could this be a coded message from Geraldine that all was not well at Rose Cottage? But surely all those crooked directors of Sea Giant responsible for the kidnap, were under arrest and undergoing trial in London.

She hesitated. Could Geraldine merely have been absent-minded speaking of Doctor Evans? No! Geraldine was one of the most precise people she knew. She lifted the phone and asked to speak to Sergeant Evans. He listened intently.

'You could be right, Mrs Walters. Thank you for contacting me! I'll get back to you later.' He sat thinking for a moment. Geraldine had previously mentioned to him that Anna and Susan were thought to be at imminent risk from the young woman's ex-partner a man called Greer, and had been moved to a place of safety. Since then he had heard nothing further. Suddenly he remembered the notification that he together with all other officers in the region had received to be on the lookout for a black Volvo—driver a man named Malcolm Greer. Of course—the same man! He had written down the words the headmistress stated Geraldine had used and checked them now. 'Charles and Melanie seem to be going down with the same bug they had back in August—but I haven't called Doctor Evans as I did last time!' He breathed a sigh of gratitude for the quick wits of Mrs Walters who had worked out a concealed message delivered in what must have been a very fraught situation for Geraldine Denton. He unlocked a drawer in his desk and slipped something in his pocket as he mentally reviewed the situation.

It had been last August that Geraldine's young grandchildren had been kidnapped and he had been involved in the search for them. Had someone taken the twins again—or was it possible that this man Greer had entered Rose Cottage, and was using the twins as hostages to pressurise Geraldine into revealing the whereabouts of Anna Lindstrom? As his mind darted about his phone rang.

'Is that Sergeant Evans?'

'Yes, who is this?'

'Colin Denton—I have Charles Latimer and Tom Lanscombe with me! Listen, I may need your help for my mother and children!' Evans listened carefully as Colin explained what had happened—that Greer was in Rose Cottage with Geraldine and the twins—that he had previously abducted Anna from a refuge, following which there had been a car crash and she had escaped. Greer had pursued her and now believed her dead from a bullet he had fired at her. But Anna was now on her way to Bramble Cottage—might even have arrived there already—or worse, have gone next door to visit Geraldine!

'So, if he believes Anna to be dead, why would he move into your mother's home?' probed Evans keenly.

'No idea—unless he considered it the last place the authorities would search for him—and where he could safely hide. He is wanted for masterminding a massive people trafficking organisation—will be arrested on sight. He's dangerous, almost killed an innocent woman in the women's refuge—and attempted to kill Anna.'

'What do you want me to do? And where are you right now?'

'The chopper has put us down in a field on the outskirts of the village. I'll describe exactly where—would appreciate it if you could pick us up in an unmarked car. We can't land closer, as Greer would both see and hear the chopper.

'Just give me the location.' He listened, then moved quickly. His old navy Rover was parked outside the station. He walked over to it, checking his pocket for the firearm he had taken from his drawer before leaving his office.

'You off somewhere, Sergeant,' called a musical voice and he gave a quick smile as he saw policewoman Julie Bird.

'Yes—you can come with me. Might be a dangerous situation ahead though!'

'Then count me in, Sergeant. Where are we going?' she asked alertly.

'To help Geraldine Denton and her grandchildren who are being held hostage in Rose Cottage. Get in if you're coming!' He judged that Geraldine might be glad of a woman's support once that miscreant Greer had been apprehended.

In the sitting room of Rose Cottage, Geraldine was sitting between the twins on the settee, listening as they read aloud to her. Greer sprawled in an armchair opposite, legs extended before him, as he watched the woman through narrowed eyes. Why was she so calm when she knew herself to be so completely helpless? She was courageous he decided grudgingly, but he still did not trust her. Nor was it natural for a woman in what must be a terrifying situation to her show no fear?

'You will go to the kitchen—make more coffee and bring it through here!' he instructed. She looked up but made no move. 'You will obey me,' he barked.

'You could at least show some civility,' replied Geraldine quietly. 'Yes, I will make coffee, but in future, I would prefer you to ask—not order.' He glared at her. It was intolerable to be spoken to like this by a woman. He watched as she rose to her feet, smiling back gently at her grandchildren as she went to the door. He lifted his gun and pointed it towards the twins.

'If you value the lives of these brats you will show respect. One false move from you and they will die!' He saw the fear in the children's eyes, as they huddled closer together, the boy placing his arm about his sister's shoulders. Geraldine made no response as she left the room. Once outside in the passageway, she took a deep breath. Had Anna received the warning she had sent to Colin? She knew he would not attempt to ring her back, and had no way of knowing what was going on and if help was on its way. She also wondered if the children's headmistress had understood the message she had tried to impart.

She switched the red kettle on, prepared mugs—and placed homemade cookies on a plate, then on impulse she slipped into the adjoining conservatory. Almost automatically she glanced out of the side window to the neighbouring cottage. At least Anna must have received her warning she thought, then gasped as her eyes swept over the upper side window of Bramble Cottage. Someone had drawn the bedroom curtain there! She went cold as she realised it could mean only one thing—Anna had returned! She experienced a sick feeling in her stomach. But how—when? Was Susan over there too? Why had she not seen them arrive? Of course, it must have been when she was in the kitchen earlier! But if Anna was indeed back, why had she not come around to see her? Maybe she had just been exhausted, that must be it. So how could she warn Anna not to show herself?

She returned to the kitchen, made coffee and carried the tray through to the sitting room, poured for Greer then handed the plate of cookies.

'I am going back for fruit juice for the children,' she said now, as she watched him devour one of the cookies appreciatively. 'Also, I need to visit the bathroom again.'

'Then be quick about it,' he jerked, as he reached for another cookie. Geraldine nodded and made for the stairs. Once in the bathroom she rescued her mobile from the pot plant and called Anna's number. Oh, no! Her mobile was dead, and needed recharging! In utter frustration she hid it again—then on inspiration rushed into her bedroom, opened the wardrobe and pulled a red shirt off its hanger. Her side bedroom window looked across at Anna's own, as she checked that the girl's curtain remained closed. She opened the bottom of her window and then shut it over the hem of the shirt, allowing it to dangle its red warning signal! It was the best she could do. Back to the bathroom she flushed the toilet before leaving and hurried to the kitchen to pour fruit juice for the children.

'Here you are my dears,' she said quietly, hoping her voice did not express her breathlessness. Greer looked at her curiously. Part of him wanted to irritate her and break down her extraordinary calm, but realised it was better that she remained cooperative however annoying her attitude.

Little Susan woke up to find herself in her bedroom in Bramble Cottage once more. She rubbed her eyes, had only slept for an hour or so, but was instantly alert. Her thoughts flew immediately to her beloved kitten Patches—desperately wanted to play with it. She went into her mother's room and found Anna sleeping heavily.

Susan knew she really shouldn't wake her up, but the need for her kitten overcame better judgement. She was going to shake Anna's arm, but decided instead to open the curtains so that hopefully the daylight would waken her mother She did so—and as she glanced out her eyes were drawn to something red lifting in the breeze from a window in the cottage next door—Geraldine's bedroom window. She stared at it puzzled as she recognised it was a red shirt. Now, why had Geraldine hung it outside her window?

'Susan—you are all right?' murmured Anna, her eyes focussing anxiously on the child and trying to remember where she was and breathing a sigh of relief on realising they were safe home in Bramble Cottage.

'Mummy—why has Geraldine hung a red shirt out of her window?' inquired Susan curiously. Anna stared at her. What did she mean? She climbed awkwardly out of bed and went to stand next to her daughter. She also stared at the shirt in amazement. It would have been quite impossible for Geraldine to have accidentally shut the window over her shirt in that way—it must have been a deliberate action. So why? Her thoughts rioted. Was it possible this was some kind of warning? As she continued to stare with a troubled expression, Susan touched her hand for attention.

'Mummy—I want to go and see Geraldine now—and get my kitten!' she pleaded.

'No Susan!' replied Anna sharply. 'The red shirt over there—I think Geraldine is trying to warn us of something. Get away from the window!'

'But Mummy!'

'Just do it!' Anna readjusted her sling as she spoke. She had slipped into bed fully dressed when they arrived and now sought urgently for her shoes, as her mind groped with this new worry. At that moment her phone rang. Taking Susan's hand to restrain her from any attempt to go out, she reached for her phone.

'Anna—is that you?' She recognised Colin's voice at once.

'Yes, it is—and safely home in my cottage,' she exclaimed

'Thank the Lord,' he breathed and listened as she continued to speak.

'I was exhausted when we arrived and took a nap in bed. Listen, Susan just woke me up—we have seen a red shirt hanging out of Geraldine's bedroom window. Maybe I'm being paranoid—but I have the feeling it's meant as some sort of warning?'

'No easy way of telling you this—but Greer is next door in Geraldine's cottage. I've got Latimer and Tom with me—came up in the chopper. We're in a field waiting for Sergeant Evans to pick us up by car.

'You said—he's there—in Geraldine's cottage?' Her eyes widened in shock

'Yes! It's vital you remain inside. We tried to warn you earlier on your mobile.'

'It went flat. We arrived here much earlier than estimated. But why is Greer with your mother? He doesn't even know her—has no reason to be there.' The words poured out disjointedly as she tried to make sense of the situation.

'We'll speak later Anna. I just want your promise to remain safely hidden away from Greer. I don't have to tell you he's very dangerous! Right now, I have to concentrate on rescuing my mother and the twins—all three with him in there.' She heard the anxiety in his voice and her heart went out to him.

'Don't worry about me! He will never guess I'm here—thinks I'm dead. Colin dear, I pray you'll manage to rescue them safely. I'm so sorry Geraldine is having to deal with that brute!'

'Must go—Sergeant Evans just arriving. Remember Anna—stay indoors!' He rang off leaving Anna looking down at the phone in shock.

'Please may I go and get Patches now,' said Susan persistently. She had not overheard the conversation with Colin. Anna held her close.

'Listen, darling, that phone call was from Colin. He told me that your father is next door to Geraldine's cottage. We are not to go outside—he is extremely dangerous, and must not know we are here. Colin and some others are going to deal with him. I know you want your kitten Susan, but you have to be patient until it's safe.' Susan's face went white with shock. She looked at her mother in bewilderment.

'Will Daddy hurt Geraldine—and what about Charles and Melanie?' she asked fearfully.

'Sweetheart, we can only pray they will be safe. Let's go downstairs and I'll make you something to eat. I think there should be some long-life milk and a packet of muesli in the cupboard—it will have to do for now.' She smiled at Susan reassuringly.

'Mummy I'm so scared!' whispered Susan.

'Don't be. We are safe in here. Your father believes I am dead. But we mustn't get in front of any of the windows.' She held the child's trembling hand comfortingly. As they went downstairs she realised just how lucky they'd been in not visiting Geraldine when first they arrived. She shuddered as she considered what the outcome might have been.

Colin Denton explained his brief conversation with Anna to his colleagues, who nodded their relief that Anna and Susan were safe, but concerned at their close proximity to Greer next door.

'I made her promise not to go outside—I'm sure there is no way she will take any risk as young Susan is there with her. They must both be terrified. Can't wait to get that bloody bastard Greer under arrest!' said Colin grimly. Latimer spoke calmingly to him as did Tom as they waited for the police sergeant to arrive.

Sergeant Evans spotted the men waiting on the grass verge—saw the helicopter in the field behind them. He drew up, waited as the three of them squeezed into the back seat of his car, as Julie Bird felt slightly uncomfortable in occupying the front seat next to Evans.

'Now—tell me what your plans are,' said Evans, after quickly acknowledging the men. 'Incidentally, as you see I've brought Policewoman Bird with me. The Denton children know her well—thought we might be better of a woman's presence.' It was Tom Lanscombe who answered.

'Glad to see you again Will—and you Julie. Our plans are somewhat fluid right now—need to find a way to get into Rose Cottage without being seen.'

'We certainly can't just drive up and park outside!' agreed Evans thoughtfully. 'I would suggest we take the car as far as that bend in the road before the cottages come into view.'

'Yes, you're right—get into the field bordering the road on the opposite side, and approach the cottage sheltered by the hedge—we would be exposed on the other side, the meadow there bordered by a wire fence,' added Tom as Colin and Latimer nodded approval.

'But how do we actually get across the road without being seen,' asked Latimer.

'The front garden of Rose cottage is bordered from the road by a low hedge and wooden gate—as is Bramble Cottage. In any case, evening is about to fall. If we were to dart quickly across and approach the house bending low beneath the hedge, Greer would only be able to see us from bedroom level,' said Colin.

'And damnably we've no way of knowing what part of the cottage Greer is holding Geraldine and the twins in,' said Tom. 'My own bet is downstairs—in case he has to make a quick getaway.'

'I believe our best plan is to access Bramble Cottage garden first— make our way round to the back, then over the fence dividing the two gardens,' said Latimer. They nodded agreement. It made sense. 'Now we must remember he is armed—will not hesitate to shoot if he sees us,' Latimer continued. He glanced at them as he gave a warning.

'We also need to be prepared in case Greer uses one of the twins as a shield—puts a gun to their head,' said Tom, He regarded Colin. 'This is going to be difficult for you in particular. Just remember not to allow anger to cloud judgement,' he advised quietly.

'Let's go then,' said Latimer.

Malcolm Greer was getting restless. So far, his hastily made plan to hide in this remote cottage had gone like clockwork—the level eyed woman who owned Rose Cottage behaving sensibly—her grandchildren quiet and obedient. None of them offering slightest challenge to his authority. But how long could it remain like this? What would happen at night for instance—how would he be able to sleep knowing that they might make attempt to escape? Lock them in their bedrooms, yes, that would be the answer.

He stared at them now, Geraldine once more seated between the twins on the settee. He realised that after all that coffee, he also needed to visit the bathroom to relieve himself, but he could not leave them alone in here. He looked at the boy—Charles, that was his name.

'Charles, I am going to the bathroom—you will accompany me,' he instructed the boy, who looked at his grandmother for guidance. Geraldine smiled at the child reassuringly.

'It will be alright, Charles,' she said quietly. It was obvious Greer wished to keep the child with him as insurance to prevent any attempt to escape, knew she would never leave her grandson in his power.

Once they had left the room she rose to her feet and stared out of the sitting-room window. The front garden stretched in front of her, autumn flowers making a splash of vibrant colour, massed chrysanthemums in red gold and white, purple Michaelmas daisies, and late yellow roses. But today her eyes ignored their beauty. She could just glimpse her beige Ford parked on the grass verge on the other side of the low hedge. She stared at it longingly. If only she could get the twins out of here and into that car and drive away from this whole horrible situation! As she stood there looking, she became aware of slight movement beyond the wooden gate. What was that? She stared again, but could see nothing. Must have been an illusion she thought.

She returned to the settee, then smiled at Melanie's quick cry of delight as their two kittens scampered in through the open sitting room door. They clawed their way up onto the settee settling on Melanie's lap.

'They are just so cute, Granny,' said the little girl as she stroked them. 'What will happen to Patches now—if Anna is really dead as that horrid man said?' her voice trembled as she put the question. 'And where is Susan?'

'It's quite possible he is mistaken, let us hope so—and I'm sure Susan is safe, so try not to worry dear.' replied Geraldine gently, wishing she could reveal the truth to Melanie, that both Anna and Susan were safe next door in Bramble Cottage. She could only hope that Anna had noticed the red shirt hanging out of the bedroom window, flapping its warning in the breeze.

But why was it neither Colin nor Tom had passed her warning on to Anna not to return as Greer was here, for obviously she would never have come back to Bramble Cottage had she been aware of the situation? She frowned pondering the problem—guessed at the answer. Anna may have been exhausted on arrival hence no immediate visit— later received belated phone warning from either Colin or Tom. If this was so she must now be aware of Greer's presence in Rose Cottage. She sighed as she imagined the terror the young mother must now be experiencing.

Another thought occurred. It was a miracle none of them had noticed Anna and Susan's arrival earlier. She must have had a lift or taken a taxi—for her grey Nissan had been left in the village garage being cared while Anna was away. She worked out that the girl must have arrived when Greer was holding them in the kitchen. She relaxed slightly realising there was no way that Anna would risk an appearance. She looked up as she saw Greer come back in the room and glanced at Charles who followed him in, his young face stiff with anxiety. Greer scowled as his eyes lighted on the kittens.

'Those creatures should be in the garden,' he said sourly, but as neither Geraldine nor Melanie responded, he threw himself down heavily in the chair he had previously occupied and stared at them. 'Well, have you nothing to say for yourself?' he asked Geraldine.

'Perhaps to ask why you should have favoured me with this visit?' she said quietly, hoping to distract him from his aversion to the kittens.

'It suits my present plans to remain here for a while. As I said before, providing you do as you're told, you have nothing to fear—otherwise!' and he patted the bulk of the gun in his pocket. He smiled as he saw the real fear in the children's eyes, but disappointingly no such reaction from their grandmother. Suddenly he felt uneasy. Why was it she remained so calm? Was she expecting someone to come and rescue them—and if so who? He jumped up and walked over to the window, stared out as Geraldine had only minutes before.

There was no sign of movement out there. He ignored the delightful garden before him, and instead glanced intently at the garden gate set between low hedges, with what must be Geraldine's beige car parked on the verge beyond. There was obviously little traffic on the road—more of a lane really. He would probably get a better view from the upstairs windows. He would check later, and meanwhile try to understand why Geraldine Denton showed so little concern at her present situation.

He returned to his chair and studied her from curious dark eyes, realising how little he really knew about her. Seemingly she had been very close to Erika—or Anna as she had known her. Suddenly he wondered why she had shown so little emotion when he had carelessly mentioned Erika's death. That had been when the child Melanie had spoken of Erika's annoyance on his handling Susan's kitten roughly. He remembered the horror on the children's faces when he stated Erika was dead—but Geraldine had demonstrated no such reaction. So, either she was one of those who feel no pity for the sorrows of others, or she was adept at hiding her feelings.

His eyes travelled around the room—strayed to the piano. She, was a musician then, creative, which combined with her interest in chess indicated a keen mind—and books, many books lining the tall bookshelves. She had also rescued her grandchildren from those members of Sea Giant who had apparently attempted to murder her son Colin—and according to the children had also killed their mother! All of it demonstrated a cool nerve. He would have to watch Geraldine Denton carefully.

How long could he stay here? Certainly, it was the very last place the authorities would be searching for him. He restrained a grin as he imagined their future chagrin when discovering his erstwhile hiding place—once he was safe away! In the meanwhile, all must be kept under rigid control here in the Denton woman's cottage. His gaze returned to the children. The twins were behaving impeccably, he admitted grudgingly. Hopefully, matters should go very well. All that was needful—patience!

Chapter Sixteen

Sergeant Will Evans slowed down the car's speed as they approached the bend in the road beyond where the two solitary cottages were situated. He jerked his head towards a rustic farm gate.

'Would one of you open that—we'll leave the car in there.' Julie slipped out and waited as Evans angled the car into the field immediately behind the hedge, then stared as he saw the young policewoman pointing excitably to another car parked just a few yards ahead of his Rover. The men piled out and surrounded the vehicle—a black Volvo! They checked the registration number, realising that without doubt it was Malcolm Greer's car.

'Let's make sure he doesn't make his getaway in this!' said Tom grimly. He groped in his jacket pocket for his pocket knife—and watched as the tyres slowly flattened, the others looking on approvingly.

'Better make sure your car is locked Evans, in case he attempts to take it instead,' warned Latimer. 'Well, let's get a move on in case we are faced with a tragedy!'

They kept close to the thick, bushy hedge splashed with crimson hawthorn berries and bright scarlet hips, glancing through any small gaps for sight of two cottages, in one of which Anna and little Susan were hiding—whilst in the other, the man who had left Anna for dead, was now threatening Geraldine Denton and her seven years old twin grandchildren!

'Look—Bramble cottage,' said Colin, as they peered through the bushes, 'Rose Cottage next door—and see, that's my mother's car parked outside. He may try to escape in that,' he warned. Latimer produced his pocket binoculars and trained them on the lower windows of Rose Cottage, but could see little as the beige Ford blocked view. He swore in frustration.

'Wait—I'll take a look,' exclaimed Julie and before the men could prevent her, squeezed her way through the hedge and darted across the road and crouched behind the low hedge bordering Rose Cottage. She could just about make out movement in the sitting room window—then gasped as a man pulled the lace curtain aside to stare out. He stood there unmoving for a few minutes, then closed the curtain, moving away. She beckoned to the men, indicating they should keep low as they joined her there.

'He's in the sitting room!'

'He will have Geraldine and children in there beside him,' said Tom. Colin nodded.

'If he dares hurt them, I'll choke the life out of him with these hands!' he breathed. Latimer grabbed his arm warningly.

'Time now for cool heads, Denton,' he said quietly. 'So, let's keep low and make our way to Bramble cottage. We need to access Anna's back garden, then across the fence separating it from your home.' He glanced urgently at the others. 'Any questions?'

'Suppose he holds a gun to the head of one of his hostages when we confront him,' whispered Julie. 'What do we do?' Latimer did not reply but gestured them to follow him.

Will Evans touched Julie's hand.

'Stay close to me,' he said, as they began to make their way crouching double, slipping into the gate of Bramble Cottage. Keeping low, they skirted the cottage to the back garden and stared up at neighbouring Rose Cottage.

'Should we let Anna know we're here?' Colin, gestured towards the back door.

'No point,' advised Tom. 'She will have more sense than to venture out—and....!' He broke off, Latimer indicating they should climb the fence into Geraldine's garden.

'Kitchen and conservatory here at the back,' said Colin. 'Back door may be bolted as well as locked. The conservatory only locked—and I have the key!' Although fraught with anxiety for his mother and children, knew he must hold rigidly onto self-control.

'Let's approach keeping close to the fence,' advised Latimer. 'Colin, you lead the way.' It took a mere few minutes to draw level with the cottage. They glanced searchingly up at the windows, but saw no sign of movement. Greer and his captives must still be round the front, in the sitting-room. They crept cautiously along the outer conservatory wall, reaching the glass door. Colin produced his keyring, gently turned the key—and as the door opened they slipped silently inside.

Latimer produced a pencil torch, played it around. He clearly remembered the layout of the cottage from his previous visit. The others were also well acquainted with the Denton home. The same thought was present in their minds now safely inside—how best to separate Greer from Geraldine and the twins, aware any false move could have fatal consequences.

'Julie, you remain in the conservatory ready to comfort the twins once released. I'll be at the top of the passage near the main entrance, watching the sitting room door in case Greer appears on his own!' He produced a cosh from his pocket. 'Tom, Colin and you Will, into the kitchen—hide in the cupboard and wait there in case as is more likely

Greer escorts his prisoners through there for something to eat—and I will follow in behind.'

'And what if he catches sight of us, snatches one of the twins?' demanded Colin urgently. 'We know what he is capable of!'

'There is a certain amount of danger— that we have to accept,' responded Latimer firmly. 'But consider, there are five of us—six if you include your very determined mother!'

Before these whispered plans could be put into effect they heard voices coming down the passageway. Greer, together with Geraldine and the twins were approaching along the passage—turned into the kitchen. Concealed there in the darkened conservatory they could hear Greer's harsh demanding tones speaking intimidatingly to the children. He sounded in a foul mood. Now Geraldine could be heard, asking him to be patient while she prepared a meal—he could have coffee and cookies in the meanwhile if he so wished. They heard Greer's grudging acceptance—but no sound from the frightened twins.

Now what?' asked Tom in a barely perceptible voice. Latimer glanced at Colin, knew it was vital that the father of those vulnerable youngsters should remain calm and objective however difficult.

'We need to draw him out of the kitchen and into the passage. As soon as he is out of the kitchen we slam the door behind him to prevent his grabbing the twins—and wrestle him to the ground. Now, all of you ready?' he whispered. Sergeant Evans ventured a question.

'How do we manage to get him out on his own?'

'Like this!' hissed Latimer. He slid the door connecting the conservatory from the passageway further open—and putting his hands to his mouth and uttered a loud, bloodcurdling yell. The result was instantaneous—the kitchen door burst open, and Greer stood framed in the doorway glancing around him panic-stricken, a gun in his hand.

'Now,' called Latimer as he hurled himself forward, knocking Greer backwards onto the red carpeted passage floor—but the man on his feet again almost instantly, still holding his weapon. Tom reached Latimer's side now. while Colin rushed into the kitchen to check on his family. Geraldine stared at him in delight and the youngsters cried out in tremulous relief. at sight of their father.

Greer raised his gun as he glared calculatingly at the two men—saw the bulky form of Will Evans coming to join them. He pulled the trigger and Latimer spun and fell, dropping his own pistol—Greer fired again, this time the shot missing Tom by merest fraction. Now Evans produced his gun, aimed at Greer's right arm, heard the man's cry of anguish as he turned away from them, and tore along the passage to the front door which was locked and bolted. Using his left hand, Greer produced Geraldine's keys from his pocket, bent, unbolted the door and was outside. He relocked the door behind him Tom Lanscombe reaching it fractionally too late.

Greer stared at the shape of Geraldine's Ford parked outside the garden gate—groped in his pocket for her keyring. He grinned painfully, his wounded arm dripping blood as he prepared to get in. But the key did not work—the car was immobilised. He could hear shouts from the cottage behind him, one of his assailants opening the sitting room window and commencing to climb out. What now, he thought wildly. He faced a life sentence if the first man he had shot died. He could run for it, climb through the hedge into the field and make his way the few hundred yards to where his own vehicle was parked. But he didn't know how many more men there might be back there in the cottage, and the loss of blood was making him feel lightheaded—they might out run him. He stared across at neighbouring Bramble Cottage, where the late Erika had made her home on taking refuge from him. It would be empty now and hopefully his pursuers might not guess he'd dare seek shelter so close at hand. He crept along beneath the low hedge, opened the garden gate and bending double, hurried up the pathway, reached the front door of Bramble Cottage.

How to get in? It would be locked of course—and he couldn't risk delay exposed here in the front—his pursuers might glance this way at any time. No—he must gain access from the back somehow. He made his way around the far side of the cottage, pressing his left hand over the bullet wound in his upper right arm that was pumping blood, as he went There were no lights at the windows, for the place empty of course. He tried the back door—also locked! The pain in his arm was driving him crazy.

He bent, grabbed a small rock from a flowerbed, broke a window—and was in! He closed the curtains, switched on the light and looking around, realised he was the kitchen. He sank down on one of the cushioned wooden chairs, found he was trembling. Gritting his teeth, he removed his jacket, saw his shirt was soaked through in blood. He had to stop the bleeding. Perhaps Erika had kept a first aid lit in one of those wall cabinets. He got up, started to systematically examine their contents, but to no avail.

In desperation he snatched a tea towel, wrapped it tightly over the wound, drawing a sigh of relief as the pressure helped staunch the flow of blood. He sat there for a long moment wondering how he could extricate himself from the precarious situation he had placed himself in. It was always possible that his adversaries might examine this cottage once they had made futile search of the area. He wondered if they had previously discovered his car parked in the meadow a few hundred yards away.

He must find a safe place to hide here in case they suddenly appeared, but where? The bedrooms might be the best bet.

Anna and Susan were in the sitting room watching a Disney film on TV when they heard the recent shots. Anna's blue eyes widened in shock at the sound, as her young daughter uttered a cry of alarm.

'What's happening, Mummy? Is my father shooting people?'

'Darling, I'm not sure. But we must hide just to be on the safe side. Now, off with the TV, and upstairs to my bedroom. Stay close at my side Susan dear, mind you don't stumble in the dark.' Susan nodded fearfully and took her mother's hand as they closed the sitting room door and mounted the stairs. The shooting had stopped but they could hear angry shouting. Anna had brought a torch up with her, glanced swiftly around the bedroom, hesitating now between crawling under the bed, or hiding in the wardrobe.

'In here, Susan!' she whispered, opening the mirrored door of the mahogany wardrobe. The little girl obeyed, as Anna slipped in beside her.

'Mummy—it's like the film about the children in that magic wardrobe—and that mysterious land they found,' the child breathed trustingly. Anna forced a smile.

'You're right Susan darling—now hush. We mustn't make a sound—just listen!'

Anna had left the wardrobe door slightly open, could still faintly hear sounds from Geraldine's cottage—then came a noise below, the sound of breaking glass, and the implication of it made her stiffen in horror. Geraldine or Colin would have used the spare key. No, this could only mean that Malcolm Greer was here, violating her home with his presence and a wave of anger swept through her. But why come here? Did he know she was still alive, or was he seeking somewhere to hide from whoever was shooting next door. But those shots might well have been his! Suppose he had already killed Geraldine or Colin or the others and she shuddered at the thought.

What was that? She heard the sound of someone mounting the stairs, one of which always creaked badly, and sound of a man's voice cursing. Greer was coming up! She froze for a moment. Should she close the wardrobe door—but he'd have no idea that she was still alive, would not be looking for her. She whispered a caution in Susan's ear as she sank down next to her.

Greer entered one bedroom after another, trying to decide which of the four offered the best sanctuary. Two of the bedrooms looked unused, the third obviously a child's—his young daughter's he realised unemotionally. There was a small bathroom—and then what must be the master bedroom. He walked in—this must have been Erika's!

Greer smiled wryly at the thought that Erika was posthumously offering him shelter. He examined the room by the light of his mobile. Comfortably furnished enough with an old-fashioned bedroom suite. Where would be the best place to conceal himself? There was little time to consider this, as he heard the sound of men's voices below, realised they had decided to search the cottage—he was bound to be discovered, unless…? On inspiration he opened the bedroom door pulling it back as far as it would go against the wall—squeezed in behind it. He still had his gun, would have to use his left hand to fire.

Once confirming Latimer was not fatally wounded, an ambulance called, and leaving the wounded man in Geraldine and the young police woman's capable hands meanwhile, Colin, Tom, and Sergeant Evans hurried outside checking the gardens of both cottages for any sign of Greer—then crossing to the opposite side of the road searched behind the thick hedge using a powerful flashlight. No trace of Greer! They returned and turned their attention on Anna's cottage.

It was Colin who noticed the heavy bloodstains on the flag stoned pathway by the light of his torch, following them round to the back of the cottage. They stared at the broken window. Colin went white with shock. Greer was in there now with Anna and little Susan. He produced the spare key Geraldine had hurriedly thrust on him before they left—opened the back door. The other two followed him inside. The kitchen door was open and they stared at the bloodstains on the floor. Obviously, Greer was badly wounded. But where was he now?

'Where the hell is he?' murmured Tom once they quickly checked the two reception rooms without success.

'And where are Anna and the child,' Colin asked in a choking voice. 'It only leaves the bedrooms now.' Tom shot him a sympathetic look, knew the strain he was under. He lifted his revolver, nodding to Sergeant Evans to do likewise, as they followed Colin upstairs.

Quiet as their footsteps were on the carpeted stairs, Greer heard them approach—the noise of doors being carefully opened. Strangely it was Erika's bedroom that was the last to receive their attention. He froze as they entered the wide-open door behind which he was precariously concealed.

The three men stared around the apparently empty room in bewilderment. Colin stooped and checked under the bed, then swung around on hearing a sudden cry, as the wardrobe door suddenly opened and Anna Lindstrom and Susan stumbled out.

'Colin! Oh, thank God,' gasped Anna, as he caught her in his arms, with Susan clutching at his legs.

'You're not hurt?' he inquired anxiously. She shook her head glancing around uneasily. 'Where is Greer?' he asked urgently. 'We know he has been in the cottage—bloodstains!'

'He was in here—in this room! I heard steps—thought he was going to find us. It was terrifying! Are the twins alright Colin—and your mother?'

'All are fine, Anna.' He released her and lifted Susan up comfortingly close. 'No need to worry any more, little one,' he said gently, as Tom now intervened.

'Tell me Anna—how long since you heard the sound of Greer in this room?' he asked urgently. She looked at him and frowned, found it difficult to think clearly, was trembling in reaction.

'I'm not sure Tom—but not many minutes before you appeared. He can't have gone very far! Please be careful all of you—he is very dangerous.' The men looked at each other. They had already thoroughly searched the rest of the house, and seen no trace of him, yet according to Anna he had been in this room only shortly before. It was Evans who spoke.

'Possibly he slipped out while we were investigating the other bedrooms. We'd better get after him.' He looked at Tom and Colin for confirmation. They nodded. Colin gave Susan a quick hug, and slipped her down at Anna's side.

'Will you manage if we leave you for a while?' he asked, looking into Anna's anxious blue eyes. She forced a smile, holding Susan close.

'Don't worry about me—just find him before he can do any more harm—and Colin, be careful dear.' Anna stared after them as they turned away, began making their way downstairs. then she sank down on the bed feeling mentally exhausted, absently rearranging the sling on her arm. Perhaps she could dispense with it soon. She reached out a caring hand as Susan flung herself down on the bed beside her, resting her head on her mother's lap.

'Why is my Daddy such a bad man—so angry? Why does he hurt people?' she asked in tremulous tones. Anna stroked her daughter hair, seeking the right reply.

'Darling I simply do not know the answer. Perhaps something happened to hurt him when he was younger, or...!' She lifted her head as she heard a sound—was about to scream, but in a couple of swift strides Greer was at her side. He grabbed Susan off the bed with his left hand, pressing his hand over the girl's mouth.

'One single sound out of you and the child dies—understand?' he hissed to Anna. She was staring at him in horror and near disbelief. He looked down sneeringly at his small daughter now. 'You wonder what makes me angry Trudy? Might it be in having your mother deserting me and filling your mind with lies! Do you think that could be it—eh?' He continued to maintain grasp on the child as his gaze swept over Anna.

'I believed you dead,' he said coldly.

'Well as you see I am not,' she replied, her eyes flashing defiance. 'Where were you, just now Malcolm?' He gave a harsh laugh.

'When those lumbering idiots burst in here? Behind the door all the time! Heard you touchingly express an interest in Denton's welfare.' He swayed slightly, anxiety and loss of blood taking their toll. The tea towel binding his arm had become dislodged—pressure released the bullet wound was beginning to bleed violently again. Everything began to swim before his eyes. He lowered Susan to the ground as he felt consciousness deserting him. He knew he was about to fall, and glanced helplessly at Anna. Her reaction was instinctive. As he released his hold on Susan, she moved quickly towards him, eased him down on the bed, managed to rip off his blood-soaked shirt.

She stared at the blood still pumping out of his arm, knew that if she did nothing, he might well die from blood loss—which would put an end to his ability to wreak further vengeance. But she was a nurse first and foremost. She jerked the sling from about her neck, and bound it tightly around Greer's wound. Anna was herself now smothered in blood and her young daughter staring at her mother in horror.

'It's alright Susan dear,' consoled Anna. 'Your father will recover—but he needs to go to hospital and have that bullet removed. Listen Susan—I want you to go to the bathroom and take a small towel, dip it in cold water, wring it out, and bring it here.' The child nodded and sped off to do her bidding.

He was coming to now, opened his eyes to see Erika bending over him, holding a cold compress to his head. He noticed his shirt was missing, his wounded arm tightly bound. He stared up as her disbelievingly.

'I tried to kill you—and you did this? But why?' he asked in bewilderment.

'The bullet pierced an artery—it's a wonder you didn't die of blood loss,' she replied quietly. He continued to stare at her. As he did so, perhaps for the first time in his life began to inwardly question all his actions since boyhood. Different scenes flashed before his eyes, as he mentally acknowledged the harm he had done to so many people—destroying the lives of countless women through his people trafficking—those corrupt business deals—and in particular his treatment of the beautiful woman above him, who had every reason to both hate and fear him. And yet she had saved his life. He shook his head.

'I'm sorry,' he whispered bitterly. 'It could have been so different between us. Why could you not have returned my love Erika?' She returned his almost desperate glance as he lay there on her blood spattered, cream bedspread.

'What kind of love constrains the presence of their partner by force? What normal person attempts to control their every slightest action?' She shook her head. 'The truth is that you do not understand the meaning of love—lust perhaps, the need to possess. You are sick Malcolm, need help.' She was speaking dispassionately, but with a deep look of pity in her eyes. As he met her gaze Greer knew that all she said was correct and having to face the truth, more than he could cope with. He struggled to his feet.

'Damn you, Erika for a self-righteous bitch! I did all in my power to give you what most ordinary women could possibly desire. Would have given even more had you shown any slightest sign of genuine affection.' He swayed there unsteadily, raking her face with his defiant dark eyes, was already banishing his faintly dawning acknowledgement of guilt. She had helped him just now and for this she should live.

'You have nothing to fear from me Erika. I am going.' His gaze dropped down, settled on his small daughter's face as she stood behind her mother for protection. He had loved little Trudy once, had named her for his late mother—but the child had rejected him. Nevertheless, she was flesh of his flesh, he thought. He looked at her regretfully. If only---!

'Look after our daughter, Erika.' He stumbled towards the door and she heard him moving erratically downstairs. He must have fallen for she heard a crash, followed by a howl of pain. She stood there petrified for some minutes, wondering if she should go to his assistance—then a loud bang shook the house as he slammed the back door and left.

'Has he really gone, Mummy?' asked Susan fearfully.

'I think so, darling. Now I want you to be very brave—I need to see if your father is out there in the garden, or has truly gone. Everything will be alright very soon I promise sweetheart. Promise you'll stay in here— right?' The child returned her gaze trustingly.

'Be careful, Mummy!' Anna bent and kissed her, then ran quickly downstairs.

Why she was risking contact with him again she was not sure—but he must have damaged his arm badly when he fell. She took a heavy torch from a kitchen drawer, and let herself out. She played the beam of light around the lawn and flower beds with sweeping movement, then ventured nervously to the end of the garden, but saw no sign of him there. He must have made his way around to the front garden, she thought, but again frustratingly found no sign of Greer. But as her torch swept over the paved pathway, she saw bloodstains—fresh, heavy. He must have left by the gate. She opened it, and stepped out cautiously onto the road. Where was he? Perhaps hiding in the field on the opposite side of the thick hedge?

She hesitated, had still felt comparatively safe in the cottage grounds. It was then that she heard the sound of a siren, the lights of an approaching ambulance blinding her for a moment. It braked outside Rose Cottage as two paramedics sprang out. She stared. But surely Geraldine and the twins were alright—so who?

She debated frantically for a moment. Should she continue looking for Greer—or offer her help in Geraldine's cottage? And where had Colin and the others gone? Suddenly she stiffened as the beam of her torch caught something humped by the side of the road lying partially on the grassy bank beneath the barrier of the thick hedge. She ran across and bent to examine the still form. It was Greer.

'Malcolm—are you alright?' she called softly as she fell to her knees beside the man. She reached out an exploring hand—withdrew it sticky with blood. She turned him gently onto his back—desperately flashing the torch over his pale features, saw those blank, unmoving eyes, felt his neck for a pulse, found none. He was—dead! She closed his eyes and continued kneeling there stunned by the finality of his death. Ten minutes earlier they had been talking—now he had gone.

She was shaking as she rose to her feet and as she did so, heard a shout. She looked around. Two paramedics were carefully carrying someone out of Rose Cottage, and along the garden path, and making for the ambulance. One of them noticed her, as did Geraldine who was following behind them, and flashing a torch towards Anna—and recognised her.

'Anna dear—you're safe! Oh, thank God—I was so worried,' she called out as she hurried towards the girl. 'But why are you out here in the dark?' Then her eyes caught sight of that still shape. She shone her torch downwards and put her hand to her mouth in shock. Her eyes asked the question.

'Yes, he's dead, Geraldine. I know I should be glad—but I just feel so confused, so tired.' Then she was sobbing in Geraldine's arms.

'Where's Susan.' asked Geraldine quietly as Anna became calmer.

'How could I have forgotten! She's in Bramble Cottage—in the bedroom. I told her to stay there. I must go to her.' Geraldine released her, patting her shoulder reassuringly.

'Bring her over to my place—it will be good for her to see the twins who are still traumatised by all they have been through. We will talk later,' she said gently.

'Who was that being carried into the ambulance?' asked Anna turning to go.

'Charles Latimer—Greer's bullet just missed the lung they reckon—he is being taken directly to hospital for surgery—thankfully he should survive!' She gave Anna a straight look. 'You need shed no tears for that reprobate,' she said firmly and watched as Anna nodded absently, then made for her own gate.

'Mummy—why did you take so long!' cried Susan as her mother hurried up the stairs and caught her in her arms. 'Did you find my Daddy—I was so scared he might hurt you.' Anna did not answer at first, but stroked the child's hair soothingly. At last she replied in a low voice, holding the little girl close.

'Susan darling—your father will not hurt anyone ever again.'

'Oh, that's good—did Colin and Tom catch him?' asked Susan in quick relief.

'No Susan——listen, you remember your father was badly wounded. Well it was too much for his heart—and he died.' The child looked back at her sorrowfully.

'He could be nice—sometimes,' she whispered, her blue eyes damp. Anna kissed her.

'Darling, those are the times you must remember. You know most normal human beings are kind and caring individuals—but very few are damaged people. Minds can become sick as well as bodies. I believe your father's mind was sick. '

'Can people with sick minds be healed by doctors?' asked Susan,

'Many can—but they have to acknowledge that they need help,' replied Anna. 'Now look sweetheart, I want you to slip a jacket on whilst I wash and change.' She couldn't wait to get rid of her bloodstained garments. 'Geraldine is waiting for us next door,' she added. 'You'd like to see the twins again, wouldn't you?' Susan's face brightened.

'Oh yes—and the kittens.' With the amazing resilience of childhood, little Susan Lindstrom concentrated on what was most essential. Ten minutes later she took her mother's hand as they made their way back to normality.

Meanwhile unaware of what had just transpired, Colin and Tom Lanscombe stood with Sergeant Evans staring at Greer's car parked in the meadow, as the officer frowned and shook his head.

'Well—he obviously hasn't made his way back here—which begs the question where the devil has he gone?' The three men exchanged glances.

'Is it possible we missed him when we searched Anna's cottage?' asked Colin now. 'We'd better get back there in case—and also check

Geraldine and the children are safe. We can't afford to relax while he remains at large!' Tom nodded instant agreement.

'Let's go—and make it snappy.' He shook his head. 'My fault in suggesting coming here, was so sure he'd have made his way back to his car—instead we have wasted valuable time!'

'Let's take my car then,' said Evans. 'No point in hiding it here now. Even if Greer should get this far later, he'll be unable to get away in the Volvo with those slashed tyres!' Within minutes they were on the road for the quick return journey.

Soon the two solitary cottages came into view outlined by the car's headlights. As they rapidly approached Evans gave a shout—noticed that still shape by the side of the road, and braked. They got out and Tom stooped, bent over the lifeless form lying in a pool of congealed blood. Colin played his torch down—no need to check if Greer was dead. They stared at each other, unspeaking for a moment, trying to take it in this bewilderingly sudden end to their search.

'He must have bled out,' said Tom quietly.

'Let's hope he did no further harm first!' Colin exclaimed anxiously. He glanced from one cottage to the other. As he did so, Anna came out of her gate, holding Susan by the hand. He stared and ran towards her.

'Anna—you're not hurt, my dear—or Susan?'

'No. Oh, it's good to see you. Where were you Colin?' she demanded.

'Down the road a bit. We thought Greer might have returned to his car—it was parked on the other side of the hedge in the meadow, just a few hundred yards back there.' He paused. 'He's dead, you know.'

'Yes. I saw him.' said Anna bleakly. 'Look, Geraldine is waiting for us—and Susan is tired, and we're both shattered.' He saw the utter exhaustion on her face, nodded and lifted Susan up in his arms as Tom and Evans came across.

'I've just phoned for the ambulance. I will stay with the body, until it comes,' said Sergeant Evans. 'I'll join you in Rose Cottage later.'

Geraldine opened the door to them, reached out and took Susan from Colin's arms and smiled at Anna, as she stroked the child's hair gently.

'She looks almost asleep, poor lamb,' she said softly. 'I've just put the twins to bed, so why not slip Susan in beside Melanie?' Anna smiled back at her gratefully.

'Thank you, Geraldine. I didn't want to keep her over there in Bramble Cottage—so much blood everywhere,' she said starkly. 'I'll start clearing the place up tomorrow.'

'Indeed, you won't—Tom and I will take care of it,' said Colin firmly.

'I've already dealt with the mess in my passageway here,' said Geraldine quietly, 'I've also phoned the hospital—Charles is in surgery as we speak. Poor man, that shot was almost fatal.' She glanced at the three men. 'None of you were hurt?' she confirmed and as they shook their heads, gave a sigh of relief, relaxed. 'Then Anna and I will take Susan up to bed—then we'll talk.'

Colin Denton found sleep difficult to come, was still wrought up after the day's violent episodes. Next door in his mother's spare bedroom, Anna Lindstrom lay in a deep slumber, her arm around her daughter Susan who had been moved there from Melanie's bed. Colin had glanced in at them at Geraldine's side before retiring himself. Lying there it was hard to relax realising how nearly he had lost his mother and children at Greer's hands—and as for Anna's ordeal, he felt a tremendous sympathy for their attractive, golden haired neighbour who had so bravely outfaced the demented individual who had caused such havoc in his many victim's lives.

Earlier, Anna had related her final confrontation with Greer—then the trauma of finding him lying dead in the road. How long would it take for her to recover from the shock of all she had endured? Then there was little Susan, who had seen and heard things enough to shatter any young mind. He began to realise that he had developed a strong affection for the mother and child. Then he thought of his own mother, who had spent so many anxious hours attempting to humour the dangerous individual who had held her hostage together with young Charles and Melanie. One man whose evil genius had master minded the largest people trafficking ring in Europe, destroying all who impeded his path, whilst outwardly appearing an innocuous businessman who enjoyed his privacy. His thoughts returned to Anna who as Erika Nicolson had endured many fraught years at Greer's side, born him a child, before finding the courage to escape—how long would it take her to recover from all this?

As he lay there, he thought back to all he had personally suffered at the hands of that corrupt organisation Sea Giant—the devastating effect on his own mind for so many long weeks. Now at last he sensed he was strong enough to put all behind him and face up to the future. But what did that future hold now that his new friend and mentor Charles Latimer was lying dangerously ill in hospital?

It was his admiration for the senior MI5 operative that had caused him to agree to join the service. Did he want to risk his own life on a regular basis in this undoubtedly exciting but dangerous occupation? But Tom Lanscombe had done just that for so many years until taking his eventual retirement with his dear wife Lottie. He thought affectionately of Tom now, sleeping downstairs on the sofa and looking forward to returning to wife, home and work at that women's refuge, Dream Echo.

At last Colin like the rest of the exhausted household, slept.

Next morning Geraldine was up early and phoned the hospital. To her relief the news was good—Charles Latimer had come safely through surgery. The ward sister added that he was asking for Tom and Colin to visit. As she put the phone down, the kitchen door opened quietly and Anna stood there. She glanced at the girl. Anna was pale, but the blue eyes that met her gaze were steady as she stood there in jeans and pale blue sweater, blond hair tied back behind her head. Geraldine walked over and kissed her.

'How are you this morning, Anna dear?' she asked.

'Trying to deal with a plethora of mixed emotions. So much happened in so short a time—and dealing with a sense of unreality.' She took Geraldine's hands. 'What about you? You must have been terrified alone here with the twins when Malcolm broke in!' She looked wonderingly at Geraldine, who showed no sign of the trauma she had endured the day before.

'How did you cope with the awful fear you must have felt?' she asked. Geraldine smiled as they seated themselves at the table.

'I did what I always do when confronted by evil—I prayed to Almighty God for help. I knew the man's mind was deranged, that I had to humour him as best I could, whilst trying to keep my little grandchildren calm.'

'I prayed too,' revealed Anna quietly. 'He had tried to kill me the day before—possibly believed I was dead, so when he saw me again I knew he would not scruple to shoot! I felt so scared for Susan. What kind of a father has no love for his child?' Anna bit her lip. 'Yet I still believe some slight affection remained in his twisted heart.' She fixed troubled blue eyes on Geraldine. 'How is my child going to deal with the knowledge that her father was a criminal and attempted murderer?' Geraldine returned her anxious glance pityingly.

'Her mother's love will compensate for all. Your little Susan is a fine child, Anna. Perhaps one day you will meet someone who will give you the love and respect you deserve—and prove a loving father to Susan. I truly hope so.' She got up. 'Well, I'd better get breakfast under way—I can hear movement upstairs—and Tom will be getting up from the couch in the sitting room. Care to lend me a helping hand, Anna?'

Tom came in as Geraldine prepared coffee. The two women smiled at his slightly rumpled appearance.

'Tom dear—how did you sleep?' inquired Geraldine.

'Oh—quite well. Must ring the hospital—see how Charles is!'

'I've already done so Tom—he's doing fine and according to the ward sister, asking to speak with both you and Colin.'

'What a relief—I'd feared the worst at first! I'll get over there right away! Oh, by the way I phoned Lottie a few minutes ago and filled her in with news. She sends her love. Look Geraldine, since everything here is ok, I'll arrange transport and make tracks back for Ivy Cottage Now what about Colin? He'll be needed back at the Sea Giant trial.' He saw her face tighten, realised how much she must long to keep her son with her at this time.

'If he must go then I understand—am just so grateful that both you and Charles accompanied him here to our rescue. Had you not, then I fear Greer's presence in Rose Cottage might have ended in tragedy. Luckily the only death was his own.' She gave a shudder. Tom took her hand and pressed it reassuringly.

'Well my dear, Malcolm Greer will never hurt another soul on this earth—and those villains running Sea Giant soon be paying for their crimes in jail. Colin's evidence is of vital importance to the successful outcome of the trial.' She brightened at his words, smiled.

'How will you get back, Tom? I'd lend you my Ford, but can't afford to be without it living so far from the village.'

'No problem, I'll arrange for the chopper to collect Colin and myself. I want to ensure that Charles is alright before leaving—see if he has any instructions. Can I rely on you to keep in touch with the hospital?' he asked. 'I hate to leave him, but I'm needed back at Dream Echo!'

'Need you ask? Once he is strong enough to be discharged, Charles will be more than welcome to recuperate here. I promise you Anna and I will spoil him,' she stated warmly. 'Now I must prepare breakfast.

Tom stared down at Latimer, as did Colin. He realised it was the first time he had ever seen his esteemed friend and ex colleague in such weakened state. But despite this, Latimer managed a faintly humorous smile from his pillows.

'Tom—Colin, good to see you both! Feel such a fool allowing myself to be downed by that mongrel,' he managed in disgust.

'Thank the good Lord you survived!' Tom's gaze expressed his intense relief as he regarded his best friend under his thick shaggy eyebrows, while Colin leaned forward and placed a sympathetic hand on Latimer's shoulder.

'Geraldine informed me of Greer's death—loss of blood she said?' Latimer stared at them inquiringly. Tom nodded, filled him in with brief account of all that had transpired. Latimer listened attentively.

'Anna must have been traumatised by that final meeting—then finding him dead so soon afterwards. Probably the best result for Greer. He would have faced years in jail—life perhaps. Personally, I would have preferred him alive still and facing justice—and opportunity to extract relevant details of his involvement with his vile people trafficking ring…!' He didn't finish the sentence as Sister appeared and stared disapprovingly at Tom.

'Mr Latimer has undergone major surgery—requires perfect peace to aid his recovery.'

'It is essential that we speak with Mr Lanscombe, Sister,' said Tom authoritatively. 'A vital matter pertaining to the Civil Service.' The woman regarded him curiously under her white starched cap, as his words registered, wondering about this patient from whom the surgeons had removed a bullet that had almost ended his life.

'Five minutes more —but no longer.' She turned quietly away.

'Well Denton,' said Latimer, casting a searching glance on Colin, 'I imagine you will be glad when the Sea Giant trial is over—and the bastards who caused you so much grief dealt with by the law! I will soon be out of this bed—then once you've completed your initial training, look forward to having you at my side.' He watched Colin's face, thought he saw slight hesitation before the younger man made his quiet reply.

'You may need to take things easy for a time,' said Colin carefully. 'Just concentrate on getting well again.' He felt uncomfortable under Latimer's direct stare. Did the patient sense his internal battle, as he balanced the future excitement and camaraderie of working at Latimer's side, in the knowledge that he was protecting his country, with the longing for a normal quiet life, spending precious time with young Charles and Melanie and the mother with whom he was beginning to be really close for the first time.

'And you Colin enjoy providing your evidence before the court that will ensure those corrupt Sea Giant Executives pay dearly for their crimes!' and he sank back on his pillows plainly exhausted. Tom glanced meaningfully at Colin, inclining his head towards the door.

'We should go I think. You need to rest Charles my friend—and make a good recovery,' said Tom feelingly.

'And by the way, my mother says you will be more than welcome to stay at Rose Cottage while regaining your strength,' added Colin. Latimer smiled back at them tiredly.

'Thank Geraldine for me—and go with God my friends. Oh, and Tom, my love to Lottie!' He watched them leave and closed his eyes. On returning to her patient, the ward sister found him sleeping peacefully.

Geraldine sank down tiredly in her armchair, had just finished tidying the cottage, checking no slightest trace of the violence so recently perpetrated there remained. But she couldn't remove the imprint in her brain—nor the memory of those long tense hours under Greer's malevolent control. She tried to reason why this should be, considering those many years she had spent facing life threatening situations in her work as a member of MI5. Perhaps because on this occasion evil had penetrated into her home, threatening those dear to her?

Colin and Tom had departed a few hours ago. It had been a wrench to see her son leave, but knew his evidence was vital at the Sea Giant trial and little Charles and Melanie had shed a few tears when he had disappeared with Tom. Anna was very quiet today, doing her best to care for Susan and the twins in the kitchen, telling them stories as they petted the two frisky kittens, then providing paper and paints to keep them busy. Geraldine thought of Anna now, worrying about the girl who had been through such a terrifying ordeal.

Anna watched the children distractedly from brooding blue eyes—they seemed to have completed their painting. She realised Susan was speaking to her, and forced herself to concentrate on the child.

'Please Mummy may we stay here with Geraldine and the twins? I don't want to go back to Bramble Cottage.' Susan was staring at her pleadingly. Anna hesitated. She also felt reluctant to return to a home desecrated by Malcolm Greer's cruelty. She knew that Colin and Tom Lanscombe had been over there and cleaned all bloodstains from the place, making sure all was back in order. But would the memories ever fade? She tried to tell herself that if she allowed recollection of Greer's malevolence to her destroy all love of her beloved cottage, then even in death he would have won.

She knew Susan was waiting for an answer and prevaricated.

'Perhaps we could stay here for tonight,' she said lightly. 'I'll ask Geraldine. Now let me see your painting, dear.' She reached out a hand and drew the painting pad towards her. As she looked at the childish depiction of a man holding a gun and standing in a pool of blood, she could have cried.

'Is that your father?' she asked. Susan nodded, small face serious.

'Yes. He really is dead now, isn't he, Mummy? He won't ever hurt us again?'

'I promise you your father is truly dead—told you so before, sweetheart. He won't ever hurt you again!' She bent over the child, kissing her gently and holding her close felt the small body relax. Was it possible for them to carry on life as normal after all that had transpired, she wondered?

Charles and Melanie had overheard the quiet conversation and looked at each other.

'It will get better Susan,' the boy said now. 'Melanie and I have been there, know what it's like. But there will be lots of happy times ahead—you just have to let go of the hurtful stuff.'

Anna glanced at the boy, he was so right. She thought of Geraldine now, first facing the apparent death of her only son, then dealing so bravely with her daughter-in-law Mary's murder, and subsequent kidnap of her beloved grandchildren. If Geraldine could cope with all this, then she surely could do likewise with her own lesser trauma. She looked up as the kitchen door opened and Geraldine appeared. The twins pointed to their paintings, calling across to her to come and look. She did so—then with a smile at Anna glanced at Susan's picture. She raised her face, her grey eyes troubled.

'Susan asked if we might stay a little longer,' said Anna quietly, as she nodded towards her daughter's painting. 'Would it be possible—I know you must need peace yourself after all that has happened?' Geraldine saw the strain on the girl's face and reached out a reassuring hand as she sat down beside her.

'Anna dear, you're as welcome as the flowers in May! Stay as long as you like. I know Colin would be equally delighted. Time is a great healer as both you and your little daughter will find.' Anna bit her lip. Yes—but how much time would it take? What to do in the meanwhile! How was she going to return to Bramble cottage with Susan after the terror they had both experienced? But what alternative was there. She could not impose on Geraldine for months or longer. But where else could she go—how to find new accommodation and employment, and then make arrangement for Susan to be cared for while she was at work?

Geraldine felt Anna's hand tighten in hers, sensed the girl had come to some sort of decision, and watched as Anna rose and walked over to the window, beckoning to Geraldine to join her so that they could talk out of the children's earshot

'Geraldine—I have this feeling that I need to get right away from Bramble Cottage. I do not mean for a few weeks or even months—but for a year at least. The problem will be finding a job and new accommodation—and put arrangements in place for Susan to be cared for whilst I work. I just had this thought—about Dream Echo? I am familiar with the refuge, understand how it operates and get on well with Amber and her staff. Then Tom and Lottie are closely involved with the running of it. My medical knowledge may be of some use there, plus my own experience of domestic abuse!'

Her face became animated as she spoke and Geraldine looked back at her thoughtfully. Much as she would miss Anna, she understood the strain the young mother was experiencing in the aftermath of recent events, together with little Susan's obvious distress. Dream Echo might indeed prove a suitable launching pad to a new future.

'I suggest you think it over carefully, my dear—make no hasty decision. But if you really feel constrained to move, then seeking a post in that wonderful women's refuge sounds the perfect answer. Your nursing experience would make you a welcome addition to Amber's dedicated team—easing you back into work in a familiar setting where you have already made friends.' Anna smiled back at her, tears forming in her blue eyes. She put her arms around the older woman who had shown such amazing kindness to her from the first moment they had met.

Colin Denton took the oath with a feeling of detachment. He made a swift glance around the court, taking in the judge resplendent in red robes and full bottomed white wig, prosecuting and defence counsels, the attentive jury consisting of seven men and five women and packed spectator area—and in the dock three well remembered faces. It was rather like participating in a strange movie—unreal. He snapped back to full attention as the Prosecuting Counsel began his detailed questioning. As Colin responded, he was aware of the malevolent glances directed at him from the dock by Richard Lancaster the Managing Director of Sea Giant, and Ross Chamberlain—Head of Security, and Director Roger Armstrong. He concentrated his attention on the Prosecuting Counsel's questions as the man skilfully led him through the sequence of events from his initial engagement by Sea Giant as adviser on the possible location of a new oilfield—his expertise in discovering what was a potentially an immensely rich find and the directors subsequent delight with him.

The questions then probed Colin's own feelings towards oil exploration, the need for it in a commercial world, his early satisfaction that he had been successful in pin pointing the location of Sea Giant's recent new oil field. Had his feelings changed—if so when and why?

He found himself describing his early incredulity on learning the effects global warming were expected to have on the planet—the ice caps melting with rise in sea levels—devastating floods, tornadoes and hurricanes—huge areas swept by uncontrolled forest fires—soaring temperatures and crops dying—famine. All of this predicted to take effect over the next twenty years and already beginning to take place. He noted the judge was watching him curiously.

'When I realised the enormity of the situation, and that the process of global warming was accelerated by the use of fossil fuels, I began to question my own position. I shared my concerns with a trusted colleague and friend, Jonathon King.' He paused. The prosecuting counsel stared at him.

'Pray continue Mr Denton.'

'One day I was flown out for a meeting to be held in the MD's private office on the oilrig. While it was taking place a fire alarm went off and the directors rushed out of the room instructing me to remain. I realised that Richard Lancaster, the Managing Director of Sea Giant, had left his computer on and some instinct caused me to behave in a way that was quite out of character—to examine its contents! What I saw shocked me to the core. I was just in time to resume my place around the oval table apparently studying a map when the members of the board returned.

As he spoke Colin realised Lancaster's eyes were glaring at him furiously. He continued.

'A month later, having spoken over my concerns about global warming with my colleague and assistant Johnathon King, I asked permission for the two of us to be flown out to the rig to discuss matters of importance.'

'So, this meeting was officially agreed to?' confirmed the barrister.

'Yes, it was. Kevin MacDuff an experienced pilot flew us to the rig. I thought it unlikely Sea Giant executives would be swayed by the facts we laid before them concerning the effects of global warming—nor that they could be persuaded to draw back from developing the predicted new secret oil field, likely to yield billions of barrels of oil and massive profits—but I just knew I had to try!' and Colin shrugged.

'What was their reaction?'

'I was as I had feared—amused contempt and disapproval. I was told I should return home and consider my position in the company. In the meanwhile, King and I would be flown back to the mainland. A chopper would be put at our disposal, piloted as before by MacDuff.'

'I take it you were to return in the same helicopter as that in which you had made the outward journey?' asked the prosecutor.

'It would have seemed logical—but no. Kevin MacDuff was instructed to use another fairly new model—a smaller craft. We got aboard, and Kevin took off, all perfectly normal. Then after about ten minutes Kevin turned his head towards Jonathon and myself—we noticed his face registering alarm.' Colin paused and swallowed, as his mind regressed to the terrifying episode that was to follow.

'I know the recollection must be painful Mr Denton, but pray continue.'

'Kevin shouted out that the controls were not responding—that we were going down! He did a Mayday. We struck the water, and I remember forcing the door open, my lungs choking on ice cold sea water! Then everything went black.'

'You managed to escape the helicopter before it sank to the seabed, bearing the pilot Kevin MacDuff and your assistant Jonathon King to their deaths.'

'That is correct. I lost consciousness, had sustained injuries when the chopper struck the water it was a miracle I survived—and one that Sea Giant had not reckoned with.'

'Then there you were, floating unconscious in the sea a tremendous distance from land. Pray explain to the court how you escaped from such dire situation,' encouraged the prosecutor. Colin gave a slight smile.

'I was spotted by the crew of a Norwegian fishing vessel—they saw something drifting in the waves. I was brought aboard and taken by the skipper to a small coastal mountain village in Norway to be cared for by his parents. There I received marvellous care from this kindly couple attended by the local doctor and district nurse. After nearly three weeks I regained consciousness, and shortly afterwards my memory returned.'

Colin was finding it difficult to carry on but did so, speaking now of making contact by phone with a minister friend in Scotland, who was amazed to learn he had survived—a memorial service had already been held. The Rev Ian MacKinnon then revealed the deeply distressing news that Colin's beloved wife Mary Denton had died in a suspicious car accident the day after the helicopter crashed—that his twin children had been taken by their grandmother, Geraldine Denton, to stay in her home in the south of England.

'I understand you have evidence pointing to the fact that your wife Mary's new car had been deliberately tampered with by Sea Giant, who believed she had acquired knowledge from your computer of certain secret plans of theirs to enter into an illicit contract with the Chinese—details of which may not be revealed here due to the Official Secrets Act.'

'That is so. Mary's car was parked outside our house as usual. A fine new car in which she was to make a short few minutes journey. My wife was an experienced driver with an unblemished record. Inexplicably the Audi hit the parapet of a bridge and immediately burst into flames. Mary did not survive.' Colin clenched his fists as he laid the facts before the court.

'I know I speak for all here when I offer our commiserations on the death of your wife, Mr Denton,' said the prosecutor quietly.

'This might be an appropriate time for the jury to take a break,' said the Judge leaning forward—and all rose as he left his seat.

Colin was exhausted by the end of that first day. Once the bewigged, hawk nosed, sharp eyed, prosecuting counsel had completed his examination, he was then subjected to a severe cross examination by

Sea Giant's portly, bristling browed, defence counsel, thrusting out protruding chin, loftily attempting to discredit Colin's assertions line by line, his dark eyes narrowing in frustration as the stark truth clearly and credibly presented by Colin continued to prevail.

He was lying on his hotel bed, fighting off recollection of those frightening moments when the helicopter had suddenly dropped like a stone, with death seeming inevitable. Revealing details of his trauma in court under the penetrating gaze of the judge and aware of the cold fury of the three Sea Giant directors balefully glaring from the dock, had forced back to the surface of his mind those images he had attempted to banish over the last few weeks. He sat up as he heard a knock at the bedroom door.

'Come in!' He smiled as he saw Latimer's tall form and steady eyes, 'Charles?'

'Thought I'd see how you were coping, and to say how impressed Tom and I are by the way you conducted yourself in court today. May I?' and he sank down in the black leather armchair beside the bed and smiled approvingly at Colin.

'Good of you to say so, Charles. Brought a lot of stuff back up in my mind, just as I was beginning to let go of it,' he replied wryly. Latimer looked at him thoughtfully.

'Once you embark on your new career, you'll find the drama and excitement of each new case tends to obliterate past memories. No place for such distractions when constant alertness and steady nerves are required to protect the lives of others as well as your own.' He watched as Colin slid off the bed and stated to pace the room.

'Look—the point is Charles, I'm no longer convinced that I'm best suited to join MI5. I'll always be proud and immensely touched by your confidence in me, but...!'

'Colin, no need to explain. If you are not totally convinced that joining the firm is right path for you, it's your natural prerogative to change your mind. However, I would suggest you take a few days to think things over.' He studied the younger man's face thoughtfully. 'Has your blossoming friendship with Anna Lindstrom any bearing on matters?' he inquired gently. Colin glanced away before speaking.

'I like Anna—but it is too soon after losing my dear Mary to say more than that.'

'I only ask as Tom Lanscombe mentioned that Anna is considering leaving Bramble Cottage in the near future. Seems she intends to approach Amber for a job at Dream Echo. Thought you might like to know in case you are in any way serious about the girl—but since you are not?' He saw Colin's lips tighten, eyes registering shock.

'But why there? I'd have thought that since she was kidnapped from the refuge by that brute Greer, the place would hold frightening memories for her!' he said in a low voice.

'Perhaps she feels Bramble Cottage has been violated by recent happenings—and who could blame her,' replied Latimer. 'There again, employment at Dream Echo offers an opportunity to use her nursing skills—and I know Amber esteems her highly.'

'But what about her small daughter? The twins love Susan dearly, as does my mother!' protested Colin as he rose and started to pace the room. Latimer watched him sympathetically.

'I've no doubt young Susan will receive the best of care at Dream Echo. Incidentally, Amber has recently employed a retired school mistress to teach the children of mothers seeking sanctuary there.' He paused, realising the information was falling on deaf ears, Colin's face fraught with frustration. If he really had feelings for the golden-haired Anna then, a year or so apart would test the depth and reality of that affection. As for the young man's rejection of a career in MI5, well this might be mere temporary reaction to recently resurrected memories of Sea Giant's cruelties perpetrated on both him and his family.

'Do you know how serious Anna's decision is to leave Bramble cottage?' shot out Colin, turning and facing him squarely.

'Only Anna can provide the answer to that!' replied Latimer.

Chapter Seventeen

Amber Marsden was sitting in her office with her husband Robert, her mother talented artist Gwenda Williams, together with assistants Connie Sheldon and Lilian Destry both with experience in psychiatric nursing, and Amber's close friends and helpers Tom and Lottie Lanscombe. The subject they were discussing this morning not as was usual the progress of the residents in the refuge they ran between them, but an application to join the team by a previously abused woman who had initially sought safety there a few months ago, and had left to start a new life, unusually needing further help only recently.

'Personally, I believe Anna Lindstrom could become a fine addition to our staff. The fact that she is an SRN as well as having experienced domestic abuse herself, makes her a very suitable candidate, together with proven ability to communicate with the traumatised women who arrive at our doors.' Amber spoke with enthusiasm, her unusual golden-brown eyes sparkling as she scanned the faces of those she had gathered about her to help run Dream Echo over the last three years.

A murmur of agreement ran around the office, Lottie's face breaking into a warm smile as she nodded her head in agreement.

'Anna possesses courage and integrity. I certainly vouch for her.'

'The very fact that she wishes to join us after all she has recently endured speaks for itself,' added Robert thoughtfully. 'Let's see, she has a little daughter if I remember rightly?'

'Susan—about four years old,' said Connie Sheldon. 'Just one query though? Anna recently suffered a terrible shock at Dream Echo when her ex-partner broke in here kidnapping mother and child. Will she be able to shake off the memory of this?' she asked inquiringly

'Perhaps not,' said Lilian Destry quietly. 'However, that memory may enhance her desire to help other women who have suffered abuse and keep them safe.' Connie nodded agreement.

'I think you are right, Lilian.'

'We are all agreed then?' confirmed Amber. 'Anna Lindstrom is to be invited to join the staff with immediate effect!'

Geraldine watched regretfully as the girl she had come to love as a daughter gave a final wave out of the car window, before driving off. She would miss Anna and little Susan deeply, as would the twins! She turned to go back inside Rose Cottage, wondering what Colin's reaction would be when he heard the news. Although still grieving his dear Mary's death she had sensed a growing closeness between her son and Anna.

It was over a week later that Colin returned from London, looking slightly weary Geraldine observed. as she released him from a fond embrace, stepping back as Charles and Melanie threw their arms about him enthusiastically.

'Careful there, children—you'll have me over!' he laughed, kissing the twins. 'I hope you have been behaving yourselves!'

'We have,' said Charles. 'But we really missed you—and now Anna has left with Susan!' he added dolefully.

'What's that—Anna has actually left?' He swung around in dismay, to stare inquiringly at Geraldine, saw from her face that it was true.

'Yes, she drove off this morning to join Amber and the Lanscombes at the refuge,' replied Geraldine. 'She intends to spend a year or so there, just could not face returning to Bramble Cottage after recent happenings! She is to visit us here when her work permits,' she added reassuringly.

He shook his head in almost disbelief. Although Latimer had suggested Anna was considering the move, he had secretly hoped to persuade her to change her mind once the trial was over. Why the hurry to get away? Certainly, she had endured a terrifying sequence of events—but Greer was dead now, so the future hers to shape without stress. He would miss her. He threw himself down in what had been his father's armchair, realising Geraldine's eyes were examining him.

'You are disappointed at Anna's decision,' she probed. He didn't reply, wondering soberly whether it might have influenced that recent decision to turn down an interesting future in the secret service. Well, possibly matters could be reversed. He tried to hide his disappointment at Anna's departure then glanced down curiously as he noticed Susan's beloved kitten with its white bib and paws, scampering after his own children's mischievous kitten Pyrites.

'They left Patches behind?' he queried. 'I thought Susan loved the little creature.' Geraldine smiled.

'She was a bit downhearted when Anna told her what was happening, but knew she'd have the kitten back one day,' she said lightly and saw his face brighten. He would have to adjust to Anna's temporary disappearance even as she had. Besides which, her son would be engrossed with the introductory strictures involved in joining MI5.

'One good thing to come out of all this mother is that you will not have to attend court in London to give evidence against Dawson and Bickerton. Both men have entered a guilty plea to all charges of serious offences against you and the children. In exchange, they have been offered slightly easier sentences, but will certainly be out of the way for some years to come!' He saw her face brighten at the news. As he looked at Geraldine he realised how much pressure she must have suffered over the last months, whilst outwardly presenting an aura of calm and tranquillity. It must be down to all those years of self-discipline as a member of MI5. Again, his thoughts returned to his last meeting with Latimer, and his decision to turn down a future in the Secret Service.

The following morning Colin posed a question to his mother.

'What is going to happen about Bramble Cottage? I mean, has Anna given up the tenancy?' Geraldine did not answer immediately, continuing to butter her toast. 'Well?' he asked impatiently. He had to know, had been brooding over the matter all night in bed.

'As I understand it, Anna does not wish to extend the tenancy once her first year's lease is up. She has asked me to inform the owner my dear friend Daphne Pearson who as you know is presently living with her son in New Zealand, explaining that Anna will continue to pay the rent until her lease expires. I am to keep an eye on the cottage and garden meanwhile.' She crunched on her slice of toast as she watched Colin's face.

'Mother—do you think Daphne might consider selling Bramble Cottage to me?'

'But why? I thought you were happy to live here with the children,' she cried in dismay.

Colin coloured as he bent his head over his plate. He couldn't explain his true motive in wishing to own the cottage—that one day he might declare his growing feelings of tenderness towards the lovely golden-haired woman who had made such an impact on all their lives. To seize this opportunity to own a property next door to his mother's beloved Rose Cottage so that when the time was right, to ask Anna to share it with him and the twins. But was he being disloyal to his dear Mary's memory even to think along such lines so soon?

Geraldine saw the mixed emotions cross his face, instinctively guessing the reasoning behind his desire to buy the place. Anna—He was in love with Anna! She turned the idea over in her mind, and liked it! But what were Anna's feelings towards Colin, she pondered? There was definitely an attraction between the two, but surely it was much too early after so much turbulence in both their lives to make a decision of such magnitude. She realised Colin was waiting for an answer.

'You could always contact her, dear. Daphne might like the idea of selling to a friend. But are you sure this is what you want? After all, your duties with MI5 mean you're likely to be away for weeks at a time. So, what about Charles and Melanie? The present situation allows you freedom of movement, whilst preventing any worry about their care when away?' She stared at him questioningly. Colin pushed his plate aside, rose and started to pace the room, then swung about and faced his mother

'Look, I told Latimer that I've decided against a career in MI5! Too disciplined for me, plus the fact I do not want to leave the twins. They're only now adjusting to Mary's death.' He looked at her almost defiantly but saw no disapproval in her wise grey eyes.

'And one day you might remarry? I know you are fond of Anna—and that she has a warm interest in you too.' He nodded slowly.

'Do you think she might come to love me?' he asked huskily.

'I do. But right now, I believe she needs time to put the hurts of the past to rest—you must remember she endured years of fear and oppression under the control of Malcolm Greer. Working to assist other women recovering from a similar situation, may help to release the pain from her own mind.' She smiled at Colin, noting the expression of delight on his face when she suggested Anna might come to love him. It was disappointing that he was turning his back on the Secret Service—but another path would beckon shortly.

She bent down carefully extricating kittens Patches and Pyrites now busily attempting to climb up her trousers. The house would seem strangely empty if Colin did buy Bramble cottage—move next door with the twins and these frisky kittens! But this decision was dependent on Anna's returning his love. Seemingly all this was a year away. Much could change in that time.

Amber had allowed Anna two days to settle into her accommodation. It was situated at the end of the passageway in that part of Dream Echo private to the family and others helping to run the refuge. It was a good-sized room well furnished with a comfortable bed for Anna and a smaller bed for Susan.

'Susan are you all right, darling?' inquired Anna, as she watched the child staring listlessly out of the window, fair head drooping. The little girl turned slowly and swept an arm disconsolately around the bedroom.

'I miss our home, Mummy. Why did we have to come back to this place again? We do not need to hide away as before! Please say we may return to the cottage. I really miss the twins and Geraldine and my kitten.' The words were blurted out imploringly as her eyes met her mother's troubled gentian blue gaze.

'Sweetheart, I have to earn a living to support us both. That is one reason for coming here to a place where my nursing skills can be put to good use. Then there's the fact that Bramble Cottage no longer feels like home after all those dreadful things that happened there.' She walked over to Susan and took her hands. The little girl merely stared back at her reproachfully.

'But Mummy—just because Daddy came to our home on that day, and—well did frightening things you said were because his mind was sick—this is no reason to forget all the lovely times we had there. I love Bramble Cottage and I want to go back!'

'I'm sorry you feel like this, but there's nothing I can do about it now, dear. I've given my word to Amber to work here assisting those poor distressed women who arrive at Dream Echo as we once did.' She spoke gently but firmly. Susan pulled away from her and flounced down rebelliously on her bed.

'I miss Colin too—he used to swing me around just as he did with Charles and Melanie. We were all so happy together.' Anna stared down at her in dismay. Had she acted too precipitately in leaving her delightful cottage in the tranquil village of Ravensnest, foregoing the friendship of Geraldine Denton and her good-looking son Colin and twin children? But how could she have returned to Bramble Cottage, tainted as it now was by Malcolm Greer's violence—and with a view from her window of the actual spot where he had bled to death on the road? No, it would have been unendurable, she assured herself firmly.

Then her thoughts returned to Geraldine, who together with her young grandchildren, Charles and Melanie, had endured hours of terrifying intimidation by Greer at Rose Cottage until mercifully released at last by Latimer, Tom Lanscombe and Colin with the backing of the two police officers in the confrontation that almost cost Charles Latimer his life—Greer himself receiving the wound that had ultimately caused his death.

Despite all that had happened at the cottage, Geraldine, the twins and their father Colin continued to live in a home where so much violence had occurred. Perhaps it was the strong bond of love binding them together that made this possible. But she, Anna, was not part of their amazing family and although little Susan might dismiss all thoughts of the terror they had endured in the neighbouring Bramble Cottage, she could not. The place had been defiled by Greer. The fact that he was now dead did not help, for recollection of that final confrontation in the bedroom continued to flash vividly in her inner vision.

A month passed, and Anna caught up in the immediacy of the vital work of which she had become a part, her nursing skills constantly in demand as fresh victims of domestic abuse regularly arrived at Dream Echo. Anna found the work deeply absorbing, realising that once the team had dealt with the initial physical damage the women had sustained, each one of their traumatised guests needed the courage and confidence to open up and speak openly of matters they had concealed from the outside world sometimes for years through fear, or even shame.

Amber who was keeping a watchful eye on her new assistant was favourably impressed by Anna's intuitive ability to get through to the abused women of all ages who arrived in deep shock and all too often with serious injuries. Today she discussed Anna's progress with Lottie Lanscombe as they sat in the small office examining the admission register. Amber pointed at the most recent entry in the book, a sixteen-year-old girl abused by her guardian.

'Anna has been successful in gaining Olwen's trust. The girl has started to speak a little—despite her painful facial injuries,' said Amber in relief. 'You know Lottie, I think we should offer Anna a permanent position at Dream Echo.' The older woman nodded approvingly.

'She's a natural for the work. I took to her over a year ago, at the time she arrived here with little Susan seeking help after escaping from that brute Greer at Enderslie House! I admired the way she managed to take back control of her life. Then when she moved to Ravensnest and I found she was living next door to my friend Geraldine Denton—was delighted that they had become friends.'

'Your friend Geraldine sounds like a wonderful woman,' said Amber. 'You said there was a hint of romance between her son Colin and Anna? If so it could affect Anna's decision on her long-term future here.' There was an inquiring glance in her unusual topaz eyes. Lottie stared back musingly.

'Colin is still grieving his wife Mary's death—but according to Geraldine, he has become very fond of Anna.'

'Possibility of close relationship eventually then,' murmured Amber and smiled. 'Although it would be great to engage Anna permanently, her happiness and that of little Susan must come first.'

'The child Susan hasn't settled yet. She was happy enough when her mother escaped Greer over a year ago and they came here—but now after making a new life in Ravensnest next door to Geraldine and her twin grandchildren, it's a different matter. She badly misses young Charles and Melanie, and the kitten she left behind.' She fixed her gaze fondly on the amazing young woman who had given her own home, money, time and effort into creating this welcoming refuge that opened its doors to women of all ages suffering domestic abuse.

'Well Lottie, we will just have to exercise patience—see what transpires!' and she paused. 'How is Colin doing now the Sea Giant trial is over? I remember how beforehand Tom and you took him into your home—that Charles Latimer was interested in him?' Lottie nodded and pushed a stray white curl back from her forehead.

'It seems Colin has declined a position in the civil service. But he's an intelligent and accomplished man with a deeply caring nature and I'm sure will find an interesting job soon—but not in the oil industry!' she snorted. Amber said nothing, but her mind was darting in a direction that would have astonished Lottie.

Charles Latimer was brooding despondently behind the leather-topped desk in the study of his Knightsbridge flat. It was hard to take in the devastating news received earlier today. He had submitted ungraciously to a thorough examination by the MI5 medic as was routine after receiving a serious injury. As far as he had been concerned, Greer's bullet which had barely missed his heart a few weeks ago had been successfully removed, and all was now back to normal.

He had stared unbelievingly at the sympathetic doctor who presented him with the stark prognosis, as he impatiently buttoned his shirt now with clumsy fingers.

'Heart failure—it's impossible! How many times have I sustained serious injuries and returned to active duty within a short time? Forgive me, but I need a second opinion, Morton!'

The physician bowed his head understandingly knowing the shock his words had been to the brave, determined character in front of him.

'That is your prerogative, Mr Latimer. Personally, however, I have no option but to submit my report to your immediate superior. Look at it this way, although possibly no longer active in the field I imagine you will still have a very responsible job. Better to accept this health issue gracefully rather than to insist on continuing to work as usual and putting your own life and that of others in danger.' He hated to put it so bluntly but had to state facts. He saw Latimer's face tighten, as he slipped his grey jacket back on, the movement slightly awkward resultant on the scarring left by surgery for his recent injury.

'I guess you are right, Doc! But I'm still only in my sixties, had expected to carry on much longer.' He sighed in frustration, then grasped the hand of the man who had treated him professionally for so many years and let himself out of the familiar consulting room.

Back in his comfortable Knightsbridge flat now, he stood in his study, staring down at a folder on his desk, then turning away with an exclamation of frustration, slammed the door behind him, and stalked into the living room. Here he glanced around, critically examining its few tasteful antiques blending well with the burgundy leather couch and deep swivel armchair, and the oval, walnut pedestal table, lifting his gaze to the three fine wall paintings, one an amazing seascape by an outstanding Cape Town artist, making a name for herself, the waves unfolding on the sandy shore so realistic you could almost hear their hiss and splash.

He walked over to the window, staring down at the expensive cars parked below as the motley crowd drifted past on the pavement, each individual with their own small ambitions, joys and sorrows. Was he going to become just another anonymous speck of humanity with no set purpose or challenge?

'So, this what I am left with at the end of a turbulent career?' he muttered with a wry smile, 'Nice enough flat, comfortable bank account—but what kind of a future? Undoubtedly, he'd be offered an administrative position, but in a life strained of all excitement?'

His thoughts sped to all that had happened over the last weeks. He remembered the pursuit of Malcolm Greer, the fanatic who had threatened the lives of Anna Lindstrom and her child as well as Geraldine Denton and her twin grandchildren— a momentary flash of pain, shock, as he received Greer's bullet and consciousness, left him— hospital and coming around from life-saving surgery. True he had taken longer to regain his strength after this latest injury, but there had been no indication that anything was really amiss.

He walked over to his drinks cabinet, poured a brandy and seated himself in his swivel armchair. He rolled the glass between his hands, his thoughts rioting as he recalled the meeting with Colin Denton during the progress of the Sea Giant trial, and disappointment on learning the young man had decided against joining MI5.

He shrugged. Just as well under the circumstances, as he would be unable now to train him up as once he had Paul Trent who had become his esteemed friend and colleague until his untimely death—Paul who had cared so deeply for Amber when she believed her beloved husband Robert Marsden had died in the Arctic. Well at least after Amber had grieved Paul's death, she had received the joy of her beloved husband's safe return from the Arctic, both now working smoothly together in running Dream Echo.

The brandy was smooth against his throat as he sat there absently recalling the equally fine brandy Geraldine Denton had offered him when spending a few days at her delightful Rose Cottage on discharge from the hospital. That place had been a little haven of peace!

He thought about Geraldine now, widowed taking everything on the chin, caring so devotedly for her young grandchildren and her son Colin whom for many devastating weeks she'd mourned as lying dead on the sea bed. A truly courageous lady who had dealt efficiently with kidnappers Dawson and Bickerton, villains in pay to Sea Giant, and remained calm when held for hours with the twins at gunpoint by Malcolm Greer. Their professional paths had sometimes crossed in past years when she had acquired the reputation of being a fine operative. Well, her work in MI5 was long over—as soon his could be also!

He frowned in growing frustration. So, what then, should he accept a desk job on a good salary—or throw in the towel and resign? Take up gardening like Geraldine! His friends Tom and Lottie seemed to have made the perfect balance between retirement and new interests—Lottie with her writing, Tom his garden, combining these with their dedicated input into the work at Dream Echo.

Perhaps he had been fortunate in reaching this turning point in life without suffering a major injury—death. Yet surely this heart condition that assailed him, was directly attributable to Greer's bullet! He thought savagely about the fellow now, not considering that perhaps an accumulation of stress over the years might also be to blame. Turning matters over in his mind he knew that if again offered a choice of his career in the Service or a happy marriage and a five-to-five job, he would still choose MI5!

Tom! He would visit Tom, and talk over his options with this trusted friend who had himself faced a similar situation a few years ago.

Tom looked up as Lottie came into his study with coffee and chocolate cake. They were taking a rare day off from their voluntary duties at the refuge, and Tom was sitting at his desk reading details of the recent Sea Giant trial. Lottie glanced at his computer screen.

'They deserve every minute of their sentence!' she exclaimed hotly, would have said more but the phone rang just then. Tom lifted it.

'It's Charles—wants to spend a couple of days here?' and he lifted his shaggy eyebrows and looked at her inquiringly.

'Tell him—yes! Great idea,' she replied happily. 'Find out when he wants to arrive because of meal times!'

Charles Latimer sat back in the comfortable armchair, feet stretched before him, after savouring the earlier delights of Lottie's delicious roast beef and Yorkshire pudding, followed by strawberry mousse. Tom was a lucky man to have meals such as this on a regular basis! Tom looked at him shrewdly now.

'Well, my friend—what is it that brings you here today? It's obvious you've something on your mind?' Latimer nodded slowly, and hesitated before speaking, knowing that once the change to be wrought in his life was put into words, it would become real—not just a notion to be discarded at will. They listened in silence as he explained his visit to the doctor's office, the news that had come like a bolt out of the blue.

'Did Dr Morton say how serious the condition is?' asked Tom quietly. 'I mean surely this heart condition can be controlled by drugs—perhaps an op?' Have you been feeling unwell recently, and I don't just mean the after-effects of the surgery for that bloody bullet wound that could have been fatal?' He scrutinised his friend's face seeking clues.

Latimer pressed his fingertips against each other reflectively and shook his head.

'Tiring more easily perhaps—breathless at times, but surely that's the ageing process Tom?' He awaited confirmation. It was Lottie who intervened now, watching him with sympathetic blue eyes. She leaned forward.

'I think you should consider Morton's advice, Charles. He's a fine doctor and has been looking after the firm's operatives for many years now, and knows most of you very well. He would never suggest you should step back from active duty unless he considered it vital for your safety and that of those you might be working to protect.' He looked back into her sympathetic face and nodded slowly.

'But they'll offer me a desk job—don't think I could cope with that, sending others out to face dangers I should be coping with! You both decided to leave a few years ago—how did you manage to deal with matters?' He glanced from one to the other of the couple. Tom smiled, reached out and took his wife's hand.

'I decided on retirement but left it open to help out in an emergency. Have only been called on occasionally as you know. Lottie who was never employed full-time, left before I did to concentrate on her writing. More fulfilling than gardening I suppose—but then the voluntary work we have taken up in helping young Amber run Dream Echo is completely absorbing. Perhaps you might find something of the same nature to occupy your own talents Charles, my friend!' He sighed, knowing how heart-wrenching the decision was facing Latimer.

'I don't suppose you would be interested in helping out at Dream Echo, Charles?' put in Lottie tentatively. She tried to hide a smile at the horrified look on the MI5 man's face.

'Not my scene I'm afraid,' he replied dismissively. 'Don't get me wrong, I admire the splendid work you are engaged in, assisting those poor women to recover from the violence and evil mind control and the subjugation of domestic abuse! But I would be better involved in bringing the perpetrators to justice than dealing with their victims.' Tom and Lottie exchanged glances. Lottie decided to sound him out further.

'Amber and Robert Marsden are considering opening another women's refuge in the near future. They have discovered a suitable building not far from Ravensnest, where Geraldine Denton lives,' informed Lottie now. She noticed a flash of interest in Latimer's eyes. 'It's an old monastery,' she added, 'The last of the monks died a few months ago, and the order has decided to sell. Amber heard of it from the Rev Michael Bonnet whom you know well.'

'But have the couple sufficient funds to buy such a property?' asked Latimer curiously. 'I thought they were already fully extended financially.' Tom and Lottie smiled.

'Correct,' agreed Tom now. 'But you see, Charles, the order has agreed to accept a very reasonable sum, given the use the Marsden's wish to put the old building to! The couple are looking at bank loans I believe.'

'How short are they at present?' asked Latimer slowly. He listened to the information thoughtfully, a weird idea coming into his head.

'You say the place is close to Ravensnest—that's about seventy miles from here! Surely a considerable distance for Amber to cope with when also running Dream Echo?'

'Amber is an amazing woman,' reassured Lottie, 'And Robert now shows as much dedication and enthusiasm for the work as his lovely young wife. No doubt they will install someone equally dedicated to running the new refuge. Hopefully, they may receive support from the council. It's a disgrace that the need for refuges so far outruns that presently provided.' She rose to her feet to prepare coffee while giving the men a quiet moment to discuss Charles's future. As she lifted the decanter she wondered at his curiosity about the old monastery. She must ask Tom if they could drive over and take a look at the place.

Geraldine looked out of the window. Those heavy storm clouds promised snow she thought. It was certainly cold enough and she pulled her dressing gown closer. Only two days to Christmas now and the twins were full of excitement. Colin had already bought and potted a splendid tall, bushy pine to stand in the living room and they planned to dress it tomorrow evening. She still missed Anna and little Susan. It would be so wonderful if mother and daughter could join them for Christmas, but a tentative phone call had dashed her hopes. Anna would be needed at Dream Echo at this special time.

Later that morning as she was just laying out the ingredients for her Christmas cake, her mobile rang. It was Lottie Lanscombe.

'Was just thinking about you, Geraldine dear. It's quite a while since we saw each other, so wondering how you would feel about joining us here at Ivy Cottage for Boxing Day, with Colin, the twins and the kittens—and staying for a few days?' She paused for an answer.

Geraldine thought quickly. This would give her a chance to see Anna—and just as importantly for Colin to do so! Although Anna had said she would visit them occasionally, so far this had not happened. It would also be good to see Tom and Lottie again.

'Charles Latimer is coming too. He hasn't been too well recently.'

'Nothing serious I hope?' exclaimed Geraldine in quick concern.

'He is retiring from the firm. I'll say no more now. So, will you come?'

'If you are sure you have enough room for us all—then yes! Look forward to it!' She slipped the mobile back into her pocket, her face troubled. It was not that she had ever been close to Charles Latimer—but had always admired him and had recently become quite fond of him. Now it seemed he was retiring from the work he loved for health reasons. He had certainly looked far from his usual self when visiting them for a few days on leaving the hospital, which was understandable considering the severity of the wound he had sustained from Greer's bullet that had almost cost him his life.

'Something troubling you, Mum?' asked a quiet voice.

'Colin! Not exactly troubling—but I had a call from Lottie a few minutes ago. We are all invited to spend Boxing day at Ivy Cottage. Charles Latimer will be there—he's retiring it seems—hasn't been too well.' She saw the surprise on Colin's face.

'He appeared OK when I saw him in London during the trial. Perhaps it just as well I didn't accept that position with MI5—it was the opportunity of working with him that attracted.' He glanced at all the ingredients on the kitchen table. 'What's all this then?'

'It will be our Christmas cake if I get peace to make it! You are happy enough about joining Tom and Lottie on Boxing day and for a few days afterwards?' He nodded and his face broke into a warm smile and she guessed he was thinking of Anna.

Twins Charles and Melanie were reluctant to leave the tree they had been helping Geraldine dress, now glittering with fragile baubles, tinsel, and fairy lights. As they climbed the stairs, the children were aware that it would be the first Christmas without their mother. They still missed her deeply much as they loved Granny, but with the resilience of youth accepted their new life.

Snow fell early that Christmas morning, the first whirling flakes giving way to dense blanket of white sweeping in on a blustery East wind. Two hours later Geraldine stared out at the garden where the twins were busily building a snowman, all the exciting gifts Santa had brought them put temporarily aside. She smiled as she watched Colin helping Charles and Melanie to set the snowman's head firmly in place, while kittens Pyrites and Patches ventured gingerly into this strange white world. Hopefully the roads would have been cleared by tomorrow morning for their trip to the Lanscombes.

They had found the roads well gritted, their journey easier than anticipated. It was just over two hours later that Tom and Lottie came hurrying down the pathway of Ivy Cottage to greet them, had seen Geraldine's car arrive, before carefully turning into the space between the garden wall and nearby historic church with its soaring tower. Soon the visitors were sitting round the cosy woodfire, as Geraldine recalled the comfortable living room from her many visits there years back, whilst working with the couple in MI5. As for Colin, his own brief stay at Ivy Cottage more recent, he immediately felt at home. They were chatting animatedly together when the door opened quietly and Charles Latimer's tall, commanding figure appeared. He greeted the newcomers warmly, smiling at the twins. Geraldine scanned him curiously. Was there a new stiffness in his bearing, then their eyes met and she relaxed.

After a wonderful Boxing Day dinner, the children reluctantly retired to bed, allowing the five adults to speak freely at last. Latimer plunged directly into the subject he knew was exercising their minds—his retirement.

'I gather Tom and Lottie have given you my news? 'he said abruptly, glancing from Geraldine to her son.

'That you may be leaving MI5?' said Geraldine softly. 'I understand it is for health reasons Charles?' He saw the sympathy in her quiet grey gaze as he nodded grudging agreement.

'Yes, my dear. A shock to put it mildly. I have been swithering whether to accept a desk job—or take early retirement. Have almost decided on the latter!'

'Not an easy decision I know,' replied Geraldine reflectively, 'But strangely stepping back from the firm can offer its own blessings.' He looked at her disbelievingly.

'What for instance?'

'Learning to look at others without suspicion—developing new hobbies. Taking time to enjoy music—gardening, all those things there was never time for in an earlier frenetic lifestyle!' She watched him questioningly. He nodded slowly, not wholly convinced.

'Or, perhaps an unusual challenge?' he said. 'Tom and Lottie drove me over to see an old monastery yesterday—not too far from Ravensnest! Sadly, the last of the monks passed away recently, and with no new novices, the Abbot has reluctantly decided sell the property!' He smiled at Geraldine. 'Well, Amber and Robert are interested in acquiring the monastery, plan to transform it into a second Dream Echo!' Geraldine's grey eyes lit up in surprise.

'I know the place—beautiful old stone building reputed to date back to Medieval times! Quite extensive grounds too. Certainly, its remote location would make it perfect for a refuge,' she exclaimed, then paused. 'Will the young couple manage to raise the purchase price? It's likely to be hefty?' and she glanced at the Lanscombe's inquiringly, before turning back to Latimer. 'And what is your own interest in all this, Charles?' she asked.

'It connects with your last question! I have money stashed away in the bank more than I'm unlikely to need in the foreseeable future—so considering donating a fair amount to this new refuge. When my late colleague Paul Trent died on duty three years ago, he left a large sum to Amber Marsden to help in the ongoing upkeep of Dream Echo! I believe Paul would have approved of my assistance now in the second stage of this project.'

'But that's extremely generous of you, Charles,' exclaimed Geraldine softly, the Lanscombes adding their own delighted surprise.

'I thought you were not interested in any involvement in the refuge?' said Tom, remembering a recent conversation. Latimer shrugged.

'Not actively—but supporting the work financially is different, perhaps in security too! A lot must depend on the agreed asking price for the building,' he replied and Tom nodded.

'Right—plus overall cost in modernising the monastery—painting and decorating—new electric wiring—purchase of furniture—security etc. Lottie and I were closely involved in setting this up for Amber at Dream Echo,' explained Tom as Lottie smiled reminiscently.

'It was a very exciting time, watching that cold, austere, old mansion house transformed into the vital, caring place that has already brought healing into so many damaged lives,' she added softly.

Colin Denton listening intently leaned forward now.

'I wonder—could I be involved in this project in some way too?' he inquired now. He turned to Latimer. 'I need another job, but not in the oil industry! Maybe I was wrong to turn down the chance to join MI5 you offered, and Charles, I will always be grateful to you for that opportunity!' and he smiled at Latimer, before proceeding, 'Look, I understand that I'm to receive a fairly large sum in recompense for all that my family and I underwent at the hands of Sea Giant. How would it be if I put some of this into the kitty for Dream Echo 2?' He glanced around the others. 'Perhaps I could be of practical use as well—in security for instance? I know that for obvious reasons, most of those involved in running Dream Echo are women, but...?' He paused, glancing at the Lanscombes. It was Tom who replied.

'Colin, the work we contribute to Dream Echo is purely voluntary—and whereas any financial contribution you might offer, would be welcomed with open arms, I suggest that what you need on a personal level is a proper job to provide for yourself and the twins.' Colin sighed knowing it was true. They continued to talk for a further two hours in a conversation that would form the basis of the project yet to be named.

Before the evening broke up and they sought their beds, Colin drew Tom aside and to ask a question in casual tones.

'I had wondered if Anna and little Susan might join the party for this get together.'

'We will see that they receive an invitation while you are here, Colin,' replied Tom with a twinkle in his eyes.

The following day Tom and Lottie having left their guests at the cottage, arrived at the refuge and were now sitting in Amber's office smiling as they watched the rapturous expression on her lovely face, her eyes filling with tears of joy on receiving the wonderful news! Just so amazing that due to the generosity of friends they could raise the asking price for the old monastery—plus sufficient to transform it into a new refuge.

'I can hardly believe it's true,' she gasped in tremulous delight as the couple confirmed it, Lottie hugging her, and giving details of that recent meeting.

'I believe you should be able to open official negotiations very soon,' assured Tom confidently. 'Charles Latimer says he's able to transfer a substantial sum immediately and Colin intends to donate his contribution as soon as he receives recompense for all he and his family suffered through the evil machinations of Sea Giant!' It was as he said these words that they heard a startled exclamation from behind them, had not noticed the door opening. Anna Lindstrom stood there and had obviously overheard the news.

'Oh, I do apologise—I should have knocked, but you said to come to the office once all was quiet.' She stared at Amber. 'Did I hear Tom say that your plans for the old monastery are possible, will be going ahead?' Amber nodded, and pointed to a chair.

'Yes—isn't it absolutely wonderful! It will take time, an enormous amount of planning, but having already transformed this place will make working on the next project that much easier.' Her heart was almost too full to say more—her dream soon about to come true through the unexpected financial help of Charles and Colin.

'You understand that all of this must remain secret, Anna,' said Tom quietly. Anna inclined her head, wondering why he had thought it necessary to make the remark but realised she was privileged to be taken in their confidence over this exciting step forward, another refuge to bring future help and hope to many more terrified abused women.

'You can rely on me,' she replied quietly. 'Anything I can do personally to help in the new refuge you have only to ask,' and she smiled at Amber, then unable to contain her curiosity burst out with a sudden question. 'Colin Marsden is helping to fund the project?'

It was Lottie who answered after first glancing at Tom.

'Yes, Anna—Colin and Charles Latimer are both contributing—and Tom and I helping out a little as well. Incidentally Anna, would you like to join us for dinner tonight, bring Susan of course—Geraldine and the twins are staying for a few days, as are Colin and Charles.' As she mentioned Colin's name she saw Anna blush and lower her eyes.

'I would love to come—if Amber can spare me?' she said softly.

'Yes, you go and enjoy yourself,' said Amber, exchanging a glance with Lottie. 'It will do you good to have a break and meet up with your friends again.'

Little Susan threw her arms round her mother in delight when she learned they were visit Tom and Lottie's cottage that evening—and that Geraldine and Colin and the twins were staying there for a few days.

'Will my kitten be there too?' She fixed hopeful blue eyes on Anna.

'I simply don't know darling. We will have to wait and see,' was the light reply. Now that it was time to get into her car to make the short journey to Ivy Cottage, Anna found her heart beating faster. Colin was going to be there. She hadn't seen him since leaving Bramble Cottage shortly after the terrible events in which Malcolm Greer the man who had controlled and terrorised her for four interminable years had bled to death on the road from a bullet wound—only some few yards distance from the cottage. Memories of all that had led up to the event that had finally set her free from the unbalanced individual who had attempted her own life, flashed back into her mind as she wondered whether she had made the right decision in leaving Bramble Cottage where she had been so happy and enjoyed the friendship of her kindly neighbour Geraldine—but her home sullied by the violence that had occurred there.

Yes, she enjoyed her work at the refuge, found deep satisfaction in being part of the group of wonderful selfless individuals who welcomed a nonending stream of terrified, traumatised women who finally made escape from their abuser and sought sanctuary at Dream Echo. And now it seemed Amber Marsden was to open a second refuge—apparently situated only a few miles from the village where Anna had spent happy months in the cottage next door to that of Geraldine and the twins—and Colin Denton.

She rang the doorbell of Ivy Cottage as Susan's hand tightened in hers, excitement on her young face as the door opened and Lottie welcomed them in, took their coats and led them into the comfortable sitting room. Anna barely registered the glittering Christmas tree and beautifully decorated room, with its log fire crackling in the grate. Instead her blue eyes sped around those seated there and now rose to their feet in greeting—Tom, Charles Latimer—the twins, Geraldine—and Colin!' Anna smiled back at them.

'It's a tight squeeze in here, Anna dear,' Lottie explained. 'Perhaps you could sit next to Geraldine—and Susan you can join the twins on that other pouffe.' Without waiting for further invitation Susan slipped down on the carpet beside Melanie and Charles, who threw their arms about her, hugging her ecstatically. Suddenly Susan noticed the two kittens hiding under a chair and uttered a squeal of delight.

'Granny brought them here in a basket,' explained Melanie. 'They were quite noisy in the car!' Susan stared at her kitten with tears of joy in her eyes, and reached down for it.

'Patches has grown bigger—so has your Pyrites,' she exclaimed in surprise.

Geraldine smiled watching the little scene. She embraced Anna, holding the girl back from her as she examined her.

'I've really missed you, dear,' she said warmly. 'Bramble Cottage seems so very lonely without you. It's absolutely wonderful seeing you again!'

'Hallo Anna,' called another well-remembered voice, and Anna turned her head to see Colin Denton watching her quizzically, as he approached. 'You are looking well—and as beautiful as ever.' His eyes examined the golden-haired woman who had constantly filled his thoughts since he'd returned from London following the trial, only to learn of her precipitate departure. 'Are you enjoying your work at Dream Echo?' He drew closer and bending gave her a light kiss on the cheek. 'May I wish you a belated Happy Christmas!' he exclaimed. As he straightened he noticed that her face had lost that tense look—she seemed different in a way he could not yet define.

'Yes, I'm enjoying my work,' she said in a low voice. 'I am extremely fortunate to be working for Amber Marsden, who is such an inspiration as are the rest of her special team,' she paused. 'What are your own plans, Colin?' she queried. 'I know you were considering joining the civil service a few months ago?'.

'Decided it wasn't for me.,' he replied lightly, staring at her admiringly, had only seen her casually dressed in shirt and jeans in the past. She looked very attractive tonight in a close fitting sapphire blue dress, flared at the hem, blonde hair drawn back under a matching headband, as her blue eyes examined him unfathomably.

'I knew I was right,' he murmured in a low voice.

'Right, Colin—right about what?' she asked curiously. They did not realise that the four other adults in the room were glancing at them.

'About you—us being right together,' he said softly. 'One of these days I am going to ask you to do me the great honour of consenting to become my wife! You see, Anna—I love you.' She looked back at him in bewilderment.

'You must have been drinking! Either that or it is a poor joke!' But despite her shocked protest, he had seen the soft expression that briefly flashed in her eyes. He took her hand in his, raised it to his lips.

'I have never been more serious. Alright, this may not have been the right time or place to express myself in this way—but seeing you again like this, I realise how deep my feelings are for you. When Lottie invited us to make this visit, I was over the moon to think I would see you again.' He continued to hold her hand, felt her fingers relax under his.

'But you are still mourning your Mary,' she said gently, as she realised he was serious. 'We have both experienced deep trauma over the recent past, Colin. Perhaps as time passes we may discuss this again, but not now!' She released her hand from his and turned away, walked across to Geraldine and perched on the side of her armchair. Her cheeks were burning with suppressed emotion. Geraldine who had watched the brief meeting between Anna and her son, was bursting with curiosity as to the cause of the girl's obvious agitation.

'The twins have missed your little daughter so very much. Look at them laughing together there—it's almost as though they had never been apart!' she said quietly Anna nodded as she directed her own gaze to the children happily playing with the excited kittens.

'Susan was very upset a being parted from Patches at first—and even more at leaving all of you behind. But I had to make a difficult decision, Geraldine—was distraught after the horror of all that happened at Bramble Cottage—had to get away. Also, I knew I had to provide a secure future for myself and Susan—and I love my work at the refuge!' She spoke feelingly, but Geraldine recognised a defensive tone in her voice.

'You needed to get away after the shock you endured. I know this—but hopefully you may return to Ravensnest in the near future. Lottie mentioned that you are to become involved in the planned new refuge—the old monastery?' she probed. 'You realise it is only a few miles away from the village?' She paused as she saw Charles Latimer leaning towards them from the settee.

'Anna—are you definite about moving to the new refuge when the time comes?' he asked.

'Why yes, Charles—if Amber wishes. It will be a tremendous challenge to be involved in a completely new sanctuary for abused women. I am completely dedicated to the work, realise how severe the problem of domestic abuse truly is—at least one in four women experiencing it at some stage in their lives.' She returned his interrogative gaze unwaveringly. 'I believe you are helping to make it all possible financially. That is truly noble of you,' she said softly. He nodded slowly.

'Yes, my dear. It will be a delight to use some excess funds in this way—but I am not the only one involved. Colin is to make a substantial sum available too—and Tom and Lottie also adding their own financial help to Amber and Robert Marsden. Have you seen the old monastery yet?'

'No—but I would love to,' she replied eagerly.

'Well, why not ask Colin to drive you over there tomorrow to examine the place. I assure you it's a wonderful old building, but will need a lot of preparatory work. You could leave Susan here with Geraldine and the twins.'

'Oh—I don't know,' she prevaricated. 'I will be needed at Dream Echo!'

'Oh, don't worry about that, Anna,' said Lottie. 'Tom and I will go over to the refuge to help out in the morning. I know Geraldine will be happy to look after Susan together with her grandchildren.' She looked at Geraldine for confirmation, which was instantly given.

'But Colin may have other plans,' said Anna awkwardly. But Colin merely raised an amused eyebrow.

'Nonsense. What about leaving at about eleven tomorrow—will that suit you Anna?' he asked. 'I'm very curious to see the monastery myself.' She found herself agreeing reluctantly, saw the warm satisfaction in his eyes. The dinner that followed was a delicious turkey roast, followed by mince tart and cream, afterwards toasts made to the new project. The evening came to an end happily, as Anna got into her car and drove back to the refuge, leaving Susan to sleep overnight with the twins. As she got into bed herself that night, her thoughts were centred on Colin Denton, his declaration of love and desire to marry her in the future.

'I can always ring up tomorrow and say I am unwell, will not be able to visit the monastery,' she murmured firmly as she fell asleep. But the next morning she dismissed the excuse. Amber gave her blessing to Anna's trip to see the monastery—saying she should take the entire day off.

She sat quietly in Colin's dark green Jeep, his concentration focussed on negotiating the many icy patches on the road due to freezing temperature overnight, and she began to relax as the miles sped by Their conversation was light, until he questioned her about her work at the refuge.

'I really do love working there—it has given a purpose to my existence,' she said softly. 'Each woman helped across the threshold, is badly traumatised, often suffering severe injuries and has a different story to tell. It would break your heart to listen to them Colin!' He heard the emotion in her voice, saw her hands tighten in her lap. He reached out a hand, touched her arm reassuringly.

'A few months back, when I stayed with Tom and Lottie, they told me a great deal about the cruel and cowardly behaviour of some men towards those who should only receive love and protection from them. It fills me with disgust this has apparently been going on for centuries, accepted as normal. This is why I offered a little financial help when I heard that Amber wanted to open another refuge! I would love to become involved in the actual running of the new project, but Tom explained that it would have to be on a voluntary basis—that I would be better advised to seek other work to enable me to support my family. He is right of course.' As he spoke he drew up at a layby, and reached for his map.

'Is it much further,' inquired Anna, glancing around at the beautiful countryside through which they had been progressing, the rolling fields sparkling with hoar frost under the thin winter sunshine, patched with wooded areas. It looked idyllic. Colin looked up from the map.

'No Anna—we're almost there. I thought it looked familiar—you remember where we turned off at the junction from the familiar road to Ravensnest—must be parallel with the village now. According to the map there should be a private lane leading off to the right around the next bend. It leads to the monastery!'

They drew up outside the arched gateway, got out of the Jeep and walked up the pathway to the grey stoned building that soared serenely ahead. Colin knocked at the heavy oak door, which was opened by an elderly man in a brown cassock, who looked at them inquiringly.

'Colin Denton and Anna Lindstrom—we're friends of Amber Marsden,' said Colin. 'She suggested we might look around.' The man nodded, smiled benignly and beckoned them in.

'I'm Friar Jerome—caring for the monastery until the new owners take over. If would care to follow me, I'll show you around.' They thanked the elderly Friar and entered behind him sensing a stillness and peace envelop them as they walked curiously around, passing through the refectory, offices, eventually entering the chapel, its ancient carved altar still in place, here they paused and sat quietly beneath the Friar's gentle gaze. They also saw the kitchens—and the many small dormitories.

They actually spent an hour exploring the old building where over long centuries past, men had withdrawn from the world, worshipping God in prayer, tending the surrounding gardens and small orchard. At last they thanked the old Friar, who escorted them down the path towards the ached gateway, signing the cross over them as they got into the Jeep. They waved back at him as Colin drove off, glancing at each other now as they exchanged thoughts.

'It will need a great deal of work to bring it up the standard of Dream Echo, but I just love it!' Anna exclaimed. Colin saw her blue eyes were shining with excitement.

'Yes—it's very special,' he replied quietly. 'I'm glad to have seen the monastery, can imagine just how suitable it will become as a refuge once the alteration work has taken place. It's wonderfully remote too—nothing around for miles apart from a few farms.'

'I wonder who Amber will engage to run it, when the time comes,' Anna mused. 'It will be a tremendous challenge for whoever she selects—and I'll do my very best to support them!' He heard the enthusiasm in her voice.

'You are really up for it then, Anna?'

'Most definitely,' she exclaimed. 'I can see my future opening up before me—but what of you, Colin? Have you any plans for a new career?' she probed, then wished she had not asked the question, recalling his last night's unexpected offer of marriage. So far today he had made no mention of anything of a personal nature, and although relieved she also felt unaccountably disappointed. She knew she was deeply attracted to Colin—had missed him and also his dear mother Geraldine and the twins. Young Susan had missed all of them too and still seemed unsettled at Dream Echo. She remembered her little daughter's delight at meeting with Charles and Melanie again last night, her joy at seeing her kitten again.

'No definite plans as yet—but working on it. Look, we're approaching the main road that leads on into the village. How would you like to stop by Rose Cottage for a cup of tea, before the drive back?' The suggestion took Anna by surprise, as before she could answer they reached the junction, and he swung the car towards Ravensnest.

She walked up the pathway to Geraldine's familiar blue door, glancing across almost apprehensively to what had been her own once beloved home, Bramble Cottage. Colin unlocked the front door and she followed him as he made for the kitchen. As they sat there sipping the hot tea and eating a slice of Geraldine's fruit cake, Anna felt herself relax. It was almost as though she had never left—the months slipping away. She realised Colin was watching her with an understanding smile.

'I shouldn't have gone, should I,' she said. 'Yet if I hadn't, I would not now be embarking on a career where I will have the privilege of helping many other women into a brighter and safer future.' She spoke softly and from the heart.

'And the location of the new refuge where you will be pursuing the work you love will be less than a fifteen minutes' drive from Rose Cottage—and your own home!' he said. 'Surely this is no coincidence. Sometimes life presents us with the most amazing answer to complex problems.' He rose to his feet, took her hands and led her towards the window. 'Look over there—Bramble Cottage, which you made such a warm and welcoming home. Won't you consider returning to it Anna darling?' She stared across at it wordlessly.

He slipped an arm about her. 'Last night I blundered out a proposal of marriage to you—and yes, it is less than a year since my dear Mary died at the hands of those murdering Sea Giant operatives. But so much has happened since then, so many changes, dangers faced. But like a golden strand linking past to presence has been your entrance into my life and that of my children. I truly love you, Anna—so will you make me the happiest of men and become my wife?' he asked passionately.

'I need time to think, Colin,' she began, then felt herself in his arms, stiffened as brief flash of the revulsion she had experienced at Greer's touch shot through her, replaced almost instantly by a longing to feel his lips over hers. He was stroking her hair, then holding her closer, as with a sob she raised her face to his and opened her mouth to his kiss.

How they had arrived on the sitting room couch neither could remember afterwards—but their lovemaking that followed would remain a treasured memory throughout life. Now at last Anna knew she was free of the past, could give her heart to a man she truly loved.

She gasped now, glanced up at Geraldine's pendulum wall clock as it chimed seven.

'What is it?' he asked,

'Look at the time—the others will be expecting us back—wonder what is keeping us!'

'I suppose we must go,' said Colin regretfully. 'Come on then, darling.' They tidied themselves, locked the cottage door behind them and hurried outside where the pale glimmer of stars now cloaked the heavens in the frosty night. As the Jeep sped smoothly along, they began to make tentative plans for the future.

'What about a spring wedding,' he suggested. Anna considered it, nodded approval.

'May is usually a lovely month—or June,' she said softly.

'I wonder if you would like a honeymoon on the Isle of Skye? I would like you to meet the wonderful couple who opened their home to me there.'

'Skye—that's in the Hebrides,' she said. 'I've heard its incredibly beautiful, soaring mountains and deep dreaming lochs. I read a book about it.'

Tom and Lottie looked at each other in relief as they heard the Jeep drawing up.

'Thank goodness, I was beginning to fear they might have had an accident,' breathed Lottie, and surprised a smile on Geraldine's face and looked at her interrogatively. 'You obviously didn't?' she probed.

'No, my Colin is a good driver,' replied his mother lightly.' They paused as Tom hurried to open the door to welcome the latecomers back.

'Come in out of the cold! Well—what did you make of the old monastery,' he asked the pair as they hung their jackets on the hallstand. He noticed Anna's face was flushed, Colin looking at her tenderly as they followed him into the sitting room.

'We both think the monastery will make a splendid refuge—a wonderful old building, seems structurally sound, suitably remote, and may not need as much alteration as you fear,' said Colin, glancing around the room. 'Where are the children?' he asked.

'All three in bed now,' said Geraldine. 'They have had a wonderful day playing with the kittens, then there was fun with Ludo and Snakes and Ladders. They have been as good as gold,' she reassured, as her eyes examined Anna's face curiously, and guessed intuitively something had happened between the girl and her son as the others plied them with questions

'You really like the old place then?' confirmed Charles Latimer, leaning forward in his chair with satisfaction. 'Good! Since we all approve the sooner we get to work on reconstruction the better. I suggest we meet up with Amber and Robert tomorrow.'

'You spent a long time at the monastery,' queried Lottie now.

'Well, after old Friar Ambrose had given us an interesting tour of the building and grounds— we dropped in at Rose Cottage, lost track of time,' Colin explained. Then he grinned and reached for Anna's hand. 'I would like to announce that we are to be married,' he said. There was a moment's amazed silence, then congratulations poured towards them as Geraldine rose and took them both into her arms,

'Colin, my darling son—and you Anna who are already like a daughter to me, I cannot be happier! This is wonderful, wonderful news!' Lottie glanced across at Geraldine, wondering if that her friend had already guessed the situation between the couple, while Tom went to the drinks cabinet and produced a bottle of champagne. Glasses were passed around and toasts made. Lottie glanced at Anna.

'I doubt if either of you have had anything to eat! We have already had dinner, but I have kept yours, just need to heat it up,' she smiled, practical as usual. 'Anna, come into the kitchen with me and help me put it in the microwave.' Anna nodded and slipped out with her. Lottie pointed to a kitchen chair. 'Now young lady, you sit down and tell me all about it,' said Lottie. 'How did it all happen my dear?' Anna spread her hands out. How could she explain the lifechanging episode at the cottage, the sudden knowledge that Malcom Greer's hold over her inner self had at last been severed. That she was free—free to love and be loved, to lead a life without fear.

'I managed to wipe Greer out of my mind forever,' she said. 'I knew I loved Colin, but was afraid I wouldn't be able to respond to him normally. When you have suffered abuse, Lottie—it's not only the physical body that needs healing. You know this from your work with the abused women who come so regularly to Dream Echo's door. It can leave a knot of deep anxiety causing you withdraw from all that's normal between man and woman. Tonight, I finally became free of fear—and can look forward to marrying a man I truly love.' Lottie put her arms around Anna, and held her close, deeply touched by her words.

'Anna—you have endured so much, turned your deep hurt into desire to help other abused women face a happier future. That you are now to be married to Colin is just so wonderful. He will make you a fine, caring husband, dear. I am so happy for you!' She released Anna and pointed to the two plates on the table. 'Let's get that food heated up now!' she said.

Chapter Eighteen

Amber Marsden looked thoughtfully at Lottie as she heard the news—Anna was to wed Colin Denton! She was delighted to think the girl who had undergone so much
trauma, was to find new happiness. But how would this affect her own tentative plans involving Anna?

'Do you think it will alter her intention to remain working at Dream Echo—and possibly becoming involved in the new refuge once the old monastery is transformed into our second refuge,' she asked quietly. Lottie smiled and shook her head emphatically.

'No fear of that Amber dear. She is full of enthusiasm for the new refuge, as is Colin who drove her over there yesterday and was also greatly impressed. You do realise Rose Cottage where he currently lives with his mother Geraldine and the twins, is next door to Bramble Cottage, Anna's rented home?'

'Yes—It had occurred to me,' said Amber lightly. Lottie glanced curiously at the attractive young owner of Dream Echo as the girl continued, 'I had already considered asking Anna run the new refuge. It would be helpful if her future husband Colin might be interested in joining her in the work which will need energy and complete dedication. Do you think Colin shows these qualities, Lottie?' Her unusual topaz eyes watched Lottie's kindly face seeking an answer.

'Strange you should ask this. As you know, when Charles Latimer offered to put up a substantial sum to help purchase the monastery, Colin made a similar commitment to donate some of the compensation money he is soon to receive. Well he also suggested he would be interested in taking an active part in the running of the refuge, asked Tom if he thought it was possible.' Lottie shrugged as she continued, 'Tom explained that the work that we both do here is voluntary, whereas Colin needs a paid job that will enable him to maintain his little family. Colin accepted this at once. But it was interesting that his thoughts were focussed in such a direction.'

'Well, if Colin was serious—I believe we could manage a reasonable salary, provided I can obtain a grant from the council.' Amber's fingers toyed with the amethyst pendant she wore at the neck of her white mohair sweater. Lottie looked affectionately at this girl still in her early twenties, so young to have created the wonderful refuge that had opened its doors to so many terrified, exhausted abused women and their children, offering a place of safety and healing. Now with the support of her husband Robert, she was about to enter upon the challenge of opening a second refuge—nor would it stop there, thought Lottie admiringly.

'What is your own opinion of Colin?' asked Amber.

'From what I have observed, Colin Denton is a courageous, honourable, determined man and devoted father. If you are seriously considering employing him, then why not invite him to spend some voluntary time here at Dream Echo. Perhaps he could learn the ropes from your husband Robert?' She leaned forward and took Amber's hand. 'Personally, I think Anna and Colin would prove a perfect pair to run the new refuge—once the purchase is complete and alterations taken place.'

Amber stared back into Lottie's kindly blue gaze, thinking of all the good advice and support she had received from this amazing writer, whose earlier years like those of her husband Tom had been involved in that special part of the civil service known as MI5. She gave Lottie an affectionate hug.

'Thanks for that, Lottie dear. Incidentally, the legal agreements for purchase of the monastery are being completed later today! All has been surprisingly easy—almost as though it was meant to be!' she exclaimed.

'I truly believe that you were guided by God,' said Lottie quietly. Amber nodded.

'I know.' She sat thinking for a moment. 'What you suggested about Robert preparing Colin through the essentials of what the work entails should he agree to work with Anna in running the new refuge is a great idea. But before he can become involved it's vital he understands exactly what trauma those who come to our door endure—the huge scale of domestic abuse worldwide—the previous acceptance by women that it had to be a hidden thing—endured!'

'Amber, even now I find the extent of what goes on behind closed doors something to shudder at—so completely abhorrent. To think that one in four women will experience it at some point within their lives just monstrous!' and she shook her head in frustration. 'But I certainly feel deeply privileged to be able to assist you here in my own small way,' and she smiled at Amber.

'Lottie dear, you have given your help unstintingly since Dream Echo became a reality, as has Tom—and your quiet wisdom supported me through many a problem. Well here we are about to open another refuge and I'm immensely excited at the prospect of all those extra desperate women we will be able to help!' Her eyes were damp with emotion for a moment, her attention focussing back on the present as the phone rang.

'Amber—it's Babs Chamberlain. Have you room for another guest? Kate Wilson is a forty- one years old business woman—was good looking before her partner broke her ribs and slashed her face with a razor. I've just collected her from hospital—police looking for the abuser now, but Kate terrified he may find her. I know it's just after Christmas, but…?'

'It's fine. Bring her here, Babs. I'll have a room ready for her.' She put the phone down and glanced at Lottie. 'Well here we go again, another poor seriously hurt woman! Perhaps Anna and my mother will help you keep watch over Kate once we have settled her in—so that I can meet with the legal types coming with the official paperwork for—for, Peace Haven!'

'Peace haven?' queried Lottie. 'Ah—you have decided on a name for the new refuge? Peace Haven—I love it!' and she tried it again on her tongue. Amber gave a soft laugh.

'It came out of nowhere—but I do believe it sounds right! Listen Lottie, as you know I've been exploring an idea on how we can disguise the true purpose of Peace Haven. People have comfortably accepted the notion that Dream Echo is some sort of Artist's commune. Well, we will put it about that Peace Haven is run by a private religious order where people bruised on life's journey can book in for a few weeks of quiet and contemplation.' She glanced tentatively at Lottie. 'What do you think?'

'Perfect! Why not contact that wonderful nun you met at her son Bruce Trent's funeral? As I remember she was a very unusual woman with as you personally experienced, a strange healing ministry. She might agree to help.'

Amber nodded soberly, recollecting the sad time when believing Robert to have died in the Arctic, she had briefly loved Bruce Trent. They had planned to marry—then within days of their decision came the violent death of the MI5 operative. Amber had met his mother at his graveside. That had been three years ago—had not seen her since.

'Lottie—it's a good idea! We will discuss it later—must dash now and prepare for Kate's arrival—get Anna to help me. You stay here in the office and mount the phone.'

And from that short conversation plans began to unfold. Anna was quietly assisting Amber as they checked all was in readiness for the anticipated new admission, when Amber looked at her quizzically.

'I believe congratulations are in order, Anna? Lottie tells me that you are to marry Colin Denton. I am truly happy for you—and I would very much like to meet your future husband.' Anna coloured as she met Amber' gaze steadily.

'Thank you Amber. Yes, it's true. Yesterday we spent quite some time exploring the monastery with Friar Ambrose, were immediately able to see the potential in the lovely old building. I would love to be part of the team you will put in place to run the new refuge.' Her blue eyes met Amber's calm gaze hopefully.

'And how would Colin view your working there once married?' asked Amber gently.

'We discussed it late last night—and he definitely approves the idea. His mother Geraldine who has become a dear friend of mine, will happily look after little Susan together with Colin's own twin children. You see, once he finds work, it's possible he will be away at certain times. It's all up in the air at the moment! I'm still on cloud nine, hardly able to believe all this is happening after experiencing so much trauma and violence in the recent past,' she admitted and Amber smiled understandingly.

'Anna, we need to talk once we have a quiet moment. Now, I think we've finished in here. The lady we are expecting has severe injuries, we'll need to get the doctor to call and assess her—and check any medication the hospital may have supplied.'

It was two days later that the small party arrived at Dream Echo's front door, to be received by Amber and Robert Marsden, Anna at their side. It was the first time that either Geraldine or Colin had actually seen the elegant old mansion house the greater part of which had been adapted into a busy refuge for abused women and their children. Now as they entered the couples beautifully furnished, welcoming sitting-room that looked out on the long driveway, they had an immediate sense of peace and tranquillity. It was not what they had expected, although completely familiar to Charles Latimer who accompanied them on this visit. Tom and Lottie had remained at Ivy Cottage to care for the twins and young Susan who was making an overnight stay with Charles and Melanie—and the kittens.

While Robert poured drinks for their visitors, Geraldine sank down in one of the comfortable armchairs. Glancing around she recognised the care that had been spent in creating this charming setting that was so much at odds with Dream Echo's true function. No one entering this room would suspect that the mansion housed a busy refuge. Charles Latimer was watching her face.

'It's quite something, isn't it,' he said quietly. 'I was privileged to meet Amber Williams as she was then, not long after she inherited the house. It was at the time that Robert was assumed dead in the Arctic.' He called across to Robert who was making himself known to Colin, with Anna looking on. 'Just telling Geraldine about the early days here—

before Amber turned the house into a refuge!' Robert turned with an amused grin on his face.

'It certainly was a shock when I arrived home where I was believed dead, to find my house so strangely transformed into a refuge—but I have only the greatest admiration and respect for my lovely young wife's achievement in creating this wonderful haven for abused women. I gladly decided to become part of the team and have never regretted it.' He looked considerately at Colin now. 'How do you feel about Anna's wish to take a position at our second refuge once it's up and running? I'm guessing you must approve, as together with Charles you're so generously contributing financially to the purchase of the monastery.'

The two men were standing beneath a dramatic painting above the mantlepiece, an amazing seascape. Robert noticed Colin's interest. 'That was painted by Amber's mother Gwenda Williams—as were these others!' and he indicated other remarkable canvasses.

'Gwenda Williams—why she's famous I believe,' exclaimed Colin, 'And looking at this beautiful work, deservedly so! Robert, you asked me my feelings about Anna working at the new refuge once it is ready. I can only say she will have my full support. I only wish I could become involved myself. Already felt this way before we made that visit to the monastery and met Friar Ambrose. Then when exploring the place, I had this strange feeling of déjà vu. But perhaps not that I had been there before—but that it was to become part of my life! Impossible, as I realise now. Eventually I am going to have to find work to support my future wife and our children.,' and he shrugged philosophically. The other man gave him an encouraging smile.

'Who knows what may happen in the near future, Colin! Just one question at the present time. Would you be interested in working alongside Anna, should it become possible? There wouldn't be a princely salary, but…?' He watched Colin's face, saw delight spread across it.

'Man—that would be absolutely marvellous,' Colin exclaimed incredulously. 'But how would I fit in—I mean, I'm guessing by its very nature a refuge is run mostly by women?' They were so intent on their conversation, they had not noticed Amber's approach. She overheard their exchange.

'So, you really are interested then Colin?' she asked quietly. 'I had a private talk with Anna earlier, sounded her out as to whether she would be prepared to run Peace Haven—yes, that will be the name of the new refuge—with you at her side! She was very enthusiastic at the suggestion.' She paused and looked at him earnestly. He gave a cry of excitement!

'You need to think very carefully before entering into such a commitment Colin,' she continued, with her topaz eyes fixed firmly on his face. 'You must be able to present a calm demeaner at all times, although you may see sights that will make you furiously angry. Even now I have to school myself to hide my fury at the suffering some brute of a man has inflicted on the woman in his life. Some injuries too horrific to describe. But our part must always be reassuring and protective at all times, helping to heal their physical hurts as well as what can be more difficult, the mental scars they are left with. It can be draining, Colin, as Anna will tell you, but with this a wonderful feeling of achievement as yet another woman leaves the refuge with her confidence restored to begin a new happier future.' She glanced fondly at her husband.

'Robert, perhaps I can leave you to explain what will be required of Colin when the time comes—while I take this chance to get to know his amazing mother Geraldine! Charles has told me of all she has been through—her remarkable courage. You must be so proud of her Colin!' She smiled at both men leaving them to get better acquainted, as she went back to Geraldine, noticing that this silver haired woman who had once been a member of MI5 was in animated conversation with Charles Latimer. She stared at them curiously. Robert smiled after her and turned back to Colin.

'Well Colin—it's early days yet, the work involved in converting the monastery into a working refuge will probably take a few months. We are looking at June as a possible date to open the doors of Peace Haven. What I suggest is that you join us at Dream Echo for a few weeks so that I can show you the ropes—explain my own part in working here and what your own future work will entail. Will that be possible?' he asked. Colin thought quickly. It would mean leaving the twins with his mother again, but was sure she would be agreeable. It would also give him the pleasure of seeing Anna each day.

'Yes Robert—it's a great idea! Anna has already told me much of what happens at the refuge—filled me in with the shocking statistics of how great the worldwide problem of domestic abuse truly is. I cannot understand the mentality of any man who thinks it normal to raise his hand against a woman. To me it reeks of the utmost cowardice. You have my promise to do all within my power to help in your work in restoring the lives of those poor women who suffer such terrible abuse!' Robert sensed the man spoke from his heart.

'Good—then that is settled. What made you consider becoming involved though?' he asked. Colin bit his lip.

'As I believe you're aware, Anna endured horrific abuse at the hands of Malcolm Greer. If I could have got my hands on the scum....! Now however, realisation that his cruel behaviour is mirrored in the hands of possibly a quarter of the male race, enhances my desire to join you in helping their victims. Work to expose these abusers for the cowards they are.' His grey eyes flashed as he spoke.

'Well said. We should get on well together I think, Colin Denton.'

Over the weeks that followed, Colin remained a guest at Ivy cottage with Tom and Lottie. His twin children Charles and Melanie had returned back with Geraldine to Rose Cottage at Ravensnest. He had the joy of seeing Anna briefly every busy day at the refuge—had decided against the opportunity to share her accommodation at Dream Echo. No matter how frustrating the wait, he did not wish to anticipate their wedding to enjoy the delights that would follow.

Anna honoured him that decision, much as she longed for the time when they would be husband and wife. How different their marriage would be to the parody her life with Greer had been. When she told Susan that she was to marry Colin—she was relieved at her little daughter's obvious delight at the news.

'Does that mean that Colin will be my Daddy then—and I will be Melanie and Charles sister? Oh Mummy, I'm so pleased!' and she threw her arms about Anna. 'When is the wedding going to be?'

'Well, either May or early June. We thought it could be at the lovely old church next to Tom and Lottie's cottage. Would you like to be a bridesmaid, darling?' She had never seen Susan look happier.

Colin enjoyed several deep conversations with Robert Marsden, as the two men paralleled their backgrounds. Both had put their lives at risk to expose unscrupulous companies, in Robert's case when as an investigative journalist he had sought to reveal the dangers posed by Oleumgeldt a rogue oil exploration company, prepared to precipitate global warming by irresponsible mining in the Arctic—with danger of a substantial rise in sea levels, causing flooding across low lying areas of the world.

For his part, Robert questioned Colin about his determined stand against Sea Giant—their murderous attempt on his life and the death of his wife Mary—their further cruelty directed against Colin's mother Geraldine and his young children.

'Strange that we both have attempted similar actions against powerful crooked companies and survived, the miscreants now languishing in jail!' said Robert reflectively. 'But who would have thought that our paths would have crossed in this way—with the objective of helping abused women and shining a light in the dark corners of a world where men have thought it legitimate to threaten and brutalise their partners and daughters.'

'We need to get the whole problem high-lighted on tv and social media,' said Colin. 'Make men realise that such behaviour proclaims them vicious cowardly bullies! Name and shame them so that normal men treat them with contempt!'

'You're right my friend. But one step at a time. In another three months when the alterations to Peace Haven are completed and we open, you will have your hands full with the everyday running of the new refuge. You know that Amber has decided to conceal its true purpose, letting it be thought as being run by a religious order, where an occasional person can stay on retreat.'

Today Geraldine and her twin grandchildren were in the garden, where her spring bulbs were a glory and the flowering cherry bending in the light breeze, a few pale petals fluttering down on the grass.

'When will Daddy come back?' asked Melanie wistfully. 'I do so miss him, Granny!'

'Just a few weeks now,' replied Geraldine. 'Listen, children, I have a secret to share with you. But first we'll go in and have some cookies and fruit juice.' Minutes later they were sitting in the kitchen. The twins looked at her expectantly as they brushed crumbs off their lips.

'What's the secret, Granny?' asked Charles, glancing at her curiously, noting her usually serene face looked slightly distracted. 'Is anything wrong Granny?'

'No Charles darling, far from it. Well as you know that your Daddy is going to marry Anna soon and that we are all going through to stay with Tom and Lottie for the wedding day!'

'Yes, and it's going to be so wonderful,' put in Melanie excitedly. 'Susan and I are going to be bridesmaids—and Charles a pageboy! Why do we have to wait so long though?' Geraldine smiled back at them.

'Because they have to make lots of plans for the future. But the important thing is that we will all be one family. Now there is something else you need to know. It's about Charles Latimer. I believe you both like Charles—have often seen him on visits to Rose Cottage.'

'Yes—he said we should call him Uncle Charles,' said Melanie. 'It's strange he has the same name as my brother. He's a nice man Granny. What do you want to tell us about him?' The little girl looked at her curiously, as did Charles. Why was Granny being so mysterious?

'Well children, the secret I want to share with you, is that Charles and I have become very good friends indeed and we've decided that we want to spend the rest of our lives together. In fact, we have decided to get married!' Her face became rosy as she spoke watching their faces for reaction. The twins looked at each other in astonishment. Charles Latimer, the tall, commanding figure, who always greeted them with a kindly smile when he arrived and whom they had become accustomed to seeing on his visits to their home—he was to marry their Granny?

'But why do you want to marry him, Granny?' demanded Charles. 'Can't he just come to visit sometimes instead. It won't be the same anymore!' His grey eyes expressed his worry. And he glanced at this sister expecting her agreement. He was disappointed.

'But it will be fun—he'll be a sort of grandfather and I really like him,' said Melanie thoughtfully. She looked at Geraldine, 'Does Daddy know about it, Granny?'

'Well, not yet, darling. I wanted the two of you to be the first people to hear the news!' She smiled reassuringly at Charles. 'It truly will be alright, my dears. Charles Latimer is a very good and brave man. He used to be a very special kind of secret policeman and saved many peoples lives. I used to know him when I was a young woman. You see I was involved in the same kind of work—as were Tom and Lottie. All of this has to be kept secret and it's important that you give me your promise never to mention it to anyone else.' The twins looked at her in amazement.

'We promise,' they said quietly, and Charles looked at her awkwardly.

'If it is going to make you happy Granny, then it will be fine for Uncle Charles to become part of out family. I was being selfish. You see, there have been so many changes,' and his voice broke. Geraldine felt a deep wave of sympathy as she heard his words. Poor children—they had indeed been through so much stress. But at least now they would be able to grow up surrounded by the love and caring of a new, extended family.

'Thank you, my darlings,' she said softly. 'I am so proud of you both.' A sudden crash made them turn their heads—the two active kittens playfully chasing each other around lost their balance attempting to leap from the sideboard to the kitchen table and sent the cookie barrel onto the floor, scattering its contents. Geraldine stared at the mess in quick dismay—then laughed as she began to clear up. It wouldn't take long to bake another batch of cookies. Such small disaster after all the real trauma experienced over the last year or so. She raised an admonishing finger to the kittens as they scampered off guiltily into the hall, the children exploding into laughter. Just then there was a ring at the door. Geraldine hastily put down the dustpan and brush, and hurried to answer it and found Charles Latimer smiling on the doorstep. He proffered a box of liqueurs and an orchid plant, as he kissed her.

'Charles—thank you! Come in dear—I thought you were arriving tomorrow!' she said softly as he embraced her. 'Listen, I've just told the twins our news.' He lifted an inquiring eyebrow.

'How did they react?' he asked, slipping an arm about her waist.

'Charles a bit worried at first, Melanie pleased—they are both happy now,' she confided as she led him into the kitchen. 'Look who is here children,' she called. They stared solemnly at the man at Geraldine's side.

'Hallo there,' he called. 'I believe you now know your Granny has wonderfully agreed to marry me. I guess it must be a big surprise to you both. Perhaps you are wondering what difference it will make in your lives.' He seated himself beside them at the kitchen table. 'I promise you there is nothing to worry about. So far, when your father is away you've had Granny to look after you, but soon you will have two of us to care and protect you.' He glanced from one to the other of them, as Geraldine looked quietly on. It was the boy who replied with a question of his own.

'Granny told us you used to be a special secret policeman, sir. Will you teach me how to become one too when I grow up?' Charles looked at the child thoughtfully. It would be so easy to make a light promise, but instinct told him this was not the right future for the boy.

'Charles, it will be your father of course who will guide you through childhood, together with Anna and your very special Granny. But I will always be ready to advise if needs be! The career I have just retired from is not for everyone, can sometimes prevent a person from pursuing a normal home life—wife, children—although some can combine both.'

'Is that why you do not have a family, Uncle Charles?' asked Melanie intuitively.

'Well, it may have been so in the past, but I am soon to have a splendid ready-made family and am really looking forward to it.' He looked affectionately at the twins, as it was born in on him that he was not only about to take a wife—but would have a close relationship with these two delightful children whom he already cared for.

Geraldine looked on with relief that they had accepted her future husband so easily. Had it been otherwise, she might not have felt justified in bringing Charles Latimer into their lives. Now she wondered how her son Colin would react at the news.

The following morning Geraldine received a phone call from her son that made her cry out in delight. His wedding to Anna was to take place in three weeks' time!

Geraldine watched as the young woman about to become her new daughter-in-law, walked serenely up the aisle on Tom Lanscombe's arm, looking extremely lovely in her long, white gown overlaid with fine lace, a chaplet of tiny white roses securing the veil over her long golden blonde hair. She was followed by her two little bridesmaids, Susan and Melanie, in blue taffeta dresses, with young Charles just behind. Her glance sped further on to her son Colin, handsome in his dark grey suit, best man Charles Latimer at his side. The congregation murmured enthusiastically as the bride proceeded up the aisle to the sound of the organ music. Colin turned about and drew in his breath at sight of the beautiful woman approaching him with a smile on her lips.

'Anna!' He whispered her name lovingly as she reached his side, then both turned their attention on the Rev. Michael Bonnet as the ceremony commenced and they made their solemn vows and exchanged rings. The quietly moving words the Minister uttered would remain forever in their hearts, as he raised a hand in blessing to the couple who had both suffered so much hurt in the past and were now embarking on the joy of a happy marriage.

The wedding reception was held at Dream Echo in Robert and Amber's charming, spacious front sitting room which had been decorated with garlands of flowers for the occasion. Geraldine stood holding her glass of champagne at Charles Latimer's side, glancing around the happy gathering of those who were wishing the couple well. As well as Amber's mother, talented artist Gwenda Williams, there were the Lanscombes, members of Amber's team who ran the refuge were present, and Michael Bonnet—and of course the twins and little Susan.

Eventually a helicopter rose up in the late afternoon sky, bearing Colin and Anna Denton to a special island in the Hebrides, where another couple were waiting to greet them. The helicopter put them down close to the spot where once a similar craft had plucked him from his temporary stay with the MacLeod's Iain and Fiona who had opened their croft home to him offering sanctuary when he was in fear of further violence from Sea Giant should those who ran that corrupt oil and gas company discover Colin was still alive, had escaped their murderous plot and not lying dead on the sea bed.

As Colin assisted Anna out of the craft, they heard themselves hailed, saw a sturdy figure waving at them. Even in the dim evening light, Colin immediately recognised crofter Iain MacLeod, closely followed by his attractive red-haired wife Fiona, their collie dog bounding in excited circles about them through the greening heather.

'Greetings to you both Colin and Anna,' called Iain as he closed the gap between them, grasped Colin in his arms and turned to beam kindly at Anna.

'Colin told me you were bonny, Anna—and so you are my dear. Welcome to Skye both of you—and congratulations on your marriage!' By this time Fiona reached them and added her own warm welcome, her blue eyes scanning Anna's own curiously and satisfied by what she saw. Colin had chosen wisely in this lovely woman, not only for her undoubted beauty but for the integrity she sensed in the girl. Anna likewise was attracted to the couple who had so generously opened their home to the honeymooners.

They enjoyed a splendid dinner of roast chicken and fruit dumpling and cream, and a delicious white wine, that was smooth on the palette, relaxing the newlyweds, as they sat in the small sitting room where Colin now attempted to relate all that had happened since previously he had sat there last year. Anna also found herself explaining the difficulties that had beset her own life, Greer's cruelties, her escape to first one, then another refuge, the assistance in renting a cottage next door to Colin's mother. As their joint story unfolded, overlapped in such extraordinary fashion, Iain and Fiona glanced at each other in wonder.

'The Good Lord has indeed had His hand on both your lives,' said Iain quietly, looking at Colin. 'Who would have thought that the deep shock and sorrow you disclosed to me when first we met last year, would have been transformed into your present joy! Your dear children rejoicing their father is alive. And you Anna, the courage you have shown in facing such extreme cruelty has brought you now to position of a happy marriage with a fine and decent man, who will always love and protect you and your little daughter.'

'Iain and I feel blessed and deeply moved that you have decided to spend your honeymoon here in our remote croft house,' added Fiona gently. 'May the days spent here prove a special starting point to your marriage a fine memory in the years ahead. Then her voice rose, 'May the wind that blows over Skye touch your lives with its sweetness, the sound of the burn splashing music between its banks wash all past hurts away, sweet, lilting melody of the lark's song lift your hearts to the Eternal love above. Be happy Colin and Anna!'

They looked at each other, hearts too full to reply, as Iain smiled. He opened the door and pointed towards the bedroom they would share, murmured a few words in Gaelic, the meaning they could only guess.

Anna glanced across at the delicate white nightdress lying discarded on the bedside rug, as she raised herself on one arm smiling down at her sleeping husband's face. All her suppressed fears that she would be unable to respond to his lovemaking had been wonderfully dispelled during the night. After those first tender embraces that led to joint, passionate climax, they had fallen asleep in each other's arms. On waking a couple of hours later, they had taken delight in intimately touching each other, tenderly kissing as they engaged again—and she had raised her hips ecstatically to his thrust, while Colin joyed in the response of this woman he knew he truly loved. Anna who had secretly feared she might disappoint him now realised such worries were groundless. The crushing mental wounds inflicted on her self-esteem by Malcolm Greer had evaporated as though they had never been.

Now she bent over and kissed him, she watched him stir, saw the look of pleasure light his grey eyes as he pulled her down gently and they kissed. She turned her head.

'Listen—I can hear something outside—sheep I think!' she said suddenly.

'Yes, the MacLeod's have quite a flock—which I imagine by now must include this year's lambs—possibly about two months old I guess, although I'm woefully ignorant about farming matters.' He drew her closer, began to kiss her breasts as her breathing quickened. Then they heard voices and realised the MacLeod's were already up and busy. Colin sighed and reluctantly allowed her to slip out of bed and pull a robe about her.

'Later, my darling,' she whispered softly and he nodded. They had the rest of their lives in front of them he realised and the thought of it so wonderful.

They spent the rest of their week on Skye exploring its dramatic wild beauty, those soaring mountains, cliffs and innumerable inlets of the sea reminding Colin of his stay on Norway, as he made mental promise to take Anna and the children to visit the kindly Schiffer family. He thought fondly of them now, Hans Schiffer and his wife Greta and their son Sven who had rescued him from the sea in his fishing boat. Between them had saved his life and Sven brought him over to Skye where he had received more wonderful assistance from Iain and Fiona the owners of this croft where now they had been so graciously received on their honeymoon.

There are so many kind and caring people in our world,' said Colin, his head full of memories, as together they climbed the hill above the croft. 'This is where Iain opened my mind when I was so overwhelmed by despair over all that had happened. Remember I told you how he spoke of the dark night of the soul—times of taking a turbulent journey, but then accepting that we need to let go and let God? He said more—much more, and his words helped me through the grief-filled months that followed.' Anna looked a him

'You know Colin, both Iain and his dear wife Fiona, are very special people. You sense it as soon as you cross their threshold. If only all men were as wise and compassionate as Iain—but they are not as we both know! Next week we have to return to the real world, where countless abused women attempt to escape the vicious behaviour of a man in their lives who controls and brutalises them.' Her blue eyes flashed her concern and he nodded.

'You are right, Anna—and although between us we have personally had to deal with the worst examples of man's cruelty, like a rainbow after a shower of rain, something happens to restore our faith in mankind. When we return home, we have a vitally important work to embark on. Peace Haven is almost ready to receive its first guests. So much will rest on your shoulders Anna—and I will do my utmost to support you in every way!' he promised.

She smiled and stroked his hand, then a slight shadow passed over her face.

'I am a little worried as to how Susan will react on being parted from me for the first time. I am sure that the twins will be happy with Geraldine, are now so used to their home in Rose Cottage—and I just hope Susan will adapt to living there with them. We will try to arrange matters in such a way that one or other of us manage to drive over to see them if not every day, then as often as possible.'

Colin did not reply at once. He was not comfortable at the prospect of being parted from the twins and Susan long term, with a few weekly visits, but what was the alternative? Of necessity he had already seen little of them whilst he had spending those last long many weeks at Dream Echo, learning exactly how the refuge was run, his own duties in particular to be focussed on security.

But then what was the alternative—move them into Peace Haven? But suppose the children should inadvertently make mention at school that their new home was a women's refuge? But surely Amber and Robert Marsden at Dream Echo would have the same problem with their two young children as they approached school age. He sighed. What was the right answer?

It was Sunday, the children playing in the garden as Geraldine finished her baking. Charles Latimer was in London—and she missed him thought Geraldine fondly. When he had first proposed marriage, she had pointed out that she was five years older than he, only to have her reservation tossed aside—and as they embraced she realised how much she had come to love Charles. Perhaps it was not the same love as that she had experienced with her late dear husband David, but it was real and would be enduring.

Their wedding was arranged to take place in two weeks' time at St Lawrence Church, arrangements made with The Rev Bonnet, also with Tom and Lottie for a return stay at Ivy Cottage. Geraldine looked up as she heard the front door open—that could only mean one thing! Her son and his new bride had arrived back from their honeymoon on Skye!

She hurried through to the hall to be caught up in Colin's strong arms, receiving an equally warm embrace from Anna. Both looked happy and relaxed if a little tired after their long journey back from the Hebrides.

'Welcome home, my dears! I made a chocolate sponge earlier—I'll just put the kettle on and I can't wait to hear all your adventures! Just leave your bags there and come through.'

'So how was it?' she asked them as they sat in the comfortable kitchen.

'Geraldine—It was absolutely marvellous. The MacLeod's are a wonderful couple—they were unbelievingly kind. As for the island, I've never seen any place so wildly beautiful or mysterious,' cried Anna, her blue eyes dreamy with recollections. 'I'm so glad Colin decided we should honeymoon there—it was very special!'

'What can I add,' smiled Colin, looking fondly at his young wife. 'We found a peace there that dispelled all the hurts and anxieties of the past. It was the most wonderful start to our marriage! And soon you will be taking a similar step yourself, Mum. Where is Charles? I must tell him about Skye—suggest he takes you there!' Geraldine smiled.

'Charles has returned to his London flat briefly —lots of loose ends to tidy up. I just hope the sudden end of his busy exciting life in the Secret Service will not leave him feeling bored. But hopefully helping with the children will occupy him. He is very fond of them you know and they have decided to call him Gramps when we're married!'

'Gramps?' chuckled Colin, 'I'd love to see his face when he hears his new name. But seriously Mother, I couldn't be more delighted that you two are to be married. You deserve some new happiness and Charles Latimer is a man of integrity whom I like and respect.' He took a mouthful of Geraldine's chocolate sponge. 'This is delicious—you must show Anna how to make it.'

At his words Anna smiled as her thoughts went back to the day she had first arrived at Bramble cottage with her small daughter, to receive a visit from Geraldine with just such a chocolate sponge as she welcomed them to their new home. The circle of change had closed—and now she was no longer a neighbour, but daughter to Geraldine Denton, who would now become the mother she had never had.

'Where are the children—out in the garden?' asked Colin now. 'Look. Before we see them, I want to discuss how we're going to cope with the situation once we start work at Peace Haven.' Geraldine looked at him, puzzled.

'What do you mean, Colin?'

'Anna and I are unsure as to whether we should move the children into what will be our private quarters at the refuge—or leave them here with you. I worry that if we take them to Peace Haven, they may unthinkingly mention the refuge at school and I know it is vitally important that the ongoing work must remain secret at all times!'

Geraldine nodded her head as she considered the problem. It was one she had already discussed with Charles.

'I believe the children would never deliberately let any information slip about the refuge. But it does present a certain risk. I am more than happy to continue looking after them here, absolutely love having them with me—and I know Charles is looking forward to his role in helping to care for them.' Colin glanced at her gratefully.

'That is tremendously kind of you Mum, when you are about to embark on a new marriage. My only reservation is that the twins and Susan may feel we no longer love them.' His expression showed his genuine worry about the situation, as Anna also looked at Geraldine for guidance. The answer was gentle but firm.

'Look, providing you manage to visit them regularly, I'm sure they will accept this new situation. I suggest you explain to them that you are working nearby at a place where people arrive to spend a time of peace away from their problems. I believe the wonderful nun who was almost became mother-in-law to Amber once, has agreed to help at the refuge, giving authenticity to the story invented to satisfy the curious, that the old monastery is now home to a small religious group, who receive guests needful of withdrawal from the world in quiet retreat.' She smiled encouragingly.

'We could take them over on a visit to Peace Haven—to actually see where we will be working. They could meet our small staff. I just feel a bit guilty that we will not be with them at all times during their precious childhood.' Anna's voice was low. 'It is just that I know how very important the work of offering sanctuary to abused women is. There are so very few refuges, Geraldine—the need far outstripping available places of safety. It is something I know I am called to devote my life to—and wonderfully Colin wishes to be part of the work. I'm so proud of him. So, if you are really sure you'll be able to cope long term, then we are immensely grateful to you for your offer of ongoing care of the twins and my little Susan—making it possible for us to run Peace Haven!'

'I love the children, cannot imagine life without them now,' Geraldine confessed warmly.

'Mum—you're amazing,' said Colin quietly. 'We'll make frequent visits to see them—after all, we will be less than a fifteen-minute drive away.' His face expressed his relief that the matter was settled although he still felt slightly uneasy at the decision they had taken. How would the twins and Susan take it?

Suddenly the kitchen door burst open and the three children tumbled in, uttering cries of excitement as they saw Colin and Anna. In the moments that followed as the couple embraced the delighted youngsters, feeling their worries evaporating. Yes, life was not going to be the straightforward vista they might once have wished for, but the bonds of love binding the newly formed family together would be able to withstand different arrangements soon to be put into place. They had brought small gifts back from Skye which they unpacked and handed out now, as they told the children about the magical island with its wild beauty.

'We promised our friends the MacLeods we would bring you there to meet them one day,' said Colin, and as he said it realised it might prove difficult to get away from the new refuge once it was up and running and looking at the children's trusting faces, the actuality of the change the work that he was to engage in with Anna would have on all their lives was borne in on him. He looked down as little Susan tugged at his sleeve.

'May I call you Daddy now you are married to Mummy,' she asked. He glanced at Anna and pulled the child onto his knee.

'That would make me very happy, Susan,' he said gently. 'We are a family now. Perhaps one day Charles and Melanie will be ready to call Anna—mummy?' It was Anna herself who shook her head warningly at him. It was too soon after the loss of their beloved mother Mary to expect this.

'I am very happy to remain as Anna for now,' she said softly. 'But this I promise, I will always love and cherish Melanie and Charles as much I do Susan!' She saw the relief in the twins' eyes at her understanding.

Geraldine watched them all tenderly. The decision her son and Anna had taken to devote their lives to the care and protection of abused women touched her deeply. She knew that it entailed sacrifice of the precious time that should be spent with the youngsters during their fleeting childhood years. She had taken a similar decision when working in the Secret Service—yet despite spells of absence in pursuing her vocation during his school years, Colin had developed into a son to be very proud of.

It was the following evening, Anna had just finished helping Geraldine tidy up after the family dinner when Colin spoke softly to her. She nodded and called to the youngsters to join them in the sitting room.

'Now children, there is something we want to discuss with you,' said Colin, pointing to the settee. 'Let's sit down.' Anna joined him as Susan scrambled on his knee, the twins plumping down on the carpet and looking up at them inquiringly. Geraldine settled into her favourite armchair aware of what was to be discussed.

'Is anything wrong, Dad,' asked Charles perceptively. Colin shook his head and leaning forward placed a hand on the boy's shoulder.

'Not wrong—but we need to talk about some changes about to take place. As you know I have been staying with the Lanscombe's for some while—have missed you both immensely. I know you must expect that Anna and I will return to live here again with Granny and with you, children. But that is not going to happen. You see, we are going to work together on a new project not far from here—but it will mean we have to live on the premises.' He swallowed and watched their faces.

'You mean the old monastery?' asked Melanie.

'It's going to be a refuge, isn't it!' put in Charles. Colin looked at them in astonishment.

'What put that into your heads—I mean, no one is supposed to know anything about it!'

'It's all right, Daddy,' said the small girl on his lap. 'I told them, but they will keep it secret!'

'Susan!' cried Anna looking at her small daughter in troubled amazement. 'Who spoke to you about it?' Susan smiled at her innocently.

'Why you did! At least, I heard you speaking about it with Amber when she came to our room at Dream Echo. I was in bed—I think you thought I was asleep. Amber said you were going to run the new refuge in the old monastery with Daddy. I told the twins about it—I didn't realise it was wrong to do so!' Anna looked after her wordlessly, then reaching over kissed her tenderly.

'It's all right, my darling,' she said quietly but glancing uncertainly at the twins who met her eyes reassuringly. Looking at their faces she relaxed

'Don't worry about it, Dad—we won't share the secret with anyone else,' promised Charles his grey eyes meeting Colin's gaze steadily. 'We think what you are going to do is splendid—helping poor women who have been hurt and frightened by bad men. We know what Anna went through with that cruel man Greer!'

'Mummy said it's because some men are sick in their minds,' said Susan, her voice tremulous as she remembered events she had tried to forget. 'I know there were a lot of ladies at Dream Echo who had escaped from men who were hurting them.' Colin looked at the three youngsters bemused at such a demonstration of mature thinking.

'Well, since you already know about Peace Haven—which is what the new refuge is to be called, you'll understand why Anna and I need to stay there to care for the guests. We hope to employ a few helpers—

which will make it possible to drive over here as often as possible to see you.' They nodded their heads, glancing at each other as they tried to visualise the situation. It was now that Geraldine rose to her feet and entered into the conversation.

'Not only will you children receive lots of love from your dear parents but also from Charles who is going to help me look after you. I promise we are going to have a very happy time here at Rose Cottage.' Suddenly there were smiles on their faces and Colin knew all was going to be fine. The future was beginning to take shape.

Geraldine made her vows serenely at Charles Latimer's side at St Lawrence Church, the Rev. David Bonnet looking at them benignly as they exchanged rings, blessing the union of this couple before him whose previous lives had been involved with the protection of the general public as members of that mysterious section of the civil service known as MI5.

How very lovely Geraldine looked in her peacock blue silk suit, face framed by her dainty hat decorated with white roses, thought Colin, while the eyes of the tall, handsome, grey-haired man at her side expressed his delight in her, while the excited children were ecstatic at taking part in the wedding. Colin, however, was slightly bemused at the notion that Charles Latimer was now his stepfather! As for Anna, she was delighted that the woman who had taken the place of a mother in her life was now to embark on what without a doubt would prove a happy and successful marriage

The reception held at Dream Echo had mirrored that of Colin and Anna's such a short time before and now the couple were already leaving for their honeymoon in a chalet near Bergen. While there, Geraldine was determined to call on the Schiffer family, who had saved her son's life and shown so much amazing kindness to him.

 Once Charles and Geraldine were back in a fortnight—Anna and Colin planned to open the doors of Peace Haven to the first abused woman to arrive seeking refuge from a life of fear and misery. The highly experienced Connie Sheldon was coming over from Dream Echo to help until Anna managed to add to the staff—and Amber's mother, Gwenda Williams had offered to spend time there too.

In the meanwhile, Colin and Anna were enjoying a relaxing time with the children. Today they were to let them into a secret. It was as Susan was looking wistfully over the fence at Bramble Cottage once her home, that Colin called to her and to the twins who were putting up a colourful wigwam on the lawn. All three ran across to the garden bench where Colin was sitting, his arm around Anna and stood waiting curiously.

'Listen, children,' he began, 'we have a surprise for you. We've bought

Bramble Cottage! For the time being, you will remain here at Rose Cottage with Granny. But in the years ahead we will make our home next door! In the meanwhile, play in the garden there whenever you want to and when Anna and I can get away from Peace Haven, we will spend some special family time in our own new home.' Susan was the first to respond—she cried with delight, as the twins took the news in.

'Well, does that please you,' asked Anna, her blue eyes sweeping their young faces. The shouts of delight they uttered made the parents sigh in relief. It had been a difficult decision for Colin. The money spent on purchasing the cottage might have been better put aside for emergencies. He had sold his previous family house at Grantly in the north of Scotland, knowing he could never live there again—it was too full of memories of Sea Giant's attacks on his family, and dear Mary's death.

'I think it's a perfect idea,' said Melanie. 'When we move to Bramble Cottage, we will still be next door to Granny!' Anna smiled down at her. Who would have thought the future could be resolved so satisfactorily? The only slight worry remaining was that the secret of Peace Haven and the security of those women it welcomed, would be in the hands of three young children—but looking at them she knew the secret would be safe.

Chapter Nineteen

Colin and Anna carefully rechecked one room after another, content that the accommodation in the newly decorated monastery looked so welcoming. A specialist company from the next county had been involved in the structural alterations—an immense job but carried out with professional expertise. Now they assured themselves that all twenty bedrooms, their walls and furnishings in soft pastel colours similar to all at Dream Echo, were in perfect order, and they smiled at each other, then turned to inspect the rest of the refuge.

They stared across the large beige carpeted, communal sitting room where comfortable settees and armchairs upholstered in black leather were grouped and where there was a large TV, bookcases offering a variety of reading, a play area for children and a large wicker box brimming over with toys. The dining room had several small tables that could be aligned to form a longer one should this be preferred. The adjacent kitchen was well equipped with all that was needful, saucepans and accessories in a cheerful red. There was also a laundry room.

This previous monastery had been changed beyond recognition—on the inside at least, but outside all remained much as before, the old weathered stone walls showing a familiar austere appearance to a casual visitor. The orchards and front garden had been tidied up, but now a containing wall separated it from the pleasant landscaped gardens at the back of the building, where benches were set amongst flower beds and a small fountain splashed—a sanded play area nearby ready for any children who might accompany their mothers.

'It's amazing how much work has already been accomplished,' Colin exclaimed looking around in satisfaction. 'I believe we are ready to start!'

'A blessing from above for your efforts to bring help to those who so badly need it,' said a gentle voice, as a tall nun in a grey habit quietly joined the couple.

'That's a wonderful thing to say, Sister Beatrice,' said Anna, glancing affectionately at the nun who had recently arrived with three of her nursing sisters to assist in the future care of the abused women who would soon appear at the door. They would also lend an appearance of authenticity to the planned cover story that the monastery was now home to a sisterhood of nuns, who on occasion welcomed women who wished to go on retreat for a few weeks. A small chapel had been designed close to the front hall and reception rooms. It contained the original beautifully carved altar used by generations of monks, complete with a golden cross and two golden candlesticks, in front of it rows of pews and to the right of the altar was a tall, carved screen. What was not apparent was the concealed door behind this screen, that led to that part of the building housing the refuge itself.

'Remember we have Gina Watson arriving in half an hour,' said Anna now. 'Apparently, she's a friend and one-time colleague of Babs Chamberlain, one of the social workers who recommend abused women for admission to Dream Echo. She says she heard about us on the grapevine—wants to look at Peace Haven and see if we can take a woman in severe need!' Anna's face was glowing as she exchanged glances with Colin. It was about to happen, the work to which they felt called.

The front doorbell rang. Sister Beatrice opened it and smiled inquiringly at the dark-haired, shrewd-eyed, dumpy figure in a navy jumpsuit who stood there.

'Gina Watson—I believe Anna Denton is expecting me?' the visitor said, offering a card.

'Why yes, Miss Watson, please come in,' said the nun, as Anna came up behind her.

'Thank you, Sister Beatrice,' smiled Anna. 'Miss Watson, I'm Anna Denton. Perhaps you would like to come through to my office. She led the woman past the two front reception rooms into the chapel. The social worker was taking everything in as she followed Anna to the front of the chapel with its ancient altar, and slipping behind the carved wooden screen Anna touched a projection in the wall beyond causing a concealed door to swing open. It led onto a passageway—which opened into another hallway with rooms leading off and a staircase leading upwards.

'I feel lost already!' exclaimed the social worker.

'Well, now you've reached my office,' explained Anna, pushing a door open. 'Do sit down Miss Watson.' She pointed to a swivel chair as she seated herself behind her desk.

'Just call me Gina! I'm certainly impressed by the religious façade you have presented. Coming in just now I would never have guessed this place housed a refuge. I must say I am very curious to see the accommodation for your future guests.' Gina glanced around the office, taking in the filing cabinet, the CCTV monitor, maps on the wall. Anna smiled and switched on a kettle.

'Tea or coffee?' she asked. Minutes later as Gina sipped her cup of tea and munched on a chocolate biscuit, the door opened and Colin came in.

'My husband Colin Denton,' introduced Anna, pouring another cup. 'This is Gina Watson dear.'

'I'm a social worker, Mr Denton—or may I call you Colin?' Gina smiled at him, having heard of this man who had exposed a corrupt oil and gas company at risk to his own life. The case had been in all the newspapers and her colleague Babs Chamberlain had explained that he was to assist in running a new refuge together with his wife who had already gained valuable experience from working at Dream Echo with Amber Marsden, who was sponsoring Peace Haven.

'It's so good to meet you both—and thrilled that you are opening this much-needed new refuge. I'm anxious to see the accommodation—you see I am desperate to find a place for a young woman who has endured three years of misery with a violent partner. The police are seeking him now—Cheryl Cahill was too scared to remain in the hospital in case he should find her there and kill her. She has a broken arm, her whole body covered in bruises, and her face—well hopefully it will look normal again before too long. As you might guess, she is badly traumatised.' Anna and Colin glanced at each other.

'Where is Cheryl now?' asked Anna.

'Sitting in my car outside! I had to speak with you first to ensure that you were prepared to take your first case. I believe the decorators have not long finished work here and...!' Anna held up her hand and cut her off.

'Just bring her in,' she said firmly. 'Is she able to walk?'

'With help—painkillers have taken the edge off things, but she needs to get into bed as soon as possible.' Her face expressed relief that the attractive golden-haired, blue-eyed woman was being so cooperative. She had immediately taken to Anna and her husband.

'We will help you get Cheryl inside,' said Colin quietly.

The woman now sitting awkwardly on the side of the bed, one arm in a sling, stared blankly before her. It was a look all too familiar to Anna, seen on many occasions when helping to receive the abused women of all ages who arrived at Dream Echo's doors.

'Cheryl—you are safe now. My name is Anna. You are in a women's refuge which I run with the help of my colleagues. Don't try to talk yet—we will help you change into a gown and then into bed, where you will feel more comfortable.' Sister Beatrice knelt and removed the woman's shoes, as Anna gently helped her out of the shirt draped over her shoulders, and eased her skirt off. The extent of the injuries covering Cheryl's body was a shock although she was well used to such sights—but in this case, barely an inch was free of heavy bruising.

Sister Beatrice held back the flowered duvet, as Anna helped her into bed.

'Drink this,' said Anna, holding a glass of medication to the badly cut swollen lips. 'It will help you to sleep dear. The en-suite is through that door, but for now, just rest—and remember, you are safe!'

'I will remain with her,' said Sister Beatrice softly. Anna smiled in acknowledgement. Gina Watson standing by the door observed the kindness and quiet efficiency of care which Cheryl received. At the same time, she noted with approval the well-furnished room, so far and above what she had expected. That small vase of flowers on the bedside table sent its own message.

'Two very experienced members of Dream Echo's staff are joining us tomorrow—Connie Sheldon and Amber's mother Gwenda Williams and will stay until we find suitable volunteers. Perhaps you would care to see the rest of the refuge now,' suggested Anna, as she quietly closed Cheryl's door. Over the next half hour, Colin and Anna escorted the social worker around the rest of Peace Haven, receiving praise for excellence in its furnishings and layout.

'I'm amazed! What you are providing exceeds that found in most refuges which are run on a very tight budget. Obviously, a great deal of care has gone into setting all this up.' They were back in Anna's office, where Gina glanced at the CCTV monitor screen, pointing to it.

'Security is of supreme importance which you will already be aware of from the time you spent at Dream Echo. Now I see you have installed CCTV which is great, but only helpful if someone is watching the screen at all times.' There was urgency in her tone.

'Security is my domain,' said Colin a little stiffly. 'You need to have no worries on that score.' She smiled back at him.

'Please do not think I have the slightest criticism for this wonderful refuge. Perhaps when I first arrived I should have mentioned that I head the social worker team covering a large area. It's part of my job to check on security—the danger always exists that an abusive partner may discover a refuge and force his way in. Some of these men are extremely dangerous.' She glanced at the couple's faces as she expressed the message.

'Gina—I was once an abused woman myself—the man I escaped capable of murder—I was lucky to escape with my life. Colin helped me during a terrifying ordeal. We are both extremely aware of the need for security.' Anna spoke quietly and saw the immediate sympathy in Gina's dark eyes, as she reached out a hand to Anna.

'I did not know. Your experience as one who has personally suffered abuse will give you a greater understanding of those who will soon start passing through these doors.' She paused, 'As it happens, I also underwent abuse from a violent husband. It was later when I realised that at least a quarter of all women suffer domestic abuse at some time in their lives, that gave me the impetus to train as a social worker specialising in this field.'

'You will always be so welcome here,' said Anna softly. 'Any advice you can offer on security or anything else will be gratefully accepted.'

'Good. For my part, I am delighted to have found such a wonderful new refuge. We need so many more of them you know. As for security, have you alerted the local police that you may need help in the future?'

'Yes,' replied Colin. 'As a matter of fact, I've already informed my friend Will Evans, Sergeant of the Ravensnest police station, of the refuge. He has visited here to familiarise himself with the layout in case we should ever need assistance. Hopefully, we never will, but at least may be sure of backup.' Gina nodded.

'I congratulate you on being so well prepared. Look, I must be going. We are short-staffed and receive calls for help day and night. Good luck to you both—and to Peace Haven!'

A little later they watched the dumpy figure get into her dusty grey saloon and drive away.

'She was very direct—but I liked her,' acknowledged Colin. 'Well. We have started officially now. That poor woman Cheryl Cahill! I find it hard to believe that any husband could inflict such injuries on his wife—bastard!' His grey eyes hardened as he spoke.

'Sadly, we will probably see many others who have suffered even worse abuse. But if we can do a little to help even a few such women recover and remake their lives, then all this will be worthwhile.' In answer, he took his young wife in his arms and kissed her.

'I promise to devote all my energy into bringing this about,' said Colin huskily. 'Perhaps the different turbulent journeys we both underwent in the past, were to prepare us for this work!'

Geraldine lifted the phone and heard the excited voices telling her that today, for the very first time Peace Haven had officially opened its doors to an abused woman. She beckoned her husband Charles to her side, as together they listened in to the account.

'Colin—Anna! Congratulations to you both!' she said warmly, Charles adding a few encouraging words of his own.

'How are the children?' asked Anna now.

'Fine—have just finished their reading homework, with Gramps supervising!'

'Don't call me that, woman!' objected Charles indignantly. Geraldine laughed.

'Sorry Charles, but I think you are stuck with it!' And listening to their light-hearted banter, Colin and Anna exchanged relieved smiles. Hopefully, it was all going to work. Suddenly the three children were on the phone, blurting out their news,

'We have a puppy,' they cried in unison.

'Gramps has bought us a Golden Labrador and we're calling him Bruce!' explained Susan, as the twins described the new addition to the family.

'He was naughty at first, chased the kittens!' said Melanie

'But then Pyrites scratched his nose—but now they are all cuddled up together in the basket Gramps bought!' added Charles. Their parents exchanged amazed glances. They had anticipated aggrieved questions as to when they were coming to see their offspring again, but the youngsters seemed happy and content. Which was of course all that they could have wished for while experiencing a slight pang of regret that they were missing out on that precious daily contact. Well, at least they could now concentrate on their work at Peace Haven with quiet minds.

It was not a future they would have envisaged a year ago, but as they smiled at each other, knew there was no way they would change the path they had taken.

Printed in Great Britain
by Amazon